Travel Page

Every publication from Rippple Books has this special page to document where the book travels, who has it and when.

Rowan and Eris

Campbell Jefferys

Rippple
Books

First published in 2018 by
Rippple Books

Music: Joel Havea
Cover artwork: Beate Kuhlwein
Cover design: Claudia Bode
Editor: Jeff Kavanagh
Layout: Susanne Hock

Rippple Books
Rippple Media
Postfach 304263
20325 Hamburg
Germany
www.rippplemedia.com

A CIP catalogue record for this book is available from the British Library.

ISBN: 978-3-9816249-6-0

Better off Red

It's early in the morning, and a slither of winter sun is coming through the curtains, painting a thin yellow streak on the wall that stays the same width, but gradually grows brighter.

You sleep, balled up on your right side in the corner of the bed, without a blanket. Knees under your chin, shins against the wall, ballerina ankles, small fists covering your eyes, your head on the smallest piece of pillow corner, and your hair fanning out like campfire flames in the wind. You're so small and round; a beach-ball in a white sea; or the sole survivor of a shipwreck, drifting in a lifeboat.

The bed appears huge with just you in it. Are you waiting for someone to get back into bed with you? Expecting it? Someone who needs space; who maybe sleeps with the lights on and hogs the blanket. A restless sleeper, tossing and turning and sweating, and getting up during the night. Someone who dreams with intensity.

Though she started on the floor, she got into bed with you at some point last night, because the pillow is crumpled and the blanket kicked to the floor is still slightly warm.

I pick the blanket up and smell it, that strange sweet musk she has, both alluring and disgusting. Or had, because she's gone and I doubt I'll ever see her again. You're here, she's gone, and that feels right.

Do you sense that too, even in sleep?

Maybe it's just what I want to believe, to justify this new mess.

You don't look peaceful in your sleep. This scares me. Little kids don't grit their teeth like that, or sleep with fists in front of their eyes. I see a child run-down and fearful, dreading to be woken and hauled away. A girl without a foundation: without friends, without a home, without a constant.

It's now my job to give you all of those things. Are you ready for them? Will you be able to handle a world that's not in flux? What will Holly think of you, and you of her?

Job really isn't the right the word. I'm a parent, not an employee. And I'm not the boss either. We're partners. A team.

I'm questioning whether you're ready for all this when really I'm wondering that about myself. It even seems weird that I stand over your bed in this way, watching and analysing you like some sinister stranger.

1

But it's me. Your dad.

This is the point we've been moving towards and now here we are. Both of us will have to factor in the other somehow. For you, that other will also mean a new country and a new culture. I'm hoping you're young enough for adaptation to be part of each day, with everything always new, in some way.

I take the blanket, give it a shake and spread it over you. No response. No movement. No straightening out and rolling over to the centre of the bed. You stay balled up in the corner, grimacing, fists up like a boxer, and in your sub-conscious defiance I get an inkling of what lies ahead. All the things I will have to help you unlearn. Because I want you to sleep peacefully, to be without worries. I want you to be a normal kid.

It's going to be difficult. Chaotic and challenging. You have your mother's green eyes, but my genes mean you're a member of the ginger brigade, though your red hair is closer to brown than mine. Your fair skin will require sunscreen all-year round to protect you from Perth's blazing sun.

I know I'm still very much a stranger to you.

But it was you who saw me, on the U2 as it pulled out of Nollendorfplatz station. From the wagon in front, you looked through the door windows and pointed at me. And you tugged at her sleeve to get her to look as well. You smiled, and I felt so relieved, because you knew who I was.

I couldn't open the glass doors. At the next station, Bülow Strasse, I swapped to your wagon, just getting in before the doors closed. We sat there, the three of us, in silence. A weird family, with parents who didn't love each other bookending the child they'd had together. This small, unwanted, auburn-haired miracle. I couldn't really talk, couldn't find the right words. So, I just smiled and tried to relax, to make you feel comfortable with me sitting next to you. Your mother stared straight ahead, in her own world, as if we weren't there, but you held my hand.

At Postdamer Platz station, she stood up and said, "There's something I gotta do."

She led us out, walking quickly, her pink daypack bouncing on her back. She had you by the hand and I followed. It reminded me of the way I'd followed you both all over America. Followed the trail of postcards, feeling the whole time I was chasing shadows. Grabbing at air. Getting close, then arriving too late, and each time feeling like I'd failed an important test.

Not this time. I had you. Both of you.

She walked up the escalators while others stood, weaving between people who looked like tourists, who carried umbrellas and were underdressed for the dry cold of Berlin in January. Outside, she knew the way, walking with purpose down the broad expanse of Ebert Strasse. When we got to the Holocaust Memorial, she put your cold hand in mine, without looking at us, and slinked between two grey pylons. I saw her head a few more times and caught a flash of pink daypack as she went deeper into the memorial, but then she was gone. And it was just you and me. I wondered if she would come back.

"We have to wait," you said, somehow aware of the procedure.

I nodded and gave you my zebra-patterned gloves to wear; they had the ends of the fingers cut off, but swallowed your small hands. You rubbed your little freckled nose with your gloved left hand.

I told you my name and you said you knew it already, which made me curious about what else you knew about me. I said that you could call me Rowan.

You seemed to like this, and you smiled a little as you looked towards the memorial, waiting for her to reappear.

About fifteen minutes passed.

I suggested we look for her. That we could make a game of it, trying to find her in the maze. You took my hand and led me through a gap between two pylons.

We zigzagged deeper. The memorial's slabs differed in size, but were arranged symmetrically, which meant we could look down the narrow alleys in the hope of spotting her, but we saw no sign of her. There also weren't many visitors.

I let you lead, as I thought this was your game to win. But in that moment, I felt it would be okay if we'd lost her. Good for both of us. For all of us.

And somewhere inside my head, a knot started to unravel. Tension eased. I was suddenly scared and happy. I knew this was how it would end up, with just you and me. This was how it was always supposed to end up.

You saw a flash of her and pulled me in that direction. Another flash, another direction. She was running, up and down the alleys.

3

We were in the middle of this block-sized memorial, or so it felt. In a very slight, man-made valley.

Your cheeks were pink from running in the cold.

I thought the memorial wasn't really as powerful as the small brass plaques I'd seen in the footpaths in front of buildings where deported and murdered Jews had lived. A life story, inscribed on a plaque the size of a cobblestone. I wasn't getting much from these grey blocks.

Then you pulled at my jacket and pointed at a sticker on one of the pylons. It had the word PATIENCE on it, hand-written, in capital letters. Another had a sticker with MANNERS. It was then I started to see that many of the slabs had stickers on them, with words like TOLERANCE, CHARITY, KINDNESS, PLAYFULNESS and MODESTY.

It made me want to find all the stickers, to piece the clues together. What was the point of writing ACCEPTANCE, GOODNESS, COURTESY, MODERATION and CIVILITY on these stickers and putting them on this memorial?

It was her. I saw it. She had the stickers in her daypack, the words already written out. I pointed, and I was sure you saw it too, but you seemed far more interested in finding her than discerning the meaning of her actions.

But then she was in front of us, her face glistening with sweat from all the running, her breath steaming, her green eyes wide and wild, and just about qualifying as crazy-eyes.

"Time to go," she said, and she took a handful of cards from the pocket of her jacket and threw them in the air. "Walk normally. Take photos. Be a tourist."

She did this, pulling out a bulky Polaroid camera to snap an instant shot of some of the stickers and the cards on the ground. Then, she was moving again.

I tried to do what she said, aiming to photograph both of you, but never getting all of her in the shot, because she moved too much, jogging ahead and looking around to see if anyone was following us. I thought she was fidgety and nervous, someone scared of being chased. But then she skipped a few times, and you copied her.

We went back along Ebert Strasse and down the stairs to the trains. The U2 again, the redline, direction Wittenbergplatz, and none of us with tickets.

She sat on the bench like a man, her legs spread and her elbows perched on the back rest. Proud of herself, as if she'd just done something of great significance, when she wasn't much more than a vandal with a message.

"You got space for us at your hotel?" she asked.

I said I only had a single room.

"Then you better get a bigger one."

So we ended up back at the Metropolitan, in this family room, where you sleep balled up in the corner of the bed, and you're mine, and mine only.

Who are you?

I sit down on the far end of the bed, carefully, to avoid rocking this delicate lifeboat. I want you to sleep, because I don't really know how to explain that she's gone. I can't just say that Holly will be your new mother, as she's not sure she wants that role, or that the three of us might suddenly morph into a family and all will be well.

I have no idea how many of these adult things you'll understand.

It's very nice to watch you sleep, to see the blanket go up as your ribs expand with each breath you take. It's calming. I resolve to bring you peace, to bring order to the chaos. And that shall start with honesty.

When you wake, I will tell you the truth.

In this quiet hotel room, as the slither of sun on the wall turns from light yellow to almost white, I'm aware that this is where I need to be. I can hear the ringing in my ears, but it doesn't bother me. It's constant and familiar. In this moment, it's actually a nice, even-toned piece of background noise. A one-note music box, in high E. Like the guitar's top string, the one I always break. People complain about tinnitus, treat it like a curse, a disease requiring a cure, but I'm good with it. For me, it's ever-present. I don't remember not having it.

Now, I think of the ringing as your lullaby. It will be the soundtrack for our first morning together.

I get up and go to the desk. She has left two things: your US passport and your birth certificate, which has me named as your father. There's no note. No money. No list of instructions. No itemising of likes and dislikes, allergies and medical issues, which I think would be handy. Because what if I gave you peanuts and it turned out you were allergic and you stopped breathing? I wouldn't know what to do.

Maybe you're some kind of super-child and there's absolutely nothing wrong with you. It's more likely you have your deficiencies, as we all do, and I will learn about them over time.

With your passport and birth certificate, I can take you back to Australia and no one can question this, except you, I guess. And maybe Holly, if she has decided she's not ready to play house yet. You will live with me and Churchill and start going to school. I'm sure Nana will help as well.

How do I explain all this when you wake up? All these decisions that have been made for you. Surely the first thing you'll ask is, "Where is she?" Gone, that's where, fleeing before dawn, without saying goodbye, and without even covering you with the blanket.

I check my wallet. My money is still there, and it seems a relief that she didn't rob me. I feel strangely lucky. But I barely have enough cash to buy us lunch, let alone the grand required to get you home. I've maxed out my credit card. This tour has cost me more than I've earned, and it would take weeks of busking and gigs to get the money together for your flight.

It's too cold to be playing outside.

Could we stay here, in Berlin? I'd find a job and we'd save up for the trip home. Things seem possible here. I'd get us a room and play gigs in the evening for extra cash, because I'd need to put you in day care or kindergarten or whatever it is they have here for five-year-olds. Maybe I could record another CD on the cheap. Bare bones again, guitar and vocals, foot snare, one hand clapping. No, that would just cost more. Better would be to sell more copies of the CD I already made. Make the money that way.

I turn to the bed. You have rolled over and straightened a little, appear more comfortable. But your fists remain in front of your eyes.

Do you want to stay here? Do you understand the concept of money? If you do, then I can be honest with you about it and say I don't have any, and that this limits our options. Then, we can decide together what our next move will be. There's always Churchill, and my parents, and Nana. I could get the money from somewhere and take you home.

When you wake, we will have breakfast together and talk about this. Your opinion matters. It will always matter. She forced decisions upon you, but I'm going to listen to what you have to say about things.

That's good. Do it differently from the start.

The Sleeping Giant

The first postcard came from Thunder Bay, which Churchill, still in his pyjamas and with his tablet in one hand and a mug of coffee in the other, said is in Ontario.

"Highest per-capita rate of homicides in Canada," he added from the kitchen doorway. "But that's probably not saying much, compared to all those cities south of the border. Still, there's a slight chance the person who sent this postcard is dead. Shot in a snowmobile drive-by."

"How is any of that information relevant?"

"Husky team and sled drive-by? Mush-mush bang-bang?"

"What's the matter with you this morning?"

"Just trying to add a bit more excitement to your little postcard there."

"It's exciting just getting a postcard these days."

Churchill, good housemate that he is, slinked back into his bedroom, which doubled as his home office. In his room, the division between bed and desk was marked by a large Japanese-style screen panel, the kind an actress might get changed behind before going on stage. The panel had a panda motif.

I went back to my cereal and stared at the postcard while I ate. Based on the main image, Thunder Bay wasn't presenting itself as an attractive place, though I assumed it had its good parts. It looked like a regional centre, where highways intersected, industrial and bland; a place people drove for hours to get to in order to buy supplies in bulk. A broad rail line cut through the centre of town. Freight cars were parked to the sides of the main track. I imagined Canadian hobos jumping in these to get across the country, perhaps to reach more inviting places. There was a large lumber yard to the left of the tracks, while the town was a flat expanse dominated by grey or white commercial-looking buildings. It struck me as a place to work, not live. The lakeside greenery in the foreground had a scattering of tents, caravans and boats on trailers, and there was something desolate about it. The same could be said of all the empty boat moorings in the harbour. Still, with all that, it struck me that it wouldn't be a bad place to be a kid, with adventure around every corner.

I racked my brain to come up with a likely sender, and drew a blank. The other side of the postcard gave no further clues. There

7

was no writing, apart from my name and address, printed in green pen. In the area were people normally write, there was the outline of a hand, traced using the same green pen, but with five fingers and a thumb.

"That's weird," Churchill said, looking over my shoulder and giving me a jump. "You know anyone with a hand like that?"

"It's not real. Can't be."

"Pretty small though. Could be a kiddie's hand."

"Yeah, maybe."

"You got any stray kids out there?"

"Not that I'm aware of."

He took the postcard from my hands and turned it over. "It's amazing they even make postcards for places like this," he said. "Chunder Bay. No, Blunder Bay, like it was a total mistake to build a city there."

"It doesn't look that bad. I bet it has some nice pockets. And there are worse places in our own backyard, Church."

"True. We do shanty, isolated, ramshackle towns very well in Australia. Wake in fright and all that."

"The lake looks nice. Clean enough for swimming, I'm sure."

This made Churchill smile. "Ah, Rowan. As always, love your positivity."

As he held up the card, I looked at the hand on the reverse side. He was right. It was a child's hand, and I figured that child had something to do with me. Otherwise, why would someone send me this?

At twenty-six years old and with a life not really going anywhere, I didn't feel at all ready to be a father.

Or it was all some kind of stupid prank.

"Coffee?"

"Huh? Oh, yeah, thanks, Church."

Since moving in with me last year, Churchill had become something like my housewife. This was Nana's house, split into two houses, with Nana living in the back part. We paid half the rent we should have, and even with that, I think Churchill wanted to earn his keep. Despite me often telling him that he should just live here and enjoy it, he took on a lot of the household duties and tried to look after me, which I really didn't mind. Nana thought we were a couple. Whenever I told her we weren't, she countered by saying we might as well become one as we were already halfway there.

8

To be honest, I loved Churchill, but not in that way. More than once I'd wondered whether I'd be considerably happier if I did and if he reciprocated.

Churchill worked from home, designing accounting software and acting as the helpdesk for those who used it. The designing part he'd completed a few years ago, and now most of his work was updating it and helping users. This was a good working situation for him, as he was borderline agoraphobic. He ordered our groceries online and had them delivered, but sometimes went down the street to do some shopping and run errands, as a way of proving to himself, and to me, that he could leave the house. He had yet to visit Janette, though they'd been a couple for over a year. They met online, and Janette always came to our house for what Churchill called "conjugal visitations". I could normally get him to come across the street to sit on a bench near Jualbup Lake, especially if I took Daphne and played some songs, but he didn't last much longer than half an hour. But he never made excuses, such as saying it was too hot or there were too many mosquitoes; he admitted that he couldn't stand the outdoors any longer.

Because to his credit, he was very open about his anxiety and tried to deal with it as best he could. He never made any medication, but did have regular appointments with an online therapist. Despite his condition, he was remarkably social, with our house hosting Sunday dinners as well as themed parties and events; Churchill's thinking being that if he couldn't go to the party, he would bring it to him.

He also encouraged others to seek adventure in the outside world when he felt he couldn't.

Which is probably why he said, "You should go."

"Go where?"

"To Blunder Bay." He put a mug of coffee in front of me. "I'll order you a bulletproof vest. You can go there and find out who sent this postcard."

"How I am supposed to do that? I don't even know who sent it. Thanks for the coffee, by the way."

"No worries."

One of the perks of his self-imposed confinement was that Churchill had learned to make excellent coffee. He ordered beans online from a supplier in Indonesia.

"Since when do locals send postcards? Whoever sent this was a tourist and is long gone."

Churchill nodded. "Yeah, probably."

"The postmark is already two weeks old. And I can't just drop everything and go to the other side of the world."

"Might be fun. A puzzle to solve. Rowan and the case of the mysterious five-fingered hand."

I was tempted. At the very least, it would break up the routine and get me out of Perth for a while.

"How about we go together?"

He shook his head. "Not for me. I like it too much here. Homebody, I am."

"Are you planning to get dressed today?"

"Sure. Nana's coming over for a cuppa this arvo. She said she's made muffins. I reckon that's worth dressing for. You around for that?"

"I'm working. I gotta go to the shop this morning. Couple of repairs to do. Some restringings. It's amazing how many guitar players out there aren't able to change their own strings."

"So, no Thunder Bay?"

"Not unless you're going as well."

Churchill sipped his coffee. "Hmm, not today."

"Must be bloody cold over there, right now. This postcard's a summer shot."

"If you ask me, this is personal," Churchill said, sliding the postcard towards him. "It's not someone making a joke. I know you're thinking that, big prankster that you are. This is a message, Rowan. A cryptic, freakish one, but someone is reaching out to you. This person knows who you are and where you live, which should help narrow down the candidates. You know anyone from Canada?"

"Nope."

"American maybe?"

"No. Well, hang on. One, but that was brief. And it was yonks ago. I don't remember giving her my address."

"Her?"

"It was the New Zealand trip. I told you about it. A handful of summers ago."

"Help me hit refresh."

It was a nice memory, one I'd happily relive through a long retelling, and not because of the girl, but because of how I'd felt on that trip. I liked the version of me I became there; a version I'd unfortunately left there.

10

I checked the time on my phone, drained my coffee and stood up.

"It'll have to wait till later. I gotta get to the shop."

"Back for dinner?" Churchill asked.

"Yeah. What are we having?"

"Roast bird, of some description. Depends on what the supermarket has that's reasonably fresh. I'm thinking duck, as Janette's coming over and duck should make a very nice lead-in to you-know-what."

"Charming."

"Will you get Daphne out and play for us as well?"

"I don't like being the soundtrack for your personal porn."

"Yeah, you do. And it needs more wah-wah guitar."

"It's better than listening to you."

Churchill laughed, then said, "Come on, I'm cooking. Could be slaughtering too, if the store doesn't have duck. I might have to go across the street and grab one from the lake."

"Just get whatever the supermarket has. See ya later."

Outside, the morning was warm, and the inside of my Smart was warmer. I zipped up Morgan Street with both windows down. It was after ten and all the peak hour traffic was gone. I love Perth, but it's very much a car town, and I get a lot of stick for driving the puny two-seater Smart. People try to cycle, even though the cyclists and drivers seemed to be at war with each other. I used to cycle to university, but gave up after sweating under the helmet and getting so many flat tyres from the bumpy footpaths. I ended up using my skateboard, which drivers seemed to more readily accept having on the road. And while Perth has more cars than ever, much of the infrastructure is the same as it always was, built for a city with half the population. The streets get clogged pretty quickly and peak hour is best avoided. The public transport system isn't comprehensive enough to enable people to live without a car, unless all the points of a person's life are dotted along the few train lines the city has.

Mine weren't. Living near Shenton Park station was handy, but I still needed my car to get to work, as the music shop was nowhere near a station. Today, I listened to some of my rough-cut demos while driving and was disappointed with every one of them. I skipped each track to the end because I couldn't stand what I'd written and recorded.

I wondered again why so much of my music was sad. I didn't think I was sad, yet those were the kind of songs I wrote. Melancholic was okay, if it had feeling and ended in a good place, but all my stuff sounded like it needed whining strings as fill-in, or really slow harmonica.

When I arrived at work, I parked my Smart in the smidgen of shade offered by the car park's lone tree. It struck me that Thunder Bay might make a great title for a song. But when I thought about potential narratives, all I could see was the five-fingered hand.

→←

After dinner, I played for an hour, serenading Churchill and Janette, which didn't feel that weird. I focused on the music and lost myself in each song. It was actually quite nice to have an audience. When I saw that there was no longer light showing from under Churchill's closed bedroom door, I went into the kitchen and made a cup of tea, using fresh mint from Nana's herb garden.

The postcard was still on the table.

I sipped my tea and thought back to over five years ago, to when, on the day after my twenty-first birthday, my parents announced they were getting divorced, which instigated the series of events that resulted in my New Zealand trip. Mum and Dad made their announcement in the manner of people saying they were going to buy a dog: with a certain amount of fanfare and seriousness that bespoke a lengthy deliberation, but with a blitheness that made it all sound like it wasn't such a big deal and no one should really care except them.

Well, we cared. I was shocked, as I felt it came from nowhere. My brother couldn't get his head around it either, and he was divorced himself. How did almost thirty years of marriage suddenly end in divorce? The lack of a clear underlying factor also made it hard for Conor and me to understand. It wasn't that Dad or Mum had met someone else, or that one had cheated on the other. They said they still loved each other, but had grown apart and wanted different things.

Conor's reaction was to try to turn it all around. He suggested counsellors, and had a sizeable list in his phone's contacts, and fashioned ways to get Mum and Dad together in the hope they would reconcile. One dinner he organised backfired stupendously when they both brought dates, and all four got along. Conor and I watched from the restaurant's bar, with Conor getting drunk enough to need carrying to my car and help getting into bed.

The divorce went through and the Claremont house we'd grown

up in was sold for a ludicrous amount of money to a couple who worked up north in the mining industry. There was enough from the sale for my parents to buy modest apartments of their own, with Mum moving to a two-and-one in Subiaco and Dad to a three-and-two in Mosman Park. Conor and I got tidy wedges of cash as well, which came as a surprise. Churchill called it reparations, like we were victims of war. Conor refused the money and withdrew into his own circle of relationships, which included dating another woman who wasn't right for him, and which was heading towards marriage and potentially another divorce.

I decided to use the money to travel, because getting away from everyone seemed like the best option. Nana said this was a good idea. She also said that the divorce was a good idea, that they were both better off. She even admired they'd had the courage to go through with it, as plenty of couples she knew had stuck it out for the long haul and ended up submitting each other to years of passive-aggressive torture.

"Love can sometimes run its course," she'd said at the time, and that sentence lingered.

I went to the east coast to visit some friends from high school, stopping in Melbourne, Canberra and Sydney to meet significant partners and make funny faces at a few toddlers. Mainly, I was supposed to envy the lives of people more advanced into adulthood than I was, but I didn't want to swap places, and getting to the airport in Sydney to fly to Auckland was a relief. I arrived in New Zealand without a list of people to visit, and wasn't really sure what to do with myself. I went to Rotorua, Napier and Hastings. I played my guitar a lot and tried to write some songs, which all had "love running out" as the main theme.

After a week, I phoned Churchill and complained my trip was suffering from aimlessness. He was still living at home in Mount Pleasant, just getting his software business started, and took it upon himself to be my trip planner. Over the next few weeks, I worked through a handful of four-to-five day itineraries. He organised everything, including accommodation, travel and tours, and even put together playlists of New Zealand music, which is how I ended up enjoying the strange-ish music of bands like Straitjacket Fits and Headless Chickens.

What he couldn't organise was me meeting people. Youth hostels are social places, and the guy with the guitar usually attracts a crowd if he sits down and plays, but I was happy to retreat. I did a lot of walking, and any time I spent playing Daphne was on the streets of whatever town I was in, with my guitar case out in front of me to catch coins. I was glad for the money, but really I was busking for the practice, to sing loud and get confident playing in front of people. My hands felt strong. The fingertips of my left hand were beautifully calloused.

At a tad over two metres, I'm tall for a busker, but this helps me get attention. The locals were generous and busking brought in quite a bit of money each day, which I then pumped back into the local bar and club economy. I went to see live music every night and got to see some very talented musicians playing in tiny bars, and saw some who were absolutely rubbish playing in big crowded bars. The concerts made the ringing in my ears worse, but as I wasn't conversing with anyone, it didn't matter. All day, I could switch off and let my ears ring in that unceasing, unwavering high E.

I drank too much. I slept late, often past the hostel's check-out time. More than once I was woken by a cleaning woman wearing yellow or pink rubber gloves.

Churchill was a massive help. I went wherever he sent me. All he asked for in return were reports and photographs, which I duly sent. He said he was making a scrapbook of our trip.

After taking the Interislander from Wellington to Picton, Churchill took me clockwise around the South Island, to Christchurch and down the coast. I liked Dunedin, enough to send Churchill's scheduling into temporary disarray by staying a week there. It had the best local music scene I'd come across in New Zealand, with a swag of venues huddled around the Octagon and Moray Place. Even the buskers were at another level, and this kept me from busking as I didn't think I could compete.

Back on track, Churchill took me to Invercargill, then north to Queenstown. It was beautiful country, the stuff of massive wall calendars. Milford Sound, Mount Cook, Fox Glacier, Hokitika, Nelson Lakes National Park. The best had been saved for last, but I was running out of island, having almost circled back to Picton.

The last itinerary was for Abel Tasman National Park. On the bus from Motueka to Marahau, I met her.

I was sitting on the back seat of the bus, in the middle, so I could stretch my legs down the aisle. She was the last to get on, running for

14

the bus just as it moved forward and slapping the side to get the driver to stop. There were plenty of empty seats, but she lugged her gear down to the back and asked me to slide across.

"Thanks," she said, dropping her big khaki-coloured backpack on the seat in front and putting her bright pink and very girly daypack on the seat between us. When she moved it, the daypack made a clinking noise, as if there were bottles or cans inside.

"Old school habit," she added. "The mean girl at the back of the bus."

"I'm here for the leg room."

"And there I was thinking you were the bus's bad boy. But it looks like you need it. How tall are you?"

"Two metres."

"Woah. That's, like, six-six, yeah?"

"I think so. Are you American?"

She nodded, not seeming terribly proud.

"From where?"

She gave me a glance, then said, "Nowhere in particular. I'm one of those kids who moved around a lot, and as an adult, I haven't stopped moving. Guess I'm kinda perpetually in the wind."

"I like that. In the wind."

"I'm Nola."

"Rowan."

She reached her hand across and we shook. I noticed her fingernails were dirty.

"You a local?"

"Nope. From Perth."

"No shit? I was there a few weeks ago."

"You like it?"

She laughed. "Does it matter? You're the one who lives there. Do you like it?"

"Sure. But it sounds like you don't."

"I had fun, but the city didn't do much for me. In the end, it's just my opinion. And if you really want it, then here it is. I thought Perth was dull. Like a tall, dumb blonde. Beautiful, great to look at, but not much pulse or brainpower. No, no. That's not right. Too harsh. Look, you got this breath-taking locale, right, this incredible stretch of coastline and this mighty river, but what do you do with it? You build McMansions. You know what I'm trying to say? Sorry. I'm bad at expressing myself. I'm more visual, you know?"

15

"Everybody says this, but they don't know the city well enough. There's more going on than you think, and it's not just about people showing off. There's a lot of live music and creativity. It's not all suburbs and swimming pools."

"You say that with conviction. Shame I didn't have you to show me around."

She stopped there, and I was glad she did, as I didn't like her bad-mouthing Perth.

The bus drove out of Motueka, but didn't pick up much speed.

Nola looked out the window, and I looked at her. She wasn't pretty, and I wondered how many days she'd gone without showering, but she was interesting to look at. Her long face was made to look slightly longer by her small mouth and nose. She had green eyes and light brown, shoulder-length hair pulled back into a pair of tight, braided pigtails. With that hairstyle and the pink daypack, she might have been trying to appear younger, but I had her at ten years older than me, maybe more. She also looked worn. I guessed she'd been on the road for a while and that not all of it had been in comfort and ease. She struck me as someone who liked to camp, live rugged and go to remote places.

Still looking out the window, she asked, "Is that your natural hair colour, or do you dye it?"

"It's natural."

"Lucky you."

"Are you serious? Do you have any idea what I went through as a kid? Carrot top, ginger, Ronald McDonald, Beaker, I got them all. Kids crowded around and laughed at me, and it didn't help that I was a head taller than all of them."

"They were jealous. It's beautiful. Like fire." She reached a hand towards me and touched my hair, sliding a few strands between her dirty fingers. "You should let it grow. Show your gift to the world. Embrace it. Flaunt it."

"I don't know about that."

"Be a shame to waste it."

She withdrew her hand and went back to looking out the window.

I took out my phone and opened Churchill's last email. According to his schedule, it was supposed to be a short ride to Marahau, but the bus was making slow progress, crawling around the corners and keeping a speed I found nauseating.

16

"What are you doing here, Rowan?" she asked, her flat tone making me wonder if she was asking herself the same question.

I checked my phone. "Well, I'm supposed to go sea-kayaking this afternoon. And tomorrow I'm doing an overnight hike to some place called Torrent Bay."

"You sound organised."

"I'm not. I've got ground control. A mate back in Perth doing it all for me."

"That must be great. A tour manager. Do you stick to every schedule?"

"Pretty much."

"Too scared to venture off the path?" She smiled at me. "Yeah, you are. Good little ginger Rowan, taking the road most travelled and doing what he's told."

"Not all the time."

"Defeats the purpose of travel, doesn't it? You should be following your nose, trusting your instincts. Sure, it can be good to have a plan, but you need to add chaos to that order. Throw all the cards up in the air and see how they land."

"Is that what you do?"

She nodded. "But I'm also on a schedule. Gotta get back to the States and go to work."

"What do you do?"

She shifted in her seat, putting her back to the window. She slipped her shoes off and put her socked feet on the seat, with her knees under her chin and her arms wrapped around her legs. This position meant she was both looking directly at me and could see past me.

"Is that your guitar?"

The case was in the corner behind me.

"Yeah."

"For fun, to impress the girls, or are you the real deal?"

"Is there a fourth option?"

She laughed again. "How about this. Do you make a living from it? You know, eat and pay bills?"

"I've been doing that on this trip, by busking. The locals are really supportive of live music. That was something I hadn't expected, that there'd be such a strong music culture here."

"Anything else unexpected? What do you think of the place, based on your impressions filtered through your buddy's schedules?"

17

I considered this, briefly flashing through the trip so far and not coming up with much.

"I guess the country's pretty much how I'd imagined it would be, all green and lush, all this stunning landscape. But what I reckon I'll take back is the overall feeling of friendliness. The people here are all nice to each other, and it seems genuine. We Aussies are nice too, most of the time, but there's something about it that's off. That we're just being nice to be nice."

She smiled. "Very perceptive, and accurate, and you could say the same about Americans. But we take it to the extreme. It's all, 'How are you today?' and 'Have a nice day'. They sound like robots. Machines programmed for niceness. Medicated to smile all the time. I think there'd be a lot less violence in the States if we stopped being so superficial with each other. Nice is okay, but fake nice makes people draw their weapons."

"You're the first American I've met, so I'll have to take your word for it."

"You should definitely go there. One day. If you think this is natural beauty, you should see what we got. You can skip the cities. Where you want to be is out in the wild. The national parks. The mountains. Off the grid."

Her green eyes really started to shine.

"Yellowstone, Olympic, Everglades, Yosemite, Denali," she went on. "And all those places are so different. You could spend a lifetime going from park to park. Lots of folks do that, when they're retired. They sell their house and buy a Winnebago. Sure they spend a lot of time driving and sitting on picnic chairs, but that's definitely better than wasting away in some suburb. They're getting something close to the wilderness experience. A national park is a place where you can escape the human race."

As she said this, I was reminded how much I missed Churchill, and my parents, and even Conor, though he'd been just about unbearable in the last few months. I wanted to see them all. I wasn't interested in escaping the human race.

She gave my shoulder a push. "Did I say something wrong?"

"No. It all sounds great. I was just thinking of some people, that's all. My family and friends. I'll be happy to see them. It's been a messy few months."

"A break-up?"

18

"Yeah. But not mine. My parents, they got divorced."

She shrugged. "Happens a lot."

"Not when they're middle-aged and when they've already celebrated their silver anniversary."

"Are they happy?"

"I think so."

The bus stopped and the doors opened.

"Looks like we're here," she said, lacing up her shoes. "Whatever here is, because it doesn't look like much."

"Yep. Nice chatting."

"Hey, can I come with you?"

"Where?"

"Sea-kayaking. Is that allowed? Can other people join your activities?"

"You'd be the first so far."

She jumped up. "Oh, I get to be the chaos that totally scrambles your schedule."

She seemed to like the idea of that very much.

→←

The second postcard came from Saginaw, Michigan, about a week later.

It was an old-fashioned, sepia-toned, drawn image, with an antique car in front of a two-storey building flying the American flag. "Michigan Employment Institution for the Blind" was printed along the top in gothic script, which made it sound imposing and prison-like. I imagined all the blind people of Saginaw, past and present, being sent to this institution, whether they wanted it or not. It wasn't a nice thought. The car in the image was driving away from the building, as if the driver had just dropped someone off.

On the back was my name and address, this time in red pen, along with a tracing of that five-fingered hand, also in red.

"I think you now, officially, have the freedom to freak out," Churchill said, taking two bottles of Little Creatures from the fridge and sitting down at the kitchen table with me. "This is already moving into weird territory."

"With two postcards? Come on, Church."

What I kept to myself was that I was feeling something. I wasn't sure what it was or even how to put it in words. Something deep in my gut was telling me not to ignore this.

"I bet you more will come," Churchill said. "Another town, in Canada or the States. Another hand."

We both opened our beers and drank. The air-conditioner hummed in the background. Outside, the sun was setting, but the temperature was still in the high thirties.

"What am I supposed to do? I need something more concrete. She's probably already gone from this place Saginaw."

"You think it's this girl, right? From your NZ trip? And that this freakish little hand might be from the love child you had together?"

"I can't think who else it could be. But I'd like to think that if Nola got pregnant and I was the father, she'd tell me about it. There's a responsibility involved. I would never ignore that."

As I said this, I wasn't entirely convinced of myself.

"Well, let's do the math. If you planted a ginger seed in her garden about five and half years ago, then this kid is getting close to being five." He picked up both postcards and showed me the hands. "I'm guessing that's just about the size of a five-year-old's hand."

"Could be."

"Forget the extra finger. That's not real. It's just to get your attention. It's a sign."

"Of what?"

"No idea. But I did do some research on Saginaw, because the postcard arrived when you were at work."

"You don't have better things to do?"

"Not really. This is way more interesting than accounting software. It's a puzzle, and I want to solve it. Anyway, Saginaw's not exactly down the road from Thunder Bay, but it's in the vicinity. Maybe Nola's on a road trip with her kiddie up there, and the next postcard you get might come from Chicago or Detroit, or someplace nearby."

"You sound certain these will keep coming."

He nodded. "They're smoke signals. She's reaching out to you. And these cards will haunt you unless you do something about them."

"Don't you think it's all too obscure? At the very least, I need a meeting place and a date. Why can't she put that on the postcard?"

"If you want my opinion, you should just go. Take the next flight to Saginaw and start from there."

"That's insane. I don't even know Nola's last name. You want me spend a fortune to get to wherever Saginaw is, then wander the streets shouting her name? Hey, excuse me, have you seen a girl called Nola? Maybe she's got a kid with her who looks a bit like me. They'll lock me up."

"Yeah, they probably would. You don't have a photo?"

"Nothing. And there's no proof that Nola's behind this. There have been other girls since. What about Odette? She disappeared off the map after we split."

"She's in Adelaide. Married."

"How do you know?"

"She invited me to her wedding. Don't look so shocked. The good swan always liked me. I was the one who looked after her in the mornings while you slept in. Because the way to a girl's heart is through a sterling cup of morning-after coffee, and you know I do that well."

"You didn't say you were invited."

Churchill made a slightly anguished face. "Well, I'm not exactly the wedding type. And who wants to go to Adelaide anyway?"

This made me laugh. "Okay. So it's definitely not Odette. I think all my other exes are in Perth."

"They are. I checked. It's Nola, and we gotta find her."

"How do we do that? I'm not going to Saginaw."

"What if I told you it's the hometown of Stevie Wonder?"

I picked up the Saginaw postcard. "Then I'd hope to hell poor little Stevie didn't end up in this place. It looks horrid."

"Rowan, I'm in on this. Yeah? Full throttle. I can do all the organisation for you."

"Slow down, Church."

"Seriously. Let's not die wondering."

"You really need a hobby."

"Definitely. And this can be it. I'll be a hobby detective."

I sipped my beer, giving it some thought. I didn't have the money for such a trip, and I couldn't just leave the shop on short notice.

"It's not enough. I say we wait for another postcard."

"Oh, way to live on the edge, Rowan. Why don't you just spend all day indoors as well? Live like that."

"Sorry, Church. That's the best I can do right now. I need more before I go rambling across America in search of a girl I used to know and her kid who I'm maybe the father of."

21

Having said it, the idea of an adventure like that actually sounded very appealing. A chance to break the monotony.

"Fine," Churchill said, and he was in a huff. "When the next postcard arrives, we'll move. Get ready for it."

We both drank some more. The beer was taking some of the edge off the hot day.

Churchill grabbed his tablet. "You'll be interested to know that while I was researching Saginaw, I came across some pretty weird stuff. There was a video made in that fair city about a week ago that's gone viral. Some urban artist or vandal, I don't know, set up this prank at a four-way stop sign." He found the video and turned the tablet's screen towards me. "You know how they work? The car that goes next is based on the order of who gets there."

"I know."

"Yeah, so this vandal parked four cars at each stop sign early in the morning, before the traffic started, and put four dummies in the drivers' seats, so it looked like the cars were occupied, and set up a camera to record the whole thing."

"What happened?"

"Total chaos. Watch."

Churchill played the video. It was a time-lapse, sped up, making it seem more comical. At first, drivers were forced to go around the stationary cars, but as the intersection got busier, the cars started to congest and clog it until no one was moving. Drivers got out of their cars to start arguing with each other. A fight began. A truck driver got out with a rifle in his hands. The police arrived. One officer fired a warning shot in the air. The other spotted the camera and turned it off.

"It's all over the web. Apparently, it turned a section of the city into gridlock."

"Who did this and why?"

Churchill shrugged. "Dunno."

"It's bizarre. That someone would go to all that trouble just to mess up people's lives."

"Maybe it was a protest. Bike lovers and all that."

I finished my beer and stood up.

"Where ya going?" Churchill asked.

"I gotta go. Travis, from the shop, his band is playing a set in Freo tonight. I promised I'd go down and show my support."

"Have fun, and don't do anything I wouldn't do."

"I'm already going outside."

"Yeah, well, good luck with that."

I walked up Morgan Street to the train station. I'd only had one beer, but as Travis likes to drink and is a bit of a bully about it, I thought it best not to run the risk of driving and getting pulled over by the police. There's a lot of breath-testing and speed-ticketing in Perth, and the police like to set up on the main roads leading in and out of Fremantle, especially on weekends.

It was Thursday, but still not worth the risk.

Halfway up Morgan I decided to cut down Fortune Street. I was early, and I needed to time my arrival at the gig so I got there not long after the start, to avoid having to down a rush of pre-show drinks with the band.

The evening was very warm. It was pleasant to walk.

I like strolling around Shenton Park. For a suburb of Perth, it's not the usual sprawl of large blocks, two-car garages and five-bedroom houses. It's got character, and it's changed a lot over the years. The small houses are old timber and iron workers' cottages. Some have been restored and are now worth quite a bit of money. When I was growing up in Claremont, Shenton Park was considered a no-go area, run-down and decrepit, criss-crossed by alleyways that Nana warned us not to go down, at night or during the day. It was a place of hospitals, mental institutions and centres for the disabled, bordered by a large cemetery and with a lake that Nana said was once an Aboriginal burial ground. The area could just about qualify as affluent now, though there were many houses still awaiting renovation.

I dawdled, zigzagging around Commercial Road, Hopetoun Terrace and Smyth Road, using the alleys and admiring the houses. A few were for sale. Nearly every house had a four-wheel drive parked out the front, making the narrow streets seem cluttered. The verges were also piled with garbage and stuff to be thrown away, as collection day was nearing. The mess seemed out of place, as if the area was attempting to put on more lower class airs. Or maybe old Shenton Park habits die hard.

At Abedare Road, I followed the edge of Karrakatta cemetery, which was gloomy as the last sunset colours left the sky, up to Railway Road. Once at Karrakatta station, I really wanted to turn around and walk home. I'd seen Travis and his band before. They were ordinary, and not really going anywhere; a bunch of drunks wailing on instruments they could barely play. They bought in hard to the idea that if you couldn't play well, you played loud. I had ear plugs with me, but even with those in, I knew I was in for some serious ringing afterwards, which would continue well into tomorrow.

I bought a ticket and waited for the train. Further down the platform, two kids were playing some kind of chasing game around their dad, who was talking on his phone.

Right then, I felt bad. If I was the father, Nola's child was growing up without me. But there wasn't much I could do about it. Nola was keeping me in the dark and most probably had her reasons for doing so.

Was sending cryptic postcards the kind of thing Nola would do?

I thought not, but maybe I hadn't sized her up that well, having only spent a week with her. Maybe she'd changed.

I had. I was twenty-one when we met, a university drop-out and struggling musician earning a pittance working the counter of a music shop. It was Nola who encouraged me to follow my passion, which was the guitar.

"You're good, but not everyone can be Bob Dylan," she'd said.

That stuck. When I got back to Perth, I became an apprentice luthier, which meant I moved from the counter to the workshop, a situation that suited me far better. Building and repairing guitars helped me expand the range of what I could with the instrument, in terms of playing style, sound and versatility. I became more inclined to experiment, with open tunings and different strings. And I built Daphne.

The train pulled into the station and I got on. Its relative emptiness made me feel a little unsafe, despite the two security guards on board. I moved down to sit not far from the dad and his two kids. He was still on the phone and using his free hand to get both kids to sit still.

I looked out the window. It was dark now. The streets were deserted, save for the cars. No one was walking or cycling. People were already home, or were driving home. The outside world was lifeless, and I wondered again why this lifeless world scared Churchill so much.

The stations came and went, all with empty platforms. Loch Street, Claremont, Swanbourne. The lack of passengers made the train seem pointless. For some of the way, the line followed Stirling Highway, which was still busy with traffic.

When the train reached Fremantle, I thought it would be very easy just to stay seated and go back to Shenton Park. I didn't want the Tequila shots Travis ordered between sets. I didn't want to stand with his friends, who spread out to make the thin crowd look bigger. I didn't want to listen to the shouted singing and the two-note guitar solos, with all the amps turned up to eleven.

The impending stress of it all was already making my ears ring more than usual, but I got off the train.

I decided to walk around Freo a bit, kill some more time and maybe give myself the feeling that the evening was mine to enjoy. The wind blew off the ocean and down the streets. Travis had said they were playing in the back of some warehouse on Phillimore Street and that there would be a sign out the front. I took Market Street, then headed down High. The National Hotel was busy with after-work types, men mostly, about my age, and more of them wandered the streets, looking for action. Down the side streets of Pakenham and Henry, I could see small groups of homeless people leaning against buildings, as Freo showed both her faces within the confines of one block. I took Cliff Street to circle back to Phillimore and followed the noise to the warehouse. It was Travis's band, without question. Teeth-shattering loud, even from outside.

I put my ear plugs in, which increased the volume of the ringing, and walked around the building in search of the entrance. On the back wall, there was a mural of a man and a shark kissing. Both figures were upright. The shark was balanced on its tail and taller, so that it was bending down to meet the lips of the man who was up on tip-toe. This resulted in something of a gender confusion. The man even had his left leg hooked around the shark's tail, to draw it closer and make the embrace more sexual. With the shark's fins around the man's upper body, almost caressing, there was something protective about the embrace, while the man's left hand stroking the gills displayed an unexpected love and tenderness.

I stood there staring at this mural for what seemed like a long time.

Despite the difference in size, I had no sense the shark was going to envelop the man. They were two beings as one in a loving, passionate embrace, and I felt once the kiss was over, the two would walk off into the sunset, hand in fin.

A tap on my shoulder startled me.

"Crap, Travis. Where'd you come from?"

He had a beer in his right hand and a badly rolled cigarette dangling from his mouth.

"What are you on? I was shouting at you and you didn't even move."

I took my ear plugs out. "Sorry. Doctor's orders. Gotta protect my hearing."

Travis looked confused. "But you're outside."

"How's it going?"

Travis was wearing his usual gig uniform of purple pipe jeans, white and green Parkway Drive singlet not hiding much of his sizeable frame, and Jamaica flag sweatbands on his wrists. His long hair was damp with sweat and strands of it were stuck inside the folds of his neck. It would be a keen groupie who would want to get involved with Travis.

"It's goin off," he said through a cloud of smoke. "You missed an awesome first set. Tight, man. I'm tellin ya. Tight to the extreme."

"Great. I was just about to come in. I couldn't find the door."

"I'll show ya. Place is jammed. Our second set's gonna blow the roof."

Travis walked off. As I put my ear plugs back in, I took one last look at the mural. Down the bottom, at the tip of the shark's tail, was a circular G, turned into a star symbol of sorts with eight arrows positioned around the circle.

I followed Travis inside. It was crowded. The band was already on stage, tuning up again. I saw they had a girl on drums.

I grabbed Travis by the arm, which was sweaty to touch. "Who's your new drummer?"

"That's Holly. She's filling in for Marlo. He couldn't get a sitter."

"She any good?"

Travis shrugged. "She's holding it. Just. We're propping her up."

He jogged to the stage and looped the strap of his bass guitar over his shoulders.

The first song had a disjointed start, but soon they got it together. It was so loud that I could just about lean forward against the sound waves coming from the speakers in front of the stage and they would hold me up.

The girl on the drums was easily the best musician of them all. I joined the throng and started dancing.

→←

When no more postcards landed in our letterbox, Churchill dismissed the first two as aberrations, gave up on planning my trip, stopped steering any conversation towards fatherhood and focused on other things, which included learning Mandarin online in the hope of adapting his accounting software for the Chinese market.

Life went on. It was technically autumn, but the weather stayed hot.

Nana had her cataracts removed. While she was recovering, we unlocked the door which joined the kitchens of the split house, allowing Churchill to take care of her. She was very grateful, and also really happy with the difference the surgery made. She talked about driving again.

I worked a lot, covering shifts for others and trying to get some money together. When I had some spare time, I worked on building a guitar which I hoped to sell. Because what I didn't tell Churchill was that I had a friend from school who worked at the Shenton Park post office. I asked Matt to put any postcards to the side, so I could collect them. They arrived, in order, from Kingston, Ontario; Columbus, Ohio; Baltimore, Maryland; Knoxville, Tennessee; Savannah, Georgia; Birmingham, Alabama; and New Orleans, Louisiana. Matt said the hand was cool, but he didn't pry further.

I wasn't proud of myself for keeping this from Churchill, but as each postcard still had just the hand and my address, there was nothing to go on. At night, I sometimes took the postcards out and stared at them. I checked the locations on the map and saw that Nola, if it really was her, was travelling clockwise around North America, which was the kind of thing Churchill would have me do, as he had with the New Zealand trip. He liked symmetry.

The child occupied my thoughts. It was difficult not to share these thoughts with Churchill, as we talked about everything.

The week I'd spent with Nola in New Zealand had included hiking through Abel Tasman National Park. There was nowhere along the way to buy condoms, and Nola had said she was on the pill. I wondered what else she had possibly lied about.

With all the postcards laid out, hand-side up, it looked to me like the hand was growing. Was it a little boy's hand or a little girl's? A redhead, tall and spindly, like me? Or green-eyed, restless and head-strong, like Nola?

All I could do was stare at the hands and wonder, then pack the postcards away and try to forget.

Perhaps that was all Nola wanted, that these postcards would bring a certain disorder to my life. She was a fan of disruption, of chaos. I remembered much. She'd talked about it a lot; that many people were stuck in rhythms and cycles which they needed to be jolted out of. They needed the unexpected to shake them awake, so she'd said.

Nola did that to me in New Zealand, deleting Churchill's last itinerary from my phone and getting me to decide what would happen each day and where we would go. That was how we ended up walking all the way to Awaroa Bay, getting butchered by sand-flies, sharing her sleeping bag and screwing in her tent each night. We walked for a week, and I was completely unprepared for it, with shoes that gave me blisters and a cumbersome guitar case that made hiking along narrow paths difficult. At the time, I wasn't that into Nola, but I was into the chaos that she brought and the experiences that resulted, right up until we took a water taxi back to the relative civilisation of Marahau.

During that week, I'd felt alive. Awake. I was aware of the possibilities of life. Yes, of course we could walk all the way to Awaroa Bay. Why the hell not?

In Shenton Park, I was coasting, drifting. Week after week, going through the motions.

Then, I came home from work one evening to find Churchill at the kitchen table with a postcard in front of him. He had his arms folded and looked a little angry.

"You got something you want to tell me?" he asked.

"What do you mean?"

He held up a postcard from Little Rock, Arkansas. "This came today. It's been weeks since the one from Saginaw, and I couldn't believe that after getting two in a row at the start, there'd be nothing in between that postcard and this one. So, where are the rest? Because they are others, aren't there? Must be."

"Yeah, there are."

I went into my room and retrieved the postcards from my bed-side drawer.

When I put them on the table, Churchill looked at each one in turn, then asked, "How could you keep this from me?"

He was hurt, and I felt bad.

"Because there's nothing on them. They're just hands. We're at the same point we were when the first card arrived. We don't know anything."

"Wrong. There could be a pattern here. We just need to figure it out. And it's also clear that Nola's still trying to reach out to you."

"Or she's just trying to bother me. If she wanted to contact me, she'd do it properly and organise for us to meet."

"Maybe you're supposed to earn it. As a way of proving you're up to the task."

"Come on. That's a stretch."

"Still, shame on you. For withholding. How'd you manage to hide them anyway?"

"I know someone at the post office."

"Ah, an inside job. I guess he was sick today, or on holiday."

"Or he just forgot. Look, I'm sorry, Church. I should've told you about the postcards."

"Yeah, you should have."

"But I wasn't ready to just drop everything and go. I didn't have the money, and it was just a hand. I was hoping she'd send more than that, but she didn't."

"How about now? Are you ready? Because this postcard has something written on the back."

"It does? What?"

"It says, 'We'll always have Awaroa'. That mean something?"

"Yeah. It's gotta be Nola. That's where we walked to, Awaroa Bay."

"Right. I think it's time for you to pack your bag and get on the next flight to Little Rock."

I looked at the postcards spread out on the table. Nola was really getting around, and it made me want to hit the road. What I hated the most was how powerless I felt. Going to the States and looking for Nola was one way to take control. But more than anything, I liked the idea of getting away from the shop and out of Perth, if only for a short while.

"Okay. Book me a flight. But I'm paying."

"Oh, now we're talking." He grabbed his tablet and started tapping and swiping. "But you're still in the doghouse. You shouldn't have kept those postcards from me."

"I know. I just didn't think there was anything we could do."

"Well, at the very least, we can have an American adventure. The problem is we're already a week behind. Somehow, we've got to get ourselves a step ahead. Where is she right now? Where's she going next? This is what we have to figure out."

29

"I think she's going clockwise, in a weird way, in and out, and not anything like a circle."

"That should narrow things down a bit. Don't worry. Finding the pattern is my problem." He turned the tablet to me. "Here. That's the damage, to Little Rock via Sydney and Dallas."

"Is that return? What happens when I end up on the other side of the country?"

"We'll worry about that later. So, book it?"

It was a lot of money, but I decided the chance to break the routine was reason enough to go.

"Do it."

"Right on. Hah, the airport's named after Bill and Hillary Clinton. Okay. Give me a credit card. I'll get everything sorted. Ground control is back and operational."

"Thanks, Church."

"Don't ever do that again."

"What?"

"Withhold. Especially important stuff like this. It's your child, Rowan, possibly. Think about that."

As Churchill worked on my bookings, I picked up the Little Rock postcard, to get a sense of where I was heading. The main image was Junction Bridge, which looked like it was for an old railway line. The elevator and stairs in the foreground made me assume it was now a pedestrian bridge. Along the bottom of the postcard in cheerful italic type was, "Wish you were here!"

I thought it was significant that Nola had written on the back of this one, making reference to our week in Abel Tasman. It made me think any postcards to come would also hold clues.

"Done," Churchill said. "You're on the red-eye to Sydney tonight."

"That quick? What'll I tell the boss?"

"Tell him the truth, that you need an unpaid leave of absence for personal reasons. Tell him it's family. You could even tell him about Nola and the kid. You can't go wrong with honesty."

I made the call. To my surprise, the only thing Jono was annoyed about was that it was such short notice. He was also honest with me, saying that if I was gone for longer than two weeks, he'd have to hire someone and that there'd be no guarantee I'd get my job back, which to my surprise, I didn't really mind.

"And?" Churchill asked when I put my phone down.

"We've got a fortnight."

"That won't be nearly enough. Anyway, we'll find you another job when you're back. Something better."

"I hope so. Because I'll probably come back broke."

Churchill put the tablet on the table. "Right, all done for starters. I've booked you a couple of nights in the Firehouse Hostel, which looks pretty cool. I'll email you the bookings and a map. I also added some data and roaming credit to your phone, so we can stay in touch while you're on the move, and I'll sort your visa waiver."

"Thanks, Church."

"Now get packing. You've got about an hour before you need to be at the airport. Gawd, this is exciting. We're going to America."

It made me excited too, and it was exactly the kind of crazy thing I needed to do to get out of the rut I was in. In my room, I hauled my old backpack out of the closet, still with the baggage stickers from my New Zealand trip around the straps. I shoved some clothes in, not really sure what I was going to need. Was it cold in Little Rock at this time of year? I put a few books in that I'd been wanting to read, plus my song-writing journal and an extra set of strings. Churchill stood in the doorway and watched me as I put Daphne in a soft bag, then placed that bag inside the hard-shell case.

"You're taking your guitar?"

"Of course. I'll try to do some busking and earn some money along the way."

"Good idea. Maybe you'll get inspired and write some songs as well." He paused, then added, "There's something about this that feels right, don't you reckon?"

"It feels good just to be doing something."

"Do you have anything more to go on? Because if we don't find Nola, then this could all be for nothing. A job, or a city, or her family? Something that can narrow the search parameters and maybe help me get her last name. Otherwise, you'll be looking for a Nola in a haystack."

Packed, I sat on the edge of my bed and thought back to that week in Abel Tasman. I remembered that Nola really knew what she was doing. She was comfortable camping rough and being out in the forest. Abel Tasman wasn't exactly the wilderness, but Nola was definitely in her element, and I'd felt safe with her.

"Our first night together, we camped on a beach and Nola made a fire without matches or a lighter. She really did rub two sticks together. It was impressive."

"And it was right about then you went completely off the grid," Churchill said. "You remember that too? I was worried."

"That was my fault. But when she made this fire, I asked her about it and she said she'd had training. To be a park ranger. It was seasonal work, normally in spring and summer, she said. I think that's what she does."

"A ranger. That helps. Leave it with me." Churchill checked his watch. "Time to go, Rowan. How are you getting to the airport?"

"You're not driving me?"

"Yeah, no, that's not gonna happen. Tempting, but not tonight. Maybe next time. Why don't you ask Nana? She wants to start driving again, now that her eyes have improved."

"She hasn't been behind the wheel in years."

"Still got the car though. Ask her. It's late. There won't be much traffic."

The car in question was a cream-coloured, early-eighties Holden Statesman, which had been my grandfather's car. He died not long after I was born, but I'd heard a lot of stories about him from Nana. Apparently, Mum had objected to Nana keeping the Statesman, as it was too big for her, but keep it she did. She drove it on the weekends while using her hatchback during the week, until that car died and wasn't replaced. The Statesman was an absolute whale, a good five metres long and difficult to park. Nana could barely see over the steering wheel. Over the last few years, as she could barely see at all, the car had stayed in the garage under a blue cover. Every Sunday morning, she went out to the garage, taking a cup of tea and a newspaper with her, started the car and sat in it for half an hour while the engine idled. At Nana's request, I'd taken it to the petrol station a few times to fill up the enormous tank and once to get the car serviced. It was a challenge just to get the thing in and out of the garage.

Short on time, I phoned Nana and asked if she'd run me out to the airport.

"Give me five minutes to change," she said.

Churchill, still standing in the doorway, must have read the expression on my face. "Told ya. She's full of surprises. It must run in the family, because I never thought you had it in you to just go like this."

32

"I want to find Nola, and I want to find this kid and see if I'm the father."

"Yeah, that's part of it. What's the other part?"

I threw the last necessities in my backpack: a bathroom bag, a hat, a couple of pens and several packets of disposable ear plugs, the kind used on construction sites.

"I guess I need something to shake me out of this funk. These last few months, I feel like I haven't been going anywhere. I'm not unhappy. I think life is generally okay, but I reckon a change of scene will do me good."

"Understandable. Nola's just the trigger."

My backpack closed, I was ready. The knock on the door meant that Nana was too. Churchill went to let her in.

I took my passport from my bed-side drawer and put on my thin, waterproof jacket. I ripped the old airport stickers off my backpack, shouldered it and picked up my guitar case.

"Taxi's waiting," Nana said in the hallway. She was wearing blue jeans and a red, green and white check shirt, tucked in, looking for all the world like she was going to an eighties rodeo.

Churchill wolf-whistled. "Who let the fox out? Pam, you look fabulous."

"Thank you, Churchill, and keep your hands to yourself."

"Bossy too. Love it."

Smiling, Nana turned to me. "Now, where are you going?"

"Little Rock, Arkansas."

"The search begins," Churchill added.

"For what?" Nana asked.

I moved towards the door with all my gear. "It's just a holiday. Following the music, hopefully."

Churchill gave me a hug. With me being a head taller, I had a brief flash of that shark-man mural I'd seen in Freo.

"We touch base every day," he said. "Phone on. I want reports. You don't lose contact with ground control. You stay on the course. Got it?"

"I got it." I turned to Nana. "Take care of him. In fact, I want both of you to take care of each other."

"We will," Churchill said. "Have a great trip. Don't do anything I wouldn't do."

"It's the outside world, Church. Anything can happen."

"I know. That's what I'm worried about. Contact me when you get to the Firehouse."

"Alright. See ya, mate."

Nana led the way around the side of the house to the garage. Her cowboy boots clicked against the driveway's paving.

"You better drive, Rowan. At least until we're out of the city."

"Why don't we take my car?"

"That thing's too small. A strong wind will blow it away. No, let's give the Statesman a run."

She handed me the key and I put my gear in the copious boot, which could easily have held a drum kit and half a dozen amps. The blue cover sent dust into the air as I pulled it off the rest of the car, and it was a squeeze just to get in, because the car filled so much of the garage. The Statesman had a bench seat and a column shift. The seat was way forward, which meant I had my knees wedged under the dash. But I couldn't find the lever to put the seat back.

This massive car had the effect of making me feel very small, especially because the Smart is always a little cramped.

I put the key in and turned it over, half-expecting the car to explode. It took a few tries, as the battery was probably close to being flat, but the engine eventually caught and I gave it a few revs. It made a fantastic amount of noise that drowned out all the ringing in my ears. I saw that there were just over seven thousand kilometres on the odometer.

I got the car in reverse and slowly backed out. The car was seriously sluggish.

Now able to open the passenger door, Nana got in as well.

"Let her warm up," she said. "A touch of choke."

"What the hell is choke?"

She pointed. "That one. Pull it out a bit. And you've still got the park-brake on."

"That explains why I had to put my foot to the floor to get out of the garage."

I found the park-brake and released it.

"That's enough choke," Nana said. "I think we can go."

"This is like being in a time-machine."

"Go easy. It's a V8."

I revved it some more, loving the sound. "This car's a beast."

"Well, unleash this beast."

I reversed down the driveway and backed straight out onto the street. Lengthwise like this, the Statesman just about filled Morgan Street. I had to go forwards and backwards, and really work the steering wheel, in order to get enough angle to straighten the car. Churchill watched from the veranda, the front door open, and with one foot still inside the house. He laughed and waved, and I knew I'd really miss him.

I got us onto Herbert Road and up to Nicholson Road, where I turned right.

"Pull over," Nana said.

"Why?"

"I want to drive."

I did so, getting out and moving around to the passenger side while Nana slid across the bench seat. Once I was inside, she put the car in drive and we took off down Nicholson.

"Jesus, slow down."

She was concentrating hard, leaning far forward, and driving in just about the middle of the road.

"Let me drive," she said. "It's been a while."

After we'd negotiated the traffic lights and the three lanes of Thomas Street, and made it onto the freeway, I sensed Nana relaxing.

"I've missed this," she said, sitting back and driving with one hand low on the steering wheel.

I had the feeling the Statesman had missed it too.

"You know the way?"

She nodded. "I'll follow the signs."

I remembered how, when I was a kid in this car, I'd felt like royalty. Now, I felt like an overgrown kid with a once rich grandmother, and all she had to show for her fortune was this antiquated form of luxury.

"What's in Little Rock?"

I considered a few lies, then decided to go with the truth. "I'm trying to find a girl I used to know. An American. That was what Churchill meant by the search begins. I met her in New Zealand, but lost track of her."

"That trip was years ago. Why are you looking for her now?"

"Well, I guess it's because she's been looking for me. Reaching out, in a way. I decided to make the effort and try to meet her halfway."

"That's nice. Girls like it when you make an effort. Dean, your

35

grandfather, he actually bought this car to impress me. We'd been married for years, but he still tried to romance me, right up to the end."

She smiled, and we lapsed into silence, as I wasn't sure what to say.

When we got to the airport, Nana didn't pull into the car park. She circled around to the narrow drop-off point in front of departures, with half the car still on the road and blocking traffic. A few drivers honked their horns.

"Have a good trip," she said. "I'll pick you up when you're back."

"Thanks. Churchill will know when that is."

I looked at Nana, in her retro-rodeo outfit and with both hands on the steering wheel, and wondered if she might point this whale east and drive clear across the country.

"Be careful, Rowan." She turned the engine off and handed me the key. "Only chase what's worth chasing."

I got out of the car, retrieved my gear from the boot and gave her the key back. She drove off, without waving.

Inside, the airport was busy. At check-in, I used my height as a reason to ask for exit-row seats for all my flights. I didn't get one for Perth-Sydney, which was booked out, but I did get one for Sydney-Dallas. I put three red fragile stickers on Daphne's case and hoped she'd survive the trip.

Security, a coffee, a quick trip to the bathroom, then we were boarding.

There wasn't a single empty seat. I was lucky to have an aisle seat, right at the back of the plane.

It was nearly midnight. I was on the red-eye to Sydney. Most of the passengers were already settling down to sleep, having brought their own eye masks and neck pillows on board, and wearing tracksuits that looked like pyjamas.

But I was awake.

Abandoned Shopping Trolleys

Because of the security cameras, a disguise is necessary. At first, she wants to don blackface, in order to make a political statement as well as cause chaos: the Little Rock Nine; Arkansas as the most racist state; the Klu Klux Klan headquarters up the road in Harrison; showing support for Ferguson; and making a point about wealth inequality and the lack of universal healthcare for African Americans.

But when she tests this in the hostel bathroom, applying brown shoe polish to her face, she sees how unconvincing and inappropriate it is. It will only bring attention, and this is the last thing she wants. She decides it's better to blend in rather than stand out.

Though she hates wearing them, she buys a dress at the Inretrospec store on Center Street. The dress is second-hand, fits perfectly, and is patterned with red, white and blue, which she thinks is a nice hint to American patriotism, but the shop assistant informs her they are also the colours of the Arkansas state flag. This makes her smile.

She adds to the disguise a black wig, purchased at Downtown Wigs and Fashions, on Main Street, and a pair of spectacles nabbed from an outdoor table of a café while the owner was inside.

That evening, while her daughter sleeps, she tries it all on. It looks right, and she gets lost in the disguise; the glasses even sharpen everything around her. But something's missing. Make-up adds nothing, and a handbag would just be cumbersome.

Then it comes: she's a Little Rock housewife, with a kid or two, and one on the way.

She pulls on black tights under the dress, and stuffs a small pillow down the front. It takes some adjusting to get just the right look, but when it's there, she sees it's perfect.

As usual, it's difficult to sleep the night before an action, and she's up early. The Saturday morning is gloriously gloomy; the weather gods are on her side. After a week of solid rain, she thinks all the locals will be keen to get their shopping done and go home, where they can laze the afternoon away watching sports. There'll be no picnics, barbecues or garden parties this weekend; not with this weather.

Like yesterday, when she did her shopping and recon, she takes her daughter across MacArthur Park to the Arkansas Arts Center, where there's another two hour theatre and creativity workshop happening for kids this morning. Parting is difficult, with her daughter threatening to make a scene, but two teenage helpers manage to distract her and lead her towards the raucous group of assembled children.

One of the girls working there compliments her on her dress.

It's a relief to get out of there without her daughter, and it means she can breathe a little easier and focus on the task ahead. She heads down Cumberland Street, carrying the wig, glasses, pillow and her camera in a plastic bag. She walks quickly, at her own pace, feeling her whole body starting to come alive: every neuron and synapse buzzing with the utter freedom this two-hour window offers. It's tempting to leave her daughter at the Arkansas Arts Center forever. She won't, but the mere thought of it gives her pleasure and makes her walk faster. To lose the baggage and burden, to get back in control, to be free.

A light rain falls. She thinks it's a beautiful day for chaos.

Map-less and time-poor, she keeps the route simple, following Cumberland until it bends into the broad expanse of Le Harpe Boulevard, which is heavy with traffic. She sweats a little as she weaves between the slower walkers on the footpath. When Le Harpe becomes Cantrell Road, she waits at the next bus stop, alone. It's here she turns her back to the traffic to put on the wig and glasses, and inserts the pillow as her baby bump. The Polaroid camera stays in the plastic bag.

The 21 bus pulls in and she gets on it for the last mile to the Razorback Square Shopping Center. The bus driver gives her a very warm smile as he says "Good morning".

Her target today is the Walmart Neighborhood Market. This will be the third time she's done something in a Walmart. She considers the stores bland and generic, and they offer an ideal blank canvas to work on.

When she gets there, she finds it already busy. Cars pull in and jostle in the car park, while the early-starters push trolleys laden with groceries out of the market. She thinks they look like they're stocking up for war. Or maybe there was another tornado warning. Either way, she finds the consumerism and excess sickening, on what is most probably a normal shopping day for these folks.

She goes into the Walmart, trying to walk normally and behave like a local. She loops a basket over her right elbow and starts shopping.

Though half the size of a regular Walmart, this store is still big, with enough aisles for people to spread out, but with not that many workers.

On her scoping trip yesterday, she only spotted three employees working the floor, all of them too young to drive. There were more employees at the cashiers and behind counters serving customers, as there are today, but they aren't worth worrying about. They won't be the ones coming to the rescue when something happens on the floor.

She starts by focusing on the ends of the aisles, hunting for a trolley left by a shopper who has gone in search of some forgotten item. The first one she gets is very full, mostly with junk food; the produce is scattered on top like it's decoration. She pushes it down to the last aisle, which has the picnic, barbecue and party supplies. She parks the trolley in the empty aisle and places her basket on the floor.

With the game afoot, she knows she has to act fast and surreptitiously, as the owner of that first trolley will soon raise the alarm.

In the dairy section, she takes the trolley of a portly old woman who's squinting at the labels of milk cartons. This trolley goes down to the last aisle as well.

The third trolley has a child sitting in the front carrier, with the boy's mother distracted on the phone. This thievery gives her a serious buzz.

Heading back down the aisles in search of another, her heart starts to race with the excitement of it all, and she wonders why she wastes so much time during the day not doing stuff like this. Getting the child is particularly good, but it raises the stakes and the alarm is bound to go off soon. As she grabs another trolley from the dairy section, she sees the old woman standing there, looking around for her trolley.

She manages to get one more down to the last aisle before sensing that staff have been alerted. From somewhere in the store she hears a woman shouting, "Jaydon, Jaydon," managing to extract three syllables from the name.

It's time for her to go, but as all the noise is coming from the other end of the store, and the party supplies aisle is still deserted, she takes a minute to mix up the contents of the trolleys. A large jar of jam falls to the floor and breaks, and she thinks this is just fine. She positions the trolley with the child in it near the mess, to make it look like he's responsible. For good measure, she places one of her cards into the folds of the drool-catching Confederate flag-themed do-rag that's tied around his neck. Cards also go into each of the trolleys, and she makes a few minor adjustments to where each trolley is placed, getting the scene just right.

She takes one photograph, then picks up her basket and sneaks to the end of the aisle. When she gets there, Jaydon starts crying.

"Stupid kid," she says.

Near the cashiers, she stops to look with a few other shoppers at the commotion happening at the other end of the store. Two boys in Walmart uniforms, one tall and skinny, the other tall and tubby, are trying to deal with the distraught mother who is shouting at the two employees and also at whoever she's talking to on the phone. The boys appear to be doing their best, but other shoppers also come forward to say their trolleys are gone, including the old woman.

None of the other shoppers intervene. They all just watch. And this means that no one is line for the first cashier, so she takes it.

"What's going on?" she asks.

The old cashier looks like he was once retired and decided to return to work because he was broke, or to give his life some purpose.

"Sounds like a kid's gone missing," he says.

"Yeah, I thought I heard crying, coming from the end of the store."

"Happens all the time."

"Don't I know it. My little girl is such a handful." She pats at her soft bump. "I'm hoping he'll be a bit tamer."

The cashier gives her a weary smile.

She turns and looks at the scene, because she thinks that's what someone would do. A woman in a business suit, with the air of importance of the store manager, is attempting to take control of the situation. She sends the two Walmart boys off to search for Jaydon and the trolleys, and does her best to calm down all the aggrieved shoppers. The skinny boy runs and the tubby boy tries to. But rather than just looking down each aisle, they actually go the full length, down one and up the next, together, moving through the aisles and slowly edging closer to the picnic and party supplies aisle. By the time they get there, she'll be gone.

"Cash or credit?" the cashier asks.

She checks the total, pays cash, and places her items in a paper bag.

"Thank you for shopping at Walmart."

It's tempting to stay and watch, but she deems it too risky. She walks out of the store, leaving the chaos behind.

Her walk this time, across the car park to Cantrell Road, is that of someone going about a dull Saturday routine. A police car goes straight past her and pulls into the lot. She finds that very satisfying, and assumes it was the mother who called the police.

It all happened a lot faster than she anticipated, which means there's time enough to walk back to MacArthur Park. She crosses Cantrell and enters Knoop Park. The wig goes into a bin, but she places the pillow next to a sleeping homeless man. She decides to keep the glasses.

As she walks, the adrenaline starts to abate, and she already misses it.

Chasing Shadows

I've never liked being tall. From beds to doorways to showers to cars, the world is just not designed for people like me. The situation is perhaps at its worst on an airplane, which is a cramped enough space even for people of average height.

Despite the exit-row seat from Sydney to Dallas, I wasn't able to sleep on any of my flights. The extra leg room was good, but the seats weren't wide enough for three tall men, meaning we rubbed shoulders for the entire flight.

So, I lost the first day in Little Rock to sleep. While short, the bunk-bed at the Firehouse Hostel was surprisingly comfortable, and I slept in the foetal position until late afternoon. It took a long shower for me to realise where I was and what I was doing.

I was in the United States of America, a country considerably larger than my own, where I knew nobody, and I was trying to find a person. Well, two people, but whether the second existed was still conjecture.

Every joint hurt from taking three flights to the other side of the world, and the inside of my mouth felt like a scungy old air vent.

Dry and dressed, I was just about ready for bed again. But I was also hungry, and very thirsty. I asked the hostel receptionist for some dining advice. He marked a few places on a map, mostly Mexican restaurants and fast food joints. I chose a place nearby, a Tex-Mex bar and grill, just over the big highway from MacArthur Park. There weren't many people, but I thought the atmosphere was welcoming. I sat at the bar and ordered a cheeseburger, a bottle of water and a beer. The water came first and I drank it all in one go, meaning I could sip the beer and enjoy it. The bartender said it was brewed locally, called Blue Canoe.

The bar had Wi-Fi. I took out my phone, signed in and caught up on the emails and messages I'd missed, giving Churchill's mails priority. The email "Yearbook 1" had a collection of headshots cropped from other photographs, which varied in size and pixel quality. A few were very fuzzy. I could see that some of the girls appeared to be wearing khaki ranger uniforms. Nola wasn't among them. I replied to the email saying as much. I had the sense Churchill was clutching at straws, sending me photos of any female park rangers he could find.

He replied immediately and was upbeat, claiming that by eliminating, we were also narrowing the search. I responded with less enthusiasm, saying Nola could be short for something longer, or a nickname, or not even her name at all, and that she was long gone from Little Rock. She probably wasn't even a ranger.

Churchill then sent a list of hotels in an attachment. Tomorrow, I was to call them or go to them and try to find her, or at least find where she'd stayed in the hope of getting more information about her.

I wasn't optimistic. Still, it felt good to be here, away from Perth and the music shop. I'd successfully escaped.

The cheeseburger was tasty. It came with a mound of fries and was all too much to finish. I ordered another Blue Canoe.

From somewhere in the back, I could hear what sounded like a band warming up. I paid my bill and took my second beer with me, following the music. I found a room that was twice the size of the bar and grill, and packed. It must have had its own entrance, because I hadn't seen any of these people in the bar. On the stage was a five-piece band, mixing country blues with rockabilly, all instrumental. The guy moving between the banjo and fiddle was especially good.

As I didn't have ear plugs with me, I stood just behind the unmanned mixing desk, as this is normally the area with the best sound quality and a manageable volume. It was impossible not to move to the catchy rhythm, and lots of people were dancing, in couples or alone on the spot. The jam involved each member of the band playing a short solo. Eventually the singer, wearing a battered yellow cowboy hat, loped onto the stage. Better said, he boot-scooted, heel-and-toe tapping his cowboy boots, with his thumbs hooked into the back pockets of his jeans and weaving between the band members as he did so. When he reached the microphone, he tossed his hat aside and tore into lyrics about having only one real friend, who was his brother and had done the dirty on him by stealing his girl, but was still his friend. A simple theme, which lent itself easily to rhymes: brother-another-lover and friend-end-bend. The chorus, which varied slightly each time, always ended with the line, "Brother always gonna be my friend," with the instruments holding their last chord and the bass drum keeping the beat and the word "friend" resonating around the room, before the singer let out a whoop and the band ripped back into it. At the end of each chorus, the banjo player stepped forward and played a short, neat solo.

In the dull light, I thought the singer looked well over fifty, but he sang effortlessly, as if it was the only thing he'd ever done in his life. A lot of try-hard singers, and I counted myself as one of them, really have to work for it: put in the hours, do the exercises and warm-ups, and concentrate when singing live. This guy just got up and nailed it, and it was as impressive as it was envy-inducing.

At the end of what was a long first song, the crowd cheered and clapped. The singer looked towards the mixing desk, patting the air down with his hand as he did so. Out of what he mumbled into the microphone, I caught the word "reverb". I leaned across and lowered the volume on the microphone monitor, getting a casual thumps-up from the singer in return.

The next song began, and it was another rollicking tale of loyalty, betrayal and love gone wrong. Just about everyone was dancing, which I assumed must have pleased the band, but I had the feeling they would have played to an empty room, they were enjoying themselves that much.

From behind the mixing desk, I started making a few slight adjustments, trying to improve the quality of the band's sound. It was tempting to turn down the master volume, but I knew from experience that loud, annoying and ring-inducing for me was simply loud and fun for everyone else. So, I left it where it was.

The band played for an hour, then the singer wandered off the stage and the band took a break. The banjo player came over to the mixing desk. He was considerably smaller than he appeared on stage, and also looked to be on the other side of fifty.

I stepped back from the desk and drank my beer.

"Who are you?" he asked.

"Sorry, mate. I just. The singer. He wanted less reverb on the mic, and there wasn't anyone here to do it. I'm sorry. I didn't really touch anything else."

He was wary, but his expression started to soften. "Wade just does that for show. Does it every time. He knows there ain't no one there."

"I did it anyway. I thought it was important."

"All good. What else you do?"

"Yeah, not much. Just a few tweaks."

"Uh-huh. The sound was good, man. You know what I'm saying? Clean. Lean. Not so heavy on the bass."

"That's what I tried to fix. It was all a bit muffled. Unless that's how you want it."

"Hell no. We want to hear ourselves."

I wondered if he had set up the desk, because he was standing over it possessively, his fingers poised above the dials, but he didn't touch or turn any of them.

"What's ya name, boy?"

"Rowan."

"You from England?

"No, Australia."

"Ho, ho. A long way from home. But you seem to know your shit. You good to keep goin?"

"Yeah. Sure."

"We got another set to burn through."

"You guys can play all night. You're tearing it up."

This made him smile; he had a few teeth missing.

"Hey, thanks, man. Ya alright. I'll let the boys know we got someone on the board. I'll make sure you get another beer too."

"Thanks."

He moved through the crowd and climbed onto the stage. I watched him tell the other four that I was there; he thumbed a few times in my direction, and I guessed he told them where I was from as well, as they all looked at me with curiosity. The bass player used his hand to shade out the glare of the lights to get a better look, while the drummer, who held the sticks jazz-style, gave a snappy little run on his snare. He pointed one drum stick towards the ceiling, requesting more volume. I gave it to him, and he did another run, happy with the result.

With Wade elsewhere, they started the second set as they did the first, all instrumental and heavy on the banjo.

There was a set of headphones looped over the desk. I put these on and plugged them in, enabling me to listen to a clearer sound and control the volume I heard, which gave my ears a much-needed break. I tweaked the board some more. When a certain band member performed a solo, I gave him a little more volume.

Wade appeared, singing this time with his cowboy hat on and clutching the microphone stand with a hand that also held a bottle of beer. He didn't drink from it, but seemed drunk.

People started to dance again. The band was really good. They played another hour-long set, with more songs of love lost, desolate towns and daggers in the back. But they started to fade towards the

45

end, as their age caught up with them. The crowd drifted away as well, until only a few dozen remained, and they looked like wives, girlfriends and friends of the band.

When it was over, the banjo player brought me another beer. He took out his phone and photographed the mixing board.

"I'm keeping this for prosperity," he said. "So we can get that awesome sound again. That was the best we ever played."

"You guys were great."

"Is Little Rock your new home?"

"I'm just passing through."

"Yeah, most folks are. Shame about that. We coulda used you again."

"I enjoyed it. And thanks for beer."

"That ain't nothing. You play?"

"Yeah, but not like you guys. And I can't sing like Wade either."

He smiled. "Ya too tall, man. You get up on stage and no one can see the band no more."

"I play on my own, usually."

"I can't do that," he said. "Playin in a band's too much fun. And banjo on its own just sounds depressin, you know? The stuff of horror films."

He started turning the dials down.

"Listen, we're goin back to Wade's for a few drinks. Ya comin, right?"

→←

So, I lost most of the second day to sleep as well, and was nursing a hangover and a pair of seriously ringing ears. The fog started to clear in the shower. Everything I remembered about the night before was positive, and that included jamming with the band at Wade's place until dawn. I was slow to get going, but it felt really good to be in Little Rock, in Arkansas, in the States, where I could have the kind of experiences that Perth couldn't offer.

I checked my email after showering, sitting on my bed with a towel around my waist. Incredibly, Churchill had found a photograph of Nola, included in the email "Yearbook 3". The grainy upper-body shot was of Denali National Park ranger Nolene Henderson. It was her, without question, possibly ten years ago or more. There were the restless green eyes, the long face, the thin-lipped smile that seemed to constantly disguise a quiet anger, and the slack shoulders that made her come across as bored, arrogant and indifferent. In my memory, she was better looking, friendlier, more desirable and less intimidating. It could have been the uniform; the khaki lending her an aggressive, militaristic streak she didn't have, straightening her curves and taking away any shred of femininity. Or maybe she was just younger, unsure of herself, still finding her feet, figuring out who she was and what she could do, and a bit angry with the world because things hadn't worked out quite as she'd hoped.

I knew that look, because I had it when I looked in the mirror.

At least, I did back in Perth. Here, as I combed my hair, I thought I was already a bit different. A bit more hopeful, despite the task ahead, and cheerier, even with my whiskey-rockabilly hangover.

A name was going to make it easier to work through Churchill's list of hotels, and I could be more forthright and convincing by using Nola's full name. If asked, I could also produce the grainy Denali photograph.

Dressed, I headed outside with enthusiasm. The search was on.

There were a dozen hotels near MacArthur Park. I could have called, but thought I might have more success doing it in person. My tinnitus and bad hearing also mean I sometimes struggle on the phone.

Though I considered these hotels more upmarket than I would have expected of a park ranger who liked to camp, I checked them anyway, engaging in fruitless exchanges with a parade of receptionists eager to help and who all wanted me to have a nice day.

It was disappointing to go through the whole list without success. I wondered if it was worth checking the local campgrounds, but they would have to wait for tomorrow, as it was time-consuming going into each hotel and already dark.

I found my way back to the Tex-Mex place from last night and had a bowl of chilli con carne served in a sourdough bowl. That, and a couple of beers, helped take the edge off my hangover. I was glad the band wasn't playing tonight, saving me from the temptation of working their mixing desk and getting happily drunk again.

As I walked back to the Firehouse, Churchill called.

"Hey, Church."

"You find her?"

47

"Not yet. I went to all the hotels. Nothing."

"What about the photos I sent?"

"Oh crap, I completely forgot about that. She was in it. You got her."

"I knew it. The girl from the Grand Canyon photo, right? I'm right, aren't I? She looks like a total fruitcake."

"No. Denali. Nolene Henderson."

"Where? Hang on. Let me check the database."

I could hear him tapping at the keyboard.

"Okay. Email. Sent last night to Rowan. You alright?"

"Yeah. Pretty good. Tired, but it's good to be here."

"What time is it there?"

"Nearly nine. In the evening."

"It's ten in the morning here. Bloody hot. Underwear and air-con weather. Nana's boat overheated when she drove to the tennis club yesterday. Turned out there was no coolant in the radiator. It had evaporated."

"Since when does she play tennis?"

"Mate, she's changed. It's been three days, but she's seriously mobile. She bragged that she even had a date, at the drive-in."

I laughed. "They still have those things?"

"I think there's one left, up in the northern suburbs somewhere."

"Good for her, that she's active."

"Yeah, well, she's seriously active. Get a load of this. On the night of that date, I was the one needing ear plugs. I even went into your room looking for some."

This also made me laugh, and I really missed him. "Must've been a few years between drinks."

"Try decades. She was screaming like the guy owed her money. Okay. I got it."

There was silence on the line. I crossed Commerce Street and went into the hostel. It was quieter in the lobby and easier for me to hear.

"I don't believe it," Churchill said. "That's her?"

"What's the problem?"

"I dunno. I guess I was expecting someone different. A bit rougher around the edges. Dreadlocks and piercings maybe, on the crazy side of life. Someone who'd send postcards with five-fingered hands to the other side of the world with no return address. This girl, she looks, normal."

"It's her. Trust me. And she's not normal."

"Alright and whacky-do. We've got her name. Well done me. This'll make things a crap lot easier."

"It didn't today. I asked at all the hotels and she wasn't at any of them."

"You use her name?"

"Yeah. But I don't think she's the hotel type. I reckon she camped here. Somewhere."

"I'll put a list together for you. And I'll scour the web to see what I can find out about Nolene Henderson. Build a profile of sorts."

"Thanks, Church."

"This is a massive step forward, and you've only been there two days. We're gonna find this girl. I know it."

Churchill hung up first, probably keen to get to work. I went upstairs to bed.

I slept fitfully, dreaming of bush tracks, sand-flies and campfires. Cramming into the sleeping bag with Nola, our mismatched bodies entwined, and the fat rain thumping the tent like a shower of pebbles. Walking all day without saying a word. Sharing meals from her one pot, sharing her spoon, feeding each other. That one day we didn't walk at all, and simply sat on a beach the colour of gold. Swimming naked instead of showering. Playing Daphne for hours and writing songs that came from a place inside me I didn't know was there. Nola wanting to have sex on just about every beach we passed. And after all of that, arriving in Awaroa Bay feeling like I'd spent years in the wilderness. Off the grid and away even from myself. Feeling older, and feeling grateful. I didn't love Nola, but I appreciated her and was thankful for the week we'd spent together. She wasn't sad saying goodbye, and neither was I.

"The chaos is over," she said on the morning we took the water taxi back to Marahau. "We need to find new chaos."

I woke with that thought: new chaos. It was just after three in the morning, and now awake, I quickly became alert and ready for the day. My head was full of thoughts.

I wondered what had happened to the person I'd become on the Abel Tasman trek? The Rowan who was creative, daring, present and sexual. Who was a desirable and wanted creature. I wrote more songs in one afternoon than I had all year, and they were good. I had more sex in seven days than I'd had all my adult life, and it wasn't merely the end result of a dinner together or some date where we both felt obliged to end it with sex. It was natural, unforced and fun: there's the tent, there's the sleeping bag, let's take our clothes off and roll around. It didn't matter that we were dirty or that our skin was dry and flaked with sea salt, or that I'd been wearing the same clothes for several days, or that I was too tall for the tent and too big for her sleeping bag. We found a way, worked around the hindrances, embraced them. When having sex, Nola did something I'd never seen another girl do: she smiled and laughed.

Travelling back from Marahau to Motueka, and eventually to Wellington and Perth, I turned back into myself. The chaos was over. I needed new chaos. I couldn't export the Abel Tasman version of Rowan back home. There, the old rhythms and ways took over. The songs were sad. Relationships were hard work and the sex wasn't much fun. Yet it was easier to continue the progressions I knew than compose something original.

I turned onto my back and looked at the bunk bed above. People had scratched their names into the wood, and the usual obscenities, but I stopped seeing the words or letters. I saw indentations in the wood, and these were paths through the forest, in New Zealand, where Abel Rowan wandered, bare-foot, his jeans torn and frayed, his hair matted into red dreadlocks by the salt. A happier Rowan, playing the guitar while he walked, composing great songs only the trees would hear. A free Rowan, laid-back and tanned, playing music for the joy of it rather than striving for success.

It made me sad to think of that Rowan. But I also thought that because I'd been like that once before, I could get to that point again. Especially with my music. I had to stop writing songs which I thought people wanted to hear and which would make me successful and rich. It had to be from the heart.

The two other guys in the room were both snoring, but not loud enough for me to put in ear plugs.

I wanted to sleep, but I was fully awake. I needed morning, for the sun to be shining. A beautiful spring day, when my ears could ring and I wouldn't care, and I would go to every campground in town.

Nola had been here. Somewhere in Little Rock. I felt a trace. A residual, lingering presence.

And this felt good, because it made me think that in America, I'd already changed; become more aware and alert, more attune to what I was feeling. There was a different rhythm here, different air, different sounds, different textures. There were different things required of me. I couldn't be the same Rowan I was back in Perth. I had to adapt.

Everything felt bigger as well. Not necessarily more substantial, but with more scope. I thought I could try things, experiment and evolve. Because this was America, a new chaos.

Here, I had a purpose: find Nola. But I could also feel something building inside me, a yearning to find this child. The task had meaning. It was bigger than me, and not just about me.

I closed my eyes and tried to visualise what this child might look like, but kept seeing myself as a kid, redheaded, gangly and grinning. I'd had a great childhood. It wasn't selective memory: Conor and I had both been happy kids, with loving parents and a stable home life in an affluent Perth suburb. I remembered months and months of sunshine, years of it. Parents who made time for both of us; who made me feel that being their child was a great gift and not some burden they were obliged to carry. Yet, with all that, it was hard not to look back at my childhood now without knowing what was coming: divorce and the sale of the Claremont house.

It felt like those family memories belonged to old versions of all of us, versions that didn't exist anymore. The endless sunny days were an illusion. A cover-up. And it all made me feel a little bit like my childhood hadn't happened, or that it had happened to someone else. Everyone had changed, moved on, and started making new memories with their new selves.

I curled up on the hostel bed and tried to sleep. I wanted to be small again, to go back in time, to when my family was whole and I was carefree and happy.

Because I loved being a kid. Claremont, with the looping bay of the Swan River's Karrakatta Bank on one side and Cottesloe Beach on the other, was like a huge park, with houses, schools and shops spread among the trees. It was our playground. Central to that playground was our house on Richardson Avenue. It had a big backyard, half of which was a deck that my parents used for entertaining, and they did that a lot. Kids were always welcome at those parties, and they often showed up with just one parent. Around the turn of the millennium, it seemed getting divorced was the thing everyone was doing. But my parents stayed together. At the time, there was never any doubt of that, and the other kids I knew envied me.

However this potential child of mine looked, I wanted him or her to be happy. I didn't want there to be any lies or cover-ups. I wanted honesty and stability, but didn't really know how to make that happen. There would be no getting together with Nola. No marriage and house in the suburbs. Nothing was stable, and Nola had already spent almost five years lying to me.

The sun started to stream through the gap in the curtains. I got up, keen for the day. I wanted to find Nola and answer the kid question. Because that child could be the new chaos I needed.

→←

Exhausted, I fell into bed. After walking all day, I had blisters on my toes and was sunburned. I saw just about all of Little Rock, which included crossing Junction Bridge. I didn't find Nola, but I thought it was a good day.

I was just about asleep when my phone started buzzing.

"How'd it go?"

It was good to hear Churchill's voice.

"I found the bridge from the postcard."

"Brilliant. And Nola?"

"No sign, Church. If she stayed here, she slept on the street."

"Or she's got friends there."

"I guess."

"Don't be so negative. We're closing in."

"I'm not being negative. I'm exhausted. I actually had a really interesting day."

"There's the positive Rowan I know. Well, you may not have found her, but we're in the ballpark. Hey, you should get yourself to a baseball game while you're over there. You know, beer and a hot dog. Have an American experience."

"Baseball? You know what I think about sports."

"Come on. You're in the States. Get involved."

"I'm trying to find Nola, not be a tourist."

"Sure, sure. Listen, I've done some research. Interesting stuff."

"Yeah?"

"It's been like following a trail of bread crumbs. There's nothing about her online. No social media, no websites. So, I got into contact with the nice folks at Denali National Park, and they didn't have much, but they did say that Nola might've worked the next year at Arches National Park, in Utah, because the people from Arches contacted Denali when Nola applied, to check her references, and they were the only park to do so. The extremely helpful Denali girl got Nola's file out and told me all of this, which was really nice of her, and we even flirted a bit on the phone, but she said she wasn't allowed to give out any contact details. So, then I called Arches and went through just about the same process, and I found out that the next year she was at Shenandoah in Virginia. I have to say that the Yanks are a super helpful bunch. They really try to please. Yeah, so, then she was at Everglades in Florida, and Cuyahoga Valley in Ohio. And a few others. Every year somewhere different, by the looks, up to Congaree in South Carolina last year. Your girl really gets around."

"She's not my girl. Did anyone mention the kid?"

"I'm getting to that. She always worked about seven months each time, from April to November. I've been wondering what she did the rest of the year."

"I guess she travelled. Like when we met in New Zealand."

"Or she did other work. Can't imagine rangers get paid that much."

"What about the kid, Church?"

He cleared his throat. "Yeah, that's where things get a bit weird."

"Why?"

"Well, there's no mention of her having a child. I asked, but all the parks from the last four years said she was there alone. They also said she listed her status as single, so no boyfriend or husband either."

I didn't know how to respond to that.

"But that doesn't mean there's no kid at all," Churchill added. "It could be that she didn't take the kid to work with her. Which is reasonable, when you think about it. You can't be a park ranger toting a kid around or pushing a pram."

"Maybe she left the kid with her parents, wherever they are. But that would be awful for the kid, just to be abandoned like that."

"Don't be so harsh. There's probably more to it than that. Needing the money or something. You don't know the background."

"I'm thinking about the kid, Church, if there actually is one. Growing up without parents. The kid's probably never with Nola. She works the season and then goes off travelling."

"Easy now. Look, I know you get angry when you're tired, and you're probably still jet-lagged, but don't be so quick to judge."

I rubbed my eyes with my free hand. "Yeah, you're right. That's not fair of me."

"Hang on," Churchill said. "That's the postman. Back in a flash."

I heard him go out the front door, glad that he did this so easily. It was only ten metres to the mailbox, but I knew even that could be difficult for him. I smiled thinking about it, missing Churchill's quirks.

"Austin," he shouted into the phone. "A postcard just arrived. You gotta go there, right now."

"It's ten in the evening. And I'm a week behind her anyway."

"Yeah, okay, well, I guess there's not much you can do tonight. The postmark is smudged. I can't read the date. Let me sort things out for you. Get up at dawn and be ready to start, in case I book you on an early flight."

"Thanks, Church. You're doing a great job."

"No probs. This is fun. It's so much better than the drudgery of my job. I'm thinking I should become an investigator of some sort. It was such a buzz following the trail, trying to track Nola down. Using a bit of charm to get the info I needed, asking the right questions, flirting on the phone. Exciting stuff."

"How can you be an investigator without going outside?"

"Good point. Hadn't thought about that. I guess I could be ground control, and have others out in the field."

"Churchill Everett, private investigator."

"Oh, that sounds awesome. We could do it together. Turn our house into central ops. You can be my man out in the field. We solve crimes, help people out, make people's lives better. That kind of thing."

"Sounds more like a TV show."

"I'd watch it. Look, you get some sleep. When you wake up, you'll have the bookings for the Austin leg."

"Okay. Thanks."

As usual, Churchill hung up first.

Too tired to shower or even brush my teeth, I set the alarm on my phone and fell asleep almost immediately.

I dreamed of my childhood: I'm six years old and I've received a guitar for Christmas. The strings are nylon and thick. They hurt my fingers when I try to press them. Another present is a book for learning the guitar. Mum opens the book and shows me the chord shapes, guiding my fingers into the right positions. She tells me to stop biting my fingernails, because strong nails and fingers will help me press the strings. The instrument's crook fits perfectly on my right thigh, and I like the feel of the strings under my fingers, even with the pain. Mum says the guitar has a body, neck and head, and that I should think of it as alive. As I try to get the chords right, the guitar speaks with me, conversing in sounds, complimentary and critical, friendly and shy. The whole Christmas morning, mum sits next to me. I feel protected and loved. All my other presents are left unopened.

The alarm woke me, with the phone buzzing in my hand. My eyes were sticky and it was still dark in the room. I checked my phone. In his email, Churchill explained he had booked me a rental car, driving one-way from the airport in Little Rock to the airport in Austin, which he said was an eight-hour drive, and a dorm bed at the Hostelling International on South Lakeshore Boulevard for three nights.

Already packed, I had a quick shower and put on the same clothes from yesterday.

I was hungry, as I had been pretty much since I arrived in Little Rock, as if there was a hole inside me I couldn't fill. But there wasn't time for breakfast.

Downstairs, the receptionist asked, "Where you off to today?"

He was about my age, maybe a little younger. Over the counter, I could see a scattering of open books, and assumed he was a student.

"Austin."

"Nice. Really cool place. I went there last year for spring break. Had a wild time." He talked a bit too loudly for this early in the morning, making me think he was wired on something. "Great live music. Even the guys playing on the streets, they're better than anyone you can see in a club here."

"Sounds good."

I shouldered my backpack, picked up my guitar and headed for the door. Then, I stopped. In all my searching, it occurred to me I hadn't thought of the Firehouse. This place was a museum as well as a hostel, and had been recently restored. It was the kind of place I thought Nola would like.

I went back to the reception desk.

"Listen, I'm looking for someone. Maybe she stayed here, a few days ago, or a week. Her name is Nolene Henderson, but everyone calls her Nola."

He checked the book. There was a computer on the desk, but all the guests were listed in a large, spiral bound ledger, with the paper crinkling and ruffling as each page was turned. He ran his index finger, the nail bitten low, down the column of names.

"How tall are you?" he asked, turning another page.

I remembered how Nola had said it: "Six-six."

"You play basketball?"

"No."

"Volleyball?"

"I'm all height and no coordination."

The truth was that I hated sports and always had, but I often keep that to myself.

His finger stopped.

"Here it is," he said, tapping Nola's name, which was written in thick black pen. "She stayed here for a week and, uh, left three days ago."

My foggy brain tried to do the calculation. Had Nola been here the morning I arrived? Had we slept under the same roof? On that first day, which I'd slept right through, could I have seen her, and the kid, if I'd managed to get myself up?

No, I'd arrived a day too late.

The receptionist's finger moved off the page and he started to close the ledger.

"Wait. Who's that?"

Below Nola's name was Eris Henderson. A girl. But the S in her first name was slightly smudged, making me wonder if was actually a C.

"I don't know," he said, shrugging. "I was on vacation and only got back yesterday. Donna would know, or Kelly. They covered my shifts."

"Okay, thanks. I'll call later and ask."

"Enjoy Austin."

Outside, I walked quickly down Commerce Street and got onto Cumberland, heading for the Marriot Hotel, from where I could catch the shuttle to the airport. I had to wait fifteen minutes and used this time to buy two egg and bacon rolls.

I wanted the open road. Austin beckoned.

><

The drive was fascinating and monotonous, in a way that reminded me of the highways of Western Australia. Straight, flat, unchanging. In keeping with the home theme, I decided to stop for lunch in a place called Mount Pleasant. Churchill had grown up in the Perth area of the same name. While that Mount Pleasant is a tidy, almost wealthy riverside suburb, the Texas version was considerably more down-market, with low-roofed buildings and much of the downtown area given over to parking and storage.

On Madison Street, my rental hatchback stood out among the pick-ups and utilities. Some of these vehicles had gun racks, with rifles visible on the inside of the cab's rear windows. Knowing many of the drivers were armed made me feel less safe rather than more, like I was entering lawless territory. The wild west. It was exciting.

I parked in a large lot near the Titus County Justice Center.

Laura's Cheesecakes looked the most appealing spot for lunch. Inside, I took a table in the corner. A few people looked my way, as I was a stranger in town. So, I smiled, and they smiled back.

I ordered a chicken ciabatta, a coffee and a slice of marbled brownie swirl cheesecake.

Donna answered the phone when I dialled the Firehouse Hostel, and confirmed that it was Eris Henderson, not Eric.

"She's a real cutie," Donna said. "Lovely red hair. But wow can she be a terror. She threw, like, this mega tantrum, with seriously loud screaming, and her mother just stood there watching. You know, observing, like she was someone else's kid."

"I'm sorry to hear that."

"I felt so sorry for the little girl. I wanted to rescue her."

Donna asked about my connection to Nola and Eris. I said "Family" and hung up. Then, I called Churchill.

"Are you in Austin yet?" he asked.

"Getting there. But you'll love this. I am in Texas, in Mount Pleasant, and I think this version is more interesting than your old hood in Perth."

"I have no doubt about that. But, I like the connection. You're finding links between Texas and WA."

"Yeah. I like that too."

"How's the drive going?"

"It's interesting. Hard work. It took a while to get used to the left-hand drive."

"Driving on the wrong side of the road."

"The novelty helped kill the first couple of hours. The car's an automatic, which makes things easier. Thanks for booking it, by the way."

"That's what I'm here for. But, Rowan, you're not even past Dallas yet. You got about another five or six hours to go. Why have you stopped?"

"I'm hungry. It's lunchtime."

"Fine. Eat up and get back on the road."

"Church, will you just listen for a second? It's a girl. Nola's kid, her name is Eris. They stayed at the Firehouse in Little Rock, and left just before I got there."

"No friggin way."

"Amazing, isn't it?"

"How does it feel? To be the father of a girl?"

"I haven't really thought about it. I just found it. And I think it won't really sink in until I know for absolute certain I'm the father. Anyway, all I feel right now is hunger."

"Load up. You got a long way to go. But Eris? Funny name. Never heard that before."

"Me neither."

"I'll do some research. Maybe there's something in it. A deeper significance, or a clue. Oh, and I put together a playlist for Austin, to keep you from listening to redneck Texan radio."

"Thanks. This road trip needs the right soundtrack. Shame you're not here riding shotgun."

"I'm there in spirit."

The waitress brought my lunch to my table.

"I gotta go. Food time."

"Dig in, and drive safely."

He hung up. My lunch was good and it quickly disappeared. I considered ordering another ciabatta, but decided to pay my bill and leave. Churchill was right. I still had a long way to go.

The no-frills rental car didn't have a fancy connectivity system which I could pair my phone with and play music through the stereo. So, as I followed the signs to the interstate, I plugged my headphones into my phone and accessed Churchill's playlist that way. The first song was Stevie Ray Vaughan's sublime version of *Texas Flood*.

The music helped the miles tick over. Churchill's Texas best-of included Buddy Holly, Waylon Jennings, Butthole Surfers, Willie

Nelson, ZZ Top and Roy Orbison, among other stuff I hadn't heard before.

Dallas came and went. The traffic was mostly trucks.

When a song from Janis Joplin came on, I thought of another screaming redhead: little Eris, bellowing her lungs out while Nola just watched. I had to do something about that. I didn't know what exactly, but I knew I had to act. And the first thing to do was find them in Austin.

I couldn't believe I'd been so close in Little Rock.

Driving in miles made my progress feel slow. The number of miles remaining didn't seem that high, but when I calculated it in kilometres, it made me groan each time.

I filled the car up at Carl's Corner and had a cup of awful coffee that I kept topping up with milk to make it drinkable. I bought a bottle of water and a couple of chocolate bars, to keep me going for the last stretch.

Back on I-35, I'd had enough of driving, of being cramped into this little car with my bent knees wedged under the steering wheel. My neck hurt, from having to tilt my head slightly forward so it wasn't jammed against the roof.

The hatchback was sluggish, lousy to drive and really guzzled the petrol.

I opened the window to let in some fresh and keep me awake.

The sun started to set, burning the sky with hazy yellow and orange. A big desert sky, like at home, but I saw it through squinting eyes rubbed red by my knuckles. I hugged the steering wheel and urged the car on.

It was dark by the time I finally reached the airport in Austin. I filled the car again, gladly gave it back to the rental car company, and got myself to the arrivals terminal to catch bus 100 to downtown, as per Churchill's instructions.

I was forced to stand on the bus, but almost fell asleep anyway. I wanted to wash away the drive and go straight to bed.

I got out at the Tinnin Ford stop and walked down to the hostel. Arriving late meant I had to take the one remaining bed in the dorm room I was assigned, and this was a top bunk. Everyone else was already asleep. I had a quick shower and got into bed still slightly wet.

I slept nine, dreamless hours. Best of all, I woke up at a reasonable hour in the morning and felt for the first time like my body clock was right. There were some aches and pains from sitting so long in that small car, but I was surprisingly energetic and ready for what felt like day one.

At reception, I checked if Nola and Eris were staying at the hostel. They weren't, and hadn't.

In the kitchen, a few guests were making pancakes on a grill. There was a large container of just-add-water pancake mix, as well as a tub of butter and a sticky-looking jumbo-sized bottle of maple syrup. I made myself a cup of tea and took this with me as I walked down Tinnin Ford Road, to the small shop I'd passed last night. I bought a bunch of over-ripe bananas, a couple of apples and a container of orange juice. I ate one apple on the way back to the hostel.

I joined the other guests in the kitchen and started making banana pancakes. As they had to be eaten, I offered the bananas to others, and we all sat together at one table, which was a refreshing change from all the meals I'd eaten alone so far.

There were two English girls, about my age, who had met in New York and had been travelling together ever since. The man from Sweden was driving around the country in a car he'd bought, attempting to visit every state at least once; he'd been to thirty-two so far, with Wisconsin being his favourite. He qualified this by saying he had distant relatives there and they'd made him feel very welcome. The Swiss couple were cycling across Texas, and they looked like it, sporting leathery tans and wiry physiques, as if they burned far more calories than they took on and didn't drink enough water each day. In their appearance, and with their far-away stares, they struck me more as brother and sister than husband and wife, which was a horrible thought. The three Japanese girls didn't say much. They smiled and ate their pancakes, eating slowly, with small bites. When any of them did talk, they spoke good English, and one was quite funny, in a cheeky and sweet way.

Impacting the atmosphere of this multi-national breakfast was an Australian couple, a bit older than me and seemingly in the middle of an extended domestic that was playing out at the table through gestures and whispers, given they were surrounded by people and unable to argue properly. They sat a fair distance from each other, and ate mostly in silence. If he contributed to the conversation, she looked up and glared at him. If she said something, he gave her a rather nasty sideways glance. It was uncomfortable to watch and awkward to be around them. They seemed ready to break into a shouting match at any point. Fortunately, our group's conversation was kept light, with everyone talking about how they'd ended up in Austin and what plans they had for the day. When the Australian girl got up and left, her boyfriend, or husband, remained. He seemed to relax with her gone and became more talkative, speaking to me as if we already knew each other well. He asked why I was in Austin and I said I was here to catch up with an old friend.

Thinking of Nola and Eris made me keen to continue the search. I cleaned up the mess I'd made, grabbed my orange juice and wished everyone an enjoyable day.

Churchill's latest email included a list of campgrounds in the local area. He suggested I rent a bicycle for the day, explaining that Austin was one of America's fittest cities and I should get involved. I got a map from the hostel receptionist and located the shop Churchill had recommended, Green Frog Bike Rental, just across the river on Frontage Street.

I took the Boardwalk along the river. The morning was overcast and threatened rain, but the air was warm and I had a good feeling about the day. Nola and Eris were here, somewhere, I was sure of it.

Up ahead, I saw the Australian girl, walking slowly and looking sad, even from a distance. I considered detouring around her, but the Boardwalk extended over the water and was very nice to walk along. Locals were kayaking, stand-up paddling and sailing small boats. There were also numerous runners and cyclists, populating the paths on both sides of the river.

She saw me coming and smiled thinly.

I didn't break stride. "Nice day for it."

"It is. Are you heading downtown?"

This made me stop. Up close, and away from the dismal atmosphere she'd help create in the kitchen, she was actually very pretty.

"Ah, sort of, yeah. Dunno. I'm gonna cross that bridge, because I need to find a bike rental shop. Not sure if that's all the way downtown. I don't really know where downtown is. I only got in last night."

"Can I walk with you?"

"I guess. Sure. What about, uh, your fella?"

She shook her blonde hair loose from its pony tail and took a floppy hat from the back of her shorts. With the hat on and her long hair out, she looked very nice, and somehow more worldly.

"He can do whatever he wants."

We started walking. While just about everyone is short next to me, she came up to my shoulder, but had her height in her upper body, not in her legs. This made her look a little strange and disproportioned, especially in the flat-soled sandals she wore.

"I'm Nikki," she said.

"Rowan."

"Where are you from again? I wasn't really paying attention at breakfast."

"Perth."

"Yeah, that's right. I'm from Brisbane. Are you just travelling around?"

I didn't want to answer this, so turned it back onto her. "Pretty much. What about you?"

"I'm currently in the middle of the worst mistake of my life."

While I could sense she wanted to talk, I didn't feel like it was my place to pry. So I said nothing. We walked for a while in silence. Nikki exuded sadness, which made me want to both help her and run away from her. The thought of pushing her into the Colorado River and running for it made me smile.

"I'm stuck," she said at last.

"No, you're not. You and, what's his name?"

"Bevan."

"Okay. Bevan. Yeah, right, you and Bevan, you're both adults, and whatever's going on between you, you're never stuck. My parents were married for twenty-six years and then they got divorced. Nobody saw it coming. They had a choice and they took it, and they were better off. Me and my brother probably weren't, but they were, and I think that matters the most."

"The problem is that we're here. This would be so much easier at home."

"Would it? All your problems would just follow you."

"Maybe, but I've got my friends there, my family, people I can lean on. We don't even want to be around each other, but we're both too scared to be the one that does the hurting."

I wasn't really in the mood for this. I started to walk a bit faster, forcing Nikki to match my pace. I'd had a great sleep and a filling breakfast, and now I was going to find Nola and Eris. Nikki was sucking a lot of the hope out of the day. We reached the bridge and

62

started to cross it. I'd thought maybe Nikki would stop there, but she stayed at my side. The sounds of cars and trucks made my ears ring louder. When Nikki spoke, I had to turn to her to listen.

"Maybe we should just go home."

"I was just about to say that. Or, you could try to fix your problems here and enjoy the trip. Or go your separate ways. Whatever. As far as I see it, you're definitely not stuck. You have lots of options."

She nodded. "I didn't expect he would be so different over here. This is our first big trip together."

As I led us under the bridge to the other side of Frontage Street, I thought about Abel Rowan and how different I'd become when dealt an obscure hand in New Zealand. I wondered if American Rowan was starting to emerge. I hoped so.

"Everyone's different on the road."

Nikki nodded again. "Yeah, I've heard people say that. Does that also include turning a normal person into a monster?"

"Now I think you're exaggerating. Maybe you both want to be in control, and that's why you're struggling to travel together. Maybe you should just give each other a break."

We were standing in front of Green Frog Bike Rental. Despite her prettiness, I didn't want Nikki tagging along and slowing down my ride.

"If you want my advice, just talk to him. Go back to the hostel, have a cup of tea and talk it all out."

"Where are you riding to?"

"I'm trying to find a friend."

"You don't have a phone number or an address?"

"No."

"What kind of friend is that? Sounds like someone who doesn't want to be found."

"Yeah, I know. It's a long story. Enjoy the day."

I went inside and set about getting a rental bike. Through the window, I could see Nikki still standing on the street, uncertain in which direction to go. While she had my sympathy, her problems weren't mine to fix. I had my own to deal with and I was intent on giving them priority.

So, I dawdled in the shop, asking about gears and tyre pressure and how to work the lock, until Nikki finally walked off.

The nearest campground was the Midtown RV Park. I plotted a course and got myself pedalling east on Cesar Chavez Street.

It was turning into a nice day. The bike was a good call by Churchill, and I kept a leisurely pace. My joints started to loosen up and the lingering pain in my lower back subsided. There were lots of other cyclists and I felt welcome on the streets. It was also great to cycle without having to wear a helmet.

The eastern area of Austin was industrial and interesting. I saw people working, but not terribly hard. There was a lot of music playing, coming from workshops and warehouses, or blaring from ramshackle houses where people sat on plastic chairs out front.

There weren't any tents pitched at the Midtown RV Park, but there were some caravans, campervans and trailers. The old woman at reception said no Hendersons were staying there, so I rode on to Oak Forest RV Park. This took about an hour and was hard going. But the story there was the same: no tents and no Nola. It was another haul to get all the way downtown and across the river to the Pecan Grove RV Park, but again I had no luck. From the looks of it, this park wasn't for camping, but somewhere people lived permanently; the trailers and mobile homes seemed to have grown roots and had sunk into the ground.

Despondent, tired and hungry, and seriously saddle-sore, I rode back to Barton Springs Road, headed left on South Lamar Boulevard, and stopped for lunch at a place called P. Terry's Burger Stand. I ordered a chicken burger to takeaway, and crossed the street to Butler Park to find a quiet place to eat and plot my next move.

Somehow, I felt this was all Nikki's fault. She had soured the day's positive energy. It was probably unfair, but I needed to blame someone.

But then I thought it was my fault. I should've just called the RV parks, rather than do all that riding.

I found a bench and sat down facing Austin's skyline. The city was considerably larger than Little Rock, and was sure to have many more hotels and motels. Doing the rounds struck me as an unappealing way to spend the rest of the day, and calling every hotel was even less appealing. There was also the lingering doubt that Nola was still here.

It was nice to sit on the bench. The skyline and river reminded me of Perth. Another connection that would please Churchill.

I wondered if I was going about this all wrong; that maybe I should be trying to get them to find me, somehow. I figured there couldn't be too many two-metre tall redheaded Australians in Austin. I just needed to get myself in a position where I'd be seen. Busking was an option, one that would also help bring in some money, as the green American bills were just running through my fingers.

I charted a course on the map to the Austin Visitor Center on East Fourth Street and rode along the river, passing the statue of Stevie Ray Vaughan. With his poncho, broad hat and boots, he looked more like an early explorer than an axe-slinger who had died too young.

Over the bridge at First Street, I zigzagged through downtown's grid, pedalling out of the saddle as it was a bit too painful to sit. It made me think of the Swiss couple. What kind of pain were they in, cycling across Texas?

I locked the bike in front of the visitor centre and went inside. A helper greeted me immediately.

"Welcome to Austin," he said brightly. "How can I help you today?"

"Hi. Look, I'm interested in busking, you know, playing music on the street, and I wanted to know which areas would be best and if I'm allowed to do it."

"Great. Austin is the live music capital of the world. What do you play?"

"Guitar. Acoustic."

"That'll work. I play bass." He pulled a flyer out of his back pocket. "We're playing tonight at the Spider House. The café, not the ballroom."

I took the flyer. "What about busking?"

"We don't do that anymore. We only play gigs."

"I mean for me."

"Right. Well, if you're on the street, try to get a spot on Sixth or Congress. But it's pretty competitive, especially on Red River, and no amps allowed. If all those places are full, try over on Second." He came close to me and lowered his voice. "If the police tell you to move along, you do just that. You can't negotiate with them. They're pretty tolerant, but if they order you to move, do it. Could be they don't like your music."

He laughed a little.

"Good tip. Thanks."

"Have a nice day in Austin. And maybe I'll see you later at the Spider House."

I rode back to the hostel and retrieved my guitar. It was awkward riding with the guitar case, but I made it to Green Frog and gladly gave the bike back.

My legs were very sore as I walked downtown, but I was proud of all the riding I'd done.

Red River and Sixth were full with musicians, spaced far enough apart so they didn't disturb each other. They were really good, so I headed towards the river and found a promising spot at the corner of Second and Congress, in front of the Wells Fargo building. I set myself up next to a statue of an artistically painted guitar.

My case open and Daphne tuned, I started by playing some Australian covers, to shake off my nerves. I'd been playing the songs of these bands for years. Midnight Oil, Hoodoo Gurus, You Am I, Powderfinger, Hunters and Collectors; it was easy to shift from one cover to the next. They had easy chord progressions, were well within my singing range, helped me get loose and were fun to play. A few people stopped, though I thought they were gawking more than listening, at the beanpole redhead busker, the likes of which they'd probably never seen before in Austin, playing weird songs from down under. As long as they dropped some money in my case, they could gawk all they wanted.

It was fun. I danced around a little, letting the rhythm guide me. I was singing well, trying to do what Wade had told me at his place after the gig in Little Rock: to sing with ease. He said that it was always better if it was bad and easy than bad and forced.

The coins dropping in my case sounded like the soft thuds of encouragement. Some people sat down on the low wall nearby and listened. I played upbeat songs, singing loudly and sticking to Australian covers, to give those listening and passing by a taste of music they'd perhaps never heard, and maybe pull those songs off as my own.

I was in Austin, playing on the street. I didn't know anybody here. I could jump around, make a fool of myself and play whatever I wanted.

It was about then that I stopped paying attention to where I was, who was listening and how much money I was earning. I just played and sang, one song after another, not really thinking too hard about what to play and simply letting each song guide me into the next; finishing one song on C and letting the chord hang, then launching into another song in A-minor.

What brought me back to Second Street was the siren of the police car that came down Congress and stopped at the corner. I figured they were here for me and started packing up, which included scooping out all the quarters and dimes and filling my pockets with them, to the point my jeans pulled at my waist with the weight. I put Daphne away and closed the case.

I looked towards the police car. The officers hadn't got out yet.

A couple got up from the low wall and came over to me.

"Y'all done for today?" the man asked.

"Yeah, looks like it. I was told to be careful of the police."

"You got any CDs? Your music rocks. You write all those songs?"

It was very tempting to say yes. "I wish. That was like an Aussie music best-of."

"Y'all from Australia?" He turned to his girlfriend, who was sipping from a large paper cup, through a straw. "Can you believe that? And he's playing here, on the street."

"Wow," the girl said, though she didn't seem very impressed.

"It's just for fun. I'm travelling around, and busking's a pretty cool way to experience a city."

At the corner, two officers go out of the police car and ran across Congress, dodging the cars, both of them holding radios.

"Looks like they ain't here for you," the man said.

The couple went to watch what was going on, joining others assembled at the corner. I followed, able to see over all the heads and getting a clear view of Second Street as two cars crashed head-on. It sounded like an old cannon being fired. The cars blocked the street enough to cause other drivers to brake and swerve. The two police officers tried to help. Fortunately, no one appeared hurt, as drivers and passengers got out to assess the damage and get their bearings. A few of them looked upwards, pointing and gesturing at one of the high-rises on Second. I looked up as well, to see what appeared to be rocks arcing through the air towards the crashed cars. To my surprise, these missiles splattered when they made contact with cars and the road. They were grey balloons filled with grey paint, and I figured one such balloon must have caused the accident. As a few more rained down on the crash area and burst, people started to run. The police officers talked on their radios and tried to locate where the balloons were coming from. But there were no more. The stillness that followed was eerie, with everyone waiting for something else to happen. And it did, because floating down from the building were pieces of paper. People moved forward, thinking, like I was, that it might be money. They turned out to be large business cards, the size of American bills. I picked one up. On one side was "Keep Austin Plain", hand-written in grey pen. On the other side was a circular G, with eight arrows positioned around it, like a compass of sorts.

I'd seen this symbol before, but couldn't for the life of me remember where.

><

We went in Vidar's car. The Swede's sedan had a lived-in smell, like he'd slept in there more than a few times. I helped him clean out some of the rubbish so all of us could get in. I sat in the front with one of the Japanese girls on my lap. Together, we tried to navigate, with her holding one side of my map. The other two Japanese girls were in the back, bookended by Nikki and Bevan. Despite the awkward vibe those two were contributing, it felt rather daring to be driving through Austin like this, the seven of us in one car, all of us foreigners, and only Vidar wearing a seatbelt.

I'm pretty good with maps, and I prefer the paper kind to the small map on my phone's screen. The uniformity of American cities made them easy to negotiate. It's hard to get lost in a numbered grid. The Spider House Café was beyond any area I'd seen today. It took a bit of detouring and rerouting to find.

Given all that had happened, it was hard to believe it was still the same day. I wanted to spend some of my busking money.

Vidar stopped to let us out. From the outside, the Spider House looked like a funky, off-beat place; a suburban house that had been turned into a bar and music venue. There were Christmas lights in the trees out front and strung along the veranda, giving the outdoor seating area a festive splash of colour that seemed wrong for late March. As Nikki said she was cold, we took a booth on the veranda, out of the wind, and split up into nations, with the three Japanese girls on one side and the three Australians on the other. Nikki was in the middle. I had no doubt Vidar, once he'd found somewhere to park, would try to squeeze in with the girls. I quietly hoped the Swede, who had made some sleazy remarks during the drive and gave of a fair whiff of desperation, wouldn't find anywhere to park.

In the absence of any serving staff, I stood up. "I got the first round."

One of the Japanese girls ordered a coke, and the other two nodded. Bevan wanted a beer. Nikki said she'd come with me and choose at the bar.

As Vidar passed us, he said, "Get a pitcher."

Nikki followed me inside. The band was already playing, jammed into a corner with just a pair of amps. The guy from the visitors centre recognised me and smiled. He was playing a big stand-up double bass, left-handed, and was also keeping the beat; his left foot worked a drum lever, which slammed against an old yellow suitcase, stood upright. His band partner, and it was just the two of them, had a battered acoustic guitar, so old it didn't even have a sound hole, and was using his left foot to beat a foot snare. Both sang, very well. The combination resulted in a fantastic arrangement of sounds, as they fused pop-type tunes with roots and blues.

My only thought was that a guy who plays this well worked his days at the visitors centre. He wasn't good enough to live off his music?

I watched and listened while waiting for the bartender. Nikki's shoulder touched mine.

There were CDs for sale on the bar. The EP that had five tracks on it was untitled, and I assumed this was Left Feet's first recording. Their second, *Beat You to the Corner,* had twelve songs and more professional artwork and packaging.

I ordered the drinks. Nikki asked for four glasses, deciding to also partake of the pitcher.

"... the suitcase?" she asked.

I had to turn to hear her and only caught the last part of her question. "The suitcase? It's their bass drum, I guess. It's cool. Makes an interesting sound."

She smiled. With some make-up on and wearing a tight-fitting shirt and heels, she looked nice. I wondered if she and Bevan had talked things out, but couldn't guess at the result, as both had come along this evening, bringing their awkward vibe with them.

"... your friend?"

"Vidar's not my friend."

She shouted into my ear: "No. Did you find your friend?"

"Nuh. But I did see pretty much all of Austin on the bike today. It was fun, and I like the city. Reminds me of Perth. Maybe more of Freo than Perth."

"Freo?"

"Fremantle. The port area. It's part of the same suburban megalopolis as Perth, but it's got a bit more going on. More street life, music, art and culture."

"I've never been to Perth. It's so far away."

"Austin's much further, and here you are."

"Yeah. Funny that. And now it's a place for breaking up."

"Really?"

She nodded. "I think you were right about the control thing. I told him I'm sick of running behind him and doing everything his way."

"So why he is out with us tonight?"

"I don't know. Probably to keep an eye on me."

I thought this was a bit weird, but I didn't have time to dwell on it, as the drinks landed on the bar and I started piling up all the quarters and dimes I had in my pockets.

"Did you spend the afternoon begging?" Nikki asked.

"Something like that. It takes talent and hard work to earn loose change."

I carried the pitcher and a stack of glasses, while Nikki made a triangle of cokes and gripped this with two hands. At the booth, Vidar was next to Bevan. Nikki sat down, giving Bevan a pained smile and filling that side of the booth. I poured the beers, standing. Vidar raised his glass in toast and we all drank.

"Pull up a chair," Nikki said.

"I'm gonna check out the band again."

I took my beer inside and perched myself on a stool at the bar. Left Feet were working hard. The double-bass player's green shirt was damp with sweat. No one in the café seemed to be listening, and the combined noise of many shouted conversations, and the resonating echoes, just about drowned out the band. I felt a bit sorry for them, as they were too good to simply function as background music.

I had a long drink and thought again about what a fickle business music is. When asked, I couldn't give a clear answer why some bands made it and others struggled; that fantastic musicians had to work in warehouses, offices and restaurants because they couldn't survive on their music alone, and that many gave up, jaded and bitter with the whole thing. They spent years playing gigs like this, often just for their drinks and for whatever they got from selling CDs. Meanwhile, bands and singers of lesser talent with bland, unoriginal songs somehow rose in popularity. And then, the long apprenticeship of becoming a musician had been condensed to soap-opera form by the casting and talent shows of reality television.

Would Left Feet spend the next few decades stuck here? They

70

could sweat onto their instruments all they wanted, and beat that suitcase until it disintegrated, but they would most probably never get the attention they deserved. Both of them looked over thirty, meaning they'd already missed the chance to be hailed as the next big young thing. Twenty-seven years old was the unspoken benchmark for making it or to die trying. I thought they were enjoying themselves, perhaps thinking they were lucky even to have a gig like this.

I sipped my beer and tapped my feet. Their rhythm was infectious, and I loved the sound of the suitcase drum. Yet, I couldn't look at them without feeling a bit depressed. If players of this calibre couldn't make it, how would I? Building and repairing guitars was looking like a far more lucrative endeavour than playing one.

And I wondered if I'd made more busking this afternoon than Left Feet would get from this gig, which given the disparity in ability, struck me as completely unfair. It also seemed to me that these two guys really wanted to make it, to get out of this café and go on to bigger things.

A musician who doesn't crave fame and fortune is a liar. We want to have attention and for people to scream and applaud. We want to be played on the radio. We want to record an album that sells millions and to be rich. We want to be on the cover of magazines. We want to write the song that defines a summer, and which people are still listening to years later and it transports them back to that fabulous summer.

But those are dreams, the musician's fantasy, because very few reach such heights. The vast majority of us are focused on survival: paying the rent, stocking the fridge, and having enough left over to buy a new set of strings. I paid my rent restringing other people's guitars.

As Nola had said, not everyone can be Bob Dylan.

I wasn't sure I even qualified to call myself a musician. Hobbyist was more accurate, especially given "struggling musician" was a job title I didn't want to throw around. I told myself to be glad I could say I was a luthier, which always proved interesting to people.

Left Feet were one band in this city. They were impressive, but there were probably lots of other bands who were better. And that was just in Austin. Altogether in America, there must have been thousands of bands better than Left Feet.

Bevan came to the bar, clutching the empty pitcher.

"You alright, mate? You look like your dog just died. Or is the band that bad?"

"No, they're good. I'm good. How's it going outside?"

Bevan laughed a little as he ordered a pitcher. "That Swedish guy, what's his name?"

"Vidar."

"He's a bit of dick. He's all over the three Japanese girls, and behaving like they're fighting over him. Plus, he drank most of the pitcher himself, then ordered me in here to get another."

"Probably thinks we all owe him for driving us."

"It was a ten-minute ride."

"Maybe he's low on money. I reckon he's a bit of a bean counter."

Bevan nodded slowly. "Yeah, he's got that about him, hey?"

The slight hint of respect in Bevan's voice and expression made me wonder if he was also obsessive about money.

"Or he's lonely. All that driving on his own, going across the country like a travelling vacuum cleaner salesman."

"Well, the American dream is in there somewhere," Bevan said.

"At least Vidar's version of it."

"In my opinion, he's all about bragging rights."

"The fifty states thing?"

"Yeah, he won't shut up about it."

A full pitcher was placed on the bar and Bevan paid for it, not tipping. He seemed like a decent guy, and not quite the cumbersome baggage Nikki had made him out to be. Still, the way he counted his change made me wonder if money was playing a role in their relationship, because something about Nikki made me think she would have much preferred a room in a swanky hotel with a continental breakfast to a double with a shared bathroom, in a youth hostel with just-add-water pancakes.

"You coming back outside?" Bevan asked.

I was quietly glad to be avoiding the booth. "In a minute."

As he topped up my glass, he said, "You better, because someone needs to keep Vidar on a leash."

He gave me a thin smile and headed outside.

Left Feet finished their song and took a break. The bass player came up to me.

"You made it. Thanks for that."

"You guys are great. Really."

This made him beam, but I had the feeling he would have been far happier if I bought a dozen copies of *Beat You to the Corner* and gave them to all my friends.

"How'd the busking go?"

"It was fun, right up until the police arrived."

"They came for you?"

"I thought they did, but there was an accident. Someone was dropping balloons full of paint on Second Street. That's what caused the crash."

"I heard about that. That's like the third protest this week."

I took the bill-sized card out of my pocket and showed it to him. "I found this on the street."

He looked at both sides, then handed it back to me. "Yep. Just like the others. Someone out there is really against our Keep Austin Weird campaign. Which is a total shame. The city prides itself on being off-beat and indie, but it's also about supporting everything local. Like this place."

The break was just long enough for him to get two drinks. He headed back to the corner, where his band partner was tuning that relic of a guitar. He got his big double-bass upright, and Left Feet tore into a song I was sure they'd already played.

Now spotted and spoken to, I felt obliged to stay and listen, when I would have preferred going back to the hostel to sleep. Left Feet proceeded to play what sounded like their first set all over again. I assumed these were the songs found on their second CD.

It appeared only the girl tending the bar and I were listening. There was no clapping at the end of a song, and no one went to check out the CDs on sale. The longer they played, the more the situation started to seem sad.

I nursed my beer, then had a coffee, hoping the caffeine would stop my yawning.

When Left Feet finally finished and started packing up, Nikki came in. I was surprised to see her still here, as I'd been hiding at the bar for nearly two hours, gladly avoiding the dramas playing out between my fellow hostel guests. As none had come in for more drinks, I'd assumed they'd left.

"Looks like you're their one and only groupie," Nikki said.

"Hey, I'm all about the music. I thought they needed some support. Not much material, but they can really play."

Nikki leaned an elbow on the bar and faced me, smiling just a little.

"Where's everyone else?"

"Vidar and Bevan got into an argument," she said. "Because he was drinking so much and was supposed to be our driver. So, they all went back. Bevan went as well, to keep an eye on Vidar, so he said."

"Good of him."

"Oh, very. He's determined to protect a trio of Japanese girls, who I think can look after themselves, all while his own relationship crumbles right in front of him."

I really wasn't in the mood to dissect their relationship. "So, what do we do?"

"Take a taxi, I guess. Have you got enough pennies for that?"

"A few. You wanna walk?"

"All the way?"

"Why not? We could get downtown and take a bus from there. Or if we're feeling up for it, yeah, walk the whole way. We don't have to go to work tomorrow, and I only beg in the afternoons."

"I'm sorry I said that." She gave me a sweet, rather childish look. "I'm happy to walk with you."

She led the way outside. I waved to the bass player, who was thankfully too busy packing up to do anything more than wave back, which saved me from having an awkward conversation with him about CD purchases.

The evening was warm and pleasant. I checked the map and saw that we could walk the length of Guadalupe Street to downtown, from where we could find the stop for bus 100, which would take us out to the hostel. We went down Furth Street and crossed Twenty-ninth.

"If there's any trouble," Nikki said, "I'll hide behind you."

Austin didn't strike me as dangerous. The people I saw on Guadalupe Street looked like students. Some were gathered in groups. They drank from red plastic cups and looked to be heading out on the town. Two athletic guys carrying sports bags went into the 24-hour Whataburger joint, while on the other side of the street, I saw four girls clutching plastic bags, having done some late-night grocery shopping. All normal, routine stuff.

As we worked our way down through the twenties, Nikki told me about her life in Brisbane. She and Bevan didn't live together, but they'd talked about it and Bevan wanted it; I assumed to save money.

I asked about her work and she said she had a job in a shop that sold one-off t-shirts, jumpers and bags.

"We take ordinary shirts, print something funny or summery on them, and sell them for four times the price. Same with the bags. The designs are cool, and no two designs are alike."

"I like the sound of that. Unique clothing."

"That's what it is. Shaz got the idea from a shop she found in Hamburg. They do all these different harbour motifs. We do surfing and beach motifs."

"Does the shop survive? I mean, how do you compete with all the cheap labels out there?"

"I'm just doing the designs. Shaz and Jules own it together and take care of the business side of things. I think they do alright. The shop's still there. We do a lot of gifts, and sometimes corporate stuff, for events and what-not. People like having something that no one else has."

Talking with Nikki like this, and without that relationship cloud hanging over her, I started to like her a lot more.

"It's fun," she continued. "Of course, I'd prefer to be working on my own stuff, but this is good for now."

"Did you study design?"

She nodded. "What about you? Did you go to university?"

There were several ways for me to tell Nikki about my studies, signposted with qualifiers and excuses which would put the blame firmly on others, namely my parents, their expectations and their untimely divorce.

"I graduate from the Australian Institute for Beggars."

Nikki laughed. "I'm so sorry I said that."

"And you're way off, because I actually spent the afternoon breaking open parking meters and public phones with a crow-bar."

She gave me a playful push. "Be serious. You're no thief."

"Okay. The truth is that I started uni, but didn't finish. My parents are both lawyers, and naturally they wanted me and my brother to become lawyers too. They weren't hard about it, but they did want us to go to uni and get a start in life. Conor managed it, just not to become a lawyer. He's a phys-ed teacher. I failed. Completely."

"Really? You don't really seem like the slacker type. What happened?"

We stopped for the light at Martin Luther King Jr Boulevard, then jaywalked, as there weren't any cars. I thought back to dropping out of university and how my parents hadn't really cared at the time, as they'd been more interested in their own problems and their respective reinventions.

"It all went pear-shaped when my parents split."

"Mine split as well."

"How old were you?"

"I think, three. I can't remember it. I lived with my mum and boomeranged between the two on weekends. For me, it was normal. I didn't know anything else."

"I was twenty-one, and I'd just finished my second year. I was studying conservation. The grand plan was that I would become an ecology lawyer. You know, to fight the green fight. But then my folks split and I lost my way."

"I'm sorry."

"Actually, Nikki, that's not right, and it's not fair. I was hating uni. I would've found a reason to drop out anyway. I shouldn't blame my parents for that. It was a miracle I got through the second year."

"It is extremely difficult for me to picture you in a suit, walking into a courtroom with a briefcase."

"I couldn't picture it either."

"So, what did you do? Because I don't think you're a person who would slip through the cracks. You're pretty grounded to me, like you've got things sorted. You're definitely more mature than Bevan and a lot easier to talk to as well."

"It all turned out okay. I had some help. My mate Churchill, he was big at the time, really supportive, even when I went off to New Zealand. I thought I could figure things out while I was there. Get away from everyone."

From Thirteenth Street, we headed up a long rise. I could feel my legs and all the riding I'd done. Visiting those RV camps seemed like a long time ago. What had happened to finding Nola and Eris today?

"And? Did you figure things out?"

"Yeah, in a way. New Zealand was good for me. I made some decisions and went back to Perth with a plan. When I was at uni, I had a part-time job in a music shop. For instruments and equipment, not CDs. I liked the job and I'd been playing the guitar since I was six, so I decided to learn how to make and repair guitars. I did my apprenticeship as a luthier and moved from the service counter to the workshop."

"A luthier? Sounds medieval."

"I'm proud to say I've already repaired a few lutes in my time."

"That's really cool. You got involved in something you're passionate about. You didn't just take some job."

We walked in silence for a bit, then Nikki clapped her hands together.

"That's where you got the coins from. You were busking."

Nikki was turning out to be full of surprises. It was enjoyable talking to her, and we seemed to have downtown Austin all to ourselves.

"That's it."

"Looks like you did well."

"I had a blast. It wasn't easy at the start, because you always feel like you're invading a bit, and you don't want to stand out there and hit bum notes. I played all these Aussie songs and people seemed to like them."

"That's really cool. Where'd you stand? Do you stand or sit when you're busking?"

"I always stand. I get more attention that way. The giant carrot-top."

"Rubbish. You've got beautiful hair."

I didn't expect her to say that, or to look at me the way she did, with such interest. We shared the nervous laughter and awkward smiles of two people realising they are attracted to each other and that something is happening. I suddenly felt like I was fourteen years old again.

We passed a small park called Republic Square, which might have been nice in daylight, but seemed somewhat menacing in the dark. A large and loud group of men clustered around the benches near the row of bikes from the city's B-cycle bike-sharing program. The group look best avoided. I guided us across the street to the relative safety of the other side.

"So, what are you then?" Nikki asked. "A busker or a luthier?"

"Uh, next question, please."

"That answers it. You dropped out of uni and became a guitar repairer, when what you really want to be is a full-time musician."

"You make it sound very straightforward and easy. Like it's a series of steps and all I have to do is just keep going forward."

"Isn't music working out for you?"

I didn't know how to answer that without sounding critical of myself, or worse, like a bitching cry-baby. It could've been because I was lazy; that I didn't practice enough or put in the time required to write songs. It could've been that I wasn't persistent enough in getting gigs and promoting myself. It could've been the industry, which mostly rewarded bands and singers who sounded like all those who came before them. It could've been that I didn't have the right look, or the necessary sex appeal.

I didn't have the courage to tell Nikki that I thought I wasn't good enough. I could play and sing. I could write songs. But I seemed to lack some magic ingredient that would bring all of that together and help me rise above the thousands of struggling musicians out there. After seeing Left Feet, I was starting to think the magic ingredient was luck.

"Come on," Nikki said. "I'm not letting you dodge that question."

"I guess I'm still learning. People think singers or bands come out of nowhere and are famous overnight. They write a big hit and everyone wonders who they are and where they've come from, like they only started singing and playing yesterday. But behind that are years of practicing and gigging and writing crap songs. I'm still at that stage, and have been for a while."

"You write your own songs?"

"I try."

"So, why do you play covers when you're busking? Why not play your songs?"

"Because they aren't that good, and then there are all these great songs that are much better than mine and more fun to play."

"I think you're being too hard on yourself, and making the wrong comparison. You should focus on doing something original and special, something that has meaning for you, and not simply copying what others have done."

This made me stop walking. We'd reached Second Street. I stood there, staring at the sign.

"Are we lost?" Nikki asked.

I took a step towards her and leaned down to kiss her. This caught her by surprise. Her blue eyes were wide, with shock and interest, and she moved back a little. Then she stopped, stepped slightly forward and our lips met. At first, it was a chaste kiss, the way kids kiss, or a couple in an old Hollywood film, but it became more passionate as we both relaxed into it.

When Nikki pulled back and lowered herself from her tip-toes, she smiled and said, "I need a box to stand on. Or bigger heels."

As my pulse rate started to slow, I wondered if I had just become the wrecking ball that would blast through the final foundations of Nikki and Bevan's relationship.

We headed down Second, holding hands and walking slower than before. Dawdling, and not really wanting the moment to end. This street was narrower than Guadalupe and somehow more romantic, with soft lighting, residential buildings and restaurants which had seating that spilled out onto the street. There were also more people around, eating late dinners, talking brightly with each other, laughing, and sitting on balconies drinking beer.

I saw a sign that said "J. B. Dumas Horseshoeing" and pointed at it.

"More medieval work," Nikki said. "You can learn to be a blacksmith while you're here. Get another ancient trade under your belt."

"Maybe I can learn how to make swords as well."

"I might have to start calling you Sir Rowan."

"Steady on. I'm not ready to be a knight."

We reached the area where the accident had happened. On the street, there were large splotches of grey paint, as well as bits of glass and metal that hadn't been cleaned up. I stopped and pointed at the guitar statue on the other side of Congress.

"I was busking over there. At that statue. And I was having a fine time until someone started dropping balloons filled with paint on this street."

"Is that what this is?"

"It caused a car accident. No one was hurt, but it was still messy. Must've ruined the day of everyone involved." I looked up at the roof of the nearby Austonian building. "They came from somewhere up there."

"What did?"

"The paint bombs."

Nikki shrugged. "Or they were launched from a catapult. Then they could've come from any building."

"Yeah, maybe."

"Any idea what it was all about?"

"A protest, I think. When the balloons stopped falling, it rained cards. People thought it was money and they went racing for it."

"Did you?"

"I had all this change in my pockets. I couldn't run without spilling it like a winning slot machine. But I did pick up one of the cards."

I took it out and handed it to her. She didn't react to the "Keep Austin Plain" side, but she stared at the G-symbol.

"Do you know who this is?" she asked, with a certain reverence.

"No, but I'm sure I've seen it before."

"It's Grilla. The urban artist."

"Never heard of him."

Nikki was taking in the scene differently, as if viewing a piece of artwork. "I'm not fully up to speed on the urban art scene, because it changes fast, but I did some work on graffiti when I was at uni. Grilla was one of the artists we studied. Rumour has it Grilla's a girl, but no one knows who she is. Apparently, she started out as Guerrilla, a graffiti artist, maybe fifteen years ago. Then she was Girlrilla, and then Grilla. My prof said she could also be the combination of several artists. You know, copycats who build on the fame of others."

"Does graffiti qualify as art?"

"Sure." Nikki smiled and handed the card back to me. "The G-star is her symbol. It's something to do with anarchy or chaos or revolution. I can't remember what exactly. I guess she's still out there, doing her art. Or someone is copying her."

"And now a car accident is art?"

"Maybe the cars got in the way. Amazing to think she might actually be in Austin."

Nikki started walking and I hustled to catch up. We crossed Congress.

"Are you planning to play here tomorrow?" she asked.

"I think so. It was a pretty productive hour."

"Can I watch? I'm not ready to be your groupie, but I'd like to hear you play."

"Yeah. Sure."

She stopped and held up a finger. "One condition. You play your own songs."

"I don't have that many."

"You're lying."

"They're not that good."

"You won't know that until you test them out on people."

While I wondered if Nikki was always this forthright, and that

80

maybe Bevan couldn't handle it, she reached her hands up and gently pulled my head down. We kissed.

"I'll compromise," she said, leaning back. "One for one. An original and a cover, and you alternate with each song."

"Deal."

"Good. Now, where's this bus you promised me. My feet are killing me."

→←

My buzzing phone woke me and made others in the dorm room stir.

"Churchill?"

"G'day, squire."

I went out of the room and closed the door. "Do you have any idea what time it is?"

"Don't care. I've got something and it's red hot. You need to act now."

While my brain was still fuzzy with sleep, it occurred to me that since busking, going to the Spider House, walking back with Nikki, kissing her on the street, and on the back seat of the empty bus 100, where things got rather physical, I'd barely given a thought to Nola and Eris.

"What is it?"

"You're so cranky in the mornings."

"I don't think this even qualifies as morning."

"I guess I got the time difference mixed up. Anyway, now that you're awake, I can tell you that Nola used her credit card in Austin."

"What? Are you sure? How'd you find that out?"

"I called in a few favours," Churchill said, sounding very pleased with himself. "Okay, Janette did. My Bankwest bombshell. I asked her if banks can track a credit card, and it turns out they can. Something about preventing fraud, or some such. I got Janette to call around and spin a story about possible fraud, and to mention Austin. And bang, she managed to get the details of Nola's last transaction."

"Is that even legal?"

"Probably not. But a lot of what banks do isn't really legal. Anyway, Nola used the card yesterday. And get ready for this. She used it at a place called the Firehouse, just like in Little Rock. I guess she likes continuity."

81

"Just like you. Where is it?"

"You didn't check it out already? It was on the list. You were supposed to go there yesterday."

"Come on, Church. It took most of the day just to get to all the campgrounds."

"You went to all of them? You didn't just call the ones further out?"

"You know how I am about talking on the phone. It's easy with you, because I'm used to your voice. Anyway, some other stuff came up."

"Well," Churchill said, sounding annoyed, "you better head there right now. That's an order."

"Alright, alright."

"I hope you appreciate what I brilliant piece of detective work this was."

"By Janette, you mean."

"Hey, I got the ball rolling. Janette was my girl in the field who executed the plan. You're my man in Austin, so get moving."

He hung up.

I went into the bathroom and splashed cold water on my face. Churchill was right. It was a promising lead and I had to follow it. A bonus being that I wouldn't be around for breakfast in the hostel, which had the potential to be seriously awkward after last night. I wanted to pursue things with Nikki, but didn't want to be in the middle of her break-up. Or worse, be the one causing it.

Dressed, I walked down Tinnin Ford Road to catch the bus. It was just after six in the morning and I was the only one at the stop, but lots people were already up and driving their cars.

It was such a nice walk with Nikki last night. I wondered if I might turn it into a song; how through the course of a conversation, your perception of a person could change, from disinterest and annoyance to curiosity and attraction, as the person emerged from the shadows to be revealed as someone you admired and desired. Unfortunately, Guadalupe Street didn't quite lend itself lyrically in the way that Thunder Road, Alphabet Street or Copperhead Road did. And as the ending might yet turn out messy, the song had all the makings of another whine-fest. Cue the minor chords and sad violins.

I got on the bus coming from the airport, joining a dozen bleary-eyed people who had taken red-eye flights. I checked my phone; the Firehouse was on Brazos Street. I marked it on my map, which was already starting to tear on its folds. Once across the river, I charted the bus's progress as we went up Congress and past the guitar statue. I got out at the first stop on Trinity Street and started walking up Sixth. It was cold in the shadows of the buildings, but the sky was clear and a very pale blue.

Plenty of locals seemed okay with the early hour, already heading to work, earphones in place and sipping coffees along the way. It was too early for me to be excited about finding Nola and Eris. I couldn't explain it, but I felt they were already gone.

The bars along Sixth Street were closed, but I could hear muffled music coming from behind the closed doors. On Brazos, I found the hostel opposite a grand-looking building called The Driskill, but adjacent to a rather uninviting alleyway. The ATM machine at the Firehouse entrance reminded me again that I was out of cash. I decided to busk every day, to at least cover my food and accommodation and to keep my bank balance from going constantly backwards.

The reception desk was vacant, but the door to the lounge was ajar. I edged inside. There was a corner stage and a long bar lined with stools. I liked the split levels, dark leather seats and wire-framed chairs. But as is often the case, an empty bar in the early hours of the morning feels like a desperate and dirty place, with the floor still sticky from the previous night's spilled drunks, and the drunken atmosphere of the last drinkers lingering.

A guy with a heavy beard and wearing a waistcoat without a shirt underneath was cleaning up behind the bar.

"We're closed," he said.

"Probably a bit too early for a drink anyway."

He stopped cleaning and took a long sip from a cocktail of some sort. "Is it?"

"Look, there was no one at reception, so I came in here."

"Someone will be there in a minute. Go and wait."

"Okay. Thanks."

"And close the door."

The door was a sliding bookcase, which I rolled into place. Once closed, I could hear music start playing from behind it.

A very tired girl was now standing at the reception desk, sipping coffee.

"Can I help you?" she asked, yawning.

"I hope so. I'm looking for a couple of guests. Nola Henderson, and Eris Henderson. Mother and daughter. Eris is about five."

She shook her head. "No kids."

"What?"

"This ain't no place for kids."

"But they were here. Nola used her credit card."

"How do you know that?"

"Uh, I, we, you know, we share a bank account."

She pointed at the bookcase and said, "Maybe in there. Had a few drinks or something. Paid with her card, I don't know. But I can tell you there are no Hendersons staying here and definitely no kids. It's not that kind of hostel."

"Right. Thanks anyway."

"Have a nice day."

Outside, I walked back down Brazos and considered my next move. The best I could think of was to call Churchill. He answered after one ring.

"Ground control."

"They're not there, Church. Well, not staying there. I guess Nola used her card in the bar, which is part of the hostel, sort of."

"Crap, but they're still in Austin. You need to start checking the hotels."

"Oh, come on. This city is huge. There must be hundreds of hotels."

"We'll start at the bottom end and work upwards, from the cheapest to most expensive. I'll put a list together for you."

"Yeah, whatever. I'm gonna get some breakfast."

And this time, I hung up on Churchill.

Going back to the hostel for pancakes was out of the question, so I went into the P. Terry's on Sixth and ordered an egg burger with ham, a coffee, and a slice of banana bread. I took a seat at the window to watch the vans and trucks driving along Sixth, marvelling at how busy Austin was in the morning. A party town without any trace of a hangover, and music still playing everywhere.

As the day had started so early, I was happy now to slow things down.

Something made me think checking all the hotels would be a fruitless exercise. The day could be better spent hanging with Nikki, busking on Second and enjoying the city.

Because I was really starting to like Austin. Any place that had guitar statues and memorials to guitar players was fine by me. I was also keen to visit more bars and see other bands and musicians. If Left

84

Feet qualified as small-time and struggling, who couldn't sell a single CD after a rollicking two-hour set, then how good were Austin's more successful bands?

Would Nikki be up for a club crawl this evening? I hoped so.

I also hoped that right about now, Nikki and Bevan were sitting somewhere, bringing their relationship to an amicable end, which would result in Bevan taking a bus out of town this morning, or hitching a ride with Vidar to the next state on the Swede's list. I doubted I would be that lucky. The immediate future I saw was me getting further entangled in the complex relationship web the two of them had spun.

I ate my breakfast slowly, thinking. Maybe it was just an evening walk and a few innocent kisses, and it didn't amount to much. Maybe Nikki had already dismissed it, and me. Was it the kind of thing she did often, testing the waters and trying to ascertain just how much she cared about Bevan? She didn't really strike me as the easy, promiscuous type. There was something difficult about her. Something that would make guys think twice before getting involved, as I had.

The solution was to let Nikki make the play, rather than me step forward and become their relationship destroyer. The one thing I didn't want to be was the interloper who ends up helping two people decide they really do want to stay together.

Doing nothing felt lame, and cowardly, but this time, it felt like the right course of action. For some bizarre reason, Bevan scared me.

The banana bread was good. I had a second coffee and perused Churchill's hotel list. I had to try, and it wasn't like my morning was packed. I decided to hit the hotels which were near the Firehouse, thinking that Nola might have gone to the lounge as it wasn't far from where she and Eris were staying. This would appease Churchill and make the morning more productive.

Outside, I headed east on Sixth, the sun shining straight down the road and into my face, a warm desert breeze coming with it. The Westin Hotel on Fifth was the closest, but when I got to the corner of San Jacinto Boulevard, I saw a woman walking with a small girl on the other side of the street. What caught my eye was the pink backpack the woman carried, similar to the one Nola had in New Zealand. The woman was about Nola's height and shape, though it was hard to remember, and hard to tell from behind and at this distance.

It couldn't be them, could it?

The little girl's red hair was tied into a pair of pigtails that swished from side to side as she walked.

San Jacinto's streaming traffic prevented me from crossing the street, and it seemed forever until the light finally turned red. I stood there, watching the two of them walking further down Sixth, in and out of the shadows of buildings. The mother walked quickly, holding her daughter's hand and forcing her to keep up.

By the time I caught up, they were across Red River Street and through the underpass. I decided to keep my distance, as I wasn't sure what I would say if it turned out to be them.

East of the freeway, the area was less attractive than downtown, with liquor stores and petrol stations. This didn't last. The neighbourhood improved once we got past San Marcos Street. The buildings were newer and trees lined the street.

We continued in this fashion for a few more blocks. They walked, I followed.

I didn't feel ready for this. Not this morning. Not after having slept so little. Not after having had such a great time yesterday, when I'd played and sang on the streets of Austin and kissed a beautiful girl. How was I supposed to do this? Just walk up to them and say, hey, it's me. Your old hiking and sex buddy from New Zealand. And oh, by the way, little girl, I think I'm your dad. Thanks for the postcards and for making me come all the way over here to find you when you could have just told me everything straight, about five years ago.

They took a left on Comal Street and I matched it, keeping to the opposite side, about thirty metres behind. Across Seventh, we walked along the edge of a cemetery, which had rows of little white headstones, making me think it was where soldiers were buried. There were suburban homes on my side of Comal, with verandas and front yards facing the cemetery. I couldn't imagine living there, waking up every day to see those headstones. It reminded me of Karrakatta in Shenton Park, with the houses along the cemetery's borders considered prized real estate.

When they stopped to cross the street, looking both ways for traffic, I turned around. But surely she'd seen me, would recognise me. How many two-metre tall redheads did Nola know?

They kept walking, still holding hands, the mother pulling her daughter along, up the hill and onto Eleventh.

It was attractive suburbia up here, with two-storey houses and lots of trees. The only blight on the scene were the overhead power lines criss-crossing the street.

We passed the Holy Cross church.

The further we walked, the more I felt it wasn't them. At least, the woman was unlikely to be Nola. I'd walked behind her for a week in the Abel Tasman; the woman in front of me now moved differently. And there was something routine about this walk, about the mother's harried stress and the little girl's reluctance. They lived in Austin, and probably did this walk every day.

I kept following, until they reached the Edward L. Blackshear Elementary School, where the mother gave her daughter the backpack and kissed her goodbye.

The mother turned and walked back the way she came. I continued along Eleventh, wondering what on earth I was doing in Austin, Texas.

God on Vacation

The city gives her nothing, so she does some research and is stunned to learn that Tulsa has well over four hundred churches. It works out to be about one church for every thousand people, but that's not counting all the dodgy storefront churches, of which she's already seen plenty. There's even Oral Roberts University, founded by the televangelist, and its on-campus monstrosity called the Prayer Tower.

She finds the rampant religiosity overwhelming, fitting and inspiring. While Tulsa's not quite the buckle of the Bible Belt, she think it's a pretty significant notch, and God is a theme worth working with.

An idea forms, and she thinks it's a good one.

As always, there's a fair bit of preparation to do. She starts with a website: www.godline.org. It's easy to register, set up and build. There are loads of free religious-themed images online to populate the site with and make it look professional. It's an evening's work, and she uses one of the computers in the Aloft Hotel's Business Center while her daughter sleeps in their room on the third floor. She sets the go-live date as midnight on Saturday, which gives her almost twenty-four hours. The automatic email response will also be activated at midnight. It includes the single sentence "You are God, so take a vacation" and a large G, which she thinks is a nice touch, as it looks like the brand of God is on the email.

The next thing to do is the poster. This has some of the same Christian-type images she put on the website and says in large type, "Church closed due to God on vacation. Send your prayers directly to God at help@godline.org."

She worries that it's all too obvious and that no one will fall for it.

The hotel has a new printer, but she can't run off four hundred copies of the poster on it. She prints one copy and deletes the file from the computer. She also prints a list of all the churches in Tulsa, which comes to seventeen pages.

Back in the room, she gets into bed with her daughter, but it takes her a long time to fall asleep, as she's buzzing with excitement.

The next day is given over to planning her route and obtaining the necessary supplies. While the Aloft Hotel isn't exactly cheap, it does have Camp Aloft for kids. She dumps her daughter on a pair of bored-looking teenagers and goes shopping. This includes buying a detailed map of Tulsa, a bucket of glue, a small roller, a dozen pairs of plastic gloves, two surgical masks and a pair of goggles. She spreads her purchases over several shops to avoid suspicion, and also rents a small black hatchback. At a deserted local library, she runs off four hundred copies of her poster.

Back at the hotel, she leaves everything in the rental car, except for the map, and reluctantly retrieves her daughter from Camp Aloft. She's glad that the day's activities have worn her daughter out; the little girl sleeps balled up in the top left corner of the bed while she sets about marking all the churches on the map. It takes a couple of hours. With all the dots marked, she wonders how she'll be able to get to all of those churches in one night, and spend two minutes surreptitiously gluing a poster on each church's front door.

She does the math, with difficultly, as she didn't finish high school: two minutes at four hundred churches is eight hundred minutes, which is over thirteen hours. Plus driving time and navigating a new city. Plus whatever hassle her daughter might cause. Plus trying to do it all without getting noticed.

There's no way she can do it, so she decides to concentrate on the downtown area, where the dots are clustered, and then branch out into the surrounding suburbs if she has time left over.

Knowing she'll be up all night, and with her daughter already napping, she thinks now is a good time to get some sleep.

A few hours later, her daughter wakes her up, saying she's hungry.

"God, it never ends, does it?" she says as she gets herself up.

The Aloft has a bar and restaurant, but she refuses to eat in hotels; she thinks the food is always terrible and that there's something depressing about eating in the place she's staying, like it's a hospital. The few eateries on the corner are all junk, so she heads down East Seventy-first Street, in the direction of the Woodland Hills Mall, her daughter trailing behind and hustling to keep up. If she took the girl's hand, she could get her to walk faster, prompt her to move and even pull her along, when required. But she doesn't want to hold that little hand.

The street has three lanes, going in both directions. The lack of traffic makes this broad thoroughfare seem out of place and unnecessary, built for a more prosperous time in Tulsa's history. It's lined with warehouse-sized shops fronted by car parks as big as football fields. There are petrol stations, fast-food restaurants, car washes, storage centres and furniture stores. It's difficult, but she tries to imagine this as prairie, an untamed wilderness of gently rolling hills peppered with wildlife; when it was Indian Territory, possibly belonging to the Creek Nation. That's a guess, because she's not that well-versed in Native American geography for this part of the States. Still, she knows there once was a time when this place looked far better than it does now. It makes her angry; that the best the invaders could do with a prairie was turn it into a strip mall with bloated six-lane roads and over four hundred churches.

She asks herself if God is the right theme for Tulsa. Destroying the temple of consumption and excess that is East Seventy-first Street seems more pertinent, but she's already done many acts that sought to bring chaos to consumerism. There are only so many ways to temporarily screw up a Walmart or shopping mall. It's too late now to change anyway. Everything is prepared, and she's running out of time, with just three weeks left before starting work, five more cities to visit and a lot of miles to cover.

A gritty wind is gusting from the east, sending small eddies of dust and lighter bits of garbage into the air. The eddies twirl through the car parks. Her daughter tries to chase one.

Despite the scene, she's enjoying the walk. It's helping to shake off the haze of sleeping in the afternoon, though it's a nuisance to have to stop and wait for her daughter to catch up.

When they reach the Woodland Hills Mall, she's not surprised to see the building's design leaning a long way to the religious side. The row of arches and columns on the white Macy's building would be more suited to a cathedral, while the Cheesecake Factory restaurant close to the street is an orange rectangle with a tower at the front and could easily pass for a church. It also has columns, plus a rounded extension on one corner that could be a nave.

Inside the air-conditioned mall, she takes her daughter to the food court on the upper level, where she hopes the range of options will reduce the chance of an argument, tantrum or scene.

The little girl wants spaghetti from the Italian place, with tomato sauce and no cheese. She takes a salad.

They eat in silence, interrupted by the occasional question from her daughter, followed by an order for her to sit still, be quiet and finish her spaghetti.

As she pokes at her salad, which is swimming in vinegary dressing, she realises her daughter could seriously sour her efforts tonight to hit as many churches as she can. She realises she'll have to drug her again.

With half the meal finished, her daughter demands dessert.

They leave the mall and walk to the Cheesecake Factory for sundaes. As they cross the barren car park, she feels like she's wasting the afternoon. It hurts to think of all the things she could be doing. The art she could create. The books she could read. The films she could watch. The murals she could paint. The forests she could wander through. The hills she could climb. The chaos she could instigate.

She knows it's incredibly selfish and callous to think like that, but she can't deny that she thinks in exactly that way. She wants to be rid of the girl.

They walk slowly back to the hotel. Her daughter finishes her sundae, then asks for the rest of hers. She complies, not wanting to eat so much sugar and dairy anyway.

There are only seven cars in the hotel car park, including her rented hatchback, and all are covered in a fine layer of yellow dust.

Upstairs, their room is a mess, and they've only been there for one night. She turns the television on and her daughter dutifully sits in front of it. She wonders what parents did with their kids before television was invented, and how they ever got a break from the constant demands for attention.

She prepares a glass of water for her daughter, adding a few drops of Phenergan Elixir. The bottle is almost empty, and she regrets not buying more when she was out shopping earlier.

Then there's nothing left to do but wait, for the time to run and for the sedative to kick in. She takes out her notebook and brainstorms ideas. She hasn't got anything for San Diego yet, and hopes inspiration will hit once she's there, as it did with Tulsa.

Her daughter wants to play a game.

"No. Drink your water and watch TV."

The girl does as she's told, but drinks slowly. Her movements seem deliberate, as if she's in control of the situation and perhaps even aware the water is drugged.

She marvels again at how perceptive her daughter is. But she doesn't feel any pride, that she's created this small human with advanced sensory awareness. She's suspicious of it, and wary.

"Brush your teeth and get ready for bed," she says.

Her daughter goes into the bathroom. Ten minutes pass and she's still in there.

She opens the door to see the girl curled up on the bathmat, like a cat, her head in the crook of her elbow.

This gives her a buzz, because it's on. She feels her body coming alive as she gathers her things together, including the map, her camera and the bottle of Phenergan, just in case. The last thing she grabs is her daughter, scooping her off the floor and carrying her piggy-back style down the stairs to the car park.

With the girl lying on the back seat, she gets out onto the Broken Arrow Expressway, trying not to speed. It's twenty minutes to ten and the evening feels electric, like anything can happen. Tulsa ceases to be a city and becomes her canvas.

The downtown area is deserted. Like so many American cities, Tulsa's centre is a place for working, not living. She hits the one-tiered wedding-cake Boston Avenue United Methodist Church first, which is just off the Expressway. She puts on the surgical mask and goggles, dons plastic gloves, and pulls the hood up of her black sweatshirt.

Posters go on all three doors. The roller makes it easy, and she's generous with the glue.

The First United Methodist and First Christian churches are next. She hits both, enjoying the symmetry of starting with the firsts, which also includes the First Presbyterian Church around the corner and the First Baptist Church of Tulsa on Cincinnati Avenue.

When driving, she keeps the surgical mask and goggles on, to save time and to keep from getting high on the glue, but takes the plastic gloves off to avoid getting glue on the steering wheel and gearshift.

The night rolls on and Tulsa is practically a ghost town. She hits church and after church, not being selective about religion or denomination. She considers them all to be evil. Affixing half a dozen posters to the door of the Scientology Church on Second Street is particularly satisfying. It's this door she photographs with her Polaroid.

She's amazed to see that there don't even seem to be homeless people living on Tulsa's streets.

The car starts to stink of glue. She places the spare surgical mask over her daughter's mouth and nose, and drives with the front windows down. The evening is warm. She feels utterly alive.

By dawn, she's down to her last pair of plastic gloves and the dregs of the glue, yet she still has a stack of posters and at least a hundred churches left, most of them in the outer suburbs. But the Tulsans start to stir early on this Sunday morning, emerging from their suburban enclaves to walk dogs and go jogging, and most probably get ready for church. The sun seems to rise quickly as well in this flat part of the country, and she concedes the game is up. A good thing, because she was running on adrenaline for the last few hours and is now exhausted.

She puts the roller inside the glue container, along with the surgical masks, goggles and plastic gloves, and puts this in a garbage bin. The remaining posters go into the paper recycling, as does the printout of churches. Though hungry and tired, she takes the time to clean the car inside and out at a 24-hour self-service car wash, so it's ready to return to the rental car company without them asking any questions. She puts the car through the car wash with her daughter still asleep inside. It's tempting to walk away, but the car has to be returned.

A quick search on her phone tells her that Sarah's on South Yale Avenue is rated as the best place for breakfast in Tulsa, but it's not open for another hour. That gives her time to take a long shower and change her clothes.

At the Aloft, she carries her daughter upstairs and drops her on the bed. The girl stirs a little, coming to very slowly.

She showers with the water as hot as she can handle. It turns her skin bright pink and steams up the whole bathroom. Her daughter comes in when she's drying her hair.

"Take a bath," she says, running the water.

Rubbing her eyes and looking dazed, and possibly on the edge of tears, her daughter takes her time getting undressed, and also asks for help.

"You're a big girl. You can manage."

In the room, she cleans up a little and packs things away, on the off chance they might need to make a quick getaway. She doubts it, but finds the orderly room offers a nice bit of closure.

The muffled sound of crying comes from the bathroom and sours her buoyant morning mood. It gets progressively louder the longer she ignores it, and she knows she'll have to act, but gets dressed first, putting on her most conservative clothes.

Finally, she goes into the bathroom and says, "That's enough. Dry yourself and put on clean clothes. We're going out for the best breakfast ever. And then we're going to church."

Goodbye Daphne

Our room at the Camelot Inn was a twin, with a bunk bed. As soon as I saw it, I was sure Churchill had organised specifically that. But Nikki, who had proven herself to be a surprisingly adaptive and tolerant travel companion, didn't seem to mind.

She dropped her backpack in a corner and said, "I'll get us some lunch from the supermarket we passed."

"Okay. Great."

I took out my wallet, but she waved me off.

"My turn," she said, and left.

It was good to have some time alone. I lay down on the lower bunk. It was wider than the top bunk, but not a full double. I knew Nikki would want to share this bed, as she liked to hold hands while sleeping, which I found kind of sweet. But it was also annoying, especially as every bed we'd shared so far, in Oklahoma City, Tulsa, Flagstaff, Phoenix and San Diego, had been too small for me. This was only made worse by having Nikki in the bed, with us joined at the hand, her moving whenever I moved. Still, she hadn't complained about the sleeping arrangements, and had even said she slept much better with me than with Bevan.

I didn't like it that she compared me with her ex, but I let her, as she was on the rebound and I was the other guy. Comparisons were inevitable.

It was just past six in the morning in Perth. I wanted to talk to Churchill, so sent him a message to see if he was awake.

I stared at the underside of the top bunk and thought about the last ten days. Since Tulsa, Churchill had been angry. Not yelling and screaming, which wasn't his way, but simmering. He was angry about Nikki, who he thought was baggage. He'd enlisted someone in the States, a private detective, to track down Nola. The first lead had been a rental car in Tulsa. Churchill booked me a ticket on the train and I was glad to leave Austin. When checking out of the hostel, I saw Nikki crying in the kitchen. I went straight up to her and told her to get her stuff and come with me. She had just a backpack, which was unexpected, as I'd thought she'd be more high-maintenance, and a battered guidebook that was a good twenty years out of date and full of incorrect information. Escaping Austin together, leaving her boyfriend behind and catching the Heartland Flyer seemed like a crazy and romantic thing to do. We both didn't think twice about it. Train delays meant we got as far as Oklahoma City, where we spent a glorious first night together in a hotel room that two afternoons of busking in Austin paid for. We stayed in bed until check-out the next morning, and didn't get to Tulsa until the afternoon. We were too late anyway, because Churchill called to say the detective had picked up a lead in San Diego; cash taken from an ATM at Seaworld. It was too far to drive or take the train, he said, so he would book me a flight. When I asked for two tickets, I was forced to tell him about Nikki. He wasn't happy.

My phone buzzed.

"Where are you now?" Churchill asked. "Mexico? No, let me guess. Alaska."

"We're here. In Salt Lake City."

"Oh, you are? That's a nice surprise. I kind of expected that girl would take you off for more sightseeing."

"Of course not."

"Getting off the plane in Phoenix and driving up to the Grand Canyon, that I can excuse. I mean, it's the Grand Canyon. But you spent three days there."

"It was the one time we detoured, Church. And it was worth it. You would've done the same."

"Yeah, probably. I guess it would be hard to resist, especially caught up in the whirlwind of fast love. But you're not there to hook up with some banana-bender broad. You're there to find Nola."

"I know, I know."

"She's slowing you down."

"No, she isn't. I'm glad she's here. Look, it's just a travel fling and it's fun. I can't see any future for us. I'm not going to move to Brisbane."

"No, you're not. But let's hope this fling doesn't produce another kid that we'll never be able to find."

Despite everything, this made me smile. "Don't worry. I'm making sure of that."

"Finally, you're turning into a responsible adult. Of course, it's pretty clear I can't do anything to stop you from travelling with Nikki."

"Nope, but you can meddle, can't you?"

"What makes you say that?"

"This twin room you booked us? Not exactly romantic. It's got a bunk bed."

Churchill laughed. "Precautionary. And, room for one more, maybe. What about her boyfriend?"

"Church, this is gonna sound mighty strange, but I've got a feeling he's following us."

"Like, stalking you? Why would he do that?"

"No idea."

"Maybe they're playing some weird relationship game. Nikki's telling him where you are, making him come find you."

"I hope not. I don't want to get involved in that. And I'm still doing everything you say, going where you tell me to go."

"Yeah, but not quickly enough. I've got us a faster lead on where Nola is. We don't need to wait for the postcards anymore. By the way, one arrived from Tulsa a few days ago. Doesn't look like the most appealing place."

"It was alright. Quiet."

"How's Salt Lake City?"

"Haven't seen much of it yet. But what I've seen is also pretty quiet."

"That might narrow down the number of places where Nola can stay. I'll send you the list of accommodation and you can start doing the rounds."

I didn't know what to say to this, as I was sick of going to campgrounds, hostels and hotels. So I said nothing.

"I'm worried, Rowan," Churchill continued. "Really worried. You've gone all the way to America to find Nola. You've just about maxed out your credit card, and I've spent a small fortune on detective Al, but we're getting close, I know it. I don't understand why you would jeopardise that for some girl who sounds for all the money like she just wants a travel companion so she can get around safely, since she ditched the one she brought with her."

"You're exaggerating. It's not anything like that. Nikki's one of the good ones. You'd like her. Now, what have you got for me here?"

"All Al said is that Nola arrived at the airport two days ago. Apparently, she's got a record in Utah, something to do with vandalism or terrorism. Al didn't have the specifics. Anyway, when she landed, her name must've flagged something in the system. I don't know how it all that works. Al said something about the Patriot Act and NSA, and he reeled off some other fancy-sounding acronyms."

"Should I go to the airport?"

"I don't think so. I'll send you the list. Maybe you should get Nikki involved. Divide the work up between you."

"That's actually a pretty good idea. She can call them for me."

"Does she even know who you're looking for?"

"I just said friends of mine, and she hasn't pressed the issue."

"Just her flesh. Do you talk, or is it all physical?"

"Church, I guarantee that you would like Nikki. And you'd like the States. It's brilliant here."

"Still busking?"

"Just about every day. I've written some songs and they're actually pretty good."

"Ballads for Nikki?"

"Give it a rest, Church. No, they're more about shadows and reaching for things that you think are there, but aren't. I think the best one is about Bevan and how he's following us."

"I get it. You made that up, for the song."

"Yeah, maybe I did. I've missed your insights, Church."

"And that's before I've had my first coffee of the day."

"Go have it. Nice chatting. Really."

"Always. Now, keep your pants on and hit the streets."

He hung up. I few seconds later, I got an email from him with the list of accommodation. It was short. I assumed Salt Lake City wasn't much of a tourist town.

I sat up on the bed and wondered if Nikki really was baggage I should rid myself of. She might have derailed the search a little, but she was fun to travel with and I was content to keep doing just that. And then, there was the superstitious musician in me. With Nikki around, I'd done well busking and written some songs. Was she an inspiration? Or was it America? Being here, being awake, seeing and experiencing so many things. Churchill was right that Bevan wasn't following us, but it had been interesting to imagine that he was, and putting that story into lyrics and chords had resulted in a song I was proud of. The sensation of chasing a shadow; trying to grab something you once let get away. That was powerful, and meaningful.

The D-major running so smoothly to the B-minor: *Following the shadow with only himself to blame.*

It was about yearning, about hope. A man coming to terms with the mistakes he made and trying to set them right. And the man wanting to change, to become better.

97

Nikki liked the song, even if she hadn't picked up on her connection to it. Interpreted another way, the song could quite easily have been about me, chasing shadows of my own, regretting past behaviours and hoping to turn myself into a better Rowan.

I hadn't said this to Churchill, but I wasn't sure I wanted to find Nola and Eris anymore. And that could have been why I had asked Nikki to come along. It was attraction, the desire to stop chasing shadows and touch someone real. But it was also distraction, a reason to maybe stop looking for something I wasn't really sure I wanted to find.

I thought of the little red-headed girl outside the school in Austin, and how at the time, I didn't want her to be Eris. I couldn't picture myself holding that girl's hand, carrying her bag and walking her to school. How was I supposed to be some girl's father? I still felt so much like a boy myself.

To Eris, I was a shadow. Maybe she considered me something frightening. A giant monster with hair like fire; the last thing she would want to see emerge from the shadows.

Did she even know who I was? Had Nola said anything?

The door opened and Nikki entered, toting shopping bags in each hand. She offered me a cheek to kiss, which I dutifully did, and let me take one of the bags. We put them on the table.

"Listen, Nikki, I need to tell you something. And I'm just gonna be straight up about it because we're both adults and it's the easiest way."

"Oh, no. You're pregnant."

We both laughed.

"Well, in a way, that's kind of right. You see, the friends I'm looking for, they're not really friends, as how we would normally think of friends. They're mother and daughter. And I don't know for certain, but I think the daughter is mine."

"I knew something was up with that, but I was scared to ask."

"I'm sorry, Nikki. I should've told you earlier."

"Yes. You should have."

It was difficult to gauge her reaction.

"Because this changes things," she added, pacing the room a little. "I'm guessing when you find them, you'll dump me on the side of the road and head off into the sunset with them."

"It's not like that. Not at all. Me and Nola, the mother, we aren't together. I'm trying to find her because of the daughter. Potentially, my daughter."

"You haven't been very successful so far."

"I know. But Churchill said they arrived here two days ago. I need to check all the hotels."

She stopped pacing. "How are you planning to do that? I mean, can I help? How old is your daughter anyway?"

"Getting close to five, I think. I haven't seen Nola since, you know, since it happened."

"You made this epic journey over here, even though you haven't seen this Nola for ages, and you're not sure you're actually the father?"

"When I got to Little Rock, I didn't even know Nola's full name."

"That sounds like a very meaningful relationship. A one night stand? I didn't think you were the type for that. And they don't produce kids in real life. That only happens on TV."

"We spent a week together. In New Zealand. That was it."

"Unprotected?"

I nodded.

"That was stupid."

"Yeah, it was."

Nikki sat down at the desk and crossed her legs. She took an apple from one of the shopping bags and bit into it.

"I'm sorry I didn't tell you."

"Stop saying sorry, Rowan," Nikki said, her calmness disconcerting. "I knew there had to be more to it, that you weren't looking for friends. Otherwise, you would've found them by now, because friends want to be found. Maybe Nola and her daughter don't want to be found. Have you thought about that? And you haven't exactly been looking very hard. You spend every afternoon playing your guitar on the street."

"I searched a lot more at the start of the trip. But I kind of lost my way."

"Is that supposed to be my fault? That's what you think, isn't it? And you're telling me now to get me to leave so you can continue searching for Nola and your love child. Build a little family together."

"I'm not interested in Nola. I want to find Eris."

"The daughter you don't know is yours?"

"If she is mine, I have a responsibility to her. I'm not running away from that. And I've got this feeling she needs me."

Nikki calmly took another bite of the apple and asked, "Where's that coming from?"

"I don't know. It's a feeling."

"What happens when it turns out you're not the dad?"

"Then, I guess, I made it all up. You know, wanted it to be like that. Told myself a story that I made true in my head."

"Has Nola told you?"

"No."

"What are you going on then? How do you even know this kid exists?"

"You won't believe it. She sent me postcards, and they had the outline of a little hand on them."

"That's it? Pretty thin. But an interesting way to say congratulations, you're a father."

"She didn't even put her name on them."

"So, how did you know Nola was the one who was sending the postcards?"

"We figured it out. Me and Churchill. With a process of elimination. Because, Nikki, there haven't been many girls."

She smiled sweetly. "That's refreshing to hear. Seems every guy I meet tries to present himself to the world as King Dick." She bit into the apple again, and asked, "Why haven't you had many girlfriends?"

"Not the right type, I guess."

"You or them?"

"Me, definitely. I'm too tall. No one likes the red hair and freckles."

"I do. Sounds like Nola did too. What do you think? Is Eris a redhead?"

I nodded. "She is. That much I know."

"That tips the balance quite a bit your way, doesn't it? Your brand, so to speak. The mark of Rowan."

This made me smile, also because Nikki had surprised me again. I'd thought she would be angry to hear my confession, but she seemed far from that.

"I'm not the only redhead on the planet."

"Well, it's pretty clear to me what we have to do," she said. "We have to find to Eris. I didn't care about you looking for your friends, and certainly not for some long lost love, but this could be your daughter. It's different. What's the plan?"

"You want to help?"

"Sure."

I took out my phone and showed her the list Churchill had sent. "Then we've got work to do. It looks like most of the hotels are downtown. We can split up and get it done twice as fast. You can call some of them, but I have to do it in person, because my hearing's terrible on the phone."

"No, no and no. We have to do this together, in person. It'll be less suspicious if it's the two of us. One person doing this could come across as a hunter or a predator. But a couple, young and nice and friendly, they're just regular people looking for someone they know. Trust me on this. Maybe you already got to a hotel they were staying at, but they wouldn't tell you because you were too suspicious."

"Yeah, maybe."

She stood up and opened the shopping bag. "You want some fruit? It's all so huge here. Fruit on steroids. The peaches are like rockmelons."

I grabbed a large banana and an apple the size of a softball, and we went outside.

→←

Before Daphne was Daphne, she was known as Lady Frankenstein. Travis, who has a talent for coming up with catchy band names, gave this one to the guitar I started building, because I made her entirely out of scraps that I found in the workshop. As a steel-string acoustic, she was a little bit of everything, a combination of different types of wood and old parts from different instruments. It was why she had her own special sound, which was part country, part blues, part pop, part punk and part medieval. She was rough around the edges, despite all the sanding and smoothing I'd done, full of character, and honest. There was no branding or false promises. No fancy decoration. Over the years, Daphne had matured to sound fuller, warmer and cleaner than top-line guitars that cost thousands.

To look at her was to see a regular acoustic guitar, in the standard shape with the usual twenty-one frets. But underneath the lacquer, it was a different story. This one-of-a-kind instrument was a monster made human. It was my second attempt at building a guitar from scratch, and I laboured over it. Lady Frankenstein spent almost a year in the workshop, as a project I worked on whenever there was nothing else to do, and sometimes after hours. I didn't rush it. I didn't cut corners. I was selective of the parts and scraps I used, and obsessed a little over the idea that a thing of beauty could emerge from trash. I wanted the guitar to be beautiful, something I would love. Something

I would want to hold in my arms and strum. Something that would make people stop and listen.

Of course, as in any relationship, we had our problems. For the first year, Daphne required a lot of tweaking and attention. I adjusted the action and worked on the saddle to find the right balance. Even with that, she retained the slightest bit of fret-buzz on the B-string between the third and fifth frets. I decided to let that be part of her character, as a way of signifying she wasn't perfect and never would be. For a pick-up, I settled on a mountable, coin-sized transducer that could be placed on different areas of Daphne's top. Affixing a bulky pick-up across the sound-hole took away much of her resonance, and I also felt she was unhappy with a permanent solution. The mountable pick-up meant I could place it on a certain area and get a slightly different sound. I learned over time where Daphne's sweet spots were for playing through an amp or PA, and found that gently finger-picking produced a sound superior to grating the strings with a plectrum.

I loved that Daphne had started out as Lady Frankenstein and evolved from my monster into my mistress. She once came between me and a girl: Candace, who I was together with for about two months a few years ago, and who was adamant that I was much more into the guitar than her. She wasn't wrong.

Churchill often teased me for having a guitar named Daphne and for treating her like she was far more than an inanimate object. For me, she could speak, and she aged. She changed with the conditions: humidity and dryness, in hot and cold temperatures, in atmosphere and mood. She responded well to care and attention, and she enjoyed being played. She certainly didn't like to be left in the corner to gather dust.

When I quizzed the manager of the Camelot Inn about potential busking locations, he warned me to stay away from Temple Square and the downtown area, where panhandling and busking has always been frowned upon. He said that yesterday, someone had rounded up a few dozen homeless people and got them all to beg at Temple Square, creating havoc, because many of them had handcuffed themselves to points around the square, as if in protest.

"Not sure what it was all about," he said, "but I'd stay away from Temple, for now. Try Sugar House."

He gave me directions. After spending a few hours bouncing from one hotel to another, all without success, Nikki and I were both keen to get something good out of the day. We took the TRAX Red Line to Central Pointe station, then switched to the S-Line and got out at Sugarmount. The Camelot manager had mentioned the obelisk in the heart of the Sugar House district, and we found this just past McClelland Street.

I set myself up at the base of what was some kind of pioneers' monument, facing away from the street. Nikki took a table in the crowded outdoor area of the Wasatch Brew Pub and started writing in her journal.

Case open, I launched into a string of covers. I moved around, danced as I played, and went up the steps of the obelisk to make myself more visible. A circle of people formed. They clapped at the end of each song and dropped coins in my guitar case.

Things were going great until I saw Bevan pushing his way through the crowd. It was a shock to see him, and he didn't look happy. He came right up to me, standing aggressively with his arms folded and making me stop mid-song.

"Where's Nikki?"

I unstrapped Daphne and placed her in the case, on top of all the money. "She's sitting over there."

"Who are you to steal someone's girl like that?"

"She came by choice, mate. No stealing."

He gave me a shove and got into what look like a boxer's stance, without his fists raised. I was a head taller, but I didn't want to fight.

"Come on, Bevan. Let's have a beer and talk about it."

He gave me another shove, the patronising, antagonising type, using just his fingers.

Nikki got between us. "What are you doing here, Bevan? You said you were going home."

He pushed her aside and took a swing at me. I wasn't ready for it, but still managed to avoid his first punch. But I didn't avoid the second, which followed quickly after the first and got me right in the stomach. Doubled over, I saw Nikki trying to pull Bevan back, but he shrugged her off.

As I dealt with the pain, I thought this was all so primitive: that someone would actually want to fight for a girl. With the crowd around us, it was like being back in high school.

When Bevan didn't throw any more punches, I thought it was

over. But then he went for Daphne with intent, grabbing her roughly by the neck. I attacked him, tackling him rugby-style, making him drop the guitar as I drove my right shoulder into his rib cage and got him to the ground, where we wrestled. Bevan was first to get his hands free and he hit my cheek hard. The force of the punch made the back of my head hit the ground, causing me to blackout momentarily.

What brought me back was the worst sound I'd ever heard: strings snapping and wood shattering and splintering.

I opened my eyes to see Daphne in pieces scattered at Bevan's feet, him still holding part of the broken neck in his hands, the strings flaying. I got to my feet and charged at him. I knocked him off balance as he tried to defend himself with Daphne's leftover neck. I swung my fists through the air. My wrists and hands felt strong after playing the guitar so much in the last few weeks. A couple of punches connected, but he had his arms up, protecting his face. Then I felt some guys grab me from behind and pin my arms. Another couple of guys did the same to Bevan, getting more separation between us and ending the fight.

As he struggled against two guys bigger than him, Bevan spat blood onto the ground. "You stealing prick," he shouted.

"Someone call the police," Nikki said, and I thought she was looking at Bevan with a strange combination of disgust and admiration, as if she'd seen a new side to him, and possibly liked it.

When I didn't struggle, the two guys let me go. I looked down at Daphne's remains and would've started crying if not for the adrenaline and rage that was pulsing through me.

I looked at Bevan. "How could you do that?"

"We don't need any cops," one of the guys said. Those who had intervened were staff from the Wasatch Brew Pub, all of them in black shirts. "You guys are done, right?"

"We're done," Bevan said. He shrugged himself free. "Come on, Nikki. Let's go."

I didn't possibly think she'd go with him, but there was a brief moment when she seemed to consider it. Maybe she was envisioning her potential future, sparked by how the normally placid Bevan had perhaps shown himself to be tougher and more forthright than ever before.

But she stood next to me and said, "Go home, Bevan."

He wiped the blood from his mouth and took a tentative step

forward, his angry face now pleading. For some reason, I thought he was more upset about walking away the loser in this exchange, in front of all these people, than he was to be breaking up with Nikki for good. I looked around and saw the crowd was far larger than when I'd been busking. The expressions on some of their faces made me wonder if they thought this was all part of the act. Music, violence and destruction. Performance art from down under.

Bevan eventually started walking away. He kicked at Daphne's remains, sending bits of splintered wood across the ground.

I felt Nikki grab my arm. "Let him go," she said softly. "It's over."

As the crowd drifted away, many of them dropped coins in my case.

"I'm sorry about your guitar," one of the Wasatch guys said. "Come and have a beer on us."

I nodded. "Thanks. For your help as well."

The staff went back to the pub and the crowd dispersed, leaving just me, Nikki, and a case full of loose change. I didn't know what to do with Daphne. I bent down and started picking up the pieces. Nikki helped. We carried the pieces to the garbage bin near the obelisk. It was entirely the wrong place to leave her, but I couldn't think of what else to do. Bevan had reduced her to garbage.

I closed the case, with all the money inside, and carried it over to the pub. I couldn't help feeling it was like carrying an empty coffin.

Nikki still had all her stuff at her table, and we sat down there.

Two beers were brought to us. I was also handed an ice pack, which I held against the back of my head. My ears were ringing like mad.

"You want something to eat?" the waiter asked.

I didn't have any appetite, but Nikki ordered the pub salad with garlic bread, and asked for two sets of cutlery.

→←

Nikki said several times that it wasn't necessary, but when the time came, I went with her to the airport.

We walked up to Courthouse station to catch the TRAX Green Line. She wouldn't let me carry her backpack.

There wasn't much to say. We'd already talked it all through. Nikki wanted to leave, and while sad, I didn't think it was completely terrible that she was going. It was Nikki who had renewed my desire to find

Nola, and with her gone, and Daphne too, I could focus all my attention on that single task.

While she said she was going back to Brisbane to take care of things, as Bevan had a key to her apartment and she was worried what he might do, I did wonder if they might try to patch things up.

It was a rather pathetic end to what had been an enjoyable, adventurous time together.

On the train, Nikki asked, "Do you think you'll find her?"

"I really hope so. But the trail's gone dead, for now."

"What about that detective Churchill hired? Maybe he'll find something."

"They could be a thousand miles away by now. We got here too late."

"Sorry."

"That wasn't your fault, Nikki. I wouldn't have done anything differently."

She gave me a sad smile. "It was fun. Still, now that I'm gone, when you get the word from Churchill, you'll be able to react straight away, without me holding you back."

"And without a guitar to carry."

"That was awful. I can't believe Bevan did that."

I was slowly getting over Daphne being gone. The strangest thing was not having a guitar to play.

"I guess for Bevan, a guitar's a guitar. He didn't know the history, or that I'd made her from scratch. From nothing."

As we went through the stations, Temple Square, Arena, North Temple Bridge, I felt myself getting over Nikki, even with her still sitting next to me. This was a shame, because I liked her, especially the version I'd got to know when Bevan wasn't around. I wanted to warn her not to try again with Bevan, but it didn't seem like the right thing to say.

"What was it worth?" she asked.

"It was a hand-made guitar. A unique instrument. How do you put a price on that?"

Fairpark station came and went. Only two more until the airport. I found it curious that it was possible to like someone, but also be happy when they were gone.

"What will you do?"

"About the guitar?"

"About Nola and Eris."

I shrugged. "Nothing, until Churchill tells me where to go next. We checked just about every single place a person can stay in Salt Lake City. They're not here. And it doesn't even look like they were here. They must've gone somewhere nearby, or booked private accommodation. I don't know. I really thought we'd find them here."

"We were a good team," Nikki said, "going around to the hotels together."

"You were good at it. Everyone was nice to you."

We pulled into the airport's station. I'd planned to say goodbye here and take this same train back to Courthouse, but I went with Nikki to departures. I was curious to see if Bevan was there.

"I hope you find them," Nikki said as she joined the long check-in line for her flight to Los Angeles. "And I hope you get a new guitar. I guess you'll make one, right?"

"Yeah, when I'm back home. I need the right tools and a workshop."

As we waited and shuffled forward, I surveyed the terminal. There was no sign of Bevan.

I tried to picture Nola and Eris arriving here four days ago. The two of them, walking through this very terminal. Nola's name was flagged and they were stopped. They must've been caught on a camera, possibly even interviewed in a back room by airport security.

The line moved quickly. Soon, Nikki had her boarding card and was ready to go. With both of us uncertain how to say goodbye, we hugged.

"Take care," Nikki said.

"Have a good trip."

I walked away and didn't look back to wave one last time. I went straight for the information counter.

"How are you today, sir?" the man asked. He had Brenton on his name-tag. One thing Nikki had taught me when doing the rounds of hotels, was to use people's names if possible.

"Hi, Brenton. I could really use your help."

"May I ask where you're from?"

"Perth, Australia."

He took a few seconds to write this down. "And how can I help?"

"Well, you see, Brenton, four days ago, my girlfriend and daughter arrived here, but I haven't heard anything from them. Is it possible I can talk with someone from security, maybe get more information about when they arrived?"

"Have you been to the police? Four days is a long time before you go looking for someone."

"I know. I've been really slow to react. And Nola, my girlfriend, she's one of these low-tech people. She doesn't have a phone and it can sometimes be really hard to get in touch with her. It's frustrating, believe me. I've been asking at hotels and motels downtown, but there's no trace of them."

Brenton gave me a sceptical look. Then he picked up the phone, dialled slowly and spoke with someone, giving a brief version of my story, with his account of it sounding dodgier than mine.

"A member of security will be here shortly," he said, putting the phone down. "May I ask what brings you to Salt Lake City?"

"Like I said, to meet my girlfriend and daughter."

Brenton picked up his pen, started writing and said, "Family reasons."

I took a few steps back from the counter, not wishing to engage with Brenton further. I thought about how I might give my story more depth and plausibility. It had to be innocent, a mix-up. A meeting point missed. The low-tech angle was good and I needed to build on it.

I couldn't come across as a hunter; this much I'd learned from Nikki.

The man from security wore a police-like short-sleeved blue shirt with black pants. He was short, paunchy around the middle and walking with a very slight waddle. While he had no name-tag, he did hold up his ID card, and I saw his name was Oscar.

"Are you the man who's lost his little girl?" Oscar asked, putting both hands on his hips.

"Yeah. Thanks for taking the time to see me. So, my girlfriend arrived here four days ago, with my daughter. It was supposed to be a surprise. They didn't know I would be here, but I missed them. And I haven't been able to locate them since."

"Have you tried calling?"

"Nola, my girlfriend, she doesn't have a phone. I know, it's incredible. But, Oscar, she really is one of those people. Low-tech and trying to stay off the grid."

He smiled and nodded. "I know people like that." Then he looked at my eye. "How'd you get the shiner?"

"Oh, I walked into a door. You wouldn't believe how often that happens, being this tall. I'm always hitting my head on something."

More nodding. "I know that too. My brother-in-law's as tall as you. You got a flight number?"

"No, I don't. But they flew from San Diego."

He folded his arms and spread his short legs a little. "So, what do you think will help?"

"Maybe, you know, something that can prove that they really did arrive here. Because I've been all over the city, hotels, motels, campgrounds, everything. I can't find them. And I'm asking myself if they're here at all. It's a bit stupid, Oscar. This surprise meeting has gone totally wrong."

"You go to the police already?"

"No. It's just a mix up. I don't think they're in danger or anything like that."

"What's that accent? Where you from?"

Brenton chimed in: "He's from Perth, Australia."

"And I've come all the way over here just to meet up with Nola and Eris. That's my daughter."

Oscar looked at me very seriously. "Do you believe in God?"

That took me completely by surprise. "Uh, yeah, sure." Judging by his tone, I felt this was the best answer. It also wasn't a lie, and I thought it good to keep going with honesty. "I haven't been to church for a while, but I did scripture studies at school, and my teacher taught us that the kingdom of God is all around."

This seemed to satisfy him. His serious look softened as he said, "I think you better come with me. We'll see if we can figure something out."

As he led us away from the information counter, I wondered if his last sentence was some kind of cue, for possibly a bribe. Did he want money? Did he want to convert me to whatever religion he was? Or were we going to some isolated room where he would interrogate me?

When we got to a door that I assumed led to the airport's restricted security area, Oscar turned his back to me and swiped his card.

"I know it was a surprise, but I bet your daughter would've been really happy to see you here," he said.

"If only Nola had a phone, none of this would've happened."

The door opened and we went down a brightly lit hallway. There were other members of security, in the same uniform, walking around, sipping coffee, chatting and staring at monitors.

It didn't appear that physical fitness was a requirement to work security at Salt Lake City International Airport. There was also a very relaxed vibe about the place; not quite the heightened state that might be associated with keeping Americans safe from potential acts of terrorism.

We went into a small room where another man was sitting in front of half a dozen monitors and eating from a bag of chips.

"Can you take five, Carl?" Oscar asked.

Carl looked at me, then got to his feet and left the room, taking his chips with him.

Sitting down, Oscar said, "So, it was SAN, four days ago."

"That's right. Sorry, I don't have the flight number. My girlfriend's full name is Nolene Henderson."

He started tapping at the keyboard.

While the security staff didn't seem quite up to the task of running after people, they did have some cutting-edge technology at their disposal. Putting in Nola's name and the date was enough for Oscar to locate footage of the two of them entering the arrivals area.

I leaned closer to the monitors. "That's them. How did you do that?"

"She was flagged," Oscar said. "That's why the system kept track of her. She must have a record here in Utah."

"Maybe some parking tickets or something. I think she mentioned that once."

"Have to be more than that. An arrest, at least."

He played the videos, getting a procession of angles and shots as Nola and Eris moved through the airport. Nola walked in front and Eris followed behind. A few times, Nola stopped and waited for Eris to catch up, and appeared annoyed. The camera angles shadowed their faces and Nola kept blocking my view of Eris. When they got to the luggage area, the light was better, the angles flatter, and I got a clear look at both of them.

Nola looked just about the same, older, perhaps not as pretty, but that could have been my unreliable memory. She struck me as sad and worn out, which contrasted with the energetic and cheeky version of her I'd met on the bus to Marahau. I remembered that Nola as being up for anything. This Nola looked just about done with the world.

Eris had red hair and looked tall and skinny for her age. I also thought she was worn out, like her mother.

I had the feeling the two of them weren't happy with each other. For parent and small child, they had a lot of distance between them. If

110

Eris got too close, Nola would move away and maintain the distance.

The man stopped the footage on one of the monitors, offering a clear shot, with both of them facing the camera.

"So, there you have it," Oscar said. "They made it."

"Would it be possible to print that picture?"

He looked at me, eyebrows just slightly raised. Then he smiled and said, "As the Lord Jesus said, 'It is more blessed to give than to receive.'"

"Thanks. That's really kind of you."

When the image was printed, he went to hand it to me, then pulled it back.

"You're on the side of good, aren't you?" he asked.

"Of course. I just want to surprise them."

"Because if you ask me, these folks need more help than trouble. They look to me like people in need."

"I know. That's why I'm here. Nola needs me. My daughter needs me."

With some more nodding, he handed me the print-out and I walked back down the hallway. It was a relief to get out of the restricted area. I went into the nearest bathroom, spread the print-out on the floor and photographed it with my phone. I sent the image to Churchill. It had been a full day since we'd last had contact. I hadn't even told him about Daphne yet.

Back in the terminal and heading for the train station, I walked while staring at the print-out. I studied their expressions and stances, looking for clues. From the way she looked, I started to think that Eris was indeed my daughter.

On the crowded train, my phone buzzed.

"Is that them?"

"Yeah, it is. That's Eris, Church."

"How did you get this?"

"From airport security. They were really nice about and very helpful."

"Brilliant work, mate. Seriously." There was a pause, then he said, "Eris looks like a peach. But you'll have to excuse me, because Nola's not much chop. Is that really her?"

"She looked different when we met. Fresher, more vibrant."

"Maybe it's just a bad angle. And everyone looks like hell when they get off a plane, don't they? But Eris, what a cutie. That red hair. She looks a lot like you. I guess that settles it, if there was any doubt."

"It tips the scales, doesn't it?"

"But you still want to hear it from Nola, am I right?"

"Yeah. I'm not ready to jump fully in just yet. So, where do I go next?"

"Well, hmm, there's a monkey in that wrench. The last postcard was from San Diego. I guess there'll be one soon from Salt Lake City."

"What about Al? Does he have anything?"

"Nothing. He said they've disappeared. Maybe gone to Canada. This all started in Canada, remember? In Thunder Bay. And I had to cut ties with Al, because he was too expensive."

"Sorry about that. But we need to do something. I can't just sit around."

"Until I get a new lead, you're gonna have to do just that. Maybe go off and see some sights with Nikki."

"She's gone. That's how I ended up at the airport. To see her off."

"Just when she was making herself useful. What happened?"

"Crazy stuff, Church. It turned out Bevan really was following us. He showed up here looking for a fight."

"I hope you gave him one."

"I did, but he smashed Daphne to pieces."

"What?"

"I know. I couldn't really believe it either. What a dickhead."

"I'm sorry, Rowan."

"It's alright. Maybe her time had come. So? Where should I go?"

"Canada perhaps?"

"That's another flight. I'd prefer to go by road, and I've had enough of cities for now."

"You want wilderness? Yellowstone's up the road. I've been analysing lots of maps, trying to guess where Nola might go next."

"Yellowstone sounds great. Can you organise it?"

"Sure. I need to reward my man's efforts out in the field. Top work getting that screenshot. You'll be able to show it around the next time you're checking hotels."

"That's right."

"I'll send you the trip details."

He hung up.

I took out the screenshot and stared at Eris.

→←

The schedule surprised me: I was to hitch-hike from Idaho Falls to West Yellowstone. Churchill qualified this by explaining there was no bus and that renting a car would be too expensive. He also said it would be a good experience; that there was no reason to be afraid, as no one would dare try anything funny with a ginger-haired giant.

I was emboldened by how I'd stood up to Bevan, and I was keen for something different. Plus, it was good to get out of the intercity buses.

From the Idaho Falls bus station, I walked to Rigby Highway. It was supposed to be about a two-hour drive to West Yellowstone, but my first ride only got me to Ucon, the next town down the road. Still, as I waited for another ride, I thought it wasn't such a bad way to get around. I was travelling light, with just a backpack and without a guitar to worry about or protect. I was saving money. And I wasn't crammed into a tiny seat on a bus, sitting next to some slobbish guy and forced to watch him consume two litres of soda and several packages of cookies.

It was farming land out here. There were fields and silos, but no animals.

The traffic on the highway was mostly trucks, and they were going too fast to slow down in time to give me a ride. I remained upbeat. The afternoon was long.

I took out my song-writing journal and went over some of my recent compositions. A couple were good, possibly the best songs I'd written.

Then I thought of Daphne, about how we'd started out together and how she'd met her demise. From somewhere in my head, I started to hear a chord progression. Five chords in all: minor, major, minor, major, and a seventh. The progression repeating and repeating, for a song all in verses. No chorus and no bridge.

And so I say, goodbye to Daphne, fare thee well, the time we shared, the stories we'll never tell ...

The music played in my head and I wrote down some verses. It was a story of a relationship cut short by an act of violence. The man then seeking revenge, hunting down the killer, tracking him from place to place, but when he finally gets revenge, it leaves him feeling empty. Maybe a verse in the middle that was whispered over soft finger-picking, that lead to hard strumming and an angry wail. The man with blood on his hands as he achieves redemption. The satisfaction of completion, but also the pain of loneliness.

A pick-up pulled over, with a woman of about sixty behind the wheel. She looked like a farmer's wife, who got up early and worked with her hands. She didn't ask me where I was headed, but said she was going to Plano and could drop me at the turn-off near Rexburg.

The cab had plenty of space, but it was loud. We made conversation and I thought she was glad for the company, but I had to turn to hear her each time she spoke. She asked me about my trip. I said I was going to West Yellowstone. When I reeled off all the cities I'd been to so far, it began to sink in just how much I'd already seen and done. I realised that on this trip, a new Rowan had emerged: a girlfriend-stealing fighter who charmed airport security and was now hitch-hiking through the mid-west. This Rowan didn't sleep away every morning. He was a hard-working musician who could earn lots of money busking and write songs without a guitar.

I liked this Rowan.

"What was the highlight so far?" the woman asked.

This was difficult to answer. Oklahoma City stood out, but only because of Nikki and the way we'd fled Austin together and taken the Heartland Flyer north, talking and laughing all the way. Then there was that first night, taking a bath together before we got into bed.

"It's probably boring and obvious, but the Grand Canyon was really amazing."

"It's something everyone should see at some point in their life. It can help to put a lot of things into perspective."

"Yeah. It did that."

"Where you're headed, it's also a beautiful part of the country. The season's about to start, so there won't be many tourists right now. In summer, they turn this road into gridlock some weekends."

"Any snow?"

"Not since February," she said. "We had some on Valentine's Day. Me and Bert went snow-shoeing out at Snoshone Lake, had us a nice picnic there. A couple of bears showed up, but they kept their distance. Bert said it meant winter was over, and I was glad to hear that."

"You don't like the cold?"

"Does anyone? Give me summer, all year round."

"You'd like Perth then. Where I'm from. It barely has any winter at all, and when it's cold, everyone's shocked by it and they don't know what to do."

"We can have summer days out here when the sky is white, like the whole thing is sun."

I thought that was nice: a white sky, all sun. I made a note in my journal.

She saw me and asked, "What are you writing there?"

"Just ideas. For songs. I'm a musician."

"Is that right? What do you play?"

"Guitar."

"Did you forget it on the road back there?"

"It's a long story. The short version is that I left it in Salt Lake. I was busking and this guy came up and smashed my guitar."

She laughed. "Are you that bad?"

"There were other things going on. A girl between us. We kind of ended up fighting over her."

"And you lost. Your girl and your guitar."

"Something like that."

"Sounds like there could be a good song in all of that. Nothing better to sing about than losing stuff."

"Or heartbreak. I'm working on it."

She gestured at a sign up ahead. "We're just about in Rexburg. You alright to stand on the highway?"

"Sure."

She pulled over and stopped near the overpass. A sign pointed to Rexburg in one direction and to Mud Lake and Salmon in the other.

"Thanks for the ride."

"My pleasure. Good luck with the music."

She turned left and drove in the Mud Lake direction. I crossed the street, humming my ballad for Daphne. At the start of the highway's on-ramp, I put my backpack down and sat on it. Journal open, I worked more on the song's verses, changing things, improving the lyrics. While it dealt with death and revenge, it was quite funny in places, in a way that harked to the songs of Warren Zevon and Don Walker, maybe even to Bob Dylan, but I didn't want to go that far. Emulating Zevon would be satisfying enough.

Cars went past. I didn't bother sticking my thumb out.

It took the honk of a horn to make me look up at the station wagon that had stopped in front of me. Another woman, this time with two young boys in the back. The passenger window was lowered.

"Where ya headed?"

"West Yellowstone."

"We're going to Warm River. About halfway there."

"Great. Thanks."

I got in the front seat, which was all the way back, giving me enough room to put my backpack between my legs. We set off up the highway's entry road.

"What's your name and where the heck are you from?"

"I'm Rowan, and I'm from Australia."

"Oh really?" She looked in the rear-view mirror to talk to her kids. "Did you hear that?"

"The capital city of Australia is Canberra," the elder boy said, though he couldn't have been older than nine.

"Henry's a whiz at geography," the woman said to me. "I'm home-schooling both of them. They're way ahead of normal kids their age."

She used the world "normal" with a certain distaste.

"So, what brings you to our part of the world?"

I felt that mentioning Nola and Eris in this situation seemed weird. "I'm just travelling around. I've seen a lot of cities so far, and I'd like to see some more of the nature."

"The boys love Yellowstone. We live right on the edge of the park. We'll probably be going for a hike this weekend." Another look in the mirror. "What do you think?"

"I wanna see an eagle," Henry said.

"I wanna see a bear," his brother said.

I turned around. "I don't. That sounds too scary for me."

"We have magic spray," Henry said, and he struck me as a serious boy. "It keeps them from getting close."

"Is that right? I might have to get some of that. I could use some magic spray in my life. Thanks for the tip."

"You're welcome."

I turned to the woman. "Nice kids."

"They are. You know, I grew up in Seattle, surrounded by buildings and streets, and I didn't want my kids to grow up like that. I wanted nature to be an essential part of their childhood. That's why we moved out here, first to Idaho Falls, then to Warm River."

"How big is it?"

She smiled. "The town's entire population is in this car."

"Wow."

"Yep. Warm River is all ours. We have a rotating mayor. Every week, we change the leadership. Henry's the mayor this week. He

116

hasn't done much, but he did decide that the house needed a clean, which is what we did last weekend."

"I cleaned up our town," Henry said.

"You sure did. And the citizens thank you."

We passed a place called Sugar City, which reminded me of Sugar House in Salt Lake City. I felt a pang as I thought of Daphne getting smashed at the obelisk.

The double-lane highway was separated by a wide median strip of yellow grass. A sign pointed to the Tetonia Experiment Station, which sounded sinister.

It felt good to be in this car, heading north. There was something distinctly American about this situation: the highway, the fields, the expanse, the station wagon, the two blonde-haired boys and their good-looking mother. This was a big country and I was somewhere in the middle of it. And I wasn't on a bus or alone in a rental car or sharing the experience with someone from my own country. It was just me, with locals, en route to a town with three inhabitants.

I lowered my voice. "I hope it's okay to ask this, but where's...?"

"Their dad? In Ogden. Down near Salt Lake City. He comes up every second weekend and stays in our guesthouse." She also lowered her voice and I could only just hear her add, "We don't really get along, but I think it's important the boys see their father."

I thought of Eris, fatherless and following behind Nola. Where was Eris right now? What was she doing? How was she feeling?

"So, not quite as planned, but it's working out okay. You know, even when you want something real bad and do everything to get it, can be it wasn't really what you wanted, or what was right for you. Does that make sense?"

"It does."

"You got any kids? I guess you're too young for that, and if you did, you wouldn't be out here on your own."

I didn't want to give my whole story to this woman.

"I haven't found the right girl yet."

"Don't wait too long. One thing I really didn't want to be was an old parent. No one should be, if you ask me. I was twenty-four when I had Henry, and twenty-six when I had Jack. It wasn't easy, but I'm glad about it. Makes me feel closer to both of them."

Which made her around thirty-three, though I thought she looked older. The way she delivered this opinion about young parenting seemed to change the atmosphere in the car. I chose not to voice my disagreement that older people shouldn't have children. Something made me think she wouldn't listen.

We passed St. Anthony, then a tiny place called Chester.

The boys in the back were very well-behaved. I wondered if they were scared to talk, or trained not to. There was something eerie about little kids who didn't ask questions, make requests or speak whatever thoughts they had.

At Ashton, the woman turned off the highway.

As we went down Main Street, she said, "Okay if we keep going? You'll be able to take Mesa Falls back to the highway to West Yellowstone. It's a beautiful route."

We were already too far from the highway for me to walk back. "Yeah, sure."

The nice storefronts and restored buildings of Ashton soon gave way to the warehouses, workshops and petrol stations that I was finding typical of small American towns. At least, of those I'd seen so far.

Soon, we left Ashton behind and started passing through more farming country, driving on the single-lane Mesa Falls Scenic Byway. The area reminded me of the farming lands south-east of Perth: the bare fields, parched grass and huge sky, and the country seeming massive and the people living there miniscule.

"It gets better than this," the woman said. "No place in the world like Yellowstone. What's he gonna see, Henry?"

"There are bears and wolves and elk and coyotes and bison," Henry said.

The woman gave me a stern look she tried to soften with a smile. "That's why we moved here."

It sounded like she was reassuring herself, and I thought there was something regimental about how she was with her boys. It was good that they were quiet and well-behaved, and both seemed reasonably clever, though Henry was more a repository of information than simply a smart kid. Their mother was certainly teaching them a lot of important things, but I wondered if she was overly strict with them, taking them from one extreme to another and forcing upon them a specific kind of childhood that may end up being as psychologically scarring as growing up in a big city. They would know about nature and animals, but would they know how to behave among large groups of people, on crowded streets and in busy offices? Would they turn out socially equipped enough to handle the rigours of high school and university, if they went?

Home-schooling sounded to me like a mistake. These kids needed more interaction with others; a balance between city and nature, which is what I had growing up in Claremont. I wanted Eris to have that kind of balance. Was she getting that with Nola? Could I offer something better? More stability? A place between the river and the ocean in the world's most isolated city?

The farming fields gave way to forest. Trees lined the road on both sides. We drove in the shadows, no one talking. The trees started to spread back from the road. The land was cleared, but undeveloped. I could see a small river following the left side of the road.

"Welcome to our little kingdom," the woman said.

A short bridge took us over Robinson Creek. The water looked fresh, clean and cold. Not quite the frothing, steaming, warm river I was expecting. There was a steep hill to the left and a backdrop of trees to the right, starting beyond a property that had a wooden fence out front.

It was scenic, but somehow scary. I couldn't imagine living out here, in this one-house town. The best I could offer was, "It's nice."

We pulled off the road and stopped. Henry got out to open the gate, doing so without being asked. Though young, he behaved like the man of this house, and seemed aware of what that role entailed.

The woman turned to me. When she spoke, her voice was bright: "Would you like to come in for some coffee?"

I was unsure about the hitch-hiking protocol of spending time with people who picked me up. A coffee sounded good, but I was keen to finish the journey.

"Uh, how far is it to West Yellowstone?"

"About fifty, sixty miles."

My main worry was that I wouldn't get a ride on this bare country road. Something also told me to be wary of this woman, living far from anywhere and raising her nature-loving army of two.

"You'll get a ride. This road goes back to the highway and all the cars are going that way."

As she said this, a car went past, heading in the direction I needed to go.

"See?"

"Alright. A coffee would be nice."

This made her smile. It looked strained, as if she was trying too hard to be cheery and perhaps wanting to mask any obvious signs of loneliness.

She drove through the gap and Henry closed that gate. The dirt driveway was lined either side by logs. The grass looked recently cut. A pair of black dogs came running out to meet the car and followed alongside until we stopped in front of the house. To the right was a smaller house, like a servant's quarters, and I guessed this was where the kids' father stayed during his fortnightly visits.

As I got out of the car and shouldered my backpack, I couldn't decide if this was a place of sublime beauty or hidden evil.

Henry opened the door for Jack, then raised the station wagon's back door. The two of them started unloading the shopping. I asked if I could help, but the woman waved me off.

"They got it. Come on in. I baked blackberry muffins yesterday."

She was tall and thin, but almost to the point she was scrawny. Her jeans were baggy, which could've been fashionable, but it appeared more that she'd bought them when she was a size bigger.

Inside, I left my backpack near the door, where we both kicked our shoes off. The house was orderly and clean, rustic with modern touches, and not without signs that two young boys lived there. Toys were scattered around, including an orange plastic racetrack winding around the living room, with a stool used as a starting ramp for the matchbox cars to get some speed. This made me relax, and had me thinking that I may have overreacted about how the woman was raising her children. A bookshelf was given over completely to board games and jigsaw puzzles. There was a stereo and a neat stack of CDs, but no television.

The boys put all the shopping away. The woman helped by telling them where to put specific items.

In the corner, near the huge fireplace, was an old classical guitar. I picked it up. It was light and flimsy. Tuning it wasn't easy, given the metal strings had flecks of rust, while the nylon strings were so old they sounded like the teeth of a comb being plucked. I match the top E-string to the ringing in my ears, and tuned the rest from there. It felt really good to have the strings underneath my fingers again, to press them against the fret board and to extract a passable sound from this cheap guitar. I searched for the right key for my Daphne ballad, settling on B-flat minor, knowing that I sing well in F-major. I played the five-chord progression, singing some of the lyrics.

This had the makings of a really good song.

The woman came in and placed a tray on the dining table. "That old thing still work?"

"Kind of. It's almost music."

"It was here when we moved in. I thought about teaching myself, but I didn't have the time, then it just became ornamental. Henry and Jack haven't shown any interest in it."

Cheap or not, holding the old guitar in my hands, I felt sorry for it, gathering dust in the corner and left to die slowly. It hurt me that people did this with instruments.

"Cream? Sugar?"

I put the guitar back in the corner and went to the table, the top of which was made of three planks of wood, not quite straight and with gaps between them.

"Just milk, thanks. No sugar."

"You're having a muffin. I won't let you say no to that."

She put one on a plate and gestured for me to sit down.

The coffee was very good. Churchill quality.

"Can I ask what you do for work?"

"Are you wondering how I managed to afford buying my own town?"

"I guess, yeah."

Standing, with her hands gripping the back of a chair, she said, "I design clothes. I've got a studio out the back. I make the patterns for mass-produced clothes. Stuff that's made in China and Taiwan. You'll find people all over the world wearing my designs."

I thought of Nikki and her one-off t-shirts and bags. She would be back in Brisbane by now. I was curious about the current status of the Nikki-Bevan relationship.

With the woman's eyes on me, I took a bite of the muffin. It was very moist, but not sweet.

"Good?"

"It is. So is the coffee."

"There's a market in Ashton," she said, "but we do all our shopping in Rexburg. Better quality. More choice. Organic produce."

The two boys came in and sat at the table, side by side, opposite me and staring.

"Hot chocolate?"

They chorused: "Yes, please."

She went into the kitchen.

Henry asked, "Can you play the guitar?"

"Yep."

"Can you play us a song?"

"I don't know about that, matey. The guitar's not very good. It sounds like a dying cat."

Jack laughed.

"The mayor orders you to play a song," Henry said.

"Okay." I took a long sip of coffee, then had another bite of the muffin. "What kind of song?"

"Something funny," Jack said.

"No, something sad."

"How about a song that's funny and sad?"

They both nodded.

I drank the rest of my coffee and got up to retrieve the guitar. I also got my journal from my backpack. While I didn't want to perform for these kids, I was keen to find out how the Daphne song sounded.

At the table, I set myself up, taking my time to find the lyrics in my journal and to tune the guitar again. The two boys watched my every move. I noticed that Henry seemed to rarely blink. I was about to start when the woman came in with two cups of hot chocolate. Each cup was personalised, with the boys' names painted on them.

It struck me as odd to be spending time with this family and not yet know the woman's name.

"You don't have to play anything," she said, sitting down and pouring me some more coffee, topping it up with milk as well.

"I've got direct orders from the mayor."

I was about to call Henry the little dictator, but thought against it.

"He can be demanding, Mayor Henry," she said.

As I finger-picked the five-chord progression of *Goodbye Daphne*, I started tapping the guitar with the last two fingers of my right hand between chords. This made the song feel more upbeat and bright.

Then, I stopped. "Okay, I think it has to be said that I wrote this song today. It's got wet paint all over it. Don't expect me to get it right the first time, but," and I looked into Henry's unblinking eyes, "you're the first people on the planet to hear it."

"That's excellent," Henry said.

I started again, playing upbeat, a happy campfire song. The lyrics weren't quite kid-friendly, so I had to improvise. In the process, the revenge-seeking hunter morphed from dogged pursuer into an idiot who kept messing things up, much to the delight of Henry and Jack.

All three clapped when I strummed the last chord and put the guitar aside.

"You really wrote that today?" the woman asked.

"That's what I was doing when you pulled over. Which reminds me, I really should get back on the road. It'll be dark soon."

"No, stay," Henry said. "Please."

I was glad to see he wasn't ordering me around anymore.

"What about dinner?" the woman asked. "You could stick around and test a few more songs on us."

I stood up. "That's very nice of you, but I need to get to West Yellowstone tonight."

"I'll drive you there afterwards."

"I couldn't ask you to do that. You've already been really generous."

"We like welcoming strangers to our town, don't we boys?"

Both nodded.

I had the feeling Henry and Jack wanted a man around the house just as much as the woman did.

"Thanks for the ride, and the coffee, but I really should be going."

I grabbed my journal and went to the door. As I put my shoes on and shouldered my backpack, I heard the woman say, "That's how some people repay your kindness. Let that be today's lesson."

The chairs scraped on the floor, so I went quickly through the door and closed it behind me. Outside, the dogs barked at me, blocking my way and keeping me in front of the house. I tossed a stick to the right, but neither went for it. So I started running, using the car as a decoy to get around the dogs. They chased me to the fence, barking all the while. The gate was locked. I climbed the fence, getting over it just as the dogs got there.

I jogged down the road, my backpack bouncing, keen to leave this place. I wondered what it would be like at night.

There was a short bridge, with no barriers. Signs said "Warm River" and "No Dumping".

The road was empty. I started up the hill, looking behind me to check if the general of Warm River and her two little corporals might

123

be coming in pursuit. They weren't, and I considered myself foolish for thinking such a thing.

Walking backwards, I looked down on the town's lone house and the river.

She dumped the body in Warm River.

I made some notes in my journal, writing as I walked.

Picked up the vagabond and dumped his cold body in the warm river.

I liked that: the cold body in the warm river. I couldn't hear a chord progression, but I had a sense of how the song might work lyrically, and from there I might get a melody to fit.

Once around the first corner and with the house no longer in view, I started to relax. The woman wasn't crazy; just lonely.

She lives at a lonely bend of the river, waiting for someone to come.

I wondered why the woman would choose to live in such isolation, then force that isolation onto her children as well. She thought she was doing the right thing, but could really have been doing all sorts of damage to Henry and Jack. Long-term damage.

Seeing those two boys got me thinking about Conor and how we were as kids. Our situation had been just about ideal, but even that turned out badly in the end. The divorce messed up both of us and tarnished many of those good childhood memories.

I decided to send postcards of my own once I got to West Yellowstone, to Conor and my parents. Word had most probably travelled from Nana that I was in the States, meaning I owed them all an update anyway. Not that any of them would be that concerned about me. Of all the people in my close circle, only Churchill was a worrier. Conor had his own problems, which always took priority, and I think my parents felt that their job was done; that, as I was an adult, they were free to pursue their own lives without having to keep tabs on me. While I was technically a university drop-out, I'd managed to piece together a life where I wasn't dependent on either of them or in need of rescuing and constant support.

Churchill had quite nicely filled the void as my surrogate parent and substitute older brother.

Thinking of home had resulted in the river running lyrically dry, for now, so I put my journal back into my backpack.

There were no cars, from either direction. I kept walking. Could I make it all the way to the highway on foot? I took out my phone to check the distance, but I had no connection. Was Warm River a communications black hole as well, where you couldn't even call for help?

I regretted letting the woman drive me off the highway, though it would make a good story to tell Churchill. I hoped he was doing okay in my absence. Given he was such a homebody, he definitely got on my nerves sometimes, but I really missed him when he wasn't around.

Could the two of us raise Eris? If it turned out that Eris was to come back to Perth with me, would that be a good way to bring up a child, with a platonic male couple as parents? At least there would be great-grandma in the house behind, driving Eris to school in that massive car of hers. It seemed an unlikely situation, but I was sure Churchill and Nana would try to make it work. They were good people and they cared about me. But would Eris try? And where would Nola fit into it all?

Where the hell were they? It couldn't be that they'd just disappeared off the map.

I didn't regret asking Nikki to come with me, but I wondered whether there was a Rowan in an alternative universe who had gone to Tulsa alone and had already found Nola and Eris.

No. That was negative thinking. I'd find them. The postcards were sent to get my attention. Nola was making me earn it, and that was what I had to do. I wouldn't give up and go home.

I took out the printed photo and stared at my little girl. So sweet, so innocent. Somewhere, she was waiting for me to appear. And I wasn't a ginger-haired demon. I was her knight in freckled armour.

At the top of a long rise, the road started to bend. I stopped to take in the view, looking out over the expanse of trees. It was spring. A haze of pollen seemed to cling to the tree tops. Yellowstone, the far western edge.

Did Nola ever work a season at Yellowstone? Where was she working next?

That was how Churchill had found out more about her, by following the trail of jobs and reference checks, which meant it might happen again in the next few weeks or so. If Nola was working as a ranger this year, her new employer would check her references and contact the previous parks. Churchill just had to contact the park she'd worked at last year and find out if another park had called. There could be more than one, if Nola applied to several parks, but it would help to narrow the search and predict where she was going next.

I just had to wait. I could slow down, enjoy my time here and stop chasing Nola's shadow. No more hotels to check. No more stories to make up.

But for some reason, it struck me as too easy. Why would Nola go to all the trouble of sending cryptic postcards and making me search only for it to require a few phone calls to locate her before the park season started?

A red pick-up truck came from the bottom of the long rise, with two guys in the cab. The truck reached me and stopped. The passenger window was lowered. Both men had beards and wore battered, greasy caps.

"Where to?" the man in the passenger seat asked.

"West Yellowstone."

The two men exchanged a glance, with the driver nodding.

"We can take ya to the highway, but you gotta ride in the back."

"Thanks."

"I hope you got a strong stomach."

I climbed into the tray, using the rear wheel to get a step up. There was a blue tarp held down by bits of wood, covering something that just about filled the tray. I stepped around it, took my backpack off and sat down with my back against the cab's rear window, which had a gun rack on the inside with three rifles. When we started moving, the wind rustled the tarp, lifting it in places.

There was an animal underneath, a large deer. I lifted the tarp a little, expecting a mess, and there was. Blood was pooled around the animal's slit gut. The two men had emptied the deer's insides before loading it, probably so it would be easier to carry.

I'd never seen a deer before, and here I was, a metre from a dead one, its eyes open.

This innocent beast would perhaps feed these two men and their families tonight, which was a way for me to justify what they'd done. As with people hunting kangaroo in Australia's outback, the locals here hunted deer in their own wilderness.

I moved the tarp enough to get a full view of the animal.

I felt sad, not so much because this animal had been killed and would soon be cooked and eaten, but that it had perhaps been in the wrong place at the wrong time. I pictured the deer in the forest, and the possible events that led up to the animal being shot: deciding which tracks to take, which grass to eat, which other deer to follow. Or could I attach

126

something human to it, something heroic? Stepping in front of others to take the shot, or standing still, long enough to let the others flee?

You take the hit and let the others live.

I took out my journal and jotted down some notes about accidental sacrifice, one which somehow takes the person to another plane of existence. Because in the song, the person would sacrifice himself without any motivation. Not for love or money or reward. It would just happen. Wrong place, right time, followed by a moment of purity. Caught in the headlights and not jumping out of the way.

Riding in the pick-up, looking at the deer's unblinking eye, I was overcome with the joy of being alive. It was brilliant out here. I was so lucky. I wasn't restringing guitars in a hot workshop. I wasn't sleeping the morning away. I wasn't sitting on my bed and composing rubbish songs. I wasn't stoned or drunk. I wasn't wondering when life would begin, when I would finally grow up and become an adult.

Life had begun. I was an adult. I had a family. I had Eris, maybe, and I had Churchill. My family didn't have to be nuclear and perfect. It didn't have to be uniform and standard. It just needed to be comprised of people who cared about each other and who would offer lots of support. Yes, of course Churchill and I could raise Eris, if he was up for it.

I leaned forward and placed my left hand on the animal's neck. It was very warm.

After driving mostly uphill and negotiating curves, which had made me queasy, sitting backwards like this, we crested a rise and started going downhill. The road straightened and the forest moved back from the verge, the trees having been cleared away. The pick-up started going much faster than before. I held onto the tray's side to keep steady as the vehicle took some bumps in the road and swerved a little. I wondered if the guys in the cab were drunk.

I kept my left hand on the animal's neck.

The trees flew past in a green blur.

I was glad when we eventually started to slow down. I looked around and saw we were approaching a stop sign. We came to a halt next to it. I took this as my cue to get out. The two guys got out as well. They ignored me and walked, not quite in straight lines, to the stop sign, where they both pissed against its post. When they came back, I thanked them for the ride. The driver acknowledged me with a casual wave of his hand. The pick-up turned left and roared off.

Standing at the corner, staring down the flat expanse of highway, I had to admit that the woman had been right: the Mesa Falls Scenic Byway was much more attractive than this. And given that nothing bad had happened in Warm River, I was glad for the experience and that I'd taken that route. The encounter with the deer had also been strangely comforting.

My only problem now was that this corner wasn't a good hitch-hiking spot. There was some traffic, but the cars and trucks were going too fast to stop, and the single-lane road meant there was no room for a car to pull over. The best chance was a car coming down Mesa Falls that would turn right, but that road was vacant. As I waited, I realised I'd been very lucky to get the ride in the pick-up.

On the main road, there was a turning lane for Mesa Falls. I shouldered my backpack and walked half-way down this lane, thinking I could safely stand here, drivers would see me early, and they would have somewhere to pull over without holding up traffic.

I'd kind of had enough of the road for one day. The passing drivers didn't even look at me.

The area around the highway was cleared and flat. There were tree-covered hills in the distance.

It felt like I was standing in the middle of an early Springsteen album. This was the America that had inspired the likes of Woody Guthrie, John Mellencamp, Bob Seger and countless others. The heartland. The land that was your land and my land, where a hard rain's gonna fall and there were scarecrows on wooden crosses, and where out past the cornfields the woods got heavy. The place of hungry hearts. Stories behind every door, ploughed into the earth of abandoned fields, trapped inside all the big American cars driving down the highways of regret.

In both directions as far as I could see, the road was straight. A wind was swirling around, not really blowing from any one direction. Gusting and dying, or spinning into a little eddy that twirled through the dusty field across the road and dissipated. The sun was warm, but was heading towards the hills to the west and would soon be gone. The sky was just about white, like the farmer's wife had described during the day's second ride.

And we're all dreaming, under a big white sky.

A light blue hatchback slowed down as it passed me, indicator on. I thought the driver was turning onto Mesa Falls, but the car stopped before the corner and I ran towards it. The passenger window was open. The driver was about my age, maybe a few years younger.

"Man, you picked a spot for it," he said. "Tough to get a ride out here."

"I came down the Byway. That's how I got stuck here."

"Well, get on in. I'm going to West Yellowstone, if that helps at all."

"That helps a lot."

I put my backpack on the rear seat and climbed in the front. The car was a mess, with a lot of rubbish on the floor, food wrappers and beverage containers. I had to move my feet a little, to part the garbage and find some floor. It looked like he often ate in his car.

"I'm Jez."

"Rowan."

We shook hands and started swapping stories. Jez was an easy talker. He said he was studying at the University of Idaho, but he lived with his dad in West Yellowstone. It meant he commuted to Idaho Falls and back every day during the week, but qualified this by saying it was much cheaper than living on campus.

"Plus, the people are nicer at home," he said. "Can't say what it is exactly. Maybe it's the park and the environment. We're just a bit more grounded and welcoming. More humble and respectful too. I mean, people in Idaho Falls think they're kings of the world. Come on. It's Idaho Falls, not New York."

"What does your dad do?"

"He runs a bookstore. It's a café too, but he only built that in because no one was buying books. It's going well."

"He built it himself?"

"Sure did. Made all the tables and chairs. Built the bar too. Did all the renovating. Everything out of wood. We got a workshop out the back of our house. It's always been just his hobby, but I tell ya, he's real good. Got all the tools."

"Nice."

We'd been driving for about fifteen minutes and had yet to make a turn. The wooden fence that started at the Mesa Falls intersection continued along the left side of the road, but was eventually hidden behind the trees.

As he did this drive every day on his own, I thought Jez was happy for the company. He asked about Australia and I told him about my life there, explaining that I was a musician and that I also had a job in a music shop.

"My dad tried to build a guitar once," Jez said. "But it sounded terrible."

"It's harder than it looks. Does he still have it?"

"Yeah, in his workshop. It's on top of his mistakes pile."

"Maybe I could adjust it a little. Get a decent sound out of it."

"You know how to do that?"

"Sure. I know all about guitars. I'm a luthier."

"Yeah? I always thought that was someone who played the lute."

Stationary Bicycles

Inspiration hits on the train from the airport to downtown Vancouver. Ignoring her daughter and looking through the window, she sees a lot of people cycling, and the weather isn't even that good for it today. It's drizzling and miserable. The grey clouds rolling in from the west threaten heavier rain, and she thinks this might be why people are cycling with such intent and vigour, getting out of the saddle and leaning forward, their faces grimacing in the mist, trying to reach their destinations before the rain really starts to fall. The cyclists come across to her collectively as an unhappy lot, if their facial expressions and body language are anything to go by.

Of course, it could just be the weather, and her own bad mood.

Still, she sees potential there: make the unhappy cyclists even more miserable. With that theme, she considers various angles, all of which include causing accidents. While that would be telling, she doesn't really want people to get hurt, because the focus is then on the injury rather than the act of chaos that caused it.

They walk from the train station to the youth hostel, down busy Burrard Street to get to Burnaby. At damp street level, she senses that there's a fair amount of animosity between cyclists and drivers, and witnesses it too, as cyclists fight for space on roads lacking dedicated bike paths. The drivers are unwilling to make space and liberally use their horns to express their displeasure at having to share the roads. Windows are lowered, heated words exchanged, the occasional bird flipped. It all comes as something of a surprise, as she's always considered the Canadians far more relaxed and tolerant than her own countrymen and women. But not when it's raining, and not when everyone has some place to get to. They're all in a hurry, the cyclists too. Road space is limited. Vehicles dominate. No one wants to be held up. Few are willing to concede, and few are accommodating.

With all this open hostility, going both ways, she wonders what further chaos she can add, as it all seems chaotic enough already.

But then a nice vision forms; placing some metaphorical sticks of TNT under this ticking time bomb in the hope of making things worse. She wants to escalate this battle for road space into a war of sorts, and make a statement in the process.

She can hear her daughter talking, but she tunes her out, brainstorming ideas instead.

Slash some tires?

Tacks on the roads?

Cut through bike chains?

Too malicious, she decides, and not creative enough. It needs to be something innocuous, almost accidental, where blame can't easily be placed, but will require conjecture and accusation. Something that might look like it was done with intent, but which might also be excused away as a person's innocent mistake.

Eris pulls at her arm, demanding attention. She pulls back, helping her daughter up the short hill of Burnaby Street, which is narrower and has less traffic than Burrard.

The small corral of bikes outside a building gives her an idea: lock them all together. And the idea quickly starts to expand as it takes hold. Lock as many bikes as she can on one lock. Lock bikes together all over the city.

She thinks this is good, and starts making a mental list.

She'll need lots of cheap locks and transport. As she knows how much Canadians love a bargain, the locks can be bought at various dollar stores around the city, maybe getting two or three locks from each store, to avoid suspicion. As for transport, she decides the only way to complete this project is by bike.

The idea fully takes holds of her and makes her walk faster. She wants to get started.

Eris struggles to keep up.

When they reach the youth hostel, they're too early to check-in, but they are allowed to place their luggage – the big, army-green backpack she lugs and the small pink daypack that Eris carries – in the hostel's storeroom. She gets a map and asks at reception for directions to the nearest bike rental shop. The receptionist says the hostel has bikes to rent, but not for carrying kids. So, he recommends Bayshore Bicycle Rentals, several blocks away on Denman Street.

"I'm tired," Eris says. "And hungry."

"Just wait, will you?"

Eris sits down on the carpeted floor.

She sees a tantrum building, so picks the little girl up and carries her outside.

"Fine. We'll get something to eat," she says, putting the girl down.

"And the little princess can choose."

They head down Burnaby, then up Denman. It's a long walk, and her daughter's slow pace and whining makes it take longer.

Bayshore turns out to be a small shop, while Denman is another street busy with traffic and lacking cycle paths. She finds it interesting that there are two bicycle rental shops across from each other on what is potentially a dangerous street for riding. She goes into Bayshore and discusses her options with the assistant.

Eris goes around the shop ringing various bicycle bells.

"Stop that," she orders, and her daughter sits down on the floor again.

"Cute kid," the assistant says with a smile.

"You can have her."

The assistant laughs at this.

"I'm serious."

"Yeah, right. So, you want to carry her too?"

As she'll be forced to cart the little girl around, as well as a pile of bike locks, she settles on a mountain bike with an enclosed mesh trailer. It's not cheap, and she rues that it would be so much easier without her daughter, but she can't just leave the girl at the hostel.

Eris climbs inside the trailer, zips the mesh door shut and appears more than happy to be ferried around in this fashion.

The helmet, required by law, the assistant says, is included with the price of the rental, but a lock costs extra, which she finds very fitting.

As she wheels the bike and the attached trailer out of the shop, she's surprised to see the clouds have cleared a little and that the drizzle has stopped. It bodes well for the afternoon and she's keen for it.

"I'm hungry," Eris shouts from inside the trailer.

She shakes her head. "For what?"

"Pizza."

"What a surprise."

Eris gets out of the trailer.

There's a pizza place next door to the bike shop. She locks the mountain bike to a post and sees two more bike shops across the street.

Inside the Rebellious Tomato, she orders a small margherita for Eris and a medium arti zucci for herself, and pays with cash. She thinks of Europe, wanting to go there again, but on her own this time:

to eat real pizza in Italy and Croatia, drink beer in Germany, smoke hash in Amsterdam, paint some murals, and bring more chaos to the staid Europeans.

In America, she's running out of ideas. The whole country seems to lack inspiration. It's why she decided to start in Thunder Bay, and added Kingston and Vancouver to her itinerary; to shake things up a bit. And this worked, because she got a great idea as soon as she landed in Vancouver. But after this stop, there's only Des Moines left, then home to Chicago.

Eris talks and talks.

She wishes the little girl would just shut up and give her some peace. She knows better than to engage with Eris or lavish attention on her, because she will then demand more.

Looking at her creation, she thinks to herself: "Attention is your drug, and you're addicted to it."

The trip is nearly over. She considers it mostly a failure. A few projects worked, many didn't. The ones she thought were ordinary and uninspired had the most impact, like Frozen Four-way Stop Sign in Saginaw. Yet the really clever ideas, the ones she felt had deeper meanings, including God on Vacation, didn't make any difference. The only real problem she'd caused in Tulsa was that the poster was hard to get off the door. It didn't stop people from going to church, her website got very few views and she only received a handful of emails, which were all nasty. It was a lot of work for very little result.

She hopes Europe will be more inspiring, but fears her creative well is slowly running dry.

With just a week left, it's time for her to line up her next park job. Leaving it so late reduces her options, but she's not worried. Her references are good, and many of the parks lack reliable, experienced staff who are willing to work seasonally and have the flexibility to move for the job. She decides to do some applying tonight.

The pizzas arrive. Eating shuts Eris up, but she only finishes half her pizza, then demands dessert.

"We'll get an ice cream later, if you're good."

"Okay."

Eris is a mess, with tomato sauce on her face and hands.

"Go clean yourself up."

Her daughter complies, waiting to be accompanied and helped, but eventually going on her own to the restroom.

The break gives her the chance to search on her phone for nearby dollar stores. She finds half a dozen and marks them on her map. It will be easy enough to buy the locks and put them in place as she goes along.

Eris comes out, half clean, requiring a wipe with a napkin.

She does this, roughly, but Eris seems to enjoy it.

Outside, the sun is shining; the chaos gods on her side.

Eris gets into the trailer, putting on a bit of a show as she makes herself comfortable.

She hopes the food will put the little girl to sleep. She gets the bike onto the road and starts pedalling. Further down Denman, there are three more bike shops.

A white van passes, close and with speed. The force of it nearly blows her off the bike. And that's just the start. It's dangerous riding on the road and hard work pulling the trailer. But the drivers, and also the single-minded cyclists, motivate her to pedal on and get this project underway.

The first dollar stores are on Davie Street, three of them close together. In each store she buys four locks, the coloured flexible ones that extend to about half a metre and are so flimsy, a strong person might be able to pull them open. In Rosalinda's Dollar Mart, she also buys a package of little car stickers, to affix to the locks and potentially give those cyclists caught in her web of locks someone to blame. And as she's fully into her project now, she also buys a blonde wig, sunglasses and a packet of latex gloves.

Each time she goes into a store, she leaves Eris outside. She's glad the slow rocking trailer has had a sedative effect, which saves her from having to administer more Phenergan.

There's another dollar store on Hamilton Street, where she gets four more locks. In nearby Yaletown Park, which is more concrete than grass or trees, she takes a few minutes to stick a car onto the connection point of each of the sixteen locks, and puts on her wig, sunglasses and gloves.

She wants to get as many bikes as she can with each lock, and that means finding places where there are lots of bikes close together. Her first stop is the Vancouver Public Library, which looks like a mini coliseum. In the racks out front, the bikes are more separated than she'd like, but she manages to get four bikes with one lock and five with another. The difficult part is doing this without being seen. Here, the trailer comes in handy, because it's while she's pretending to be checking on Eris that she loops the lock between the frames and wheels.

It doesn't really matter, as no one's watching her anyway. People have their phones and their goals, and are immersed in their own little worlds.

Back on the bike, she drops the two sets of keys in the nearest bin and heads down Robson Street, pedalling with more vigour as the chemistry of chaos kicks in.

It's possible Eris has said something from the trailer, but it's hard to hear above the traffic and with the wind rushing past her ears, and easy to ignore.

The next stop is City Centre station, where she again uses the trailer as a decoy for putting the locks in place. Then, it's on to Granville station. It becomes a challenge to see how many bikes she can get with just one lock, setting a record of nine at Waterfront station. But the real boon is getting five very flash racing bikes outside the New Amsterdam Café on Hastings Street. While securing the lock, and she uses two for good measure, she can see the five riders inside; middle-aged men all in colourful, too-tight spandex, caffeinating up for the next leg of their ride.

She finds it fascinating how no one notices her. Sure, people prioritise their own concerns, but she concludes few would ever suspect a blonde-haired mother riding around with a child in a trailer of committing any devious acts.

As the afternoon turns into evening and the work day finishes, there is more traffic on the road, more cyclists and more pedestrians. It's easy for her to get lost among the rush, even with the cumbersome trailer.

To reward Eris for her good behaviour and for cooperating so well all afternoon, she buys her a big ice cream at Soft Peaks in Gastown, and has a small one herself.

She stops at a few more dollar stores in Gastown and locks more bikes together, hitting the most crowded bike racks and corrals she finds. A minimum of four bikes on each lock becomes the benchmark.

With no more locks left, and tired from all the riding, she circles back to the library. Before getting there, she stops to remove her wig and sunglasses, and drops the gloves in a garbage bin. Eris wants the wig, and she helps put this on, the sunglasses too. In her buoyant mood, she finds this very funny.

Eris laughs as well. It's a rare nice moment for them.

Over an hour has passed since she was at the library. She gets a buzz when she sees the large group of people assembled around the bike racks and the police car parked on Robson Street. One police officer is searching the car's boot; for bolt cutters, she assumes. The other officer is trying to calm people down, smiling a little as he does so, thinking it all some harmless prank. She can spot the people whose bikes have been grounded, because they look frazzled and annoyed. Some stand with their arms folded, some remonstrate with the police officer, and others pace while talking on their phones.

It's all very satisfying, and she'd like to photograph the scene, but realises her camera is in her backpack, in the hostel's storage room. She also wonders if the main impact the locks have had, both here and at other points around the city, is to make people late for something. Instead of instigating chaos and trying to ignite war between cyclists and drivers, she's only caused tardiness. No one seems to notice the little car stuck on the lock. She's also surprised by the lack of fraternity between the cyclists, who argue with each other and point fingers. Their individual concerns and wrecked schedules far outweigh the importance of cyclists banding together against drivers everywhere.

The police officer uses a large pair of wire-cutters to remove the two locks, though it takes a while, as the cheap locks prove more stubborn than expected. There's a bit of push and shove as the cyclists grab at their now freed bikes, with the odd pedal getting caught in the spokes of another bike's wheel, and handle-bars tangling up. The remains of the locks are put into the nearest bin, which is where she dropped the keys earlier. The cyclists disperse in a hurry, potentially late for whatever is next in their lives.

"I'm hungry," Eris says from the trailer.

"You're kidding. My God, you're American to the core. All you do is consume."

She rides down Robson to Thurlow Street, saddle-sore and tired, but elated. The road is busy. The cars, trucks and buses all demand first use and dominate the space available. There are parked cars that pull out suddenly, without indicating and without their drivers looking, and car doors are opened without checking the street first. It's hard work, dangerous, and she feels the spite. The trailer takes up more room and makes her slower than on a regular bike. It requires more space for a car to get around her, though some pass precariously close, as do faster cyclists. The fact she's a mother hauling a child in a trailer makes little difference. She doesn't feel at all welcome on the road.

She decides more locks are required, more bikes strung together, at more locations around the city. What she did today wasn't enough, and she needs a stronger link between the locks and vehicles, so that drivers will be blamed. The little car stickers weren't blatant enough.

It's a relief to arrive at the hostel and place the bike in the storage room.

Eris climbs out of the trailer. "I want pizza."

"But we had that for lunch."

"I want pizza."

Having been at this juncture many times before, normally post-drugging, she recognises that her daughter is overtired and will make a scene if unable to have her demands fulfilled. She's really not in the mood for tantrums, tears and having everyone stare.

"Fine. You win. Pizza it is. But let's go to the room first and get cleaned up."

"I'm hungry now."

"It'll just take five minutes."

"Now," Eris shouts.

"Why are you so needy?" she shouts back, and she immediately regrets it.

Eris stands still for a few seconds, then starts to cry. This time, it's the grating wail that stretches her mouth wide open and turns her cheeks pink. It echoes in the bicycle storage room, and the more she cries, the more this one sound seems to fill the room, in layers.

Watching her daughter cry with the blonde wig on has the strange effect of making her think this is someone else's child; that this little tumbleweed of chaos is not her responsibility, and she can simply turn her back and walk away.

"That's enough. Please, stop crying."

She says this with feeling, but doesn't move closer to her daughter, which she knows is what the crying is really for. A hug, a kiss, any kind of physical contact. Attention, and lots of it. The little girl is crying hard for it, really working her lungs, desperate.

The stand-off goes on for another minute or so. She's glad no one comes into the storage room, but wonders if her daughter might also want that: an audience.

138

Finally, she steps forward, removes the blonde wig and picks Eris up. Immediately, the crying stops and the little arms are tight around her neck.

As they exit the storage room, she says, "I'd say you cried yourself clean."

Outside, she carries her daughter for a while, then puts her down. They walk along Thurlow Street holding hands. At Davie Street, there are three pizza places in view. She lets Eris choose, and so they go into Yummy Pizza.

"I like the name," Eris says.

The greasy pizzas in the front window look less than appetising.

Eris wants margherita again.

She makes the order, but gets just a lemonade for herself, because she doesn't want to eat what Yummy Pizza has to offer. Vancouver's traffic has also driven its way under her skin and covered it too, with grime and exhaust fumes. She wants a shower and to eat a decent meal. She considers buying a few things from the organic market next door and cooking herself dinner in the hostel kitchen. But then, there's the problem of what to do with her daughter. The hostel has a TV room; maybe she can dump the kid in there and let other hostellers take care of her.

She likes that idea. A reprieve. A break. Something real to eat. Hopefully, cooking in the kitchen will give her the chance to interact with other people; to be herself for a while, among adults.

Eris eats happily.

She looks through the window at busy Davie Street. The traffic continues to stream by. It's unrelenting.

She asks herself if she's gone about this project all wrong; attempting to bring cyclists to a halt when what she'd like to do is somehow bring the whole city to a halt. Make everything stand still. But how to do that?

Yummy Pizza has a TV on the wall, showing the local news. A reporter is interviewing an angry middle-aged man in spandex. Though not riding, or even standing with a bicycle, he's actually wearing his helmet, making him look like a person with special needs. Behind him is the New Amsterdam Café.

"Can you turn that up?" she asks.

The server looks around the counter and shakes his head. "Sorry. Don't know where the remote is."

On the screen, the interview finishes. It cuts to a montage video, showing different points around the city where bikes were locked together, the groups of angry cyclists and short interviews with some of the victims.

She says to Eris, "We made the news. That's something."

It motivates her to really step things up tomorrow.

"I want dessert," Eris says.

"Of course you do. We'll get it in the store next door."

"Okay."

"But we're going to bed early. Tomorrow's gonna be a busy day."

One Hand Clapping

It was mid-morning and the café was going through a lull. I called Churchill. He answered after half a dozen rings.

"This better be very important. I've got one eye shut."

"Is it that late?"

"After midnight."

"Time to let it all hang out."

"Time to sleep. What's up? Before you ask, I've got nothing to share. I'm still waiting to hear back from Congaree National Park. And I can't keep bugging them. They might get suspicious."

"Any postcards?"

"One, from Vancouver. I guess that's how Nola disappeared. She fled to Canada."

"I'm not going there."

"Shame. It's been in the news lately. There was this mass protest by cyclists. It just about shut down the city. And it got a bit violent too, with cars getting rolled over and set on fire."

"News to me."

"Well, you're out in the wilderness, aren't you? Might as well stay there until Nola gets a park job, then you can pick up the trail again."

"Thanks for chasing that up, Church."

"That was some pretty clever thinking, but don't expect Eris to be at the park. Nola never took her to work."

"I know. But if I find Nola, then I should be able to find Eris."

"There's no guarantee of that."

"Or I'll be able to figure out what happens next. What Nola's grand plan is."

"If she has one. Anyway, how are you spending the days? Are you still staying with that family?"

"With Curt and Jez? Yeah. They've been real generous. It's been good to work in Curt's café and earn some money. Curt's also got a workshop, for woodworking."

"Can you make a guitar in there?"

"He doesn't have the right tools. And it would take too long. Plus, I think I've just about worn out my welcome."

"What makes you say that?"

"Just a feeling. I think Jez doesn't like it that I get along so well with his dad. A couple of nights back, I heard them arguing. They didn't use my name, but I was pretty sure they were arguing about me."

I heard Churchill yawn. "Is this why you called, to tell me your problems?"

"I wanted to know how you are."

"I'm tired. I got too much sun today."

"What, outside?"

"Yes, outside. Look, I'll follow up with the park tomorrow. But for now, let me sleep."

He hung up.

Talking briefly to Churchill convinced me it was time to move out of Curt's house. Working in the café was good, and finding a room in West Yellowstone was an option, but I wanted the road. I'd been standing still for too long. The songs had dried up. While travelling, I was seeing stories everywhere and hearing chord progressions in my head. I wanted that again.

Two construction workers came in and ordered coffees, which they drank standing at the bar. The taller one asked where Curt was. I explained he was in his workshop, building a crib for a friend. This made them both smile.

"That sounds just like Curt," the tall one said. "Tell him we said 'Hi.'"

I didn't know their names, but figured the town didn't have that many construction workers. "Okay. Sure."

They paid and left, both dropping their change in the tip jar. That was nice, as Curt gave me all the tip money I earned. Still, I was already tiring of this work. I wasn't the serving type. I knew this from my time working at the counter of the music shop in Perth. My back got sore from standing for long periods and my hearing often let me down. Curt's café was a good travelling experience, one which made me feel a bit like a local, but it wasn't one I wanted to keep going.

It was fascinating how things had gone in West Yellowstone, how quickly I'd got settled in just over a week, and how long that week had seemed. From the initial ride with Jez, I'd thought we would become friends, but Curt was the one I'd bonded with more. Now, I think Jez considered me more a rival than a friend. There was probably more to it, some key piece of family history I didn't know about; something that had come between Jez and Curt, and which now I was a reminder of. I didn't want to mess up their relationship. It could have had something to do with the café, with Jez not being involved at all, and he also showed no interest in carpentry. When I'd offered to help out, Curt had jumped at it, like he'd been waiting a long time for such an offer.

I'd worked seven days straight since arriving, and hadn't even been into Yellowstone National Park yet, beyond walking one afternoon down to Madison River. Curt had promised to take me deeper into the park, to see the Old Faithful geyser, but I had the feeling that trip would never eventuate. Already within a week, me working in the café had given Curt the chance to take on more woodworking projects and do more favours for people.

With the café empty, I went to the book section and browsed the travel titles. Many of them had a fine layer of dust along the top. I found a USA guidebook, and smiled as I recalled Nikki's severely out-dated edition of the same guidebook and all of its false information.

Seeing the maps and options made me want to get moving again. But I was also really missing playing the guitar. Not just Daphne, but playing and singing. Curt's guitar had turned out to be a disaster, one which a few tweaks couldn't fix.

I needed a new guitar.

The next sizeable town was Bozeman, to the north. There, I could probably get myself a cheap one. I would have preferred building my own, but I knew that would have to wait until I got back to the workshop in Perth. That is, if Jono hadn't given my job to someone else.

A quick search on Curt's office computer told me there was a handful of music shops in Bozeman, plus a couple of luthiers. This sounded promising. I could leave this afternoon, if I wanted, which would probably mean disappointing Curt, but pleasing Jez. I would be honest about it: my time in West Yellowstone was up and I wanted to move on.

This felt very good, to be leaving.

Three women came in, two of them pushing prams. They set themselves up at the café's centre table. I got to work serving them, and did so cheerfully, knowing that in a few more hours, I would be done with this.

Curt arrived before noon, smelling of wood and his hair covered in a light sprinkling of sawdust. Together, we handled the lunch crowd. Some of the regulars already knew my name, and it felt good to be like a local in this foreign place, even if the exchanges tended towards the superficial.

By two, the crowd had dispersed, leaving just me and Curt. While he had grey hair and was rather short, there was much about him that reminded me of my father. Curt was a few years older, but I thought they shared a demeanour; a quietness that could quickly erupt into energy and eagerness. They were men past middle-age who were still firmly in touch with their inner child. While they were not quite grasping for the glories and vitalities of youth, they wanted to keep elements of simplicity and fun. Like my dad, Curt often looked at things with an almost child-like wonder. It was something I wanted to replicate, as I could already sense I was turning into too serious an adult. I hoped that having Eris in my life might help me keep in touch with my inner child.

"Rowan, I can handle the afternoon," Curt said. "You're free to go for the day, if you want."

It was a relief to hear him say that, but now that the time had come, I was sad saying goodbye. So, I decided to be honest and get it over with.

"Thanks. Listen, Curt, I don't want to put you in a bind, but I've decided to head up to Bozeman and continue my travels."

"Oh, yeah? Itchy feet?"

"This is the longest I've spent in one place since I landed in the States. I kind of feel the need to get moving again."

"What about Yellowstone?"

"I'll probably circle back down, at some point."

He nodded slowly. "Been good having you around, Rowan."

"I really appreciate how you and Jez took me in. That was generous of you."

"You're not leaving because of Jez, are you?"

"No, no. I just think it's time."

"I know he can be difficult sometimes. He's like his mother. Wants things. But you working here, that's been real good for me. People like you. You're friendly and personable. You really add something to this place."

"Maybe more height than depth."

He smiled. "Don't sell yourself short."

We both laughed.

"Why don't you hire someone? To do the mornings, like I've been doing. I mean, it's pretty clear to me woodworking is what you'd rather be doing."

"True. I guess I always hoped Jez would get on board. Or that James

144

would come back home. Keep it all in the family." When I didn't say anything, Curt added, "That's Jez's older brother. He's about your age. Joined the army straight out of high school. Did a couple of tours of Iraq."

I assumed James was the void I'd temporarily filled. "You sound very proud of him."

"Do I? That's interesting, because I'm not so sure. He's based at Fort Harrison now, up by Helena. Working in the training facility doing God knows what. We saw more of him when he was doing his tours. At least he came home to us then."

"He alright?"

"I guess. He left a leg over there."

"I'm sorry to hear that."

"Well, he survived. That's more than can be said for others." He shook his head. "Don't know what we're doing over there."

Curt sat down at the café's centre table. I joined him.

"Me and James," Curt said, "we had a lot of disagreements. About politics. You know, people call Montana the purple state, because it's just about an even split between republicans and democrats. James was red before he finished elementary school, and I've only ever been blue. We could never find our purple. I think he went off to fight just to show me what colour he was willing to bleed for his country. And what happens? He loses a leg and they give him a Purple Heart."

He chuckled softly.

"Why don't you reach out to him?"

"Not sure he wants that."

"It's family, Curt. You have to try. Maybe you should put the politics aside and just be people."

Curt looked down at his hands, which were dry and calloused from working in the workshop.

"You know why I'm in the States? I'm trying to find my daughter."

"What? You never said anything about that."

I took out my printed photo and placed it on the table. "That's Nola, and that's Eris. I met Nola in New Zealand, and I had no idea that we'd had a child together. I've come here to find her. To find both of them. I've been following them all over the country, because I feel I have a responsibility to this little girl. Okay, James is a grown man, but I think you have a responsibility to him. You should reach out to him."

In saying all that, I realised that was something I wanted from my father.

Curt looked at the photo, then at me. "You're not some kind of crazy stalker, are you? Because if you are, you hide it very well."

"It's a long story. I don't know what Nola's doing, if she's testing me or something, but she's making it hard for me to find them. Making me prove myself, I think."

Curt sat back. "You know what? I'll drive you. To Bozeman."

"You don't have to do that."

"Sure I do, because it's on the way to Helena."

"Great. Thanks."

"We'll close up early and get going."

He stood up and went behind the counter to pack things away.

I sat there, mentally adding another item to my to-do list for when I got back to Perth: have it out with my father.

→←

Things weren't looking too good financially. I used the computer at the Treasure State Hostel to check my bank account and saw the damage the last month had done. Staying with Curt and working in the café had temporarily stemmed the flow, but that was now over. There was no going back.

At the music stores in Bozeman, I had no joy. I couldn't bring myself to buy a cheap guitar, as they all sounded rubbish, and I couldn't afford to splurge on an expensive one. The shop assistants pushed hard to get me to buy one of their mass-produced branded acoustics, but none of the guitars I played could compare to Daphne.

I wanted to make my own guitar, so I checked out the luthiers in town, to perhaps negotiate a trade: do some work in exchange for time in the workshop. I figured I would need about ten days to finish.

Unfortunately, one luthier was closed, while the other was run out of a suburban garage and looked more like a weekend hobby than a thriving business. That luthier offered to build a guitar for me, which I declined.

The third was outside of Bozeman, on Cottonwood Road. I got an area map from the visitors centre and started walking. I took a more scenic route, through the Montana State University campus instead of along busy Main Street.

It was a sunny morning, good for walking. It also mattered that I saved a few dollars on bus fare.

Past the campus, there were fewer buildings and more open spaces. Once I got onto Stucky Road, it felt like I was heading into the countryside. The scattered buildings on the left looked like apartments, but they soon gave way to fields on both sides of the road, with hills in the distance. The single-lane road had no footpath, but the traffic was light.

It was nice to stroll like this, through the countryside; to take it slow, feel the sun on my neck and forget all the debts I'd run up back in Perth.

The scenery sparked a memory: walking a road like this with my father, somewhere down south, near Collie. A long, straight, bare road. I was twelve years old. We were spending the weekend with old neighbours who had done the treechange thing, having sold everything in Claremont, quit their jobs and moved to the country. Conor was on a school trip and I was alone with my parents, relishing their collective attention. But they argued a lot over that weekend. After an afternoon swimming at Wellington Dam, they had a big fight on the drive back, one that resulted in Dad pulling the car over and the two of them getting out. I got out as well and watched. I wanted to intervene, but didn't know how to. I wasn't even sure what they were arguing about. Then Mum got in the car and drove off. Dad was annoyed and angry, but he also laughed as the car disappeared down the road. He didn't explain anything to me and simply started walking. I followed. It was hot. There was no shade on the road. I could feel the road's heat through my thin sandals. He gave me his hat to wear and it was huge on my head. We walked, neither of us talking. A few cars passed, but Dad didn't try to flag any down and get us a ride. When a car did stop, Dad told the driver we were happy on foot.

That walk, which we did mostly in silence and took hours, was one of my favourite childhood memories, as I'd felt very close to my father then.

When Collie's buildings came into view, he said, "This was much better than sitting in the car. Thanks, Rowan, for walking with me."

His face and neck were lobster-red, but he was smiling.

Now, recalling that smile, which I wondered had perhaps disguised a certain melancholy and resignation, it occurred to me that their marriage might actually have ended there, on that road, over that weekend, and all the years that followed simply marked the time until Conor and I were both grown up and out of the house.

147

I decided to ask Dad about it when I got back to Perth. There was a lot we needed to talk about.

When I reached Cottonwood Road, I stood at the intersection, unsure which direction to go. I was very thirsty, unprepared for what was turning into a long walk.

An old pick-up came from the Bozeman direction and stopped in front of me.

"You lost?" the driver asked. He looked about sixty and struck me as friendly.

"I'm looking for Cottonwood Guitars."

He smiled. "My boy, you got a long way to go. Charlie's place is down by the canyon. I can take you most of the way, but you'll have to walk the rest."

"Okay. Thanks."

I went around to the passenger side and climbed in. The dog lying in the middle of the bench-seat sat up.

"Easy, Cleo," the man said. "He looks harmless enough."

We drove off, the dog sitting close to the driver. He put an arm around her.

The road was straight and cut through farming land. There were bales of hay near fences, narrow tracks leading to farmhouses, and large devices for watering the fields. What I didn't see were people. Most of the fields were a brownish yellow, as if the grass was burnt, though there were some fields that were very green, and these stood out in stark contrast.

"How do you know Charlie?" the man asked.

"I don't. I need a guitar. I want to build one, and to do that I need a workshop."

"You know how to do that?"

"It's what I do, back home in Australia. I build and repair guitars."

The man smiled and shook his head a few times. "I didn't think people did that sort of thing anymore. Everything's made in factories these days. In China. Always nice to hear people still actually make things with their hands, rather than just using their hands to take money from someone else's pocket."

We drove down the unbending road that bisected the farms. Eventually, he slowed, turned right and stopped. The street sign for this dirt track said Pasha Lane.

"I'm going this way." He pointed down the track, then thumbed in

148

the direction of Cottonwood Road and the hills beyond. "You keep going about another mile. Charlie's place is on the left, not far around the first bend. Big red house, in front of a hill. There's a sign too."

"Thanks for the ride."

"Tell Charlie that Anthony says 'Hi.'"

"I will."

I got out. The pick-up's tyres tore at the loose stones of Pasha Lane and sent up a cloud of dust.

Back on the road, I was weary and thirsty, but as I'd come this far, there was little point in turning back. Even if Charlie couldn't help, the least he could do was offer me a drink and tell me how to get back to Bozeman.

More hay bales. Some cows. A long section of old-fashioned X-shaped wooden fence. No cars. No people. No corner-store to buy a drink.

I crested a short hill and saw the first bend in Cottonwood Road. There was a cluster of houses on the left, spread out from each other, at the foot of a yellow hill. The last house, behind all the others, was red.

I assumed I'd already passed the entry road, Derek Way, a few hundred metres back. I climbed the fence and started walking across a field in the direction of the red house. The ground was hard and dry; not exactly the plush soil required for growing crops. I wondered how many decades had passed since something had grown here.

I walked slowly, trespassing, fearing a local might emerge from one of the houses, brandishing a rifle. But as I got closer to the houses, I didn't see anyone. They looked empty. Only the red house had a car out the front; a yellow, two-door Wrangler. There was a sign hammered into the lawn: Cottonwood Guitars, in fancy cursive script, red on yellow.

I wondered if Charlie had a thing for colours.

It was strange to see all these houses so void of life, yet they didn't appear abandoned. They actually looked to be in good condition, as if waiting for a family to move in or to come home from holiday.

Charlie's house was different to the others. It had an older style and seemed more established.

I went up and knocked on the red door. After a few seconds, I rang the bell as well. No answer.

There was a tap attached to the front wall, for watering the garden, with a hose coiled on a hanger.

Was it safe to drink the water out here?

I decided not to risk it.

The car made me think Charlie was home. I walked around the side of the house and heard what sounded like an axe striking wood. Behind the house, there was a red barn, which was closed and secured by a chunky silver padlock that caught the sunlight. A woman was chopping wood. She wore dark blue overalls with a white, long-sleeve undershirt, and swung the axe with precision and strength.

"Uh, hi."

Startled, she turned to face me, both hands gripping the axe. "Who the hell are you?"

"Sorry. I knocked on the door."

"I heard it."

She looked to be in her mid-forties, but might have been younger, and was tall and in good shape. The overalls were a good fit and they really suited her. She also had a fantastic head of blonde curls, parted down the middle and shoulder-length.

"I'm looking for Charlie."

"Why?"

"I want to build a guitar."

"You mean you want Charlie to build you a guitar."

"No, I want to. I'm a luthier."

"Are you now?" She drove the axe cleanly through a piece of wood. "It's all really simple, isn't it? Just cut and paste. Where's your wood?"

"I haven't got it yet."

"What are you planning to use?"

"I was thinking about Hawaiian Koa."

"Ugly, but a good sound."

"Look, do you know where Charlie is?"

"Sure." She slammed the axe into the chopping block and took her gloves off. "Right here. "

We shook hands.

"Don't look so shocked. Girls can build guitars too. And they can chop wood."

"I'm Rowan."

"You walk all the way here from town, Rowan? I'm guessing you did, and you should've worn a hat."

"I got a ride for some of the way, with Anthony and his dog. I can't remember the dog's name, but he told me to say hello."

"It's Cleo. As in, the greatest love story ever told, even if Ant's name is slightly wrong. You know, Antony and Cleopatra. What? You don't read the classics? Oh well, who does these days?" She headed towards the house's open back door. "You want a drink? Because you sure look like you could use one."

I followed her inside, going through the spacious living room that had two black sofas, cornered together, and an open fireplace. There was also a huge television on the wall. The kitchen's counter separated it from the living room, and there was a pair of yellow stools in front of the counter.

"Take a load off," she said.

It was good to sit down. I could feel my feet throbbing slightly. Charlie put a glass of orange juice in front of me and I downed this in just about one go.

"Some more?"

"Yes. Please."

Still standing on the other side of the counter, she refilled my glass.

"Thanks." I sipped it this time. It was fresh orange juice.

Charlie eyed me curiously. "You're Australian, am I right?"

"That's right."

"You guys down under make some decent guitars. Matons are good. Why on earth have you come all the way to Montana to build one? In Bozeman, of all places. Did you get lost on the way to Mount Rushmore? Or are you on the run? No. Maybe you're on this spiritual journey that a lot of you young guys think you just have to take. Going into the wild and all that crap. Leaving your money behind and relying solely on luck and the generosity of strangers for your survival."

"None of that."

"So, then it's about the music? You're on some globe-trotting quest to find all the great guitar makers. To learn all their secrets and build the best guitar the world has ever seen. You've taken Leonard Cohen's idea of the 'secret chord' to the extreme. You're trying to find it."

I wondered if Charlie had a few screws loose.

"Come on. Speak up. Confess."

"Alright. It's like this. I had a beautiful guitar that I'd built myself. Daphne. I was busking in Salt Lake City when this guy grabbed her and smashed her to pieces. Nothing spiritual about that. It was pure violence, and I beat him up for doing it. That was nearly two weeks ago. I want a new guitar, so I can keep busking and writing songs, and

I don't want to buy something mass-produced. I want a guitar made with attention and care."

Charlie listened to all of this with her arms folded and a slight grin on her face.

"Ah, you're a troubadour," she said. "You're rocking and rolling around America, following the ghost of Johnny Cash. Well, let me be the one to tell you, red hair doesn't go too well with black. Maybe you should be following in the footsteps of Axl Rose instead."

"If I'm going to emulate a ginger rocker, I'd rather copy Willie Nelson."

"Hah. Ginger rocker. I like that. Walking all the way out here from town makes me think you're just about off your ginger rocker."

"I know. I had no idea it was that far."

"It's about ten miles. And you still got to get back."

"Is there a bus?"

She shook her head. "This is Montana. A bus is something you put dirty dishes on in a restaurant."

"I guess I'll hitch-hike then."

"I tell you what. You chop my wood, and I'll drive you back."

"Are you serious?"

"You heard me. We'll trade. Wood for a ride. Big strong buck like you should get it done in about half an hour. What are you, six-six?"

"About that."

"With that height, you must've played some ball. I'm guessing a hoops star can chop some wood."

"Why does everyone think I play basketball?"

"Walk around." When I didn't move, she added, more forcefully, "Walk, to the fireplace and back. And make a spin move."

"A what?"

"You heard me. Do it."

I complied, and nearly tripped over trying to execute a spin. Charlie laughed.

"That was more a pirouette than a spin move," she said. "You don't move anything like a baller. I should've seen it already. You're more suited to the dance floor. Not much of an athlete, are you?"

"Sounds like you are."

"I played some basketball, years ago."

"They tried with me, when I was a kid, because I was always the tallest in my class. But I was hopeless at sports."

"I can picture it," Charlie said. "You being this big kid and always getting picked first for sports, but then failing and letting everyone down. Must've been hard."

"Something like that."

"What about timber-sports? Wood chopping. I'll throw lunch into the bargain."

The promise of food was motivating. "I can try."

"That's the spirit. I'll make lunch. You chop the wood. I got to go into Bozeman later anyway."

"What about the guitar?"

"I don't let strangers into my workshop." She went to the sink and started washing her hands. "You can use my gloves. They're on the block."

Outside, I looked at the pile of wood. From the scattered pieces on the ground and the collection of sawn stumps, I guessed Charlie had only just started. Along the wall of the barn was a neat low stack of chopped wood.

I didn't want to do this crazy woman's work. I could easily walk down to Cottonwood Road and wait for a ride.

I took a few steps towards the barn. The big padlock on the door made me think the workshop was inside. That was motivation enough. So, I put Charlie's gloves on. They were warm and slightly damp. I picked up the chopped wood on the ground and placed it in the wheelbarrow. It took a bit of jimmying to get the heavy axe out of the block. I placed a sawn stump on the block and started chopping.

As a city boy, I had no idea what I was doing. I tried to cut the stump in half, but the axe only got stuck in the middle. While I'd never swung an axe, I knew a lot about wood and how to work with it. So, I cut around the edges, cutting with the grain and making the stump small enough for me to slice in half. The wood was dry and cut easily, when I cut it the right size. The axe was also very sharp.

I started to get the hang of it and swung the axe with more confidence. The wheelbarrow full, I took this to the barn and stacked the wood.

With the next batch, I found a rhythm, working the edges and cutting each stump to the heart. I also started to hear something: the sound the axe made when it struck the wood and cut through. A crisp, clean smack. Like the hit on a tight snare drum. It gave me a beat. Repeating this beat helped me to hear a song. It had a simple progression, three chords, all majors. Something like G-D-C, or A-E-D, played big and loud, the smack of the wood coming between the chords.

You're walking in circles around me again, and cut to the heart, cut to the heart.

The wood piled up around the chopping block as I tried to maintain the rhythm.

You're leaving me in pieces, no loose ends, and want a brand new start, a new start.

The song's narrative quickly took shape: the "you" was a man, leaving his girlfriend or wife and heading off on a journey to find himself, to find bigger meaning. Or, it could have been the woman leaving the man, which I thought could be more interesting.

I recalled my mother, on that highway near Collie, driving away from my father, leaving the two of us out there, and Dad preferring to walk. And I thought of myself, hitch-hiking to West Yellowstone, plotting my own course. Then there was Nikki, back in Brisbane, free of me and hopefully of Bevan as well. All these examples of people splitting up and finding their own way, better off than before.

But my journey wasn't about escaping people. I was travelling towards people, not away from them. I wanted all my roads to lead to Nola and Eris.

I reached for the next stump and saw that I'd chopped all the wood. There were pieces scattered all around the chopping block. Pieces on top of pieces. I was sweating.

I took the gloves off and went inside. There was no sign of Charlie. On the coffee table in front of the sofas, under some sports magazines, I found a notepad and pen. It was a yellow legal pad, with red lines. I wrote down the chord progression and some rough lyrics to *Brand New Start*. I also added "wood-chop" to the top right hand corner. Somehow, I had to record the sound of chopping wood and use it for the beat of this song. I left the notepad on the coffee table and went back outside to finish the job.

It took three wheelbarrow loads to clean up the wood. I thought the whole time about the song and the story it should tell; about how I might shape it into a really good song.

At the end, I stood admiring the stack against the barn wall, proud of my work.

Back inside, Charlie was in the kitchen. She was standing at the counter and holding the notepad, and looked up briefly as I came in.

"'I, I felt so lost with you, was missing that spark.' Laying it on a bit thick, but at least it's from the heart. That's where the best songs come from. And it's relatable."

"Can I have that?"

"No. Go get clean. And by the way, you were really wailing at that wood, like you were splitting some evil person's head in half." She continued reading my lyrics, and smiled as she did so. "Bathroom's down the hall. Second door on the left."

Filthy and sweating, I was glad to do as I was told. The bathroom was very large, with a separate tub and shower, and two sinks. It wasn't overly feminine. There were also signs of male life. On a shelf was a razor, shaving cream, aftershave and a wooden hairbrush.

I washed my hands and splashed water on my face and neck, towelling off with a plush green hand towel. My face was sunburned, close in colour to my hair.

In the kitchen, Charlie was sitting on a stool. There was a big bowl of salad on the counter. I sat on the remaining stool, shifting it a little away from her so we had more distance. She used the wooden utensils to fill our bowls. The salad had apple, walnuts and slices of radish, which gave it some nice colour. There was also garlic bread, just out of the oven and steaming slightly.

I was very hungry.

"Dig in," she said.

I took the fork in my left hand and went to attack the salad when Charlie grabbed my wrist. She pulled it towards her a little and inspected it.

"You have great hands," she said. "Do you finger-pick? You finger-pick, don't you? With fingers like these, you better. What about taking the bass note with your thumb? You do that? Hook your thumb over the fret board? It frees up your fingers and gives you more room. You don't? Put the fork down and show me your thumb."

I was flummoxed by this exchange. I tried to pull my hand back, but Charlie held on.

"Drop the fork," she said.

"Let go of my hand."

She didn't. "Drop. The. Fork."

I let it clatter onto the counter. Charlie turned my hand over and looked at my left thumb.

"If you're not getting the bass note with this whopper," she said, "then you're letting an exceptional gift go to waste. You need to take a look at Jimmy Page. Or Jeff Buckley, God rest his soul. The sounds he could get out of a guitar. Angelic. He barred the E with his thumb. It meant he could find all sorts of shapes and harmonies around a chord's structure, throw in bits of magic whenever he liked."

She let go of my hand and I went to pick up the fork again.

Charlie ate a little and spoke with her mouth full: "Try to hold it with your thumb?"

"Excuse me?"

"Grip your fork with your thumb." She demonstrated. "I can't really do it because I don't have the thumbs for it. But try to get it in that deep groove between your thumb and index finger. And hold it in there."

I tried it.

"You got to really bend the thumb. Lock it in there. That's it. Now eat."

The fork wouldn't stay in my hand that way. I was too hungry and gave up.

We ate for a while in silence, then Charlie said, "If you make that thumb strong, it will completely change your playing. It'll make you look at the guitar differently, and write songs differently, because it'll all sound different. Please don't tell me you're another one of those earnest strummers, running through the same old open chords and singing with your eyes closed and wondering why all your songs are so dull and unoriginal."

"I finger-pick. And I've actually written some pretty good songs on this trip."

"Oh, yeah? Were you playing one when your precious Daphne got smashed?"

Halfway through my salad, I put my fork down and stopped eating.

Charlie laughed a little. She tore off some garlic bread and chewed it. "That's not good," she said.

"What isn't?"

"Being so sensitive and precious. You're a musician. If you want to write songs and play them in front of people, then you better accept there'll be people out there who don't like it. Maybe some will. Maybe they'll say you deserve to be a star. Maybe one guy will hate your music so much, he grabs your guitar and breaks it just to shut you up. That's how it goes. There are plenty of people out there who don't get

Bob Dylan and others who think Amy Winehouse was just kind of okay. It's music. Everyone can choose what they like, and they can all have an opinion on what they don't like. But if you're gonna be so sensitive about it, you should stop right now. Because if you put your music out there, you better be ready to get torn to shreds. Now, grip that fork with your thumb and eat."

I didn't move.

"And come on," Charlie continued. "If you really loved that guitar, you would've fought to the death for it."

"I did."

"And lost."

"It wasn't about the guitar, or what I was playing. There was a girl involved. The guy smashed Daphne just to prove himself to the girl and try to win her back."

"That's a bizarre way to say I love you. And I have to say that this Daphne business is also not good."

"What? Why?"

"Giving your guitar a name? I mean, Daphne? What player leaves blood on the fret board of a Daphne? It's a guitar. It's not a person and it's not your pet. It's your instrument. An artist doesn't name his paint brushes and a sculptor doesn't name his chisels. The guitar is your tool. For Jeff Buckley, it was a magic wand. The way he conjured special sounds, he was more magician than musician."

"A lot of players name their guitars."

Charlie nodded. She appeared to be really enjoying the conversation. "They do. Very famous they are too. Stevie Ray Vaughan had Lenny. Keith Richards has Micawber. The list is long. But they all mastered the guitar long before they named it."

Finished, Charlie stood up and took her bowl to the sink. She rinsed it and put it in the dishwasher.

"I'm gonna get changed," she said, taking a piece of garlic bread with her as she walked away. "We'll go into town when you're done."

Alone in the kitchen, I stared at my salad. Then, I tried to grip the fork with my thumb and index finger. It was difficult, and painful, but I made myself eat the rest of the salad that way.

I tore the sheet off the notepad and put it in my pocket.

Charlie came back in just as I finished eating. She was wearing jeans and a baggy white t-shirt.

"Ready?"

"Yeah. Thanks for lunch."

"Sorry about the lecture. I get carried away sometimes. Music is something I care about very deeply. No, leave your bowl. I'll clean it up later."

I followed Charlie out the front door and we got in the Wrangler.

Before she started the car, she asked, "You wanna stay with me?"

This took me completely by surprise and I couldn't formulate an answer.

"We can get your stuff from town and move you out here. There's plenty of room. And you wanna build that guitar, right? Daphne II, or whatever her name is. Does she already have a name?"

"Not anymore."

"Good. If it remains nameless, I might even help you build it. And you can help me with some other stuff. You did a great job with the wood. Got a solid work ethic. I like that." She started the car and backed down the driveway. "We'll figure the trade out later."

→←

I used Charlie's laptop to Skype with Churchill. I got comfortable on the sofa, in front of the fireplace, which was burning the wood that I'd cut three days ago. The television was on, showing a basketball game, the sound on mute. Charlie was in the kitchen, cleaning up and watching the game from there. I'd done the cooking, which had been the evening's trade.

Churchill came on the screen. "G'day, Rowan."

"What the hell, Church? Did you buy a tanning bed?"

"I'm happy to see you too."

"Seriously. You look like, uh, like a lot of people in Perth do."

"Leathery?"

"Not quite, but the tan suits you."

"Janette took me to the beach."

"And you went?"

"Well, I only lasted long enough to end up looking like this, which doesn't take long in this part of the world."

"Yeah, a couple of minutes if you're me. Still, I'm proud of you, Church."

"Things are kind of changing here. The outside world hasn't been looking too bad of late. Some days."

"I'm happy to hear that. How's Nana?"

"She's on a road trip down south with some fella. He's retired, but a fair bit younger than her. Your dad was here too, looking for you. I told him you're in the States."

"Did you tell him about Eris?"

He shook his head. "I think that's something you need to say yourself."

"I'll do it when I'm back. It might even include an introduction."

"Hey, no kidnapping."

"I won't do that. I know it sounds crazy, but I wouldn't rule out seeing if I can bring Eris back with me."

"Really? Where's that coming from? You haven't even found them yet."

"Just a feeling. What about Nola? Anything on her yet?"

"Nope. It's about time I followed that up again. But there was a postcard. From Des Moines."

"Where's that?"

"Iowa," Charlie shouted from the kitchen.

Churchill got closer to the webcam, close enough for me to see the skin that was peeling on his neck.

"Was that Charlie?" he asked quietly.

"Yep. Hey, Charlie. Come and meet Churchill."

She wiped her hands on a tea towel and came over to the sofa. She checked the score on the television on the way, then bent down and got into the webcam's shot. I sat back, to give her room.

"Hey there, Churchill."

"Nice to meet you, Charlie."

"Rowan's said so much about you, I feel like I know you already."

Churchill grinned a little stupidly. "He's all talk. But it's nice to see you in the flesh. And may I say that you have the single most awesome head of hair in the history of the human race."

Charlie gave me a glance. "Is he always this charming?" Then, to Churchill, she said, "You should've seen me in my younger days, when I was playing college ball. I had like a blonde fro. All the sweating and showering just made it frizzier."

"It's glorious."

"Why thank you."

"You take good care of my boy."

"He doesn't need care. He needs educating."

159

"You got that right. We need to put together a curriculum for him."

Charlie went to the fireplace, picked up the empty wood basket and went outside.

"I like her," Churchill said. "I'm very glad to see you've got yourself another teacher in your life."

"Who are the others?"

Churchill looked a little offended. "What kind of education is she giving you? Not the kind I'm thinking of, I hope."

"Come on, Church. She's old enough to be my mother."

"Yeah, and? She looks good. I wouldn't blame you. It's just the two of you out there, in the wilderness, bonding out in the barn of hers. And is that a crackling fire I can hear?"

"It is. It turned cold a few days ago. We had a frost one night."

"So, you're not, uh, you know, relearning bedroom skills?"

"Her boyfriend lives here too. Nice guy. Melvin's his name. A commercial pilot. He's away working now, but it wasn't weird at all when he was here. I think he sees me more as a live-in worker than any kind of romantic threat."

"Is that your education? Work?"

"I'm relearning some stuff, with Charlie's help. She's made me pretty much throw everything I know about guitars out the window. It's been a revelation so far. Everything's changed."

"With playing or building?"

"Playing, mostly. I was a bit sceptical at first, but I tell you, Church, she knows her onions. She's made guitars for some pretty famous musicians. She can't tell me who they are because they have contracts with big brand names and they have to use those guitars when playing live. But they use her guitars on albums and in the studio."

"What about your new guitar? What's its name again?"

"No name this time. Charlie gave me one of her guitars. It's better than anything I could make. It's a small-bodied mahogany, and it sounds sublime. I know this is weird, but it sounds just like I always wanted a guitar to sound."

"Don't they all sound pretty much the same?"

"No way."

Churchill scratched the back of his head. "She just gave you a guitar? And you didn't have to complete any sexual favours or anything?"

He said this just as Charlie came back in, carrying a basket full with wood.

"I heard that," she said. "The boy's hands are for working and playing, not fondling."

Churchill laughed. "Mate, she's awesome. So, you've been working then?"

I waited for Charlie to go out of the room. "Bloody hard. Garden work and cleaning. Charlie owns a bunch of houses here and rents them out as holiday homes. They're normally booked solid during winter and summer, but not so much the rest of the year. I'm helping her get things ready for the summer crowds."

"Is she loaded, owning all those houses and making guitars for the rich and famous?"

"Not really. Well, not that I can tell. She bought the houses during the financial downtown, for a bargain. This was her dad's house and she inherited it when he died. She was working for Martin then, which is basically the best guitar brand in the world, but she decided to quit and move back home to take care of her dad, until he died."

"She sounds like a fascinating creature. Did she say she played basketball as well?"

I picked up the laptop and turned it to show Churchill the television. "She watches games just about every evening. It's the playoffs, or something. I don't know. She keeps talking about March Madness. She told me she got a scholarship to Lehigh University, in Pennsylvania. When she graduated, she went to work in the communications department of Martin. Turned out she was more interested in making guitars than pushing the brand, so she went to work in the factory instead, really starting at the bottom and working her way up, so she said."

"Amazing. And she plays the guitar as well?"

I put the laptop back on the coffee table, on top of all the sports magazines. "Oh, yeah. She leaves me for dead. My garden and cleaning work is also earning me a half-hour lesson with her each day."

"What about building them?"

"She won't let me in her workshop. No one's allowed in. Even Melvin said he's never been in there."

"A secret lab. Must be good."

"It has to be, because she makes fantastic guitars. The one she gave me sounds like nothing else I've ever played. And with the stuff she's taught me, I'm writing lots of new songs. Or I'm rewriting my old stuff, making it better."

Charlie came back in.

"Time to make your first album, I think," Churchill said.

"Yeah. Maybe."

"You can record it here," Charlie said, tossing a few bits of wood on the fire. "I've got a studio in the barn."

"There you go. I'll leave you two to nut out the details. I'll follow up on Nola and the park."

"Thanks, Church. Nice chatting."

"Always. Take care of yourself."

"Wear sunscreen."

He hung up.

I closed the laptop and turned to Charlie. "I thought the barn was off limits, even to Melvin."

Charlie gave the basketball her attention. "He was just messing with you. Lots of people have been in there. How many songs you think you got?"

"About thirty. I'd have to think about it. Maybe take the best ten."

"And you know which ones are the best?"

"I think so."

"What you think is good may not necessarily be good when someone else hears it. Go grab your guitar. You can play me everything you got, provide the soundtrack for this blowout. These guys aren't even trying. Garbage time, put in the benchwarmers. Don't just stand there dribbling it. Pass and move." She turned to me. "You see? This is the problem with college basketball. They all think they're being scouted for the pros, so they hog the rock and try to be a star. Ruins the game, and it ruins their chances of actually being scouted, because they show they're not team players. Selfish is the worst thing a baller can be. Come on. Get your guitar. Play for me, minstrel."

I did so, tuning it in my room and grabbing my journal.

Back in the living room, Charlie had moved to the floor, sitting on the rug with her back against the sofa and her socked feet close to the fire. She had a tumbler of whiskey in her hand, with lots of ice. The bottle was on the coffee table, as was a second tumbler, full of ice.

"Pour yourself one," she said. "It'll help loosen the larynx."

I didn't think I needed it, as I'd played in the garden for an hour before cooking dinner and my voice still felt warm. I didn't need the courage either, as I believed in my songs, most of them, and was eager to play them. Still, I poured some whiskey and had a sip.

"Okay, I think we need to set some rules," Charlie said, her eyes on the game. "So we both know where we stand and we can avoid having what might turn out to be a special experience ruined by expectations. Rowan, you play. That's all you need to do. You don't have to tell me about each song and what it's about and where you got the inspiration. You just play. At the end of each song, I'll say yes, no or maybe. But don't count on there being any maybes. It's either good or it isn't. But there's a big difference between good and great, and an even bigger difference between great and fantastic. Led Zep had plenty of good songs and a couple of great ones, but they had only one *Stairway*. And no musician worth their salt puts a maybe song on an album. You want a record that people will listen to entirely, where each song gives them something. Yeah, I know, people today buy singles more than albums and music has been reduced to snack-sized form, but for you, the musician, the creator, it's the album that matters. You want a complete record, not just ten maybes and one good song. Are we clear?"

"I think so, yes."

"Good. Now, you may begin."

I started with my Daphne song, which I'd recently changed to *Goodbye Daisy*, as this name lent itself better to rhyming and ended up giving the song a more country feel. Daisy also hinted at a character who was younger, more girly and more innocent than the mature-sounding Daphne.

Charlie gave me a no before the last chord of that song faded. I was stunned.

"What? Why no?"

"It's just a bit silly, and it doesn't really go anywhere. I can tell you like it, but sometimes what you like the most is the first thing that has to go. Next."

Disappointed, I noted the rejection in that song's page in my journal. The next song, *Chasing a Shadow*, got a yes, which was heartening. So did *Brand New Start*.

"I shouldn't say this, but that's pretty good," Charlie said. "Could even be a hit that one. A kind of sleeper song, that sneaks up on you. Got a nice hook. And you have an interesting voice. Not perfect, which is a good thing. Perfection is boring, like it's a machine singing. Or it's the result of software like Auto-Tune, which is infinitely worse. Your voice is different. Like Dave Matthews, or Gord Downie of the

163

Tragically Hip. You ever heard of them? Canadian band. Really good, and they're huge across the border. They play football stadiums. And because it's just you and the guitar, your voice needs to be interesting. It needs to stand out, become an instrument itself. You should do more vocal training. And that last song needs something that'll get into your ear. Maybe mandolin, or even a banjo? Can you play those?"

"No."

"That's a shame. You should learn. Expand your playing. I can play the mandolin, and I think that'll suit the song best. Next."

On the television, another basketball game started. I continued to play, but couldn't be sure which held the most attention for Charlie: the game or my songs. Still, the more songs I played, the more I started to trust her verdict. I also got less annoyed when a song was rejected, which was good, because out of the twenty-nine songs I played, twenty-two were nos. I was surprised that two of the songs I wrote in Abel Tasman made the cut, including *Two Sticks*, which I'd always thought was cheesy and lame. Charlie's yes made me see the song differently. She also commented that the song needed sticks as percussion, or a very light clapping.

"Like someone tapping on your shoulder," she added, after I finished that song, which was the last. "Maybe just a fingernail on the guitar's body. Like a bird hitting its beak against the window. Inviting, and just a bit on the intriguing side."

I was amazed by what Charlie could hear, and potentially hear, in my songs.

It was half-time in the game and I had no more songs left. Charlie hauled herself up.

"I need ice," she said, and she took my tumbler to the kitchen as well. Her walk was slightly unsteady.

From the yeses, I made a list of songs. The seven would just about make an album. A short one, but it was still something.

This felt really good.

Back on the rug, Charlie poured us both some whiskey and we clinked glasses.

"Wanna start tomorrow?" she asked.

"Start what?"

"Recording. We'll do a song a day, see how it goes. You know your way around the studio? Can you use a mixing desk?"

"Yeah."

164

"Good. That means you won't need too much of my help. But I wanna be involved anyway. This could be something."

I couldn't quite believe it.

"What about a trade?"

She laughed, a bit drunkenly. "Oh, man. You've been here like half a week and you already know me so well. Yeah, this'll need a trade. A pretty big one. Franchise player, number one draft pick, just about. We might need agents to complete it."

"I'll work. I'll paint every house, if you want."

"Let me sleep on it." She took a long drink. "Now, tell me. Who's Eris?"

I swirled the whiskey and ice, then drank.

"And Nora? I heard you talking about them with Churchill."

"It's Nola. And she's the reason I'm over here. Well, both of them are."

"Ah, so your journey has a cause. But your buddy said no kidnapping. What did he mean by that?"

"Eris is my daughter, I think. I don't know for certain, but I'm pretty sure."

As the game continued on the television, I told Charlie about meeting Nola in New Zealand, the postcards, my trip around the States, and how I was waiting for Churchill to find out where Nola was working next, in order to finally track them down and meet Eris.

"Then what?" Charlie asked.

"I guess that will all depend on Nola and what her plans are. I've got a feeling she's got all of this planned out."

"She that kind of girl? A control freak?"

"Maybe. Yeah."

"And you holing up here is part of the plan?"

"That's an added bonus. A big bonus. Thanks for everything, Charlie."

"Gratitude is not necessary. We're trading. You're earning every good thing that comes to you. But you'll leave the minute you get the word, right? Yeah, you probably should. You've come all this way, and it's your kid. But I'll miss you, Rowan. Amazing how fast I got used to having you around. You're so handy."

"So, it's useful to have a live-in slave?"

"Easy, boy. I wouldn't throw that word around. Everything we've done so far has been fair trade."

"I have to ask. What is it with this trading?"

"You don't follow sports, do you? No, you were picked first and played worst." She gestured at the screen with her glass, its ice clinking. "Okay, in American sports, trading is a big part of getting a team together. Moving the pieces around to get what you want. It's normally like for like, but sometimes a team will try to get rid of a player they don't need, or who isn't a good fit, and use him to get a player they do need. I always liked that. It sounds straightforward, but it opens up lots of possibilities. A trade might give a player the chance to prove himself, or to get a second chance after a bad season. It works the other way too, with a trade resulting in a player going downhill and getting worse."

She watched the game for a bit, drinking her whiskey. I tried to follow the action as well, but didn't really see the appeal of giving so much effort and deploying such elaborate means just to put a ball through a net.

"But, for me, it all comes back to the simple fact that, for a long time, I had trouble saying no to people. It was like I didn't want to let anyone down. It came from playing hoops, though it drifted into all aspects of my life. Play your role for the team, whatever that role is, even if you don't like it. Put the team first, always, and be willing to make sacrifices. So, the trading was a way to stop my one-way generosity. Anytime people asked me to do something, I said we had to trade, because I wanted to keep saying yes, but wanted to stop being a pushover. You know, because then people just walk all over you. The trade was a way of asking for something in return. And guess what happened? Pretty soon, people stopped asking, because I stopped being someone who you could get something from for free."

"What about people open to trading?"

She smiled. "You mean folks like you?"

"Yeah. I'm into this. I have trouble saying no to people as well."

"That's not what this is about. You don't want to turn into a no person. Saying yes and trading became a way for me to separate out the selfish people. A kind of filtering system. And I got to stay a yes person." She pointed at the screen. "You take these guys. They're too selfish to make it playing basketball. You don't want to be on a team with guys like that. You want people willing to work with you, to share the ball and take a hit. Those willing to trade are those willing to do just that, to meet you halfway, to compromise. And those are the people I like having in my world."

I nodded, thinking this a good strategy to take back to Perth with me.

Charlie drained her glass. "By the by, you know who Eris is?"

I took the printed photo from my shirt pocket. Since Salt Lake City, I'd carried the photo with me everywhere, to the point the paper was starting to fray.

"That's her."

"She's cute. Same red hair as you. But I mean the Eris in mythology. The ancient Greeks. I did a few courses on the classics at Lehigh. Interesting stuff. Eris is the Greek goddess of chaos and discord. She's strife, causing problems wherever she goes."

"I don't know why, but that sounds like it totally fits."

Charlie got up and turned the television off. "Think on that. I'm going to bed. We're recording at dawn. If you're not awake, I'll start doing something else, so you better set your alarm if you want to make music."

→←

I was reluctant, but Charlie was forthright with her trade: drive to Dinosaur, Colorado, pick up a load of weed, bring it back to Bozeman and finish recording the album. As we'd already recorded five songs, and they sounded great, I agreed. I couldn't not agree. My first album was shaping up as something decent. Charlie was happy; she promised to mix the first five songs while I was doing the drug-run to Dinosaur.

The dope was for Melvin, who had a side-line business selling it to people in Bozeman and the surrounds, for medical purposes, he claimed. Normally, he picked up the dope himself, when he had two days off, but he had been too busy to manage this, and he also said his supplier wasn't willing to drive the fifty kilometres to meet him at the airport near Vernal, as the police in Utah were clamping down on drug trafficking. Melvin explained this was because there was an election coming up in Utah, crime a key campaign point.

Charlie wouldn't let me take her Wrangler, so I booked a rental car. The plan was to fill this car with as much dope is it could carry, while being inconspicuous enough to not attract the attention of highway patrol. Melvin said the marijuana laws in Montana and Utah were considerably stronger than in Colorado, which worried me.

"You'll be fine," he said, and he seemed very relaxed about the

167

whole thing. "Just don't rush. Drive like a normal person. Be a tourist, if you want. Take a look at Yellowstone and check out the Green River Canyon. That's in Utah, so you want to do that before you pick up the goods. When you're loaded, best to drive straight back, and only stop for coffee and gas. And don't speed."

Charlie took me into Bozeman, where I picked up the rental car. She didn't say much. Maybe it was because this trade was all about Melvin, and she was getting nothing from it. She didn't even smoke dope.

"Just think about the record," she said. "And hey, maybe you'll get a song out of all this."

My biggest fear was ending up in jail. "Maybe."

"Good luck, Rowan."

She drove off. I got my rental and headed south as the spring rain started to fall.

From Livingston, I went through Yellowstone. It was beautiful, despite the bad weather, and busy. I stopped at Old Faithful and wandered around the sulphur pools while waiting for the geyser to erupt. The tourists milled about, posing for photographs. Many of them had extendable selfie sticks.

I'd thought the park would be a place of animals and nature, but Yellowstone was very much dominated by humans. I also wasn't in the mood to be a tourist and to be among tourists. I wanted to get this trip over with, to get through unscathed. The studio was waiting for me, and I had two more songs to record.

The eruption of Old Faithful was impressive.

Back in the car, I was struggling to believe that I would soon have my very own CD, with my name on it and seven original songs. It was a huge step forward. Even if no one bought it, I was still proud to have accomplished something I'd wanted to do for years.

Charlie had a lot to do with the songs being good, but I wondered how I could ever reproduce live all the amazing sounds she'd already added to the songs. It wasn't just her mandolin playing; there was also the strange percussion elements she'd deployed. So far, she'd used the resonating twang of a bent fork prong, the smack of me chopping wood, the hollow stomp of two wooden clogs being hit together, and me clapping my guitar with one hand. Charlie somehow knew precisely which sound was needed for each song. But apart from the unique percussion and Charlie's occasional mandolin, the songs were mostly me singing and playing guitar. I really liked the raw, bare-bones nature, as did Charlie, but I'd found it hard work to get more out of my voice. I would need vocal lessons when I got back home.

My Perth to-do list was getting seriously long. I wondered how much of it I would get done if I had Eris in tow.

From Yellowstone, I drove all the way to Vernal, stopping for lunch in Jackson, and for petrol and supplies in Rock Springs. I kept to the speed limit. I didn't take any risks. I didn't listen to music. I spent almost the entire drive trying not to think about all that could go wrong on this misadventure.

I'd smoked my share of dope, especially as a teenager floating between various bands, but I wasn't a fan of the drug, and I also didn't want to be Melvin's courier.

I told myself that all I was doing was driving. An American road trip. The miles slowly ticked over.

It was close to eleven when I pulled into the Sage Motel in Vernal. I showered and collapsed. The bed had a serious dip in it, and was also short, to fit this smaller-than-usual motel room. I got myself comfortable, diagonally, and fell asleep with marijuana on my mind.

I dreamed of car-less suburban garages, with oil stains on the floor and bikes that had chains rusted stiff leaning against dusty work benches. Where spiders had spun elaborate webs between unused garden tools and old drinks fridges hummed loudly. Maybe there was a pool table set up, or a ping-pong table, or there were boxes of stuff the parents just couldn't throw away. It often meant backing a car out of the garage to make way for instruments and band members; pushing the car out, as none of us were old enough to drive. We sat on fold-out chairs, or on plastic chairs that first had to be unstacked and cleaned, with the redback spiders hosed out from underneath the seats. The band would meet with promise, spend the first few weeks smoking dope and trying to agree on a name, and talking big about how we would do something so original and memorable and brilliant that we'd conquer the music world within just a few years. Girls, money, fame, it was all right there for the taking. We just had to pick up our instruments and start playing. Instead, we filled the garages with dank smoke and talked about the music we wanted to play, the bands we wanted to emulate, the sound we aimed to achieve, and what we would do when we were rich and famous. We sat with our instruments, forever tuning up and adjusting, passing the joint or bong around, practising our poses and not our playing. An hour might be wasted deciding on a cover that everyone knew and wanted to play, because we were all ludicrously precious about which bands we would and wouldn't play. And then there was the problem that no one could really play their chosen instrument, beyond the basics, or sing all that well, or write a song. Which led to arguments and insults and stand-offs, with band members walking out; though staggering out was more accurate. Leaving members would threaten to start their own band that would crap all over this one. So I might end up a few weeks later in another garage, going through the same motions; wanting to jam and make music, but getting stoned and staring at the fishing rods hanging from the wall or at the old cricket and golf trophies. Each time, I wanted the band to work, to gel. At the very least, I wanted us to play; to pick up our instruments and tear into a cover of an Aussie band we all loved, and who cared if we got the chords wrong or the drummer couldn't keep the beat or the singer hit bum notes. Let's make some noise and see where it takes us. But it was easier, and safer, to take another pull on the joint and talk music.

I woke with this thought: it wasn't about being in a band and playing music, it was about being able to tell everyone that we were in a band. We wanted to brag, to be cool.

I lay on my back, my knees bent and my spine in the bed's dip, staring at the ceiling.

All I ever wanted was to play music. Through high school and my first few semesters of university, I drifted from one band to another, from garage to garage, bong to bong, but never finding a place. I was always welcomed into these new bands, because I could play beyond the basics and I knew a lot of covers. The other guys were normally bigger on ambition and dreams than ability and discipline. If any of these try-hard bands got a gig, it was some friend's party or event, and none of them went very well. We'd just end up making a lot of noise, the listeners hopefully drunk enough to hear it as music. Or the neighbours called the police, complained about the disturbance, and we were forced to stop.

I gave up on bands around the time I gave up on university. Both weren't for me. I didn't want to smoke anymore dope or waste my evenings and weekends in dank garages. It was better, more enjoyable and more productive to make a cup of tea and sit on my bed playing the guitar.

I got myself out of the motel's cot. My joints ached. I felt rusted. I had another shower, and I stood under the water for a long time, daunted by the prospect of another full day of driving, this time with a rental car full of drugs.

What was I doing out here?

Yesterday, I'd kept a lookout for police cars, counting almost a dozen on the various highways I drove. The police had a presence here. They weren't just about speeding tickets and driving under the influence, as they were in Perth. They patrolled the highways. I saw them pull cars over. I saw helicopters.

I didn't want to go to jail. Not here, not back home, not ever.

I towelled off, regretting that I'd negotiated such a bad trade with Charlie. I owed her a lot, but I didn't owe Melvin anything. Still, after five days of successful recording, playing in Charlie's studio and using a guitar she'd given me, I would've agreed to anything she propositioned. And it was just dope, the nothing drug. It wasn't heroin or crystal meth; the kinds of drugs that destroy families and ruin people's lives. It was for medical purposes, as Melvin had said. I'd be helping people.

As I got dressed, I thought about the last time I smoked marijuana. It was with Nola. We were on a beach somewhere in Abel Tasman, with a campfire going, looking up at the stars. She expertly rolled a joint, using a small stash of dope she said she kept for special occasions. It was good quality, dense and rich, only requiring a few tokes to make me light-headed and languid. Perth weed, by comparison, really was that: weed. It was weak and dry. A lot of deep inhaling, and a fair bit of acting, was required before the walls started to move and things got blurry. This was local dope, Nola had said, and it was smooth and mellow. The situation was also right for it, with the beach and the stars. We talked a lot that night; getting stoned helped Nola drop a few of her barriers and made her more talkative. She told me a bit about her background and childhood.

But all I could remember now was the scene and not what she'd said. I tried, picturing the water and the fire's flames. Nola lying next to me, our shoulders touching, our legs entangled. The heavy smoke hanging in the still night air. Nola tried to draw shapes in the smoke before it dissipated. And she hummed a song, over and over. An old power ballad. The kind of song that brought groans when it was played on the radio, but which everyone secretly liked despite its cheesiness.

What was that song? Was it some kind of clue?

I spent more time than usual combing my hair, to make myself presentable. I didn't want to look like a stoner when transporting a car full of marijuana.

"Baby, please don't go."

That line was in the song, somewhere. But it wasn't the blues track of that name. It was just a line from the song. A slow song, a sad song.

Outside, the morning was foggy, but warm. It was early. I had to ring a bell at the motel's reception in order to hand my key in. When I asked, the receptionist recommended Bwana's Café in Jensen for breakfast. As it was on the way to Dinosaur, I could stop there before picking up the dope.

I got myself into the rental car. My shoulders, neck and back were all sore. Still, part of me was glad not be chasing Nola and Eris across this huge country.

Eris. Where was my little Greek goddess of chaos? How was she doing? Had Churchill found out the location of Nola's next park job?

I found the café and had blueberry pancakes. I ate quickly, wanting to be back in Bozeman before sunset.

Dinosaur was fifteen minutes down the road. There wasn't much to the town. The makeshift houses and squat buildings seemed to hunch against the wind.

I thought the place was too dry and arid for growing marijuana.

The street names were fun. From Brontosaurus Boulevard, I turned onto Antrodemus Alley, then onto Triceratops Terrace. As I drove through the town, I saw few signs of life. There weren't even any dogs roaming from one fenceless yard to another.

I wondered if the locals were collectively slow to get started in the mornings.

The house was just off Triceratops. Up close, I saw it wasn't a house, but three trailers combined to form an L-shaped structure that resembled a house. Behind it was a large building, which I assumed was the greenhouse where they grew all the dope.

Out of the car and under the shade of one trailer's awning, I saw a sign next to the door: Morganic Jam.

I was struck by the awful thought that this could all be the set up for some twisted prank, organised by Charlie and Melvin. I imagined Melvin going to such lengths, but not Charlie.

I knocked on the screen door.

It was good to be in the shade. The morning was already hot, and the rental car's air-conditioning didn't work.

The door was opened by a young girl, about seven or eight, but she stayed behind the screen door. Through the mesh, I saw that she was wearing yellow pyjamas that had small fish on them and, somewhat appropriately, was clutching a stuffed dinosaur. One of the big herbivores, with a long neck and tail. She held it by the tail and swung it back and forth.

"Are you Rowan?" she asked from the doorway.

"Yes, I am. It's cool that you know my name."

She gave me a smile, then pouted. "You're early."

"I know. My bad. I have a long way to go today and I kind of wanted to get started. I have to drive all the way to Montana."

"I've been there."

"Is that right? You're quite the little traveller."

She nodded and swung the dinosaur. "You talk funny."

"I don't mean to. It's just my accent. I'm from Australia. We all sound like this."

"Oustraya," she said, aping me.

"Hold your nose and say it."

She did so, repeating the word, more nasally, and following through with a giggle.

"Perfect. Sounds just like me."

She grinned.

A woman appeared behind her, wearing a purple robe. She placed an arm around the little girl's shoulders.

"This is Rowan," the girl said, looking up. "He's from Oustraya."

"Are you Shelley Morgan?"

The woman nodded. "What did Melvin tell you to say?"

"He never came back from Cottonwood Road."

She rolled her eyes. "Yeah, he sure does love his eighties rock, doesn't he? Well, it's all right here, packed and ready to go."

"Great."

She swung the screen door open. The little girl stepped down from the trailer and came up next to me. She hit me softly in the leg with her stuffed dinosaur, still swinging it by the tail. I looked down and gave her a smile, and she craned her neck to look up at me, like I was a giant.

"You want some coffee?" Shelley asked. "Stop that Lacey."

The dinosaur continued to beat against my knees. Through the open screen door, I could see several stacks of boxes, all with Morganic Jam written on the side in old-fashioned lettering. I wondered if it would all fit in the car.

"Actually, I really don't mean to be rude, but I'd like to load up and get going. I have about ten hours of driving ahead of me."

"Nervous?"

"A little, yeah."

"Good. You're not one of these arrogant kids who suddenly thinks he's the king because he's delivering a few boxes of jam. They're the ones most likely to get caught. But you, I think you'll be alright."

I found this very good to hear. "I hope so."

"Don't worry. The first time is the easiest, as long as you keep your eyes open and act normally. You got guys out there, they've been driving dope for years, but they're lazy. They make mistakes, think they'll never get caught."

"I just want to get this over with."

"You sound like it'll be just this one time."

"It will be."

"Yeah, they all say that. A shame, though. Lacey seems to like you. And she's pretty picky about who she hits with that dinosaur of hers."

As she said that, Lacey stopped.

"You want to see my room?" the little girl asked.

"Come inside, sweetheart," the woman said. "Let him get to work."

She motioned for me to come in as well. The little girl followed me up the two steps. Inside, the trailer was cool, the air-conditioner running, but the air was still musty with sleep. I had Shelley in her early thirties. She was pretty, in a homely kind of way; looking more like a school teacher than a dope grower. Given the derelict state of the town, I wondered if she was the prettiest girl in Dinosaur.

I pointed at one of the boxes. "Is this for cover?"

"No. It's real. I make jam. And I grow marijuana. You get one guess as to which brings in the most money."

She opened one of the boxes, showing the Mason jars of jam stacked inside. She removed a couple, revealing more jars underneath, which held the weed.

"It keeps better in these jars, stays fresh," she said. "They also make it harder for sniffer dogs to pick up."

"That's clever."

174

"And don't think the jam's for nothing. A bit of weed goes into my jams as well, which is why Melvin sells a lot of it to his dopeheads."

"I think I've had some of that jam."

"Did it make the morning seem longer?"

"Yeah."

"Then you had it. Lot of people say my jam makes the time stretch, which is one of the reasons they like it." She taped the box shut, and added, "You better take one of the back roads. The police have been patrolling the highways near the state lines. That's why I can't meet Melvin at the airport in Vernal anymore."

"What do you suggest?"

"Go south, on the Sixty-four. Then take a right onto the Twenty-one. There's no sign, but if you cross the railroad bridge, that means you've gone too far."

"Okay. Thanks for the tip."

"You should be fine to take the Twenty-one all the way to Bonanza, then circle back up to Vernal. Your safest route would be Snake John Reef, but that's all dirt and I don't think your little car can handle that. You might get lost as well, and then you'd be in real trouble, with nothing but my jam to survive on."

"It would be an interesting trip, though."

She laughed, and was even prettier when she did so. "You sure you don't want some coffee? I can make you a cup while you're loading up."

Chatting with Shelley was calming my nerves. "That'd be great. Thanks."

"Good," she said cheerfully. Then, to her daughter, "You stay out of the way, Lacey."

I grabbed the first box. It was heavy. I got my hands underneath it, as I was worried all the jars might fall through the bottom. Lacey tried to help, but as she couldn't carry a box, despite having a go at it, she held the screen door open for me.

Three boxes went into the small boot. I then started putting boxes on the back seat. Even with Morganic Jam on the sides, this struck me as exceedingly suspicious, and I rued not renting a van. The last two boxes went on the front passenger seat. I secured them with the seatbelt, to prevent them from moving around.

When finished, I stood with Lacey under the shade of the awning.

"How come you're so tall?" she asked, craning her neck again to look up at me.

"I don't know. I just am. I always was."

"You're like a dinosaur."

"That's good, isn't it?"

She nodded.

"But you know what? My brother's not nearly as tall as I am. And I'm a head taller than my dad, and two heads taller than my mum. No one knows where my height comes from. I'm a freak."

"An Oustrayan freak."

"Yep. Australis Freakasaurus."

This made Lacey laugh really loudly, and it was such a nice sound to hear. I lumbered after her a little, trying to move like a dinosaur. She squealed with delight as she evaded my grasp.

Shelley came outside, cups of coffee in her hands. "What's going on out here?" she asked, smiling.

"We're just playing. A kind of dinosaur game."

Lacey ran around me saying, "Freakasaurus. Freakasaurus. Freakasaurus."

"If I didn't know better, I'd say she's in love," Shelley said, and she handed me a cup.

"One good joke and I'm suddenly popular."

"Well, she's a little starved of male attention."

I expected Shelley to elaborate on that, but she said nothing more and watched her daughter circling me. Lacey eventually got dizzy and had to sit down on the trailer's bottom step. Her cheeks were red. She leaned back and put her elbows on the second step.

Shelley and I sipped our coffees and looked at the fully loaded car.

"Maybe you should think of yourself as my travelling sales rep," she said. "You're out there, on the road, selling my jam. It's all business."

"I promise I won't do any sampling on the way."

"Be careful, Rowan. It's no secret what I'm doing here. The local police are alright. Some of them even buy my stuff, the jam and the dope. But once you get out of Colorado, you'll need to be really watchful."

"That's reassuring."

"I wouldn't want to see a nice guy like you get busted."

I drank the coffee quickly, wanting the road, and handed the cup back to Shelley. "Thanks."

"Good luck."

As I walked out of the awning's shade and towards the car, Lacey ran after me. She stopped in front and wrapped her arms around my legs.

"Goodbye, Freakasaurus," she said.

Family Disunion

It costs more, and there's some hassle involved, but she decides to take the train. This requires getting up very early for the ninety-minute bus ride from Des Moines to Ottumwa, then a switch to the California Zephyr. The bus is just about empty, given the early hour, enabling her to lay her daughter across two seats at the front of the bus and let the little girl sleep with her head on the pink daypack.

That journey passes without event.

When on the train, she tries to relax. It's more comfortable than the bus, but the train's big plus is that it stops in Naperville, which will save them from going all the way to downtown Chicago. Her daughter can also move around and engage with the other kids in the wagon, which means she can stop being a parent, if only for short bursts.

She's appreciative of the temporary respite, but also conflicted. Since Vancouver, and that brilliant project she executed, they've been a pretty good team. Eris has behaved herself and been less demanding. Letting loose all those paper coffin boats on the Des Moines River, each with a little plastic pig inside, was fun. They folded all those boats together, and her daughter came up with a name for each pig, which was then written on the side of the boat.

She reminds herself that the good times won't last. That's been her experience; any good week is normally followed by several bad ones, when her daughter morphs into a demon who cries and whines and requires drugging. It's during those weeks she just wants to leave the kid wherever they are and walk away.

The fact that she'll now get to do that in Chicago makes her smile. She wonders if her daughter is aware that their time together is coming to an end, for now; that the next six months will be spent in the Hinsdale house. It's doubtful, though the little girl has previously exhibited a level of perception and awareness she considers unusual for a child of such an age.

At least the house will be familiar. Once there, she thinks it won't take long for her daughter to settle and become aware of her surroundings and what it means. Then she can leave, without fanfare, when everyone's asleep.

She assumes that Warren will be the one to meet them at the

station in Naperville, as he loves driving that old Mustang of his, and he's also the one who likes Eris the most.

In previous years, she'd been only too glad to arrive at the house on Glendale Avenue, dump Eris and drive away in her old Bronco, without even lowering the window to wave goodbye. But this time, something's different. Something more final. Whatever it is, and despite any closeness she might be feeling, she knows she needs a break from the kid. She needs silence, to focus all of her attention on herself. To make decisions just for her and without having to factor in her little girl.

The journey takes most of the day. Through the window, the world that flashes by is both exceedingly plain and fascinating in its plainness. The cornfields and dusty lots. The ample spaces for farming and working, but where no work is being done. The mid-west, in stasis. They pass through small towns with buildings that huddle around the train station or a bend in a river. There are trucks on the interstates, following close behind and looking from a distance like they're strung together.

It doesn't inspire any sense of homecoming. It doesn't fill any kind of hole inside her. It only reminds her of what she's always felt: that she'd been born in the wrong place. And it was from that very first day that the chaos began. Chicago was never right, and she was always a disruptive element, out of place, lost, angry and confused. On all her travels and at all the different places she'd worked and through all the cities where she'd tried to bring her particular brand of chaos, she'd yet to find the place that felt right. That place where things made sense; where she could sit and breathe and be calm, and the chaos would stop.

Her enthusiasm for searching for that place has waned. And with age has come cynicism. She's starting to think that such a place doesn't exist and that she'll spend a lifetime searching for something that's not there and never was.

Since Eris was born and they started travelling together, she feels like she has experienced every place through her daughter. So many decisions have been made around the little girl, and nearly every day shaped to meet her never-ending needs.

Being a mother, for her, is hard work, but it's not the work that makes her yearn to be free. She simply wants to stop experiencing through her daughter. She wants to see the world and feel things unfiltered. For the next six months, she'll get that, and she can't wait.

She wonders whether permanent separation is the solution. This has been on her mind for over a year. With her daughter due to start elementary school next year, she knows she'll have to make a decision on this. It's a decision that might also require a settling of sorts, for a life and a location, in one place. She has no idea what that life would be or where it would be lived. Chicago is not her world, but it would be handy being close to the Hinsdale house. This would mean giving up being an artist and a park ranger. It would also mean potentially living the next two decades in frustration, as she'd spent her first two.

She decides that this can't be an option. Her daughter's stable life be damned: she would go crazy living permanently in Chicago, becoming something like her own mother, who she considers the last person on the planet worth emulating.

She needs freedom, she knows this. Inspiration requires different scenery and different challenges, and the search has to continue. Her place is out there, somewhere in the world. It's just a matter of finding it.

And there's still so much art for her to create.

Her daughter comes back to the seat and plonks herself down, explaining something about a family at the end of the wagon, with games and a boy who doesn't like to lose, whose parents just let him win.

"It's not fair," Eris says.

The little girl goes on to talk about the dad, who kept making funny faces, but who actually looked scary, when he was making faces and when he wasn't.

She finds this interesting: that a man with a scary face tries to pull a funny face, so he doesn't look as scary anymore, but looks scary no matter what he does.

But then she gives her daughter a marshmallow and this shuts her up.

"We're going home," she says. "You know that, don't you? The house. Helen and Warren and Cyril. They are all excited to see you."

Eris chews and nods.

She finds the girl's blank expression hard to read.

"How do you feel about it? Does it feel nice to be going home? You'll have your own room again. All your toys and stuff. Your own bed."

She says all this without any emotion in her voice; she doesn't try to make the place sound inviting. Her daughter shrugs and holds out her hand for another marshmallow.

She complies, taking two from the sticky bag. "They'll be happy to see you. Maybe they'll be happy to see both of us. No. More you than me. I'm barely a blip on their radar. That's probably a good thing."

Eris puts both marshmallows in her mouth and screws up her face a little, not understanding.

She turns away from her daughter's rather disgusting chewing and the white globule seen through the gap in her little mouth, and looks out the window. Once past Aurora, the train starts to slow down. Chicago's western suburbs show the affluence and poverty of the city, and how there's not much in between: the big houses on the winding avenues, lanes and crescents, and the derelict buildings, grimy apartment blocks and wrecking yards on the broad streets and roads. The front yards immaculate or strewn with trash. Cars washed and shiny or rusted and up on blocks. It's something she's always hated about Chicago, but she's come to learn over the years it could be applied to the majority of America's big cities. The people are either doing very well or seriously struggling.

Eris wants another marshmallow.

She puts the bag away, but the little hand remains extended and insistent.

"We're nearly there," she says, standing up. "We need to get ready. Don't make that face. Get you daypack on. Eris, I'm warning you. When we get there, you can eat all the sweets you want. I'm pretty sure Warren has stocked up for your arrival."

"I like Warren."

"I bet you do." She grabs her big backpack from the rack above. "The sugar daddy is always the king."

"Is Warren my daddy?"

"No. Lord, no, no, no. A sugar daddy is someone who, uh, you know. Oh, forget it. He spoils you. Simple as that. But Warren's not your dad."

The mere thought of having sex with someone like Warren causes her to feel ill.

As usual, her daughter feigns helplessness. She is forced to assist with getting the little girl's arms through the straps of the daypack. She does, however, feel some satisfaction that Eris hasn't once complained about having to carry the bag. She wouldn't call it pride, but she's relieved that in this one case, the girl didn't make trouble.

She gets her own pack on, working in a tight space as other passengers preparing to disembark in Naperville put their jackets on and get their luggage down from the racks. Some talk on phones and lean across other passengers to look out the window, trying to locate the people picking them up. Others move forward, wanting to be the first off the train. She finds it disappointing that she has to get back into big city mode, which involves extending her elbows a little and being more forthright and physical with her personal space. Because she knows that in Chicago, as in other American cities, getting pushed around just results in getting even more pushed around, so it's necessary to stand firm and push back.

She's glad it will only be for a few days. Then she can escape north.

As the train slows and pulls into the station, she sees Warren's cream Mustang in the parking lot, its black top up. But there's no sign of Warren. In previous years, he stood in the car park, leaning against the car as if waiting to be photographed. She assumes he's on the platform.

When the train comes to a complete stop, people are rather impatient to get off, and those wanting to be first have the most luggage.

The platform is crowded and chaotic, as people try to find each other or weave between others blocking the way. In the crowd, she holds her daughter's hand and walks towards the car park, pulling the little girl along.

The train inches forward and slowly departs.

It's good to get off the platform and away from the people.

The Mustang is a beacon of style and class in a car park full of SUVs and pick-ups. When those vehicles start moving, they jostle in a way uncannily similar to how the people behaved on the platform.

"Sweet home Chicago," she sings to herself.

She puts her backpack down and leans it against the Mustang's front bumper. She sits on the bonnet, the car's suspension creaking under her weight. Her daughter runs around the car park. She should tell the little girl to be careful and watch out for cars, but doesn't. Eventually, Eris climbs up onto the Mustang's bonnet and sits next to her.

"Don't move," a voice says from behind her.

She turns. "Helen? What are you doing here?"

"I'm happy to see you too." Helen, wearing an expansive red and purple dress, raises her phone and taps a few times at the screen. After checking the shot, she adds, "Nice. That's a keeper."

Eris jumps off the car and runs to Helen. "Grandma."

The little girl wraps her arms around Helen's legs, almost getting lost in the folds of the dress. Helen recoils just slightly, then gives the girl's head a solitary pat.

It hurts to watch her mother behave like that, as it sparks so many bad memories.

"Why does she keep calling me that?" Helen asks.

"I guess she forgot, Grandma."

"Don't you do it too. Last time, I told her to stop it."

"Eris," she says, pulling her daughter's arm back from Helen's legs, "from now on, Grandma will be Helen. Okay? That's what she wants. Call her Helen."

"My, my. Sounds like this little family's turned into the military. Are you gonna make her drop and do a hundred push-ups if she calls me Grandma?"

"It's more likely that you'll say something like that. You're the one who doesn't want to be Grandma."

"Ouch."

"It's the only way she understands," she says. "Honesty works."

Helen takes a few steps backwards to appraise the little girl.

She knows this look only too well: the arms folded, the eyes narrowing, the left leg slightly forward and her weight on the right as she leans back, valuing. Every detail is taken in, every change noted, the person or thing given a monetary value.

"And? How much would she go for?"

"Stop that," Helen says. "You can be so nasty sometimes. Anyway, she's about the same. What's different is you. Not exactly proud of your work, are you? Or are you just worn out from all the touring?"

"There's that, because we did a lot of miles." She lowers her voice and adds, "I think I've moved on too. Just about."

"Yes, it happens. One day's all-encompassing passion is tomorrow's passing whim." Helen offers a thin smile, then looks at Eris. "But you could at least try to take better care of her."

"How would you know what that is?"

"She looks wrecked. And so do you."

"We've been on the road for months. That's not easy when you're dragging a little kid around."

Helen scoffs. "Well, she looks sufficiently dragged around. I assume she's my problem now and you'll go off and live in a cave somewhere."

"I'm working, and I start in a few days. No doubt my income will come in handy."

"For Eris, yes." Helen moves around the car and opens the boot. "Where are you going this time?"

"Isle Royale. Up near Thunder Bay."

"Is that the island park in Lake Superior?"

She puts the backpack and daypack in the boot. "Yep."

"I think we went there once. Hard to recall, as we were all on mushrooms. I remember it was very green. Cyril kept saying, 'Everything's so green,' and giggled like a little girl. I do remember Warren trying to swim back to the mainland. He shouted, 'I'm gonna swim to Canada.' He nearly drowned."

"Where is Warren? He never lets anyone drive his car."

"Yes, Warren." Helen closes the boot. "He died."

"What? Why didn't you say anything?"

"As if you'd just drop everything and come rushing back for the funeral. You didn't do that for Arnie and I seriously doubt you'll do it for me."

The fact that Helen's right makes her smile. But it also makes her angry, as it reminds her of that awful childhood in Wicker Park, growing up in that massive loft with parents far more interested in their own artistic endeavours and projects than in raising a child; the loft that was divided into three working areas, with hers the smallest, and the other two places more for fighting than working. From the earliest she can remember, she had been left pretty much to fend for herself.

"I'll take your complete lack of denial as agreement," Helen says, getting into the car.

She opens the passenger door and moves the front seat, allowing her daughter to climb into the back seat, where she lies down and gets comfortable. She gets in the front.

"With Arnie, I was in New Zealand, way off the track. It would've taken me days to get back, and there was no way I could've made it in time."

"Yes. That's true. Though I'm sure you would've used the same excuse if you had been nearby." Helen puts her sunglasses on and starts the engine. "But I guess it said a lot more about Arnie than it did about you. He was a terrible parent."

"Speak for yourself."

"Arnie had the time for it. I didn't. We agreed from the start he would take care of you."

She doesn't reply, in order to avoid digging further into that can of worms, and she knows it's useless trying to talk about the past with Helen.

From the station, they drive down Washington Street and get onto Ogden Avenue. It's mid-afternoon and the traffic is reasonably light.

Helen drives fast.

Eris sleeps in the back.

She thinks Helen looks very comfortable behind the wheel of Warren's car, which is appropriate, as her mother always liked the nice things she got for nothing. Helen has the window down and her left elbow perched on the door. The wind blows her hair around her face.

She finds it curious how driving this old car has the effect of making Helen seem younger. The long, loose and recently dyed hair also helps.

"What happened to Warren?" she asks.

Helen tucks a few auburn strands behind her ears, then moves her sunglasses up onto her head.

"It was just one of those things," Helen says. "We went to bed together, the three of us, and everything was normal. The next morning, he didn't wake up. They said it was his heart, or something. I wasn't really listening, because I was in shock. Warren always slept in the middle, and he had been there all night, dead between me and Cyril. It was awful."

"I'm sorry."

"That's nice of you to say, even if you don't mean it. Cyril was very sad, and he's still suffering. They were together for nearly forty years, do you know that?" Helen looks at her. "No, you never really cared about them, or their story. And you look to me like you've already got one foot on Isle Royale."

"Helen, it's been a really long day. I'm just tired."

"I bet you can't wait to dump this kid on me. Well, there's a problem now, because it was Warren who always took care of Eris. Who's going to do it now that he's gone?"

"I can't take her with me, you know that."

"No, you don't want to take her. There's a difference."

She looks out the window, at the passing churches and car washes and wheel-balancing centres, hating Helen because she's right. It was

Warren who made it possible to leave Eris in Chicago. She's intrigued by what chaos will result when Helen takes over Warren's role.

Ogden Avenue is no place for putting her thoughts together. She can't think straight when looking at all these petrol stations, pawnshops and fast food joints. There are also several specialist megastores, including a huge shop selling just cleaning supplies, another for pet food, and one that rents out garden machinery. She finds the excess stunning, and gets a pang of guilt that she's leaving Eris among all this excess, and now with Helen as her main guardian.

It's a rare moment, but she feels sorry for her daughter.

"I've been thinking," Helen says.

That sentence, heard at critical junctures in her life, makes her shudder. "Please don't do that."

"I want you to move in with us."

"Oh God, no freaking way."

"Hear me out."

"No, don't start."

But Helen is already off on her tangent and can't be stopped. "It's better than it sounds, and it could solve a lot of problems in one hit. We cleared out Warren's workspace, so you could have your own studio."

"To do what? The world is my studio."

She notices that Helen is so stuck on her own train of thought, that she's not listening, and might not even being paying attention to the road ahead, as the car is drifting in the lane.

"You'll need to kick in some money," Helen continues, "as any live-in artist would. You'll have access to a fantastic studio, and you can get expert advice from Cyril and me. I'm pretty sure you could also get a job at one of the local parks, to earn a steady income, because there's really not much money in art at the moment."

"Helen, stop it."

Her mother ploughs on: "I think this would be very good for Eris. You need to think of her, to put her first. But it would also be good for you. Both of you would benefit so much from settling down and spending all your time together. It must be terrible for Eris to have you leave for half the year or longer."

"Not as bad as being flat out ignored by both parents when they're in the same apartment."

"That was a long time ago, Nolene. Things were very different then. We were living from hand to mouth. We worked so hard. It was a constant struggle, and you were seriously demanding."

"Please, don't talk about my childhood like that. You're completely rewriting history as you speak. And don't ever make it my fault that you and Arnie were the world's worst parents."

"That's so harsh."

"But if I understand you correctly, you just want me to replace Warren and save you from having to take care of Eris."

As Helen's anger rises, the car begins to speed up. "She's your daughter. You should be the one taking care of her. I want you to give her some stability. She needs it, and so do you."

"That's super interesting coming from you. What do you think? Shall we give Eris the same stability you and Arnie gave me in Wicker Park? You know, a loft full of alcohol and drugs, with strangers sleeping on the floor and people coming and going at all hours."

Helen smiles, looking like she recalls those days fondly. She slows down and moves the Mustang into the right lane.

"You should be glad that I didn't get fooled around with by one of those strangers. But if I had, you never would've noticed."

"You're exaggerating," Helen says. "It was never as bad as you think it was. And look at the life it gave you. You didn't grow up like other kids did, with helicopter parents full of expectations. Those kids already had their lives lived for them, and now they're all in the therapy. But you, you were lucky that we let you take your life in whatever direction you wanted."

"Alright then. Good. This is the direction I chose. You helped to put us in this situation, so now you're going to have to deal with it. But, if you don't want to take care of Eris, then just say so. You don't have to come up with an elaborate plan to get me to stay, one which makes you into some kind of art guru dolling out favours to a selected few. Because you're not that. You're far, far, far from that."

"Don't talk to me like that, Nolene."

"I'll talk however I want. Warren's gone and I'm sorry about that. But if you're hell-bent on continuing to live your totally self-centred life, then we can call this the last time, because I'm committed to the Isle Royale job and have to go through with it. In the fall, I'll come back, pick Eris up and you won't have to worry about either of us again. But what you really shouldn't do is conjure this whole scheme about us all living together like a big family, or make it sound like you're gonna turn me into the artist you want me to be."

"I would never do that," Helen says. "You are already the artist you want to be."

"Thank you. That might just be the nicest thing you've ever said to me."

Helen gives her a look, one that's almost loving, then turns back to the road. "I just think you should stop wasting your creative energy on the temporary."

"It's not temporary. I photographed everything. There are videos too."

"This isn't all some kind of master plan to get you to stay. A studio would allow you the space to create something lasting and substantial. Much more than some mural on the side of a building that gets painted over, or some act of chaos that's forgotten a few hours later."

"Hey, they're still protesting in Vancouver."

"That's not art. What you did was art, but the fallout isn't. You should be making something you can sell. Something people want."

"Are you really someone to give this kind of advice? Helen, you only ever made one big sale, and that's because you slept with the rich old bastard whose portrait you painted."

"It was enough to buy my house."

"My God, you sound proud of yourself. That house is a permanent reminder of how you got it."

Helen laughs a little and lowers her sunglasses. "You always were such a moralist."

They drive for a while in silence, this last sentence hanging in the air.

She's reminded of how fruitless it is to argue with Helen, or even to discuss things with her. And it seems every argument refers back to some past event or memory that she doesn't want to relive.

"Is this part of it?" Helen asks at last.

"Part of what?"

"One of your acts of chaos. Are we in the middle of it? Are we living your art? If we are, it's going well. You should photograph this."

"Helen, as you already thought all of this through without discussing it with me or even considering how I might react, or even what Eris might think, I'd say you're making this chaos all by yourself."

They pass through Lisle and Downers Grove, and under the bridge of the Kingery Highway, from where they leave the megastores behind and the roadside scenery starts to improve. It's all familiar, but not exactly comforting. She's a stranger here, a transient.

When they reach Hinsdale, Ogden Avenue is lined with trees. The area is nice, but she knows that's just the exterior. There are plenty of secrets and lies beneath the handsome packaging.

Helen turns onto Madison Avenue when the traffic light is red and drives along the cemetery. The Mustang struggles a little up the hill.

"Is Warren buried in Bronswood?" she asks.

"He's currently on the mantle above the fireplace," Helen says, and her voice is flat and cold. "He wanted to be cremated, and we couldn't just put him in the earth. Cyril can't bring himself to do anything with Warren's ashes. I keep telling him he needs to move on."

She wonders if Cyril might have cause to leave the house on Glendale Avenue, as bisexual Warren was the threesome's linchpin. The adapter.

"Didn't Warren ask for his ashes to be scattered somewhere?"

"Not that I know of," Helen says, turning onto Glendale. "I'll talk to Cyril. Maybe you can take the urn up to Isle Royale and scatter Warren in the lake. Let him float to Canada."

"I'm not doing that."

"You are so unreasonable, Nolene. You're like a brick wall. If I'm going to devote my life to your kid for the next six months, then you can do this one very small thing for me. And because you're working nearby, I expect you to come back every couple of weeks and help me out."

"It's a day's drive from here to Copper Harbour, and the ferry takes three hours as well. I can't just pop down for the weekend. I'd need at least three days off."

"I'm sure you can manage that once a month. It would make Eris happy, I'm sure."

"Stop using my daughter as a means of getting what you want. Look, I'll try to visit, and I'll send you the money for preschool."

"You need to sort that out before you leave," Helen says, pulling into the driveway and stopping in front of the house.

"I know. I will." She looks over her shoulder to see if her daughter is still asleep. "It would be good for her to get some discipline and mix with other kids. I'll find it for you, but you'll have to be the one who takes her there the first time, to set the rhythm."

"I don't know if you remember, but I tried to take you to day-care once. You made such a scene."

She thinks Helen is lying. "You and Arnie never had enough money for day-care."

"For a while we did."

"Well, I don't remember that, but I can understand it if I behaved that way. Everything was wrong when I was kid, so it's no wonder I tried to protest, in my own way."

"Your whole childhood was one long protest," Helen says. "It was like a permanent sit-in. You even made signs. You remember that?"

"I do. You sold them at a flea-market."

Helen smiles. "It's good that Eris isn't too much like you. I'm guessing her father's a placid type, not nearly as restless or antagonistic. Will I ever get to meet him? Or is that not part of the project?"

"We'll have to see what happens."

"Hard to believe she'll start school next year. What will you do then?"

"To be honest, Helen, I don't know. But it looks like I won't have to factor you in. I'll have plenty of time at Isle Royale to think about it."

"You want some mushrooms, to help you get some clarity? They always help me get my thoughts in order."

She laughs at this, loud enough to wake Eris.

They all get out of the car. Eris is slow to get going and wants to be carried.

As it's been a long day of travel, with the last half hour proving particularly stressful, and because having to deal with one of the girl's tantrums is the last thing she needs, she complies. But with carrying Eris and the backpack pulling at her shoulders, she struggles under the weight.

Helen grabs the pink daypack, shuts the boot and leads the way inside.

She finds the house remarkably changed; not because furniture has been moved or any renovations done, but because the atmosphere is so different. She can't quite believe that Warren's absence would have such an impact. On the mantle above the fireplace, a lone candle is flickering next to a silver urn; she assumes this holds Warren's ashes.

Helen drops the daypack on the table. "Make yourself comfortable. No borders in this house," she says, breezing through the living room and heading for her studio.

"Isn't she wonderful?" she says, putting her daughter down. "One day, you're probably gonna blame me for a lot of things, but I hope we can sit together and blame her."

"Where's Warren?" Eris asks.

"Well, hmm, Warren's on a trip. A long one. You can ask Helen about it, because she's an expert on trips."

Eris goes straight for her room. It's in the same state they left it: orderly disarray.

She puts the backpack on the floor. "Why don't you continue your nap? I have some errands to run. When I'm back, we'll have dinner with Helen and Cyril."

"Okay."

Eris climbs into bed.

The sheets smell fresh, which make her conclude, along with the candle and Cyril's mourning, that it's not that long ago that Warren died. He was already preparing for their arrival. As her daughter gets comfortable, she's tempted to lean down and give her a kiss, but doesn't.

In the kitchen, she's surprised to see Helen standing there, and even more surprised that her mother has prepared two glasses of Chai tea, with frothy milk.

"For you," Helen says, sliding a glass across the counter.

"Thanks." She sips, tasting nothing but cinnamon. The act of generosity makes her wary. "Where's Cyril? I'd like to say hello."

Helen, with both hands around the glass and the froth inches from her nose, shrugs. "Not here. I checked his workspace. He's probably out walking. He does that a lot these days, in Bronswood, of all places. I'm starting to think he might need to go into a home."

"And then there was one," she says, thinking Helen would be quite happy with that; not to be alone in the house, but to be the survivor, the last one standing.

"I'd certainly miss Cyril," Helen says. "Of course, with him gone, and with you not moving in, I could rent the studios out to other artists. Bring in some youth. Turn the house into an artist's colony, and maybe even set it up as a foundation. To get some state funding."

"Sounds like you thought that through as well. You had a contingency plan for me turning down your offer."

"I knew I wouldn't be able to rely on you. You're impossible to plan around. But, as this is clearly not what you want, then I'll respect that and bring in people who actually appreciate the house, and me."

191

The milk has taken the heat out of the tea and she drinks it quickly, leaving a finger of froth at the bottom that's tan with cinnamon.

"Thanks for the tea," she says. "I'll be back in an hour. I'm going to check out a few local kindergartens."

"Good. Make sure it's close by, and that it doesn't have any kind of religious angle. By the way, I liked what you did in Tulsa."

The compliment is hard for her to take. "That barely made a dent in God's very thick armour."

"It was clever. Can't imagine how much work it was."

"I was up all night in the hope I'd shake people awake, and failed completely."

"They don't want that. I'm pretty sure the potential wrath of God and their unanswered prayers are what keep them awake at night. Funny how some people can think they're saved when they aren't even worth saving."

She thinks this is a horrible thing to say, but keeps that to herself. "Where are my keys?"

Helen puts down her glass and opens a kitchen drawer. "I hope it starts. I haven't driven it for a few weeks."

She has two keys: one for her old Bronco and one for the safety deposit box she has at the Liberty Bank on Logan Square. It feels good to have both keys in her hand. Things seem possible with these two keys.

"Have you been driving the Mustang instead?"

Helen gives her a demure smile, one that offers a glimpse to the beautiful woman she remembers from her childhood; the woman who was always so distant and out of reach, like a Hollywood starlet.

"Wouldn't you?"

"I guess I would. But shouldn't the car now belong to Cyril?"

"He can't drive," Helen says. "Warren wanted me to have it."

"But he didn't let anyone drive it. Why do you think he'd be happy that the car is now yours?"

"Better me than a stranger."

She lets it go. "I'll be back later."

"Bring dinner. Thai preferably, but not too hot. Cyril can't really stomach spicy food anymore."

"Yes, ma'am."

The Bronco is in the garage, with a fine layer of dust covering its water-green paint. She's missed it.

The engine starts, and she lets it idle while removing all traces of her mother from the car. Helen, as is her habit, had taken over this space and made it her own. She takes a cardboard box and fills it with her mother's detritus: a pair of sunglasses, flyers from art exhibitions, two coffee cups, one sandal, some clothes, and plenty of rubbish.

She does a quick search on her phone of pre-schools in the area, and they come up as points on the screen's map. The closest to her mother's house is the Village Children's Academy on Elm Street, which prompts all sorts of nightmarish thoughts.

Out of the garage, she drives down Glendale Avenue with all the windows open, to get Helen's smell out as well. On Washington Street, she heads south, through a neighbourhood that's leafy and attractive, the front lawns trimmed and neat, the large houses in excellent condition.

Not for the first time, she thinks about how there's something quietly evil in this suburban presentation; the horror behind the lustrous facade. The residents of Hinsdale putting on a show, living the way they think they're supposed to, and in a way that everyone expects them to; behaving that way as well. Playing a role for their entire lives, and maybe even aware of it. She knows this is a harsh assessment, but it's one that justifies her decision to not live here.

Because Chicago will always be a place she escapes.

At the Village Children's Academy, all the children have already gone home for the day. She's shown around by a matronly middle-aged woman wearing a floor-length floral dress who exudes a kind of scheming control. She talks a lot about child enrichment, emphasises the importance of diversity and outlines their dynamic program of learning opportunities, speaking in a bright, sing-song voice as she would to a five year-old.

This well-delivered pitch comes down to money in the end. Enrichment, opportunity and diversity don't come cheap, but she thinks the Academy will be good for her daughter's development. She likes the order and scheduling; this isn't a place where kids are let loose and tasked with discovering what it is they're good at. She enrols Eris for the next six months, from nine in the morning to one in the afternoon, and signs all the forms, saying she'll come back later and pay cash. The promise of full payment, in cash, results in the matron cranking her friendliness up a notch.

"Would you like some coffee? A cup for the road?"

"I'm good, thanks."

"We can offer you a ten percent discount if you pay cash."

"Great. I'll go to the bank and be back shortly."

"We cannot wait to welcome your beautiful daughter into our fold."

She can't get out of there fast enough. While presented as the epitome of order, she wonders how much chaos her daughter will bring to the Village Children's Academy.

Getting the cash requires a trip to the Liberty Bank. So, for the next half-hour, Chicago is all roads: the Tri-State Tollway, the CKC and Kennedy Expressways, lots of traffic. She gets off at Fullerton Avenue, hating the city, and loving it as well. Loving its unstoppable chaos. Fighting with the traffic makes her aggressive, makes her local. She becomes just another person in a vehicle trying to get somewhere, like all the other one-person vehicles on the roads.

The Liberty Bank offers some respite, once she finds a place to park, which requires fifteen minutes of circling. As she circles, she imagines she's scoping the bank ahead of robbing it.

She continues scoping inside, checking where the cameras are and counting the security guards. It's fun.

Eventually, she gets down to business, and a bank teller leads her to the quiet area behind the counters, to where the safety deposit boxes are. She's left alone. While no one seems to use these anymore, the throw-back nature of safety deposit boxes appeals to her: a secret hiding spot. It's somewhere to store an escape plan. In such a box, another identity can be kept in a secure place, along with a pile of cash to start anew. She finds something exciting about all these boxes holding other identities, and not simply old family heirlooms too precious to keep at home, or important documents like wills and deeds. She wants each box to hold a new person, like hers does, and not the remnants of old people.

She opens her box and takes out the unused passport, the fake documents that back up the alter-ego on that passport, and the three yellow envelopes, each with ten thousand dollars inside. She toys with the passport, flipping through the blank pages, contemplating the freedom it offers and enamoured by the possibility of escape. Not just the chance to wipe the canvas clean and get a new start, but to become a completely different person. She imagines creating and crafting that person, adding colours and layers and texture, perfecting herself; a living work of art.

It's difficult, but she puts the passport back in the box.

"Only in case of emergency," she says, taking one of the yellow envelopes instead and closing the box.

More roads, going back the way she came, and more traffic, as she joins the mass exodus from downtown to the suburbs; people making their own daily escape. She's tempted to detour down Milwaukee Avenue, to drive past the old loft on Le Moyne Street, and to see if the Wabansia Avenue building where she, Kim and the W-Crew squatted is still there, but decides the past is best left alone. She thinks it's all probably been laid to waste anyhow, all those old buildings, to make way for some kind of money-generating urban renewal project. And as it's been over an hour already, her mother is probably wondering where dinner is.

On the way back, she makes two stops. The first is at the Village Children's Academy, where she hands the matron a wad of cash.

"Now, you take good care of my precious little daughter," she says.

The second stop as at the Thai place on York Road. She considers ordering extra chilli, for the added chaos it might bring to Cyril's stomach, but thinks this would just be cruel, and Cyril's already suffering enough, having lost Warren and now living alone with the unbearable Helen. This is something she's about to subject her daughter to as well, but she can't quite muster the required guilt and sympathy to do something about it.

She just wants to leave. Every hour spent in Chicago seems like wasted time.

Back at the house, the kitchen and living room are empty. The candle continues to burn. Nothing has been set up for dinner.

She puts the bags on the counter and goes to her daughter's room. The bed is empty, the room already more of a mess than it was before. She finds them both in Helen's studio, which is packed with projects: pottery, paintings, sculptures, even wood carvings. Some are quite good, but she likens the studio to a storage room where a more accomplished artist stores failures.

Eris has found some space to sprawl on the floor, lying on her stomach, her small feet kicking in the air. She's drawing with crayons. Helen is hunched over her old pottery wheel, working the lever with her foot as she shapes some kind of elaborate vase.

Her mother, who has clay up to her elbows, bits of it in her hair and a streak down her left cheek, doesn't look up as she comes in. It's tempting to back out of the studio, unnoticed, and eat dinner in peace. But she looks down at her daughter's rather impressive drawing.

"Pigs in boats," she says. "Just like in Des Moines. That was fun, wasn't it?"

Pointing with an index finger smeared with red crayon, Eris says, "This one is Harold and this one is Benji."

The pigs look more like dogs. "You've done the boats very well," she says. "Excellent lines."

She looks at her mother, who continues shaping the vase, her head tilted forward and ever so slightly bobbing to the rhythm of the wheel.

"I brought dinner," she says loudly, but her mother doesn't look up.

Eris drops her crayon, breaking it, and gets to her feet.

"There are paper plates in the kitchen," Helen says. "I'll be there in a minute. I want to finish this first."

She keeps her distance from her daughter, not wanting to get smeared by those crayon-covered fingers. "What about Cyril? Is he back from his walk?"

"I don't believe so."

"Should we wait for him?"

"I think not."

She sends her daughter to the bathroom to wash her hands and goes into the kitchen to set up dinner. In one drawer, she finds a stack of paper plates, along with packets of plastic cutlery. She serves herself and Eris, and they eat together at the table in silence. The takeaway Thai, steaming from plastic containers, combined with the disposable plates, makes this meal feel like a rained-out picnic; the promise of an outdoor dinner in the sun replaced by a makeshift dinner indoors.

Being in the house makes her skin crawl, but she's glad that her daughter appears comfortable, as that will make things easier.

Cyril's absence is also unsettling. Despite thinking her mother a complete whack-job for hooking up with a gay couple and inviting them to live with her in a house earned through art-whoring, she still finds it sad that the Glendale Avenue household is disintegrating. Despite everything, it also hurts that Helen stays in her studio, more interested in shaping some crappy vase than eating with them and asking about their cross-continent escapade. The hurt she feels is old and painful, dating all the way back to when she was her daughter's age, because hurt is her earliest memory. She'd like to turn the hurt into anger, which she could let loose on her self-centred mother, but she knows all too well it's not worth the trouble, as Helen doesn't get it, never got it, and won't listen in order to get it.

When finished, she puts the paper plates and cutlery in the garbage. All the leftovers get resealed and put in the fridge for microwaving later.

Eris demands dessert, but the fridge only has a few essentials, while the freezer is full of frozen meals.

The best she can do is retrieve the bag of marshmallows and hope a handful will be enough to sate her daughter's sweet tooth. She takes the bag into Helen's studio. Eris follows, already happily chewing one. As they enter, Helen comes from the other direction, now with streaks of clay on both cheeks, as well as one on her forehead.

"I'm ready for dinner," Helen says. "Let me have a shower and then we can eat."

"We're finished."

"Why didn't you wait? It was only five minutes."

"More like fifty."

Annoyed, Helen goes into the bathroom and closes the door.

"And you think you got it tough," she says to Eris. "Look at what I had to deal with growing up. Imagine having that every single day, and Arnie was no better."

Eris chews, her mouth slightly open.

"Now try to picture those two in the same apartment together. Both living in their own worlds, on their own time, doing whatever they wanted, and expecting everyone to adapt to them. Like two suns, each with their own solar system. And the rest of us were planets expected to circle them forever."

"I want another one," Eris says, holding out her hands.

"They even talked about their circles. Arnie had his ice-sculpting circle and his drift wood whittling circle and his experimental noise circle, and Helen had her Tunisian mosaic circle and her penis photography circle and her evil-twin self-portrait circle. These circles changed from year to year, but often they interlocked, like Venn diagrams, and those few who were in all the circles made a special little circle of their own."

She proffers the bag of marshmallows, leaning down to her daughter who is back sprawled on the floor, drawing with crayons again. The little fingers smudge red onto the two marshmallows she takes.

"Of course, I had no idea what it was all about, or how messed up the situation was." She wanders around the studio, looking at the various works-in-progress, picking items up and putting them down again. "By the time I was teenager, and having seen the way other kids my age lived, I started to understand. It was all for show. They never really got anything done. They talked way more about art than they ever produced anything. And selling, well you can forget about that. Arnie's family owned the building, so we got to live there for free. The only money he ever made was from making miniature wooden railway engines and carriages, but he hated doing it. Helen sometimes got photography jobs for *Pink Magazine,* which was how she met Cyril and Warren."

She looks down at her daughter, drawing happily and not listening.

"But this house, my little one," she continues, "this is Helen's greatest achievement. And it had nothing to do with artistic merit. Because your grandma was once very beautiful, and she used that beauty to become a high-class art whore, who screwed for projects and big commissions. She worked her way up, and down, until she landed one very big client."

Eris raises her head and looks confused.

"Yeah, I don't really get her either. She's a total sell-out. I've tried my best to forget it all, but being around her, it all comes back. My chaos childhood."

She's tempted to completely trash the studio. To break every single thing in there. She picks up what looks like an old-fashioned piss-pot and gets ready to hurl it against the wall, but something stops her. It's the realisation that destroying all this so-called art would result in giving the art, and Helen, more attention than deserved.

She gently places the piss-pot back on a shelf, now feeling sorry for her mother. Actually, feeling really sorry for her. To live as a struggling artist is hard enough, but she can't quite fathom how hard it would be to spend a lifetime as a struggling bad artist. It's an unusual feeling, to have sympathy for Helen, who was always far more interested in being an artist than actually producing work of value and merit, and who relied heavily on those more appreciative of her physical beauty than of any beautiful objects she might create.

"I remember there was this one exhibition, for the evil twins. The only people who came were in one of her circles. So, it was basically just a love-in for Helen. An alignment of her planets. I guess it's too bad all those planets are slowly dying off. But Helen lives on, continuing to put her art above people."

She wonders what Cyril will do. Has he already picked out a plot in Bronswood and now spends his days patrolling it?

Not my problem, she thinks.

From the kitchen, she hears Helen opening and closing the refrigerator, and getting the microwave going. She knows her mother would like some company while eating, but as sitting at the table with her could potentially lead to more arguments, she decides to stay in the studio. She sits down, takes a blank piece of sketch paper, the rough, cheap kind, and grabs a brown crayon from the scattering on the floor.

The trunks of trees come first, then the branches, as she sweeps the crayon across the paper with fluid strokes. The lines are perfect, the dimensions exact. Her daughter stops her drawing to watch.

The foliage is shaded in with the dark green crayon, denser here, thinner there, making it appear that the trees are moving with the wind, or maybe leaning close together, like people chatting. The light green crayon gives the trees more texture, more variation, because each tree is different, in age and character. Then, the blue crayon surrounds the trees with water, and the dark green on the blue shows the reflection of the trees shimmering on the water.

"That's nice," Eris says.

She stares at it. "I think it might just qualify as better than anything in this studio. But you probably shouldn't tell Helen I said that."

She wants to go to this place: an island of trees. Alone in nature, cut off from the world by water. A place without suburbs, expressways and schedules. Without planets and circles.

The overwhelming desire to hug a tree makes her smile. She decides to leave tomorrow morning, at dawn.

"Eris, listen to me."

The little girl looks up.

"I promise you that this will be the last time you stay in this house. I have to go away and work again, so you and Helen have some money, but when the job is over, I'll come back and we'll leave this place forever. Okay?"

"But I like it here."

"Good. That's really good. I'm happy about that."

"I miss Warren."

"So do I." She stands up. "I'm going to take a shower. Are you alright to keep drawing in here on your own?"

Eris nods.

"That's my girl."

She leaves two marshmallows on a blank area of her drawing and takes the bag with her. Passing the kitchen, she sees her mother eating from a paper plate and reading from a magazine, as if she and Eris weren't even there.

It's a relief to wash away the day: the buses, trains and roads. But she doesn't dawdle in the shower, because there's a lot of sorting to do, which includes getting all her park ranger gear together. She does this wrapped in a towel, and does it ruthlessly, throwing a lot of stuff into a large garbage bag. This feels good, to remove the clutter and free herself from this house. She doesn't want to be dependent on Helen, and she also wants to shorten her final departure later in the year.

But she thinks her mother is also right: it's not so bad that Isle Royale is reasonably close by. Something is bound to go wrong in the next six months, as Helen will definitely put her own art and lifestyle ahead of Eris. She sees her mother forgetting to take Eris to pre-school, or forgetting to pick her up; Helen so caught up in herself that Eris gets forgotten altogether. An empty fridge, take-out for dinner eaten off paper plates, clothes worn once and then thrown away to avoid doing laundry until there are no more clothes left.

Her only hope is Cyril, but he has yet to surface.

With the backpack repacked and ready, and two garbage bags full, Eris comes into the room, holding a drawing in her hand.

She assumes it's something her daughter did, but it's her sketch of the island of trees.

"You like that?"

Eris nods.

"That's where I'm going. I'll be working at a park that looks like that."

"Can I come?"

"No, you have a job of your own here. To look after Grandma. Uh, Helen. To look after Helen. It's a big responsibility. Do you think you can handle it?"

More nodding.

"You're becoming such a big girl. I know you can do it, and Helen needs a lot of help. With Warren on his long trip, you could now be the most responsible person in this house."

And that's a pretty scary idea, she thinks.

Still wrapped in the towel, she grabs a garbage bag in each hand.

"Go clean yourself up. Have a quick shower and brush your teeth. It's time for bed."

"Okay."

The way Eris so easily complies in the familiar surrounds of this house, after weeks of making trouble on the road, convinces her that the little girl needs more stability. Which means Helen was right about that too.

She takes the garbage bags outside and puts them in the back of the Bronco, to be dumped somewhere on the way to Copper Harbour. With few remnants of her life left in the house, she's getting a sense of finality, and also thinks the household won't last much longer. She envisions her mother dumping Cyril in a care facility for seniors and renting the studios out to other, younger artists; or, Helen will sell the house and move back to Wicker Park, in an attempt to recapture the glories of those days, though the rents there have become astronomical since all the yuppie hipsters moved in, and Helen would struggle to afford it.

Back inside, she stands in the doorway of her mother's studio. Helen is sitting at her pottery wheel, hands at her sides, just staring at the vase as it slowly spins around.

That glazed stare makes her wonder if Helen added a few magic mushrooms when reheating the Thai dinner.

A small hand grabs hers and pulls her out of the doorway. Eris is clean and dressed for bed.

"Good girl," she says. "You did that all by yourself."

They walk hand in hand to Eris's room.

"Tell me about the island," Eris says, getting into bed.

She knows too well that her daughter doesn't like stories and has an acute awareness of when things are made up. Eris prefers to have things described, like places, situations, past experiences and memories. Having researched the park extensively before her Skype interview, she has a lot of information to share.

"Okay. North of Chicago, there's a really big lake," she says. "So big, they call it Lake Superior. We were at this lake not long ago, together, when we were in Thunder Bay. Do you remember? The rock that was called the Sleeping Giant?"

"I remember."

"In the middle of this lake, there's an island. It's about fifty miles long, but only nine miles wide. It's like a long thumb. But there are also lots of smaller islands nearby. The islands are covered with trees, and there are wolves and moose. Because the main island is hard to reach, there aren't that many other animals. The moose can swim there, and the wolves walk across the lake when it's frozen. But bears aren't able to swim or walk that far. It's an isolated place, and not so easy to get to."

She stops, as her daughter is asleep. She pulls the blanket up a little more. Again, it's tempting to bend down and kiss her, and she does it this time, closing the chapter. With her mat rolled out, she gets into her sleeping bag, naked, enjoying the hardness of the floor. It feels like it's straightening her spine, and makes her imagine that she's floating.

Eyes closed, she pictures being at Isle Royale, alone among the trees, surrounded by silence.

She sleeps better than she has in weeks, on her back, but wakes before her alarm goes off. She rolls away the sleeping bag and mat, doing this slowly and carefully, in order to not wake her daughter.

At just before six, she's dressed and ready to go, her backpack on. She takes one last look at Eris sleeping in the bed, then walks out.

In the kitchen, Cyril is sitting at the table, a bare paper plate in front of him. He looks up when she enters.

"Good morning," she whispers.

"Trying to escape before anyone sees you?"

"That's about right."

Cyril smiles and says, "Don't worry. I won't sound the alarm."

"I'm sorry about Warren."

"Thank you. He loved Eris, you know, like she was his own daughter. He always wanted to have kids."

"What about you?"

While he looks sad, she thinks Cyril is not quite the quivering bundle of potential senility that Helen made him out to be.

"I like kids, but Eris doesn't like me. At least, not in the way she liked Warren."

When he stands up, she sees Cyril has lost quite a bit of weight. "You look good."

"It's the walking. Shall we talk outside? I can see you don't want to wake anyone."

She leads Cyril out of the house and to the garage. She puts her backpack on the Bronco's rear seat and gets in the front. Cyril sits in the passenger seat.

"You wanna go somewhere?" she asks. "I can drive you."

"There are so many places, I don't where to start. Warren hated to travel."

"Well, now's your chance. You pick a place and go there."

"You sound like Helen."

This comment nearly makes her kick Cyril out of the car. "Careful," she says.

"So adamant that things are easy and doable," Cyril continues. "As if she's an upstanding example of that."

"Yeah, Helen's full of the worst kind of crap, and always has been. You should know her well enough to be aware of that."

Cyril stares straight ahead. "I was never really into this. Moving out here. But I didn't want to lose Warren. At the time, it seemed like a wild thing to do, a new kind of family, one that would spice things up. We thought we'd reinvent the American dream."

She's not really interested in hearing Cyril's confession or in bonding with someone else whose life Helen has screwed up. She wants the road. She wants breakfast in a ramshackle diner halfway to Milwaukee, crispy bacon and syrupy pancakes. She wants to hear college radio pumping through the Bronco's speakers. She wants to make the last ferry leaving Copper Harbour, and to be surrounded by trees and water by nightfall.

"So, what's next then?" she asks. "Will you leave? I wouldn't blame you."

"Do you want that? It will mean leaving Eris alone with Helen."

"I guess I'll have to see how Helen responds. Maybe she'll surprise me. Maybe it'll be complete chaos."

"You sound like you want that," Cyril says. "The chaos."

"It would be interesting."

"Well, it's coming, because I'm moving out. I've met someone. I just don't know how to tell Helen."

"I wouldn't worry too much about breaking her heart. She only ever cares about one thing and that's Helen. So, I suggest you go in there, wake her up and tell her straight. She was always for this bohemian lifestyle and sleeping with anything and everyone. And if I were you, I'd get out of that house and start again while you're still young enough to do so. In a couple of years, that motivation might be gone. You don't want to grow old with Helen, that's for sure."

"But you say all that and you're leaving Eris here. With her."

"It's the last time. I'm pretty sure that in six months from now, they'll both be happy when I come back and take Eris away for good. Sure, it would be nice if you stick around for a while and help out, but if you'd rather run, and I wouldn't blame you if you did, then do that."

Cyril gives her a studious look. He's still handsome and boyish, and given that Warren was no looker, she wonders how they ever ended up together.

"What did Helen do to you?" he asks. "There's something off about you. I've always been a little scared, to tell the truth. I never know what's going to come out of your mouth or what you're going to do next."

"I think that's the nicest thing you've ever said to me, Cyril. Now get out of my car."

She starts the engine and has the car in reverse before Cyril gets out. She thinks he looks confused and shocked, and more than a little helpless, but tells herself not to care.

Not my problem, she thinks, backing out of the garage. She heads down the drive and turns left onto Glendale Avenue.

The Middle Eight

Nana picked me out of the crowd of arrivals, as we were funnelled towards the assembled family and friends. She was almost unrecognisable under her broad-brimmed hat, and she waved at me with the back of her hand, her fingernails painted dark red.

I put my backpack and guitar down so we could hug. Given all that had happened in the last few months, it felt really nice to wrap my arms around a member of my family.

"It's so good to see you, Rowan," she said. "But you look a little different."

"So do you. I mean, you look great."

"And you look tired. Was the flight that bad?"

"It was three flights in all, plus five hours lying around the airport in Sydney. But I was tired before I got on the first plane. The last few days really wore me out. A lot of travelling."

"Well, it's good that you're home."

"Yeah, it is."

"Are you ready?" Nana asked. "I think I could stand here all day. It's fascinating watching all these people go through their overly emotional welcomings."

I shouldered my backpack and followed Nana outside. She carried my guitar, having brushed my hand away when I tried to take it from her.

The sun hurt my eyes. It glared off shiny cars and windowed walkways. I was also struck by the dryness as I breathed in the desert air and looked at the locals who appeared to have had all the moisture removed from their skin. They were weather-worn and squinting, freckled and tanned. I'd missed that look, and it reminded me I was one of them.

As I'd taken the first flight from Sydney, I was in Perth around mid-morning. But I had no idea what time it actually felt like, or what day it should be. Or even what season. I'd gone from rainy Isle Royale to humid Minneapolis to the very cold Sydney airport, and was now in Perth, where it was supposed to be just about winter, but everyone was in shorts and t-shirts.

Nana crossed the street and paid for her parking. "You won't believe it, but Churchill is here."

"What? I don't believe it."

"He's in the car. He really wanted to be here to meet you, but when we arrived, he couldn't get out. I didn't know what to do with him and your flight was landing, so I left him there."

"Did you lower some windows? He might cook in there."

"Oh, I left him some water, just in case."

"But seriously, he's here, out of the house? That's a huge achievement."

We started walking across the car park. The people arriving and departing pushed trolleys laden with luggage, with the bags piled on top requiring one hand to steady them while the trolley was pushed with the other. The people looked more like they were relocating than going overseas for a holiday. But as Perth is so isolated, it's no wonder any journey away from here is more an expedition than a trip, requiring more luggage.

"I had to park further away," Nana said. "All the spaces here were too small."

"Have you been driving a lot?"

"Yes, but it's not so easy around the city."

"Maybe you should sell the Statesman and get a smaller car."

Nana shook her head. "I'm not selling. Rory and I drove down to Denmark together, and the old girl was great on the open road."

"You or the car?"

"I'd say both."

We crossed the road to the second area of the car park, which was empty except for Nana's boat, parked diagonally across three spaces. I could see the Statesman's rear windows were halfway down.

"Is Rory your boyfriend? Is it serious?"

"We've been seeing each other for a few weeks. No need for you to learn any wedding songs just yet."

"That would require going way back to before Elvis."

Nana gave me a playful scowl. "Careful, you."

"Churchill said you've gone through a few blokes in the last couple of weeks."

"Well, it's hard to find a good man these days. You could say a lot of them are seventy going on ninety. They're lonely and behave a bit too much like very old men. I think most of them are just looking for someone so they don't end up dying alone. I can understand it, but there's not much that's romantic about that."

"What about Rory?"

"He's younger. Got a bit more life in him."

We reached the car and Nana opened the copious boot. I half-expected to see Churchill in there. I put my backpack and guitar inside and closed the boot.

Before getting in, I looked through the half-open back window. Churchill was lying foetally on the seat. He had sunglasses on and wore the grey hoodie that was his preferred article of clothing for venturing outside. He had the hood up over his head.

I was very proud of him that he'd made it this far from Shenton Park. It had to be a record.

When I got in the car and closed the door, Churchill asked, "Is that you, Rowan? I've managed to get myself into an imaginary bubble, but if I open my eyes, I think the bubble might disappear and all hell will break loose."

"It's me, Church. Thanks for coming to the airport. It makes you some kind of a superhero in my book."

"I wanted to come inside. Really, I did. I had it all worked out. Pam did a drive-by when we got here, but there were too many people. Too much stimuli. It was like a mosh-pit in there. I couldn't do it."

Nana started the car and manoeuvred the Statesman out of the car park, driving with her broad-brimmed hat still on.

"Hey, you made it all the way out here. If you couldn't manage the last few metres, I don't care. We're a long way from home and I'm impressed."

"Thanks, Rowan."

The wide Statesman only just made it through the barrier to exit the car park. But the car's size did put Nana in close proximity to the ticket slot, while other drivers in smaller cars had to reach or lean out the window to insert their tickets.

"Jeanette's been pushing to get me out of the house more," Churchill said. "Dare I say that woman is trying to change me."

"For the better, I'm sure. How's it going?"

"It depends."

As we negotiated the first roundabout, Nana giving a couple in a white rental that was all over the road plenty of space, Churchill sat up. But he did so like a blind man, moving slowly and feeling for the seat's edge.

"I find it easier at some places," he said. "The open spaces are okay, but not when there are lots people. I can do the beach, for short periods during the week, but whenever there are people, I feel like they're closing in on me. Like, getting really close to me even if they're not moving at all. It's hard to explain, but I can say it's not a nice feeling."

"I think it's great that you're trying."

"So do I," Nana said. "You're never too old to change. I came home a few weeks ago and found him on the roof."

"That was a test," Churchill said. "I was trying to gauge if the world was different up there. And what I can report is that our neighbours get up to some pretty weird stuff in their backyards."

Nana turned the car onto Tonkin Highway and floored it.

I put a hand on the dashboard. "Take it easy, Nana."

"This is the fun part," she said. "This is what she likes. Open road."

It was amazing to see how confident my seventy-two year-old grandmother was behind the wheel of this huge car.

"How fast are we going?" Churchill asked. "It doesn't feel like much."

"We're over the speed limit."

"You're both such wimps," Nana said, passing a truck.

Churchill slowly leaned forward and rested his elbows on the front bench-seat. I could see through the sunglasses that he still had his eyes firmly closed.

"What happened at Isle Royale?" he asked. "When you said you were coming back, I wasn't expecting it to be just you."

"Oh, did you find that girl of yours?" Nana asked.

I looked at Churchill. "How much does she know?"

"Not everything."

"He kept me updated. I can't wait to hear this record of yours."

"It's not ready yet. Charlie's still doing the mix. And I've got to do something about the jacket before I can start printing any CDs." I turned to Churchill. "Did you tell her about Eris?"

He shook his head.

"Is Eris your old girlfriend?"

I gave Nana a quick version of the New Zealand story, meeting Nola, and how I'd gone to the States to find Eris and confirm she was my daughter.

"Why didn't you say all this before you left?" Nana asked.

"Because I wasn't sure if Eris really was mine. A lot of it was just conjecture. And I wasn't even sure I'd find Nola."

"Okay," Churchill said, "now that our chauffeur is up to speed, can you tell us what happened? You went to Isle Royale and found Nola. Then what? You wouldn't tell me on the phone and I've been dying to know."

"She said Eris was with her mother. Nola's mother. But she wouldn't say where that was."

Nana turned off the highway and stopped at a set of traffic lights. "So, you went all that way and didn't meet your daughter?"

I nodded, feeling the disappointment all over again. "Nola said it wasn't time. We had a big argument about it, standing at the top of a lighthouse, of all places. I pleaded with her, but she wouldn't listen. She said I wasn't ready."

"That's a stupid thing to say," Nana said, moving the car forward when the light turned green. "When is anyone ever ready to become a parent?"

"Well, according to Nola, I'm not. She was very clear that she didn't want me to meet Eris. At least, not yet. The postcards were just to get me thinking. She didn't expect that I'd try to find her. It was a real shock for her when I showed up at Isle Royale. Her plan was to contact me at the end of the year. She was amazed when I told her I'd followed them across the country."

"We followed them," Churchill corrected. "We chased them across America. I felt like I was with you every step of the way, except when you had Nikki with you."

"I'm getting lost in all these names," Nana said. "Who's Nikki?"

"You don't need to remember that name, Nana. It was just a travel fling."

"I'd call it a mistake," Churchill said. "And it cost you your guitar as well. Precious Daphne."

"Not such a bad thing in the end. The guitar Charlie gave me is way better. And if Daphne hadn't got smashed, I never would've met Charlie."

"Which makes Nikki part of that equation too."

"Yep. Meeting Charlie was the best thing that happened on the trip. She got me more interested in playing than building. She taught me a lot of good stuff."

"I gotta meet her one day," Churchill said. "Sounds like a hell of a gal. You're still in contact, right?"

"We are, but I didn't exactly leave in a good way."

"Because you just dropped everything to go to Isle Royale?"

"No, it was, uh, I'll tell you later about that."

This annoyed Nana and made her drive faster. "You think I can't handle your dirty stories? Did you have an affair with this Charlie?"

"She's old enough to be my mother."

"So? She can be young of heart and you can be old of mind, and you meet in the middle."

"I didn't put it so eloquently, Pam, but I told him pretty much the same thing."

"We didn't have an affair. God, you two are like a couple of gossiping housewives. Anyway, I had to do something for Charlie, to pay her back for helping with the record and for using her studio and a bunch of other stuff."

"What was the trade?" Churchill asked.

"Her boyfriend, Melvin. I told you about him."

"The pilot."

"Well, he's more than that. Turned out he's got a side-line business selling dope, and jam too. But the dope's his focus. It's supposed to be for medical purposes. He said something about the laws of Montana not allowing people to use it that way, and that he's actually helping out lots of people and not just some drug dealer."

"That's good of him," Nana said. "I have a few friends who smoke medical marijuana. They say it helps a lot."

"Did Charlie make you sell dope?" Churchill asked.

"No, I had to get it, which involved driving to Melvin's supplier in Colorado, and driving all the way back with the car full of it."

"That's mad," Churchill said.

I decided to tell Churchill more about that trip later. "It was."

"But you're here, so it all went okay."

"I was lucky. I certainly didn't drive like this. Nana, there are speed cameras all over the place around here. Slow down."

We were now on the freeway, with Perth's skyline in view. It felt really good to be home; to be in this car, with these two people, en route to my house and my bed.

"I never drive more than seven over the limit," Nana said. "Rory told me to do that."

"Rory," Churchill said disdainfully. "Pam, you can do so much better than him."

"You should give him a chance. Or are you just jealous, Churchill?"

"You wish." He shook his head. "But if you did the dope run without any harm, what went sour when you left?"

I thought back to my last night in Bozeman, arguing with Charlie about Isle Royale. She was adamant that it wouldn't make any difference, and that Eris wouldn't be there, as a remote national park was no place for a little girl. She also said it would be better for me to stay and work on the mix with her.

"I guess you could say our trade negotiations broke down. She said I was wasting my time chasing after Nola. If people want to be found, they let people find them. They don't send cryptic postcards with nothing on them. That's what she said."

"And it turned out she was right, but I still think it was awesome how we followed that trail and found Nola in the end."

"Yeah. It was. Thanks to you, Church."

This made him grin. "But she's stilling working on your record."

"She is. I'm going to write to her, try to fix things. We became good friends while I was there, and I don't want to lose that. But I really didn't like doing that drug run for Melvin. I think that's what got me angry in the first place."

"Well, even with all of that, and despite not seeing Eris in the flesh, I'm calling your trip a massive success. And I'm very glad you're back."

This was really nice to hear. "Thanks, Church."

"But now you're back, what's the plan?"

Through those three flights, I'd thought very hard about this: what was I going to do in Perth? I was sure Jono had given my job to someone else, as I'd be gone for so long. That was fine, because I didn't want to go back to the shop. I wanted to give music a shot. Busk on the streets, sell CDs, try to get some gigs, write more songs, and turn myself into a full-time musician. If it failed, I could always fall back on repairing and building guitars, if not in Jono's shop, then somewhere else.

"Rowan? Since when did you become so quiet and thoughtful?"

"I think for the next few months, I'm going to concentrate on my music."

"Great. Lot of money in that," Churchill said. "I'm all for conjugal serenades, but I'm not supporting you through your struggling artist phase. And according to your bank statements, you should be going straight back to work. Tomorrow."

I hadn't expected such a response from him, and couldn't really reply. Churchill was way out of his comfort zone and not coping well, and I had to be lenient because of that, but his lack of support made me defensive, and my fatigue turned this into anger.

"Did you contact Jono already?" Churchill asked.

"No. I'm not working there again, and I'm not asking you to support me. I'll find a way. I'll teach little kids how to play the guitar, if necessary. And you wait until you hear my album. It's actually pretty good."

"It better be, if you want to live from it."

"Don't listen to him," Nana said. "If you want to follow your dream, you go for it. If you don't, you might spend the rest of your life wondering. And that's no way to live."

Nana's vote of confidence calmed me down a little. "That's what I was thinking. I want to try, especially now with a CD of my own. This could be the only chance I get."

"Alright, alright," Churchill said. "I'll help where I can."

That was good, but I was still annoyed with him. "I can manage things on my own for now."

"I think we can quite easily get ground control into the music business. How hard it can be? Look at what we managed to achieve while you were in the States. I turned travel arranging into detective work."

"This is different."

Nana exited the freeway at Loftus Street. "You're a great team," she said. "I'm sure you'll find a way to make it happen."

I wasn't so sure. I felt like this was something I needed to do myself. There was also the fact that when I hooked up with Nikki and when I was hitch-hiking, meeting people, and surviving on my own, I didn't really need Churchill's help anymore. I was actually better off without it, as I could follow my instincts, make spontaneous decisions, stay in control and see for myself where the journey would lead, and that journey had led me down Cottonwood Road in Bozeman.

I wanted the same for my music journey. It had to be mine.

"What about Eris?" Churchill asked. "I hope you haven't given up on her."

"Nola wants to meet again, at the end of the year. In Europe."

"Jesus, she sure does get around."

"She liked the idea that I was following them, and she wants to do it again. She said, 'Find us in Europe,' and I think this time Eris will be the reward. She didn't say it outright, but I have a strong feeling she wants me to take care of Eris. Permanently."

"She hasn't even let you meet her yet? And now you think she just wants to give her to you? What kind of mother is she? You make Nola sound like a total fruitcake."

"You're not far off, Church. When I got to Isle Royale, I was stunned to discover that she was a lot weirder than I remembered. Just about with a screw loose, you know, but somehow functional. I don't know what I saw in her in New Zealand, but she was definitely different then."

"Less unhinged?"

"Yep. And I reckon it's Eris. Nola doesn't want to be a parent. She told me all about what a relief it was to leave Eris with her mother. But she also said her mother's not able to take care of Eris, and that this would be the last time she would stay there. That's where I come in, I think."

"She's planning to leave Eris with you while she does her park ranger work?"

"No, I reckon it'll be for good. I know it's all just an assumption, but my instincts tell me I'm right."

"Sounds to me like you're okay with it," Nana said.

"I would be, if it happens like that. But I'm not committing until I meet Eris and I'm sure it's right for both of us. Most importantly, it has to be right for her."

"Smart move," Churchill said. "You want some kind of safety net if your kid turns out to be utterly bonkers like her mother."

"Or she'll be as grounded and nice and caring as her father," Nana said.

We went down Nicholson Road. The trees were tall and the houses neat. Nothing had changed, and I wondered why I might have expected it to. Would Eris like my neighbourhood? Would she feel comfortable here?

At the house, Nana let us out on the street and gave me the key so I could retrieve my backpack and guitar from the boot. Churchill sprinted inside. From the driveway, I watched Nana reverse the Statesman into the garage, expertly getting the car in as if threading a needle. I helped her close the garage door.

"Thanks for picking me up. It did me a massive amount of good to see you standing there, waiting for me."

"My pleasure, Rowan." She took of her hat and ran a hand through her hair a few times. "Do you think you're ready?"

"For what? Being a musician or a father?"

"Both. Because I think each will require a lot of commitment, and could take you into new territory."

I shrugged. "I don't know. In both cases, I want to try. The music is for me, but being a father would be for Eris, so maybe that makes it more meaningful."

"I'd help," Nana said, giving me a smile. "But to be honest, I'm not very happy about being a great-grandmother. That makes me feel old."

"We'll think of a new title for you."

"Nana will do." She looked at the plants that lined her driveway, then at the house, and finally at me. "I think Eris would like it here very much."

→←

Churchill helped me stay awake. We sat in the kitchen and he asked about my trip.

"What about this drug run, Rowan? I could sense you were holding back in the car."

"It's funny, Church. When I think about it now, it's kind of a good memory. But at the time, I was shitting myself. The dope I picked up was in jam jars, with actual jam stacked on top. You know what I mean? In each box, the bottom row was all dope, the top was all jam. Shelley, the supplier, said this made it harder for sniffer dogs to pick up."

"And Shelley is the perfect name for a dope dealer."

"She was totally normal, not what I expected at all. And she gave me some advice for the drive back, so I could avoid the police."

"And? Did you avoid them?"

"I was a nervous wreck for the first couple of hours. I was looking all around for police cars and highway patrol. The car was full of boxes, and all the drivers and passengers looked at me when they passed. Once I crossed the border from Utah to Wyoming, I started to relax. I even enjoyed it, a bit. It's beautiful country."

Churchill stood up and put the kettle on. "I've got a feeling something bad's about to happen. Tea?"

"Yeah, thanks. And you're right. On the way to Jackson, there was some kind of forest fire and the highway was closed. You should've seen it. I go around a corner, and then there's this blockade of police cars and emergency vehicles. I really thought they were all there for me."

Churchill laughed. "So, you turned around?"

"I couldn't. There were cars behind me, and cars driving back the other way. All I could do was go right up to the police cars, like everyone else. Then I get there and one of them flags me down."

The kettle boiled and switched off. Churchill got up to make the tea. "That's not good, but you're sitting here with me, so I'm thinking nothing bad happened."

"You wouldn't believe it, Church. The cop comes up to me and I lower the window, trying my best to look innocent, but I was seriously sweating. He asks me where I'm headed, and I tell him Bozeman. He says the highway's closed and I have to go to Idaho, following the highway next to Snake River."

"That all sounds so brilliantly exotic. Driving to Bozeman on the Snake River Highway. Almost like a song, that is."

"Yeah, I'm in the process of writing about the drive. Anyway, the cop saw all the boxes and asked me what I was doing. I said I was delivering jam for a friend. This wasn't completely a lie, but I thought it came out like one. And he gave me this suspicious look, like some typical Hollywood cop, and he said, 'Got any rhubarb jam? My wife, she's pregnant, and she's just craving everything with rhubarb at the moment.'"

"No way. Did you have it?"

"I had no idea if I did. I had to pull over and get out, so I could open all the boxes. There I was, surrounded by police, with a car full of dope, trying to find a jar of rhubarb jam."

Churchill laughed again.

"I gotta say, the cop was really nice. He even tried to help, but I kept positioning myself so I only I could open a box. Anyway, turned out there was rhubarb in there, and it was, I think, in the last box I opened. He took three jars and paid for them. I couldn't bring myself to tell him there was dope in it."

"She puts dope in the jam? What kind of impact is that gonna have on the guy's baby?"

"I don't know. But I couldn't tell him. He was happy he had the jam and I was happy to get back on the road. But I had to make a massive detour through Idaho, and I didn't get to Bozeman until midnight."

"What a story."

"I know. Like I said, now it seems funny."

We took our cups of tea into the living room and got comfortable.

Churchill asked more questions about the people I met and the things I saw. He was very interested to know more about Charlie.

I also played him a couple of songs. He wanted to hear something that was on the album, but I only played what Charlie had rejected, as I wanted him to experience the fine production of the CD without having first heard the songs played acoustically and sung with my dried out, jetlagged voice. Still, he thought the songs I played were pretty good, and those were ones that hadn't made the cut.

It was really great to see him. But the excitement of hanging out again couldn't stave off sleep. I went to bed just before ten and slept for five hours. At three, I was wide awake, and it was that awful kind of wakefulness that can't be overcome. My brain was active. I was hungry. I wanted to do things. It felt wrong to be lying in bed, so I went into the kitchen and put the kettle on. I left the lights off, as I didn't want to wake Churchill, and lit a candle instead. I took this outside to pick some mint leaves from Nana's garden.

Outside, it was warm, quiet and dark, the streetlights off and not a single light on in any of the nearby houses. I could see things moving in the darkness, moths and mosquitoes drawn to the candlelight. The humans were asleep, but the insects were awake. There were ants on the ground and spiders on the walls. I felt like an insect as well, a big red moth, fluttering about, following the light, never really settling down in one spot, perhaps destined to be devoured a big spider. Or maybe I was the spider, a hairy red one with eight very long legs.

I went back inside and made the mint tea, adding a spoon of honey to make it go down more smoothly and hopefully trigger the tiredness required to draw me back to bed. I doubted it, because I was fully alert. I toasted two slices of bread and spread Vegemite on them, staring at the flickering candle as I ate. I recalled how Conor and I had dubbed Vegemite "blackbird shit" when were kids, with the term becoming so ubiquitous in our household that my father had used it too.

My dad. I had to contact him. He was at the top of my to-do list.

The combination of the yeasty paste and the white bread made me feel really glad to be home. It was the middle of the night, but I was in my house in Shenton Park, drinking mint tea from Nana's garden and eating off one of my plates. This was my table, my chair and my candle.

I'd enjoyed the States, and it was a great place to visit, but there was no way I could live there. Nola had asked me what I thought about America at Isle Royale, but she bulldozed in and ranted about the country's addiction to excess and consumption, not letting me get a word in. She clearly had her own American axe to grind, but what she complained about wasn't what troubled me, as there was just as much excess and consumerism in Australia. What I had found unnerving was that while everyone wanted to be helpful and for me to have a nice day, I thought there was nothing genuine about it.

The country was like a cheap guitar with an elaborate design: all style and no substance.

America was hollow wood.

But Charlie wasn't. She had depth. She was solid and genuine, and America was sure to have more people like her, which meant my hollow-wood judgement was perhaps unfair.

Thinking of Charlie reminded me of something else on my to-do list: stop saying yes to people and start trading.

From the kitchen drawer, I took a notepad and pen. But instead of writing out that list, which had been my intention, I started a letter to Charlie. I explained how things had gone with Nola, and that she'd been right, and that I was sorry I hadn't listened to her and stayed in Bozeman to help with the mix. I confessed that she was my best discovery in America, more memorable than even the Grand Canyon.

As I started on page two, I realised there was something wonderfully archaic about sitting in the kitchen in the early hours of the morning and writing a letter by candlelight.

I wrote that she was welcome to visit anytime she wanted, and that Churchill really wanted to meet her. There I got stuck, with not much more to say.

I sat back in my chair, drank the rest of my tea and looked around the kitchen. Churchill had put all the postcards on the fridge, including the ones I'd sent. He had mine showing the picture side and place name, while Nola's showed Eris's five-fingered hand. It made for an interesting collage, and already gave the impression that a child lived in the house.

That little hand, which I never even got to shake or hold, which Nola had said had four fingers; she thought I was crazy to think the hand was real.

Her red hair that I never got to touch. The long trip I took to find her, when I only really found myself. And my music.

I took a postcard from the fridge. This one was from Vancouver, with the hand traced in yellow. In my letter, I told Charlie I wanted to title the CD *One Hand Clapping*, and that this yellow, five-fingered hand should be used on the cover. On the postcard, I used a red pen to write "One Hand Clapping" at the top.

It was perfect.

I finished the letter by saying I really hoped we'd see each other again and continue trading. The letter and postcard went into an envelope, which I sealed and addressed to Cottonwood Guitars.

It was now close to four, and I was even more awake than before. I made another cup of tea and booted up my laptop. I figured as long as I was up, I should endeavour to use the time productively and try to kick-start my music career.

I began with the clubs, bars and venues which I knew booked live acts playing original music, checking their websites to see which musicians they had on their schedules. To that list I added other venues I found from searching online. In the end, I had thirteen, which wasn't many given Perth's strong live music scene. But most of the bars wanted cover bands playing classic rock or acoustic duos who churned out *Country Roads* and *Sweet Home Alabama*. While there was a strong market for this, I wanted to give my own music precedence.

Perth also had big music venues, but these were the reserve of those famous enough to fill them.

The best chance I felt I had was to start off with a mid-week slot in a bar or restaurant. Playing on my own, I couldn't fill a large place with music and required something more intimate and relaxed. I felt my songs needed that too. A café or dining vibe would be more suitable than rowdy Friday night revelry.

I sent emails to each of the venues on my list, including in the mail a short bio and a link to *Brand New Start*, which Charlie had kindly placed in mp3 format on the Cottonwood Guitars website. It felt good to do this, to actively seek gigs, but I didn't think anything would come of it. I needed to be present; to go to these places with a CD in my hand and speak with the people who booked the acts. Still, having sent these emails, I could then visit the venues once my CDs arrived, under the pretence of following up.

Churchill had left a set of earphones on the table. I plugged these into my laptop and listened to *Brand New Start*. I couldn't quite believe I had actually written that song. I thought it would stand up to anything currently being played on commercial radio.

The song was sparked by adventure, by an unexpected experience: walking to Charlie's place and chopping her wood, getting the sound of the axe and the wood inside my head, and writing about my own feelings as well. The sense of being let down and abandoned by someone I trusted, and wanting to put the past behind me and start anew.

I realised that if I wanted to write more songs like that, I needed to get out into the world and experience things, as I had in America. I would need to suffer and feel, to take risks and embrace adventure.

The dope run for Melvin had all the potential for being a song. It was still in my head, though I had jotted some lyrics on the flight from Sydney, on an air sickness bag using a pen borrowed from a flight attendant. I would have liked to work on it, to get my guitar out and try some chord progressions, but didn't want to disturb Churchill.

I turned my laptop off and took the slowly diminishing candle into the living room. On the wall next to the television, Churchill had pinned a large map of North America. All the places Nola had sent postcards from were circled. Looking at them, it struck me that she had taken a strange route: changing direction, back-tracking, bypassing bigger cities in favour of smaller ones, and mostly staying in places that had little redeeming value for tourists. Why had she gone to places like Saginaw, Tulsa and Des Moines?

There was something about the route that looked planned. This wasn't a spontaneous trip where Nola just went where she wanted, with Eris in tow. It was a point-to-point schedule, with each place chosen for a reason.

But what were those reasons?

I stared at the map in the flickering light, looking at the cities and places I'd visited, the roads I'd travelled, the routes I'd taken. My eyes stopped on Oklahoma City; being there with Nikki felt like a very long time ago. It was almost the experience of another person. Oklahoma Rowan. A guy with no money who road trains, slept with girls on the rebound and had the audacity to give his guitar an old lady's name.

Then, I looked at Salt Lake City, where Nikki and I split, and the highways I took to get up to West Yellowstone. I thought about the two young boys in Warm River with their home-schooling mother, and about Curt and Jez, who I hoped had reconciled.

Austin was way down on the map, closer to Mexico than I realised at the time. Were Left Feet still beating their suitcases at the Spider House Café? Had they graduated to higher-paying gigs?

And what about Nola? What had she been doing in all these places? It couldn't simply have just been travel for the sake of travel.

Poor Eris, getting dragged all over the continent. Sitting on buses and trains, maybe even in planes and cars. Nola had subject this little girl – my little girl – to long, tedious and tiring days of travel. For what?

There were sixteen places circled on the map. Nola had travelled clockwise, starting from Thunder Bay in Ontario. I put the candle down and used a pencil and ruler to draw a line from that city to Saginaw. Something about this made sense, so I drew another line, this one from Saginaw to Kingston, then from Kingston to Columbus. I moved around the map, connecting the dots, ending in Des Moines. The pencil didn't leave much of an outline, and it was hard to see in the candlelight. No pattern presented itself.

I wondered if Nola had chosen these places based on visiting family and friends; doing the rounds and catching up with people. Maybe even introducing them all to Eris.

She hadn't let me meet Eris, but our time would come. I just needed to be patient and to get myself ready.

I went over the pencil lines again, making them thicker, but this didn't make any perceivable pattern more visible.

Still, I couldn't accept that this was random.

Did Churchill still have any glow-in-the-dark pens left over from the time we decided to graffiti the lounge room, before we repainted the walls? Because a fluorescent marking would really make the lines stand out.

As I tip-toed into his room, the candle flickered and almost blew out. Churchill always slept with the windows open, regardless of the temperature.

I checked his desk, fingering through the coffee mugs full of pens and opening the drawers.

The bed-side light came on.

"Looks like America turned you into a thief," Churchill said, lying on his stomach and his voice slightly muffled by the pillow.

"Sorry. I didn't want to wake you."

"Garbage. You've been puttering around the house for hours. You think I can't hear the kettle? When the toaster popped, I just about reached for my gun."

"I tried to be quiet."

"Guys as big as you can't be quiet. Your huge feet thump around the house like an elephant. Now, what are you looking for in your ultra-creative jetlagged state?"

"Glow-in-the-dark pens. Wait a minute. You have a gun in here?"

"Under the bed. You didn't know?"

"I do now. Is it loaded?"

"Probably best I don't answer that. It's just for security, against the Shenton Park crime-wave. Been a lot of home break-ins lately."

"Including us?"

"Not yet. Don't worry. I got one for Pam as well."

"Nana's got a gun?"

Churchill sat up in bed. "That sounds like a pretty good title for a song too."

"Aerosmith already took it, and it was Janie who was armed."

"Well, if you ask me, I think it's more interesting if Nana's got a gun, not Janie. But what the crap do I know about music? Now, if it's pens you're looking for, bottom drawer."

I opened that drawer and found them.

"Can I ask what on earth you're doing?"

"I'm, yeah, I guess I'm vandalising your map."

"I think I need to see this. To supervise."

Churchill followed me into the living room. He turned on the light and I blew out the candle.

"Looks like you already ruined it," he said, tracing the pencil marks with his fingers. "Are you trying to get this to mean something?"

"It just doesn't seem random to me. All these places. Why did Nola go to these specific places?"

I went over the pencil lines with a fluorescent yellow pen. It left a shiny trail, like a snail.

When I got to the places I'd visited, Churchill asked, "What was the absolute highlight of the trip? And don't say hanging with Charlie."

I traced the line from Austin to Tulsa. "You won't like it, but the first night I spent with Nikki really stands out. Not just the night, the whole day. How we escaped the hostel and evaded Bevan. Then jumping onto the Heartland Flyer. It was like we were on the run. Bonnie and Clyde, kind of. And it wasn't that Nikki was all that special. It was the situation we were in. It was wild."

"Until Bonnie turned into baggage."

"It wasn't like that. Nikki's a good one. I'm glad I met her."

I followed the line to Salt Lake City, then up to Vancouver, and finished the rest. I stepped back from the map. Churchill turned off the light.

"That's weird," he said in the darkness. "It doesn't really look like anything."

"I'm seeing a severely deformed flash a lightning."

"Maybe it needs one more line, up to Thunder Bay." He turned the light on and took the pen from me. "There. Closing the circle. Back to the start."

This time, I switched off the light and we looked at the map.

"It's not a circle," Churchill said.

"No, I'm now seeing a severely deformed star."

"With eight points. And look at them. They're points. The angles are sharp. It's a star."

"Or a compass. You've got Thunder Bay to the north, New Orleans to the south, and three points either side."

"Could be. Or it's nothing at all. Come on, Rowan. It's a bit of a stretch to think Nola sat down with a map and plotted a course across the continent specifically to create a shape like this. Is she really that clever?"

"I don't know. The Nola I met in Isle Royale, I didn't feel like I knew her at all. But don't you think there's something uniform about this? Is an eight-pointed star some kind of symbol?"

Churchill went into his room and came back with his tablet. The screen illuminated his face.

"It's on our flag," he said.

"That's a seven-pointed star."

"No, the Union Jack." He showed me the screen. "See? Eight points. And this apparently is the Star of Ishtar, also known as the Star of Venus."

"Okay, we're getting somewhere. What do those mean?"

Churchill swiped the screen. "Ishtar, Venus, the gateway to the gods, blah-blah Babylonian times, something about the Great Mother."

"Nola's not that."

"Bloody hell," he said, still swiping. "This goes on and on. There's barely a religion that hasn't used this symbol in some way, and just about every society since we stopped walking on our knuckles. Get this, Rowan. It's the Great Celestial Conjunction. And it's the Mayan

Cross of, crap, I can't even say this, Quetzalcoatl? The eight immortals in Chinese tradition. The eight paths in the ways of Buddha. The Star of Lakshmi. The seal of the prophets of Islam. The eight deities of Egypt. The symbol of chaos magic. The Wiccan Wheel of the Year. The list goes on."

"Wait. What was that last one?"

"The Wiccan thing?"

"The thing about chaos. That rings a bell. Research that."

More swiping, with Churchill's eyes darting across the screen as he took in a lot of information quickly.

"Let's see," he said. "Chaos symbol. Okay, here we go. Chaos magic, eight-pointed symbol with arrows. Hmm, that's interesting. First used in the *Eternal Champion* stories by Michael Moorcock. Maybe Nola's a fan, but I've never heard of him. Though he does have my eternal sympathies. School must've been hellish for a kid with a surname like that."

Suddenly exhausted, I tried to stave off the jetlag and find the connection. "The chaos part means something. I know it."

"What about Nikki? She caused a fair bit of chaos."

"Not her. And that was a good kind of chaos. But I remember she said something about it. Some artist, who's represented by a symbol of anarchy or chaos. She told me about it in Austin, because the artist did something while we were there."

"Do you mean Grilla?"

I snapped my fingers. "That's it. I was busking in Austin and there was a car crash across the street. Someone was dropping balloons filled with grey paint and that caused the crash. It was Grilla. That's what Nikki said."

"Did she leave a card? Because that's how she normally signs her work. She leaves these business cards behind."

"She did. I think I've still got it somewhere. But how do you know about Grilla, Church?"

"I read up on her, after that Saginaw video went viral. The four-way stop sign. That was her, remember?"

"Yeah."

I stared at the map. Then, I turned to Churchill, and at the same time, he looked up from his tablet. It appeared we were thinking the same thing.

"No way," he said. "That's too wild."

"But they were both in Saginaw, and in Austin. At the right time too."

Churchill searched and swiped. "Could just be a coincidence. We need some time to see if we can match the other places with Grilla. But before we do all of that, is this the symbol that was on the card in Austin?"

He showed me the screen. On it was the rounded G-symbol with eight arrows.

"That's it. And look at it. Eight points, just like on the map."

"True."

"I'm positive I've seen this symbol before."

"Okay. But do you really think Nola's capable of this kind of stuff? Because from what I read, Grilla's out there. Like, way out there. I think she's even been arrested a few times and thrown in prison. Does that sound like Nola to you?"

"To be honest, Church. I really don't know."

Churchill was thoughtful for a minute, then said, "If this is true, it's a massive story. No one knows who Grilla is. I'm pretty sure I remember reading that she's wanted in some places. Like in Ecuador or Vietnam or Greece. She's been everywhere, and pulled off some seriously daring stuff."

"Nola's travelled a lot. I do know that. But if she is Grilla, we need to keep it a secret."

"What? Why?"

"We just have to."

"I think we should use it to our advantage," Churchill said. He pointed at the map and added, "This could be our prime bargaining chip. You know, something along the lines of, give us the kid or we'll tell the world."

"We're not going that far. I'm going to get custody of Eris anyway. It won't require blackmail. And Grilla's just an artist, not a murderer."

"Still, it's a pretty big ace for us to have up our sleeve." He looked at the map. "It's a shame we didn't work this out earlier. It could've made it easier to find her."

"We did find her, and it was easy in the end. She intends to tell me where she is in Europe, so we can meet."

"No fun in that."

I rubbed my eyes, wanting sleep. "Sorry, Church. I gotta go back to bed. I'm fading. Let's talk about it in the morning."

He gestured with his tablet to the front window, through which the first light of day was creeping. "It is morning."

"Give me few hours."

"How can you sleep now? This changes everything. If Nola is Grilla, and I reckon I need about fifteen minutes to prove it, then it means she's not a fruitcake. I'm sorry I said that, because she's a freaking genius. She's like, the Picasso of our times. She's thrown the art rulebook out the window. Have you ever seen one of her murals?"

I yawned. "I don't think so."

He tapped at the tablet and moved closer to me, so we could both see the screen. "Look at these. This was before she started doing live art, like shutting down an intersection and throwing paint bombs."

"Yeah, they're good."

"Good? They're brilliant. If they were on canvases, they'd be worth thousands. They're on the sides of buildings. I don't know how she painted them without getting noticed."

Another yawn. "Maybe she wasn't famous back then. Wait. Stop. Go back."

Churchill swiped the screen backwards three times, to the mural of the shark kissing the man.

"That one. I've seen that. In Freo. I couldn't stop staring at it. And that was where I first saw the symbol."

"She was here as well. In Perth, of all places."

"Yeah. I'm sorry, Church. I can't go on. I'm going to bed."

"Fine. You weakling. I'll find out what Grilla did in each place. Maybe that'll help make sense of things."

"Alright. Thanks. There's something else, about this chaos thing, but my brain is a total fog right now. Maybe I'll have it when I wake up. Good night."

I left the living room.

"You mean good morning," Churchill shouted after me. "And the fact we've discovered that you impregnated a world-famous artist, and produced a red-headed bundle of sweetness with her, makes this a very good morning."

→←

For the first week, my sleeping rhythm was all screwed up, and I found myself wide awake at around three every morning. It was only when I tagged along for a very short early morning swim at Brighton Beach with Churchill and Janette that I started to feel like I was back on earth.

But things didn't go so well that first week. I received one reply to all the emails I sent, and this was a rather loose invitation to join a songwriters' night at Clancy's Fish Pub in City Beach, held every Tuesday. There was no money involved, and I told myself to be happy even to have a gig. My attempts to busk on the Hay Street and Murray Street pedestrian malls had been disastrous. I got heckled by teenagers, and even had a pathetic amount of change scooped out of my guitar case by a girl who looked barely old enough to go to school. I also tried my luck in Fremantle, but got told to move along by the police everywhere I played. They appeared so quickly, I wondered if they were following me around.

It wasn't a promising start.

The arrival of a package full of CDs from Bozeman, the day I was due to play at Clancy's, lifted my spirits. It came two weeks after I'd sent the letter to Charlie, which meant she must've acted fast to get them printed. It was exciting and a relief to get them. I'd been worrying all week that I would be forced to play at songwriters' night without any products to back up my endeavours and possibly sell. The CDs gave me more credibility. I wasn't just some guy having a crack on open-mic night.

They were beautiful. The cover was exactly as I'd sent to Charlie, with Eris's hand traced in yellow. It was my first album and I was very proud. Receiving the package was a bit like getting a baby in the mail.

Charlie included a letter in the box, along with a USB stick attached to a little dinosaur key ring, which was a nice touch. It made me think of that drug run to Colorado and smile. In her letter, handwritten and hard work to decipher, she explained the stick had the master mix and the jacket on it, meaning I could start printing my own CDs here. She said she had five hundred copies of her own, and that Melvin had used some of his dope profits to cover the costs of printing, as a thank you for doing the pick-up from Dinosaur. She was distributing them to her contacts, including a friend who worked at KBMC, the radio station of Montana State University, with *Brand New Start* and *Two Sticks* already getting some airplay.

"Holy crap."

It was just like Charlie to save her big news for last: she'd given a copy to a friend in LA who organised music for television shows, and he was interested in using *Chasing a Shadow* as the theme music for the pilot of a new police drama.

I couldn't believe it. Just like that, with Charlie's help, things were happening.

The trade for all this, as outlined in Charlie's P.S., was that I had to perform my first ever North America gig in Bozeman, for free, and that I was to do it before the end of the year. She suggested this gig could kick off an extended tour of the States and that I should start planning.

It occurred to me that I could do this trip to the States, then go from there to Europe to meet up with Nola and Eris.

I took a CD from the box and went outside. I stood on the small patch of grass that was our front lawn until Churchill saw me. He was up on the roof with his laptop and headset. Since I'd come back, he'd spent most mornings working from up there, which I considered a very positive development, as he was now on top of the house rather than enclosed inside it. Our roof was only slightly slanted, which made it easy to sit on. He didn't even need his grey hoodie anymore. Today, he wore a hat and sunglasses, and was shirtless.

"What was in the box?" he asked. "Gwyneth Paltrow's head?"

"You can keep you movie references today." I held up the CD and waved it in the air a little. "This is real."

"No way. Put it on. And bring the speakers outside. We want the world to hear this."

Back inside, I placed one speaker in the open living room window and the other just outside the door, as far as the cable would allow. I got the CD playing and returned to the lawn, where I sat down. Up on the roof, I saw that Churchill had put his laptop aside and was lying on the tiles with his hands behind his head. I didn't think I'd ever seen him so comfortable and content in the outside world. He even had one up on me, as I wasn't brave enough to climb the ladder and join him on the roof.

The album began with the barely perceptible tapping of two sticks on the track of the same name. It had been Charlie's idea to lead off with this song, because of its slow-building, attention-grabbing intro. Through the speakers, the tapping got louder and more incessant. Then the guitar came in, clear and crisp, backed by the bright twang and rootsy feel of Charlie's mandolin.

227

I heard myself sing the opening lines: "*Alone on a beach, far from ourselves, and far from sight. She took two sticks, put them to work, and lit up the night.*"

While it was me singing and playing, I felt somehow removed from it, as if this was the album of someone else.

I heard the bum notes, the times my fingers ran along the strings between bar chords and when my fingernails hit the guitar's scratch-plate. Charlie had been adamant about keeping those mistakes in, as this all gave it an edge and removed any possible studio-made gloss of perfection. There was no Auto-Tune for the vocals, which helped to make bad singers sound okay, and no computer-generated instruments or sounds to fill in for a lack of band-members. It was real, hand-made and from the heart.

It was hard not to be proud. Sitting on the grass, hearing my album, with a gig coming up that evening and a box of CDs on the kitchen table, I was happy. Possibly the happiest I'd ever been.

Because I'd done it. I wrote some good songs and made an album. The next step was to line up more gigs and get people listening. With the CD, I could follow up at the venues in person and visit local radio stations. And I was motivated to get out there and get started.

Through it all, Churchill said nothing. He simply lay there, listening.

When *Heartland Gypsy* came to end and the album was finished, Churchill sat up. He crossed his legs and leaned back a little, his hands on the tiles.

"Rowan, mate, I really don't know what to say. I'm stunned."

"I can't really believe it either. That was me."

"It's great. You sound great. I think I've heard a few those songs before, but not like that. What happened?"

"Charlie changed them. She's got an incredible ear for music, knows exactly what to add and what to remove on each song. There are two I wrote when I was in the Abel Tasman, including the opening track. But they're basically different songs to what I wrote. It was Charlie who made them so good."

I thought Churchill was looking at me a bit strangely. I saw uncertainty in the hunch of his shoulders and curiosity in his sideways glance.

"Did you play all those instruments?" he asked.

"Just the guitar. Charlie played the mandolin. And we both got involved in the percussion. Some of it was really strange, like me chopping wood."

"How rustic." He watched a white SUV drive down Morgan Street, then asked, "Where did all those songs come from?"

"I don't know, Church. I was out there, in America, and sometimes I just started hearing them in my head. At the start, I thought it was just me, you know, playing music back internally to fill the silence. But they were songs I'd never heard before. And when I was on the road, on my own, I felt like there were songs everywhere. I didn't need a guitar, because I could hear it and visualise it."

"Was that after Daphne got smashed?"

Hearing the name made me cringe a little. I'd been such a fool to name my guitar.

"It was. One time, I got picked up by a couple of hunters and they made me sit in the back of their pick-up. There was this huge deer in there as well, under a tarp, dead. I looked at the animal and a song came to me. That was the inspiration behind *Still Afternoon*."

"Well, don't be too pleased with yourself." He picked up his laptop and put his headset in place. "This is just the start. It's a bloody good start, I'll give you that, but we've got some work to do to get that CD of yours out there."

"I know. I know."

"I'm tied up this morning, at my desk," he said, spreading his hands out and gesturing to the roof. "But I could find some time this afternoon if you want some help."

I didn't. "I got it, Church. You focus on your work. Now that the CDs are here, I can start hitting places in person. I think I'll do that today, until it's time for the gig."

"Get into it. Janette said she's coming tonight, and she's bringing some friends with her. You might want to keep an eye on them, in case they get rowdy."

"What about you?" This was a long shot, but I thought I'd ask anyway.

"I looked at some pictures online, of Clancy's. I want to, believe me, but I don't think it's a good idea. Too crowded and closed in."

"No worries. You're on the roof. That's a big step up."

Churchill smiled and nodded. "The world seems surprisingly safe up here. It's best in the mornings, after all the neighbours have gone to work. In the evenings, it's a different story. That's when all the weirdos come out."

229

"I never thought I'd say this to anyone, Church, but I think it's great you're on the roof. Work hard, and try not to fall down."

I went inside and grabbed the box of CDs. I liked that the box was so heavy, because I felt what I'd done was substantial. A digital file didn't quite capture the significance the way all these CDs did.

I waved to Churchill as I backed my Smart down the drive.

The rest of the day was a blur of radio stations, music venues and traffic jams. I shied away from commercial radio, as I knew I had no chance of infiltrating their set playlists, and focused instead on indie radio and the universities which had radio stations of their own. But despite me standing there, brandishing a CD, no one was terribly interested. I couldn't get past the reception area to talk to someone responsible for airplay and programming. Each receptionist took my CD and tossed it somewhere: in a box with others, into someone's pigeon-hole, in a drawer, or just left it on the desk. The music venues weren't much better. They asked for a list of places I'd already played, but I couldn't say more beyond the upcoming gig at Clancy's. And I didn't have any Facebook fans or Twitter followers. It was tempting to talk myself up more, to lie in order to secure a chance, but I chose to stay true to my current situation: it was early days, I was just starting out and I'd appreciate any opportunity to prove myself. Most of the people I spoke to took my CD with looks of exasperation, as if they received hundreds of such CDs each day.

After leaving the house motivated and confident, I returned dejected, discouraged and tired. Churchill was working in his room, so I took the chance to have a nap, wanting to be fresh for my gig. But I just lay in bed, staring at the ceiling, wondering how I was supposed to generate interest in my music when I wasn't popular to start with.

How did unknowns get discovered?

If a radio station had a fixed playlist of music, how did a new artist get played on the radio?

If a venue only hired musicians who had already played at that venue or others, how was a new artist supposed to get a gig?

As I didn't have any contacts in the local music industry, beyond acquaintances who played in struggling bands, I wondered if I would need a manager after all. And possibly a PR person. And a booking agent. I couldn't ask Churchill to fill all those roles, and it was clear to me that I couldn't have the same success as a marketing professional.

Charlie had already had more success getting things going through her contacts. I somehow needed to replicate that here, but the only real contact I had was Jono at the music shop. I wasn't in his good books, as he'd had to hire someone new in my prolonged absence, but I figured I had nothing to lose by giving him a CD; it could be something like a peace offering, my way of saying sorry, and proof that I hadn't wasted my time off.

I didn't sleep, but it was good to lie down and rest. My feeling was that joining songwriters' night at Clancy's would be a waste of time. I got up anyway and put new strings on my guitar. I used the extra-light phosphorous bronze strings that Charlie had recommended. They helped bring out the warm, light and clear sound the guitar had.

I sat on the edge of my bed and played a couple of songs to help settle the strings and to get my fingers and throat loose. At the end of each song, I flexed and rotated my left thumb. It was getting stronger, and my ability to bar the E-string with it was improving, but the joint was constantly sore.

"Sounds just as good live," Churchill said, standing in the doorway.

"Thanks. Feel free to prop up my self-confidence as much as you like."

"You don't need it. You're gonna kill it tonight. I'm just sorry I won't be there to see it."

I put the guitar in its hard-shell case, along with a capo and an extra set of strings. "Maybe next time."

"Yeah. So, how'd it go today? I felt a bit guilty leaving you to do all that running around."

"It wouldn't have mattered if you'd helped. I reckon I'd have more chance selling vacuum-cleaners door-to-door."

"I bet. You know I want to help with all of this, but it's the end of the financial year and accountants all over the country are pulling what's left of their hair out. They need my help."

"It's alright, Church. This is my ship to sail, and I think you do too much for me as it is."

"I kind of got that impression from you while you were in America. You wanted to take control of things yourself. Of course, I'm terribly hurt, but it's about time you started behaving like an adult."

"Agreed. Hopefully, it wasn't all for nothing today and I managed to plant a few seeds. Charlie's already had some success in the States."

"Oh yeah? That's great."

"I'm proud to say I'm on the radio in Montana, for whatever that's worth. She said she gave my CD to some of her other contacts as well, which is really good of her. Maybe something substantial will come out of that."

"Let's hope so. But all that shouldn't stop you from trying here. As in, looking a bit more motivated and up for tonight's gig."

"I guess I'm still a bit jetlagged and tired."

"That's no excuse," Churchill said. "You've been here long enough. This is a chance to get a restaurant full of people to listen to your songs."

"I know. You're right. And it's better than busking. Because I really don't want to be one of those guys playing the same spot on Murray Street every day, and fighting off rude teenagers and little kids who steal my coins. I want to make this happen."

"That starts tonight. Go to Clancy's and show them what you got."

This was exactly what I needed to hear. I shut the case and stood up.

"But, Rowan," Churchill said, his voice dropping, "are you really going to wear that shirt?"

I had on a plain white shirt. "Not anymore. What do you suggest?"

"Something else. Look, I may not know much about music, but I pride myself on being an expert on colour. You need something red, or failing that, a shirt in black or dark green. Those colours will go best with your fiery locks."

"My fiery locks?"

"Come on. You're a rock star now, just about. This is your first public appearance. You want to look the part."

I went through my closet and drawers. The only thing I had in red was a sleeveless muscle-shirt, and I didn't have the arms to pull that off. I held it up and Churchill laughed.

"That'd be perfect if you were in an eighties hair band. Where'd you get that thing?"

"It's a remnant from my garbage band days. I mean, garage band days."

Churchill laughed some more. "Good thing I didn't know you back then."

I put on an emerald green, button-up shirt. "How about this?"

"The colour definitely works."

"I wore this to my school ball, because I didn't want to be just another guy in a tuxedo with a white shirt."

"How'd that turn out?"

"Surprisingly good. My date ended up wearing a dress that was almost the same colour. She thought it'd be disastrous, but everyone thought it was cool the way we matched. She was a redhead too, and in a weird way, it was a bit like going to the formal with a cousin. As you can guess, nothing happened between us, and I can't even remember her name. I was so stoned that night."

"You sure do babble when you're nervous."

"Sorry."

"We'll let it slide, this time. Maybe roll up the sleeves. A bit more casual. Make yourself look like a hard-working musician."

I did so, looking in the mirror in the process.

"That's good," Churchill said. "Suits you."

"Then I think I'm ready. Thanks for the pep talk, and for the fashion advice."

"No probs. Relax, you'll be fine. By the way, I asked Janette to film you. She might be too drunk to remember, but if she does, I'll get to see your set after all. Just pretend I'm the camera."

I picked up my guitar case and grabbed my keys. "That's not weird at all. I better ply her with drinks."

"Good luck, mate. What about some CDs?"

"The box is still in the car."

"Melting in the winter sun." Churchill gave me a smile. "Rowan, you're totally up for this. One day, the world will look back on this night."

"Or just you and I will. Janette will be too drunk to remember."

"Either way, give it your best. You've got loads of talent and great songs to play. I mean it. Your album is fantastic. You'll probably end up selling all your CDs tonight."

"Thanks, Church. See you later."

I drove to Clancy's, heading up Selby Street, then taking Oceanic Drive to City Beach. In my nervousness, I drove fast, and had to make myself slow down, as I couldn't afford to get any speeding tickets.

A light rain started falling. The purple-grey clouds approaching from the west looked to be bringing heavier rain. It wasn't the best weather for sitting in a beach-side restaurant. And as it was Tuesday, I feared I would play to an empty room.

The wind was churning the Indian Ocean into soapy-looking bath water and a serious swell was rolling in, slamming right on the beach.

I pulled into the car park wondering if songwriters' night meant playing to a roomful of other musicians, and their friends and family. I had told my parents, but both were unable to come. Dad promised he'd find some time for me on the weekend, as I wanted to talk some things out with him. But I hadn't invited Conor or any of my friends, as I didn't want this gig to be a sympathy show. The extent of my promotion included telling Churchill, who practically ordered Janette to attend with as many friends as she could muster, and Nana, though I didn't expect her to be there.

When I entered Clancy's I was surprised to find it full, and to see Nana sitting at a small corner table with a man I didn't know. She waved when she saw me. I was just inside the entrance, carrying my guitar and my box of CDs, unsure where to go next or who I should talk to. The air was thick with the smell of fried fish, and conversations were shouted. In the middle of the seating area, near the big windows, a musician was playing. He was dressed all in black and strummed his guitar earnestly, putting lots of wrist into it, the way someone who learned to play on an electric guitar does. Even from this distance, I could see he sang with his eyes closed, kissing the microphone. He had decent guitar skills and a good voice, but lacked range. He was doing his very best to show his passion, stomping his bare feet and shaking his hair around, and nodding his head from shoulder to shoulder with the rhythm whenever he wasn't singing. All of his efforts were just about drowned out by the collective hum and echo of dozens of conversations. This was more pronounced when he finished his song, as no one clapped; he was merely background music.

While disappointing, and making me feel sorry for the guy playing, it had the interesting effect of making me less nervous.

I went up to the bar and told the barman who I was. It was hard to hear his reply, so he leaned over the bar and shouted at me.

"You can be on next. The others aren't here yet."

"Okay. Sure."

I put my guitar case on the floor and placed the box on a bar stool. "Can I put some CDs out?"

"Have you got some?"

I held one up.

"There's a table near the stage. Use that."

"Okay. Thanks."

The stage he was referring to was a single amp on the floor. It had the microphone and the guitar going into it, which made the sound rather fuzzy from the bar. There was also a stool, pushed to the wall, as this player had chosen to stand, presumably so he could stomp his feet. The small table had a glass of beer on it, almost empty, and a scattering of CDs.

The musician in black was building towards some kind of big opening to a two-chord song. He tried to get the patrons to clap along with him. No one obliged.

I turned to the bartender. "How long?"

"Half an hour, max. Lot of musos to get through tonight."

"No, how long till he's finished?"

"About five minutes. You need to get up there straight away. People sometimes leave when the break's too long."

"Gotcha."

I left my stuff at the bar and weaved between the tables to where Nana was sitting. I got there without Janette seeing me and crouched down beside Nana's table.

"Thanks for coming. I'm on next."

"You're going to be great."

The man introduced himself as Jack and extended his hand across the table. Although he had lots of grey hair and the bulbous, veiny nose of someone who possibly drank too much, he looked a fair bit younger than nana.

"Nice to meet you, Jack."

"It's Jock," he said, annoyed.

"Sorry, mate. I got bad hearing, especially when there's a lot of background noise like this."

In this part of the restaurant, far from the stage, the sound was muffled and static, like a radio just off the right frequency. I could hear more voices than music.

"How does someone who's deaf become a musician?" Jock asked, and he appeared to think his question funny.

"I'm not deaf. Anyway, it didn't stop Beethoven."

Saying this made me hear the ringing in my ears, which was louder because of all the noise.

"We already ate," Nana said. "Jock doesn't like to eat after it gets dark. We'll stay and watch you play, but we'll have to go straight after, because there's a do at Jock's bowling club."

"No worries. They said I've got half an hour. And it's great that you're both here."

Jock took a hefty sip of his beer and looked towards the musician. I leaned closer to Nana.

"What happened to Rory?"

"Churchill was right. I decided I could do better. And I found out Rory was cheating on me with his mixed doubles partner."

I laughed. "Bastard."

"Forget him. Get up there and play with all your heart. I've been waiting for someone to yank this idiot off the stage with a big hook."

"He's doing alright. Not his fault no one's listening."

The big two-chord song had all the makings of being the musician's last, so I stood up.

"I gotta get ready. If it sounds crap, then it's the amp and the acoustics, not me."

"Good luck, mate," Jock said, raising his glass to me and drinking.

I moved between the tables. Janette saw me this time and waved, already looking well past inebriated. She held up the camera that was to be surrogate Churchill, then dropped it on the table.

When I got close to the bar, a woman grabbed my shirt and asked for two glasses of Chardonnay. I didn't have time to explain I wasn't a waiter, as the all-in-black musician had already unplugged his guitar and was scooping up his CDs from the table. At the bar, I gave the order, pointed at the table and took my stuff over to the stage.

The parting musician sized me up as he slid his guitar into its soft case.

"It's dead in here, mate," he said, his face glistening with sweat. "Didn't sell a single CD."

He shouldered his case and walked away, going straight past the bar and out the door.

I decided not to bother with the CDs. I put the box under the table and started setting up. The last guy had the amp all wrong, with the bass and treble up way too high, and even the chorus on. No wonder he had sounded like he was playing in an elevator shaft. I adjusted the dials, switched the chorus off and lowered the gain, hoping this would remove some of the fuzz. At the very least, Nana and Jock were listening, and I wanted them to hear me properly. To test the sound, I plugged in my guitar and played the opening riff of Nirvana's *Come As You Are*. A few people cheered, recognising it and possibly wanting to hear that song. Happy with the sound, I rigged the microphone stand for my height and slowly turned up the volume of the amp, strumming each time to be sure it was right.

The wind splattered rain against the windows that faced the water.

Ready, I looked towards the bartender to see if there would be an introduction or a cue of some sort. He raised his right arm and fired a starter's gun shaped by his hand.

I thought I'd be a lot more nervous than this, but as I was background music, I had nothing to lose.

"Come on, Rowan. You're on the radio in Bozeman."

I put my fingers in a standard A-minor shaped and gently plucked the strings while surveying the restaurant. Only Nana and Jock were looking in my direction. Everyone else was eating, drinking and talking. I needed to get their attention. I had to take a risk.

From A-minor, I moved through the chord progression of *I Will Survive*. When I got to the last chord, an E-seventh, I let it resonate and hang, and stepped to the microphone.

"This one's for you, Nana."

I started singing Cake's cover version, going as low as I could in the A-minor key and keeping the rhythm slow. As people recognised the song, they turned to look and the hum of conversation started to die down. This gave me confidence and I allowed the song to take me over.

After the first chorus, I hammered the E-seventh with all four fingers and picked up the tempo, muffling the strings to get a beat. In the far corner, I saw Nana and Jock get up to dance.

I kept the tempo and launched into the second half of the song, really belting out the lyrics and feeling every bit of the passion and liberation of the song.

At the end of the second chorus, I stepped around the microphone and really gave it some on the guitar. A few people cheered. After going through the chord progression two more times, I broke it back down to finger-picking; nearly everyone had stopped talking.

As I strummed the last A-minor, there was a surprising amount of applause. I went back to the microphone.

"Thanks. Right, I think I'm warmed up now."

With its strong beat, full chords and broken-heart theme, *Brand New Start* was the ideal follower. People clapped that song at the end, but the hum of conversation had returned. From there, I flew through the album, really enjoying myself, until the next musician came to take my place.

It was Holly, the girl who had stood in as drummer for Travis's band. She had her brown hair parted down the middle and hanging around her shoulders. She looked pretty, but was wearing a bit too much make-up.

"Hey, what are you doing here?"

"Um, sorry, I can't remember your name."

"It's Rowan. We met a few months ago. At the gig in Freo. You were drumming for Travis. We all hung out after."

"Yeah, I got it now," she said, nodding, and I wasn't sure if she actually remembered me. "Rowan. I liked your cover of the cover. But your own stuff was good too."

"Thanks. I think the punters like covers more."

She plugged in her small-bodied guitar and tested the sound, strumming with a pink, heart-shaped pick. "Good to know."

"I wouldn't mess too much with the amp. I got it sounding right."

"I know what I'm doing," she said, adjusting the microphone stand. She seemed nervous.

I put my guitar away and retrieved my box. "You want to do a trade?"

"A what?"

"One of my CDs for one of yours."

"Oh, yeah. Okay."

She took a CD from her guitar case. The cover was all butterflies, pinned to a board like specimens. The CD was titled *Butterfly Dreaming*.

She looked at my cover and asked, "Do you really have a hand like that?"

I held both up. "Completely normal. Though that extra finger would help me play the guitar better."

"You don't look like you need any help with that." She looped the guitar strap over her shoulders. "Are you sticking around?"

"Yeah. I think I'll have something to eat. Have a good set."

I took my guitar case and box to the bar. As Holly launched into a lyrically liberal version of *Crazy* by Gnarls Barkley, Nana and Jock came up to me. They had their jackets on and looked ready to leave.

Nana gave me a hug. "You were fantastic."

"I'll second that," Jock said.

Nana took her purse from her handbag. "I want a CD."

"You can have as many as you want."

"I want to buy them. How much are they?"

"For you, a dollar."

She gave my shoulder a slap. "You'll never get anywhere with that attitude."

"Seriously, take as many as you want." I opened the box. "Give them to your friends and spread the word."

Nana handed me a fifty dollar note. "I'll take five. And you're not saying no."

As I handed them to her, I saw her give Jock a nudge with her elbow.

"Yeah, I'll take five too, thanks."

He reached into the box and grabbed a handful, actually taking six. I didn't stop him, because I now had a hundred dollars in my pocket. The money changing hands resulted in a few other people coming up to the bar to buy CDs. Nana and Jock waved goodbye and headed for the door. The barman gave me a black pen, and I signed the CDs bought by those who asked me to.

While Holly played, singing very well, I sold twelve CDs, plus the ten Nana and Jock bought. The cash felt good in my pocket. I was officially an earning musician.

When everyone had drifted back to their tables, I stayed sitting at the bar. I thought about joining Janette and her friends, but was happy to give my ears a break. I ordered a plate of fish tacos and a beer. As the barman slid the glass across the bar, he said it was on the house.

I held up a CD. "Thanks, but let's make it a fair trade."

He took the CD and gave me a smile. "I'll give it to Scaff. He books the musos for Clancy's in Freo. Reckon you could get your own slot there, maybe mid-week. Hard to get a look in on the weekends. Same story here."

"Thanks for that. Much appreciated."

"You wanna play again next week?"

"Definitely."

"Alright. You raised the quality a fair bit tonight. And you didn't just rack off like that other guy did."

I raised my glass. "Cheers."

I drank my beer and turned to listen to Holly. I noticed quite a few people were looking at her and listening, and I didn't get the impression they were all family and friends. Her music was enjoyable and she was good to look at.

Someone hugging me from behind made me jump.

"Rowan the rock god," Janette said, spinning my stool around and sitting in my lap. "You were all kinds of awesome."

"And you're all kinds of drunk."

She put her arms around my neck and tried to give me a serious, sober look. "I'll admit it. I may have had a few, but I think, this, night, is something to celebrate."

I couldn't argue with that.

"Thanks for coming."

"We're here for you."

I'd had girlfriends in the past who weren't nice to be around when they were drunk, and who didn't like to be told not to drink. But Janette, even though she was just a friend, was always fun when drunk.

To the barman, I held up two fingers.

"Vodka," Janette shouted. "And only vodka. So cold it's frozen over."

"Don't you have to work tomorrow?"

Janette got herself more comfortable on my lap. She nodded, pouting. "I think I might have to call in sick," she said, tapping my chest with each word.

"Sorry for that. I'm not yet famous enough to play on weekends."

"You were fabulous, darling. Soon, you will own the weekend, and we will party all the way through it."

The vodka shots arrived. We toasted glasses, with Janette spilling a fair bit of hers onto my fingers, and threw them down.

"Now. Rowan." She got off my lap and I helped her keep her footing. "You. Come with me. Sit at my table. Now."

While Janette was a fun drunk, I didn't want to try to converse with her friends. It would be a hearing nightmare, and I was quite content to stay at the bar.

"I've gotta chat with the barman about next week."

Janette pouted some more, which actually made her look rather sweet. I could imagine lots of guys wanting to take her home. Churchill had already told me she had cheated on him a few times, and that he was okay with it. I just didn't want to be one of those guys.

"That's very disappointing, Rowan." She gestured towards her table. "They all wanna meet you. The famous musician."

I was pretty sure I'd met most of them, at one of our house parties or dinners.

The barman put my fish tacos on the bar.

"Look, let me eat and I'll come over when I'm done."

"Deal."

She held out a hand and we shook on it. She moved unsteadily between the tables. I had the nasty thought that she was putting it on as much as feeling the alcohol; a subtle sending of signals to any unattached guys present that she might be flesh for the taking.

I listened to Holly as I ate. She had an impressive voice, with plenty of range and control. The way she sang so confidently made me think she'd received training as a child, or had attended music school. Her voice sounded like it was the result of years of practice, and for some reason I envisioned her as a pony-tailed pre-schooler running through scales at six in the morning, accompanied by a parent on the piano.

While she sang the house down, her guitar playing was scratchy. She fumbled around the basic chords, having to look where to place her fingers and hitting plenty of flat notes. It made me think of Charlie and her insistence that music should never sound perfect. For some bizarre reason, I imagined that Charlie and Holly would get along very well.

Holly played bright pop songs which all sounded rather similar. At the end of each song, I led the clapping from the bar, prompting others to applaud as well. When I clapped, she looked in my direction and gave me a smile.

I ate slowly, to give me a reason to avoid Janette's table and maintain a place at the bar where I hoped Holly would join me.

A young guy entered the restaurant toting a guitar case. Though he didn't look old enough to drink, he went straight to the bar and ordered a small beer, which he drank in one go. He looked around the restaurant with the trepidation of someone about to dive into a pool full of sharks.

I turned to him. "Don't worry. They're more interested in eating, drinking and talking than listening to music."

"I've done this before," he said, and I didn't think he was convincing.

"Even more reason to relax."

He looked around some more, then stopped on Holly. "She's good."

"Yeah, but she hasn't got that many listeners either. Just get up there and enjoy yourself."

"Are you next?"

"I already had my go. Looks like it's you."

He nodded.

The barman gestured and pointed, and the young musician headed slowly for the stage, where Holly was already unplugged and packing up. I watched them exchange some words. Holly gave him an encouraging pat on the shoulder. As she walked to the bar, I noticed that quite a few people were taking advantage of the break in the music, with the young guy slow to get set up, to pay their bills and leave.

At the bar, Holly said, "Thanks for the apple sauce."

"You deserved it. You were great."

"I forgot how hard it is playing in here. And the guitar ain't really my thing."

"You prefer the drums?"

She smiled, revealing a slight smudge of lipstick on one of her canines. "Guess I should stick to what I do best. But you can't be a singer-songwriter with just a drum kit."

"You'd be interesting though. Definitely something different. You want a drink?"

She looked towards the door, then at the nervous musician, who was fumbling his way through the opening chords of a complicated first song. He got it wrong and stopped. He even said "Sorry" into the microphone, eliciting a slight squeal of feedback that made a few people wince, before starting again.

"He's gonna die up there," Holly said. "You can feel it. The tension's building. It's almost like everyone in here would rather see him screw up majorly than nail a song to the wall. And I feel like I need to stick around and see it."

"Not a good move to start with a complex song."

She put her guitar case down next to mine. "He might just blow up the amp. That'd be something. Like performance art."

"He'll survive." I tried my best British accent: "The amp goes up to eleven."

Holly let out a short laugh and perched herself on a stool, wiggling a little as she got comfortable. I was glad she sat down, not only because it gave me a reason to avoid Janette's table, but also because I found it easier to talk to girls when sitting, as the height difference was removed and I stopped feeling like a praying mantis.

"What will you have?"

"Do not laugh at me. You promise?"

"I promise."

She gestured for the barman and ordered a hot lemon with honey. I tried not to laugh. "You want some cough syrup with that?"

"It's for the vocal chords. Keeps them nice and lubricated. You should try it. Or are you trying to cultivate a kind of gravelly baritone?"

"I'm happy when I sing in the right key."

"You were a little off a few times, but I'm probably the only one in here who could hear it."

"Work to do. I should get some lessons."

"That just might ruin you," Holly said. "So, how's Travis?"

I shrugged. "Haven't seen him for months, pretty much since that gig in Freo."

"I remember you now. You were that guy really letting loose on the dance floor. What were you on? People, like, cleared out of your way, because they thought they might get hit by a stray elbow or something."

"That was your fault. It was your drumming that made Travis's band decent. And once I started dancing, I just let go."

"That must be fun, to be able to let go like that and not give a crap what anyone thinks."

"It is. So, do you play in a band as well, or do you just fill in for others?"

"I do, I do. And that's an appropriate answer, because, again, don't laugh, I'm in a wedding band."

"Get out."

"It's true. We're all girls. And we're called the Maids of Honour."

I couldn't help myself. I laughed really loudly, enough to make the musician look in my direction; from the expression on his face, I guessed he thought I was laughing at him.

"You promised not to laugh," Holly said.

"Yeah, about your drink. But the Maids of Honour? That's brilliant."

"You mock me, but it pays the bills and then some. I don't have any shame in calling myself a working musician."

"I can't argue with that."

"What's your day job?" Holly asked. "Come on. We've all got to have one."

"I'm a luthier."

"No, you're not."

"Seriously. I repair guitars. I was working at Jono's shop, on Stirling Highway, where Travis works as well."

"I know it. I grew up in Mosman Park."

"Yeah? I'm from Claremont."

Holly seemed to like this. "Hey, neighbour. You still live in the hood?"

"Just about. I'm in Shenton Park. Anyway, I quit the job at Jono's to take a trip to the States and record my album. I got back a few weeks ago and haven't found a new job yet."

"Get into the wedding business. Lots of money in it. The Maids make a killing."

"What about all the desperate guys who hit on you at the reception? That must happen a lot."

She smiled. "Yeah, the wedding groupies. They can sometimes be sweet. But the Maids are all business. If we got a slutty reputation, we'd lose a lot of gigs. The Maids really do have honour."

The barman placed Holly's hot drink in front of her. "I'm just about to pull this joker," he said. "What do you guys think?"

While talking with Holly, I hadn't really been listening to the musician. I looked at the stage, where the young guy was trying to pull off more complex stuff on the guitar, and singing unintelligibly.

"Give him a chance," Holly said, stirring honey into her drink and turning the cloudy yellow liquid light brown. "Maybe he'll find his groove after a few more songs."

"He's driving everyone away," the barman said.

I felt sorry for the kid, but I was also glad it wasn't me up there, bombing. His songs were rambling, strange and not quite working, as if he'd tried to put music to bad narrative poetry and had spent too many years listening to Radiohead. He was definitely skilled on the guitar, creating chords in unusual ways, but he didn't have nearly the required musical nous to turn weird into catchy the way Thom Yorke could.

"Where were you in the States?" Holly asked, taking a sip.

"Around the mid-west, Texas and California. I spent a fair bit of time in Montana. I got to know a luthier there and she helped me with the album. She also made the guitar I play."

"I was wondering about that. Never heard of Cottonwood, or ever seen someone playing one, until tonight. It sounds really nice."

"What about you? Why do you play a small acoustic?"

"Simple. It's easier to carry. I spend so much time and effort lugging around my drum kit. I needed a guitar that was light and which doesn't take up much space."

"Fair enough."

Holly took another sip and said, "All I need to do now is learn how to play it properly. When did you start?"

I smiled, recalling that Christmas morning. "I got a baby guitar when I was six. It had these really thick nylon strings that were agony to press."

"Then you got no excuse, boy. You play that long, you better be good. By the way, what were you doing with your thumb on the fret board?"

"Playing the bass notes." I tried to demonstrate, holding an imaginary guitar. "If you hook your thumb over, it frees up your other fingers."

"I don't think I can do that," she said, looking at her hands. "My thumbs are too small."

"Better for holding drum sticks, I reckon. Do you do the whole toss the sticks in the air thing as well?"

"Please. You saw me. I drum jazz style."

"Really? I didn't notice that. Like Levon Helm?"

Holly gave me a quizzical look. "Who?"

"You don't know him? He's one of the greatest singer-drummers of all time. The Band? Cripple Creek?"

"I'm screwing with you. Of course I know who he is. Love The Band. And us singing drummers gotta stick together."

"You sing for the Maids of Honour too?"

"We all do. When you're playing for three or four hours straight, you have to share the load. We all think of it as practice."

The music stopped, quite suddenly, what sounded like mid-song, and this made us both look towards the stage. The young guy unplugged his guitar and headed out of the restaurant, his guitar still over his shoulder and the case in his hand. He walked with his head down.

"Oi," the barman shouted. "Where are you going?"

The musician went out the door.

"And don't ever come back," the barman said.

The restaurant was still about half full. Following a short lull, the conversations continued and the voices got progressively louder, competing with each other. No one seemed too concerned that the music had stopped. The barman went to put a CD on.

I leaned over the bar. "Hey, is that it?"

"There's no one else. The other two guys didn't show."

"I'll go on again, if you want."

"That's not how it works," the barman said.

I looked at Holly, then at the barman. "How about we go on together? We'll play covers, please the punters."

He had a CD in his hands, ready to load. "Alright. Screw it. Get up there and give it a go. The night's pretty much done anyway. Let's see how much more we can milk out of it."

I stood up, keen to play some more, but Holly didn't move.

"What's wrong?"

"We've never sung together," she said. "What are we supposed to play?"

"I don't know. Wedding songs? You must know a ton of covers. I'm sure we'll find stuff we both know. And I can't believe someone who regularly plays weddings would be scared of playing in front of this lot."

"I'm not scared. I'm just not sure I trust you enough to play with you."

I grabbed my guitar. "Now's a good time to find out. Come on, Holly, there's not much out there in rock'n'roll land that's difficult to play. Let's try it."

She still didn't move.

"We've got absolutely nothing to lose."

"Alright," she said, getting off the stool. She downed her drink. "But you're gonna do all the playing."

"That's a fair trade. Let's go."

She left her guitar at the bar, next to my box of CDs, and led the way to the stage. It took me a few minutes to get the amp back to the way I had it, as the young guy had changed everything.

Because of our height difference, I grabbed the stool and sat down. This way, we could both sing into the microphone without me putting out my lower back.

I strummed a few times, getting the amp's volume right. Some people in the restaurant turned to look.

Holly put her hand over the microphone and asked, "What the hell do we play?"

246

"Let's start with something easy. How about *Dead Flowers*, by the Stones. I bet you've played that before."

"I have. A surprisingly popular wedding song."

I started strumming the chord progression. "You do the first verse, I'll do the second. Chorus together."

While I played us in, Holly grabbed a tambourine that was hanging on the wall above the table. It seemed more ornamental than anything else, but she managed to get a beat from it.

She let me play the opening progression a few times before finally singing the first verse. Every note was perfect. On the chorus, she took the lead and I sang harmony. It sounded great. I noticed Holly's eyes were starting to shine as she realised this too.

At the bar, the barman gave us two thumbs up. I also saw some of the kitchen staff standing with him and listening.

I sang the second verse and we did the chorus a couple of times at the end. When it was over, everyone clapped, including the Clancy's staff. Holly shook the tambourine and looked at me for the next song.

"Do you know *Everybody Moves Away*, by Died Pretty?"

"I love that song."

"But upbeat, yeah? You first again. Me second. Here we go. One, two, three, four."

Holly tapped the tambourine against her hip as she sang. The lyrics of the chorus were a little complicated, and we messed it up the first time, but we both smiled, thinking it funny. On the second chorus, Holly hit a perfect seventh harmony as we got the words and timing right.

Janette and her friends came over and danced in front of us, pushing a few empty tables and chairs to the side to make space.

We got applause and cheering at the end of that song.

From there, one song seemed to follow another. We played Iggy Pop's *Candy*, Gotye's *Somebody That I Used to Know*, and *Riptide* by Vance Joy. Holly was faultless with her vocals, including a beautiful rendition of *Will You Love Me Tomorrow*. I let her do most of the singing, but took the lead on *1,000 Miles Away*, my favourite Hoodoo Gurus song. We wanted to stop there, but the people clapped loudly for more and the barman urged us on, as the longer the patrons stayed in the restaurant, the more they drank.

Holly started asking for requests. We did our best. If we couldn't play the requested song, we played something by that band or singer.

And we'd reached that fabulous point where it didn't matter if we got it wrong, messed up the chords or improvised the lyrics.

We played for an hour, and it was probably the most fun I'd ever had playing music.

The barman eventually told us to stop, as it was closing time. He put beers on the bar for us, and Holly also ordered tequila shots.

"What about lemon and honey?"

"Screw that," she said, and we downed the shots.

At the bar, I sold another ten CDs, and Holly sold some of hers as well. Nearly everyone said we should make a CD together. The barman said this was the best songwriters' night they'd had and we would always be welcome back.

We were the last to leave. Outside, the rain had stopped. I saw Janette get into a taxi with some guy, while others dispersed to their cars, whether they were sober enough to drive or not. Those walking down Challenger Parade staggered a little as they sang bits of the songs we'd played.

Holly and I stood in front of the entrance; she seemed as unsure as I was how to end the evening. I wanted to keep the night going, and thought of suggesting we go somewhere for another drink. But the moment seemed wrong, and I was pretty sure I was already over the legal limit. Plus, performing together wasn't quite the same as meeting, flirting and going home together. It occurred to me that Holly might have seen this more as a professional engagement than a potential hook up.

I decided not to push it and ruin what had been such a fun evening.

We walked together to her car.

"Great night."

Holly nodded. "And totally out of left field. I sold all the CDs I had with me."

"That's awesome."

"How'd you go?"

I thought my box felt considerably lighter than when I'd carried it into Clancy's. "Pretty good. I just hope they listen to it."

"They will. You're really talented. I should get you to join the Maids."

I laughed. "I don't think two-metre tall redheads look so good in dresses."

"It would give the band a very modern edge."

Holly stopped at an old white hatchback, bubbling with rust along the bottom, and unlocked it. She put her guitar case on the back seat.

"Thanks for making me get up there," she said. "I know this sounds strange, but I really needed that."

"You don't strike me as someone who needs to be pushed to perform."

"No, not that. I mean enjoying music. Just getting up there and playing and having a blast, without all the insecurity and uncertainty that comes with playing my own stuff. You know, are my songs any good? Am I any good? Am I gonna make it? Is anyone listening? Does anyone care? All that crap."

"I know exactly what you mean. But playing with the Maids isn't fun?"

"What do you reckon?"

"I'd say it's seriously hard work. You might get to play some songs you like, and as you said, you're getting good practice, but it still must be tough. I reckon you'd have to play some absolute rubbish, all while trying to satisfy whoever's paying the bill."

"That's it. If I didn't know better, I'd say you've done a few weddings yourself."

"I know the drill. And every one of these events has some guy who fancies himself and gets up on stage to sing or play or make an idiot of himself. Then you've got grandma saying it's too loud, teenagers telling you all the music's too old, and some drunks bullying you into playing *American Pie* and *Wonderwall*."

To my surprise, Holly hugged me.

"I needed that too," she said. "You gotta get me out of that band. When I hear a wedding march, I want to scream."

"That won't be the end of it, not when you're the musician in your family. You always get asked to play, at birthdays and Christmas and events, and you can't ever say no."

Holly hugged me harder and said, "People think you're their own personal minstrel and they can call on you any time they like."

"Sure. But then you do it and it goes alright, and everyone's really impressed. You can't help but feel good about it, especially when everyone tells you how good you are. Yep, that's me. The talented one in the family."

"I know that too."

She pulled back from the hug and we stood there smiling at each other.

"Do you still live in Mosman Park?"

"Just about. North Fremantle, near Leighton. My dog likes the beach, and Leighton's one of the few beaches where dogs are allowed."

"Nice. I like dogs."

She got into her car, closed the door and lowered the window. "Thanks again, for tonight."

"We should do it again some time. Are you coming next week?"

"Not sure yet. You?"

"Yeah, I think so. It looks like whoever shows up gets a set. It's good practice for me."

Holly went to start her car, then looked up at me. "What about, you know, meeting like normal people? In the real world. Without instruments."

"We could definitely do that."

"Sweet. My website's on the CD I gave you. Contact me that way."

"I will. It was nice seeing you again. I'm a bit annoyed with myself that I didn't talk to you more at Travis's gig."

"Yeah, well, let's make sure we get another chance. Goodnight, Rowan."

She drove off.

I put my guitar and CD box on the front seat of my Smart and started the drive back to Shenton Park. I kicked myself a little for not taking a risk with Holly, and wondered what had happened to the Rowan who boarded trains with girls he barely knew.

I focused instead on night's successes, which included playing my own songs at a gig and not getting shoved off stage. I'd been invited to come back next week and might even be up for a slot at the Clancy's in Fremantle. I'd sold some CDs and played a show; I now had something to tell people.

It was solid start.

I got home just after midnight. All the lights were out, save for a lamp shining in Nana's bedroom window. When I turned off my headlights, I saw the reflection of another set in the front windows of my house. I got out to see who had followed me home.

Holly jumped out of her white hatchback.

"I was at the traffic lights at West Coast Highway," she said. "The light was green and I was just sitting there, totally angry with myself. Because this was such a fantastic night, and I drove away from you because I don't want to be the kind of girl who meets a guy and goes home with him and everyone thinks is a slut. I've been there, and I don't want to revisit that. But then I saw you drive past and I thought, what the hell kind of tiny car does that really nice tall guy drive? And what the hell is wrong with me? We made great music together. We clicked, and it wasn't just chords and lyrics and putting on a show. There's something more, I know it, and I think you know it too. That doesn't happen every day. Maybe people live their whole lives and it never happens. And I hated myself for having this happen and then just dismissing it because I don't want people to think I'm easy. Why should I go home and wait for you to contact me, which you might never do? And let me tell you something, boy. I'm not easy. I'm hard. Very hard. I haven't even made you pass the dog test yet, because Charlie always knows when a guy is good or not. He can smell it on them. So, I'm sorry for following you like some crazy stalker, but this was the best night in, like, ages, and I completely killed it by taking off the way I did. I've been promising myself for, like, ages, to stop sabotaging everything good that happens to me. That's why I'm here and I want you to ask me to come inside and you're not allowed to say no. Nice house, by the way."

I laughed a little. "Thanks."

"This isn't funny. This is very serious. You don't laugh at a crazy person."

"You're not crazy. I drove home thinking basically all the same stuff."

"You don't want to people to think you're a slut?"

"Yep, and I think you're fully brave, to push aside all that crap about reputations and how people are supposed to be. And I want to pass your dog test."

She stepped towards me. I thought we'd kiss, but we hugged again.

"Would you like to come into my nice house?"

"Yes. But tell my first how you even get in this matchbox car."

"You'd be surprised. Easily. Better than in other much bigger cars. So don't talk bad about my wheels, because I love my Smart."

"I thought you'd be in some big off-roader. Anyway, are we going inside?"

"Definitely, but the thing is, I've got a roommate and we need to be quiet. So, if you have any more ranting to do or automotive queries to make, you should do it out here. We can also sit in my tiny car for a while and you can rant some more."

251

"We won't both fit. But I'm all ranted out." She clicked an imaginary remote control. "I'm now on mute."

I took my guitar and CD box from my car. "Your dog's name is Charlie?"

Holly nodded.

"I think I'll pass that test."

→←

I woke to the sound of laughter: Churchill and Holly. While I couldn't quite decipher their conversation, I stayed in bed, enjoying the sound of their voices and their laughter. It made me think of my parents, and those weekend mornings when they were up early and getting breakfast ready for me and Conor. It had been so comforting to hear them talking, while the kettle boiled and whistled, to hear the clink of plates and cutlery being set on the table. The sounds of a once happy family.

It was Wednesday morning, just before eight. My clothes from last night, except my emerald shirt, were strewn on my one chair, together with Holly's clothes. I could see a slight bulge in the front right pocket of my jeans, full with the money I'd made last night selling CDs.

So, it was real. I was a musician, with gig experience and an album in circulation. And from my first solo gig, I'd brought home a fantastic girl.

No, she followed me home, and she wasn't just some groupie or hanger-on.

I smiled, recalling our exchange from last night, and how nervous we both had been once we got inside. As we had undressed, Holly had remarked how interesting it was that while we had no problem getting up in front of strangers and giving them a window to our souls through music, when it came to getting naked for the first time with someone we liked, all that confidence and brio disappeared.

She was some kind of a miracle, Holly, but I couldn't help thinking what bad timing this was. Things were just starting. I could already feel momentum building, and I wanted to believe it was real and not just my hope. Yes, there would be more gigs coming in Perth. Yes, there would be a tour of the States later this year, even if it was just a few shows in Bozeman. And yes, there would be a trip to Europe to meet and potentially take delivery of Eris.

Where was Holly going to fit into all of that? Could two up-and-coming musicians be in a relationship together?

This wasn't some dismissible one-night stand. I didn't do those, and I didn't think Holly did them either. She was right; we had clicked. There was something more here and it would be stupid not to pursue it.

More laughter came from the kitchen. It sounded like Churchill was at his charming best, and had probably made Holly one of his sterling morning-after coffees.

I got up, pulled on my jeans from last night and took a clean shirt from my closet. I went to the bathroom first, to splash water on my face and give my mouth a rinse. It would've been good to see a slightly different Rowan looking back at me in the mirror: the hard-working musician with the sleeves of his shirt rolled up who sold CDs by the handful. But it was the same old me. It was a stern reminder that I still had a long way to go, and all I'd taken were some baby-steps forward.

In the kitchen, I leaned against the doorway, regarding the two of them, both with mugs on the table. Holly was wearing my shirt from last night. It was huge on her, a button-up dress.

"There he is," she said brightly. "We were just talking about you."

Churchill turned to me and smiled. "This girl," he said, pointing at Holly, "is a keeper. I got up this morning and she was in kitchen making coffee. I very nearly threw her out, but," and he took a sip from his mug, "it's divine. Better than mine, if you can believe that."

"You want a cup?" Holly asked.

"Yeah. Thanks."

She already knew where the cups were and went to work on my coffee, stirring in milk she heated on the stove. In her bare feet, her waist was just below the level of the kitchen counter, and the shirt hung past her knees.

"You probably thought I'd be in here drinking more lemon and honey," she said, handing me the cup.

"No tequila shots?"

"Let's wait another hour or so."

I laughed and shook my head a few times. I couldn't quite believe this girl had followed me home.

"You sexed up teenagers are making me feel really crap," Churchill said. "What kind of brilliant evening did I miss last night?"

"Holly, this is Churchill. Be tolerant, please. He's a complete weirdo, but I love him anyway."

253

"I don't want to interrupt whatever bromance you got going on here," Holly said, giving me a playful smile. "Can I have a shower?"

"Sure. There are towels in the bathroom. Just take one."

She took her mug with her and gave me a kiss as she went through the doorway. I sat down at the table with Churchill.

"I like her," he said. "That's some girl to bring home after your very first gig."

"She didn't tell you?"

"Tell me what?"

"She was playing last night. Came on after me. And we played together at the end. It was great."

He put his hands together in prayer. "Please, God, tell me that the wonderful Janette got all of that on video."

I decided not to tell Churchill that I'd seen Janette get into a taxi with some guy at the end of the night. "Probably not. She was pretty far gone, even before I got up to play."

"Still, sounds like it went well."

"It did. Really well." I let out a long sigh. "This is it, Church. This is what I want to do. I want to play music. Just the thought of standing in a workshop and repairing some guy's guitar, seems like, you know, a total waste of time."

"You need some more gigs then."

I nodded and sipped my coffee. "You're right. This is good."

"Told you."

"I know I got a lot of work ahead of me, and I'm starting at the bottom, maybe even a little too late, but I'm going to make this happen. I'll even start taking gigs where I have to play covers."

"Weddings, parties, anything," Churchill said, and he laughed.

"You're not far off. Holly pays her bills by playing at weddings. She's in a band and they pretty much play a wedding every weekend."

"Can't quite imagine what that must be like. Never been to a wedding."

"The Maids of Honour supply the soundtrack for a lot of them."

"That's the name of the band? That's dynamite. No wonder they're popular."

"Holly plays the drums."

Churchill laughed some more. "Holy crap, Rowan. Your first gig and you bring home far and away the best and most interesting girl in the joint. How did you manage that?"

I wasn't sure how to answer that, because I didn't really know myself.

"Don't do that, Rowan," he said, lowering his voice.

"Do what?"

"I know what you're thinking. She's out of your league. I'm telling you that you're plenty good enough."

"Thanks, Church. I can't really explain it. We just clicked. And get this, we'd met before. She played at a show I went to a few months ago. She was subbing on the drums for Travis's band. But we didn't talk much that night, and she left not long after the show."

"A good thing too."

"Why?"

"Because if you'd clicked then and the sparks had flown, you can be pretty sure the postcards would've been dumped in the garbage and there'd have been no trip to the States, which would've meant no Eris, no Charlie and no album."

I thought about this, sipping Holly's superb coffee. "Did you find religion while I was in the States?"

"I'm just saying to be thankful that everything happened the way it did." He leaned forward and lowered his voice again. "That is, if you are actually keen on Holly."

"I am. I'm just trying to figure out where she's going to fit in my musical equation."

"If it's love, all the maths in the world won't help you. Trust me, I'm an accountant. Sort of. Look, you'll find a way. You both will. And you said she played last night, so she's probably thinking about all the same stuff. Talk to her about it." He put his cup on the table and stood up. "Now, if you'll excuse me, I better get back to work."

"Are you on the roof today?"

"For the morning shift, I reckon so." He went to leave the kitchen, stopped, turned and said, "Well done, Rowan. I'm proud of you."

"Thanks, Church."

In the hallway, he nearly collided with Holly, who was wrapped in a white towel and heading for my room.

I helped myself to the last of the coffee. I noticed Churchill had removed all the postcards from the fridge door, and I wondered why he'd done that. We hadn't talked about Nola and Eris since my second day back, when he had confirmed Nola was Grilla and I'd told him Eris was the Greek goddess of discord. We'd both agreed to keep Nola's alias a secret and to wait until the end of the year's meet in Europe. Until that trip, there wasn't much else we could do.

Back at the table, sipping, I saw Jock wander past the window, leaving Nana's place.

My phone was still in the pocket of my jeans. I took it out and scanned my emails. There was one from Charlie. She had replied to the email I'd sent yesterday, in which I'd informed her that the CDs had arrived and thanked her for all the work she'd done. The inquiries were coming in so fast, she wrote, that she'd enlisted a friend to handle things. This friend was also a booking agent. Charlie said I should be ready to come back to the States soon, once the dates were finalised.

It was almost too early in the morning to comprehend what big news this was. An American tour. People hearing my songs and liking them. Venues wanting me to play, maybe even charging punters to come in. A booking agent lining up gigs.

Ludicrous.

"Did someone die?" Holly asked, coming into the kitchen. She wore her clothes from last night, but hadn't put on any make-up. She looked fresh and lovely.

"It's just, yeah, some really good news. I seem to be building a bit of a following in the States. My producer's lining up a whole bunch of stuff."

"That's great, right?"

"It's unbelievable."

As Holly stood there smiling at me, I wondered if she would want to come with me on tour. Maybe we could play together.

For some reason, that felt like a bad idea.

"What's wrong?" she asked.

"Nothing. I'm stunned. A couple of days ago, I was nothing and going nowhere. Now, things are starting to happen."

"That's a good thing, and you should go with it."

"Yeah. Listen, you want to get some breakfast somewhere?"

"Well, I think you owe me breakfast for scrambling my morning routine," Holly said. "I'm usually up at dawn to walk Charlie and do my drumming practice. Poor dog's probably scratching at the walls and wondering where I am."

"How about we pick him up and go to Leighton? We'll get some breakfast on the way."

"I like the way you think. That'll give me a chance to change as well."

I drank the rest of my coffee. "Let me put some shorts on. I want to take a swim."

"We'll take my car."

"Sure."

I gave Holly a long kiss. In my room, I threw a beach bag together, with a towel, hat and sunscreen. I also grabbed a CD from the box, thinking I could drop it at Jono's on the way back, as an apology for leaving him in the lurch.

Outside, Holly was leaning against her old white hatchback and staring at Churchill, who was already on the roof.

"He is weird," she said with a smile.

We both got in the car and Holly drove us up Morgan Street.

→←

Four months passed in a blur. The spring was hot enough to feel like summer.

All the gigging was tiring, and it was hard to get up for playing covers all the time. But the money was good and I needed the funds for my trips to America and Europe. I took all the gigs offered to me and played whatever songs they told me to. The only problem was that I couldn't get any gigs for my own music, beyond being a regular at Clancy's on Tuesdays.

My relationship with Holly seemed to mirror my music career. After a strong start, we went through some rough patches as the demands of life got in the way. We were both frustrated. Holly was playing more for the Maids of Honour than for herself, and I was churning out acoustic covers night after night. It was a struggle to find time for each other and to muster the support we both needed. Not helping our cause was that we lived to different rhythms; Holly's dawn drumming practice and dog walking clashed with my preference for sleeping in and easing into each day.

My end of October departure date sat on the horizon like a huge carrot, drawing me forward, until that day arrived.

On that last morning, we walked from Holly's flat on Wellington Street to the Victoria Street station to catch the train to Fremantle. There wasn't much to say, but we tried to smile at each other. We were both sad, but my sadness was tempered by excitement. I thought

Holly was feeling a fair bit of worry, and possibly envy. Following my flight, I had a week-long stretch of gigs at various venues in Bozeman, then two months of touring, with dates in Canada as well. The schedule was set up, on my request, for me to work my way east. At the end, I would fly from New York to London for more shows there. It all meant no more cover gigs, at least for a while, and being separated from Holly for the better part of three months.

In the previous week, as everything started to wind down for me and I prepared to leave, I repeatedly said to Holly how great the last four months had been and that she had no reason to worry. Most of the venues on my itinerary were small places. I figured I'd be lucky to get more than ten people on any night, given that I was still a complete unknown. Churchill was calling this the "Intimate Tour". It was my first and could well be my last, but I had to give it a shot.

After a picnic dinner at Cottesloe Beach last night, we'd argued on the walk back to Holly's flat: about my trip and the potential temptations I'd face. Nothing I said could reassure her, and in the end, she said we should stop discussing it and just enjoy our last night together, which we had, with a sad kind of urgency. We got physically close while we both drifted emotionally apart, preparing for three months of separation.

We sat on the train in silence, our shoulders touching as the wagon rocked.

I was in love with Holly, but I hadn't told her yet. I hadn't told anyone, not even Churchill, whose council I always sought on such matters. He'd been very helpful in getting me to repair things with both my parents, which in turn enabled me see my childhood in a more positive light.

The impending tour made me hold back from confessing my love. Music took priority. I feared telling Holly how I felt would make it harder for us to be apart.

I also wasn't completely sure about how Holly felt about me. For her, music also took priority. I had the sense she resented my burgeoning success, as limited as it was, and wondered if she, like me, thought that two struggling musicians couldn't make it as a couple, as any success would throw the dynamic out of whack.

And then there was Eris, potentially waiting for me somewhere in Europe. I hadn't told Holly about my daughter, and I hadn't heard anything from Nola. As there had been no artistic acts attributed to

Grilla since the pigs-in-boats thing in Des Moines, well over four months ago I assumed Nola was still at Isle Royale and her chaos art had been shelved for the entire park season.

When we got to the station in Fremantle, I took Holly's hand and led her down Phillimore Street.

"I want to show you something."

"Okay."

It was a beautiful day, warm, with the south-westerly wind just starting to pick up. It blew Holly's skirt in the air a little, revealing her shapely, tanned legs.

We walked past the new fire station, built close to the street. The old fire station, with freshly painted red doors, was now a youth hostel. It made me think of Little Rock and Austin; chasing Nola, which now felt like a long time ago.

"I remember when this area was seriously run down," Holly said. "There were some streets you couldn't even walk down, during the day or at night."

"It looks good with all the renovations, but I think it's lost some of its character. It looks a bit like a film set."

Holly put her arms around me as we walked. "Spoken like a true romantic. I'm gonna miss you."

"I'll miss you too."

"You'll be too busy screwing college girls to think of your crazy drummer."

"Don't start that again. That's not me."

She let me go and we walked in step, holding hands.

"I want to believe that," Holly said. "Churchill told me about the long stretches you've had between drinks in the past. He's a wonderful source of information."

"Good old Church. He keeps everything secret. Trust me. This trip will be all about the music. I'm planning to give everything on stage and collapse into bed each night. I want to write some new songs too."

I said this sincerely, and I believed it myself, but it didn't appear to appease Holly, who might well have been more worried I'd come back a successful musician than one who'd shagged a different groupie each night.

We walked behind the warehouse where Travis's band had pulled the paint from the walls with their thunderous music and Holly's superb drumming.

"What are we doing here?" she asked.

"There's a mural I want to show you."

We stopped in front of it.

"Wow," Holly said, taking it in. "Now that's a different kind of shark attack."

As we stared at it, I sat down on a stack of pallets. This brought me down to Holly's height and took the pressure off my lower back. All the gigging had taken its toll.

I took Holly's hand. "I've got something very important to tell you."

"Oh, no. Don't you go breaking up with me. Not now. Don't you dare."

"That's not it. I'm not breaking up with you." I pointed at the mural. "I know who painted this. She goes by the name of Grilla, but I know who she really is. We met, six years ago in New Zealand. We had a short affair, and that affair produced a child."

"What?"

"I only found out for sure when I was in the States earlier this year. That was why I went there in the first place. To try to find them, mother and daughter."

"You have a daughter? Why are you telling me this now? Why did you wait so long?"

"I'm sorry. I guess I never found the right moment. We've both been so busy."

"That's a lame excuse."

"Yeah, it is."

Holly pulled her hand free. "Oh, I get it. You're actually going back to hook up with this Grilla chick and build a little family with her."

"No, that's way off. We have nothing to do with each other. The plan is to meet in Europe. And that's why I'm telling you this, because I think I'll be bringing Eris back with me."

"Your daughter?"

"I know it sounds strange, but that's what I think. I'm telling you now so you won't be shocked when you meet me at the airport and I've got a little red-headed girl in tow."

Holly took a few steps away from me. "Then what?"

"What do you mean?"

"When you're back and your daughter is with you. What happens then?"

260

"To be honest, I really don't know. It'll probably be chaos, at least for the first few weeks. Everything will be completely new for her, and for me, and for Churchill too."

"Don't forget me. I'm part of this, aren't I?"

"Yes, of course you are. Holly, I want to be with you. I also have this really strong feeling that Eris needs me. I'm not exactly sure what that means, but I do know I have to become part of her life, somehow. Probably the main part. Nola pretty much said that the last time I saw her."

"When was that?"

"Just before I came back."

"Nola is Grilla?"

I nodded.

"And her last name is?"

"I can't tell you that."

"Why not?"

"Because Churchill and I both agreed it was best to keep Grilla's identity a secret."

"I don't see why you should do that." Holly turned her back on the mural. "It doesn't matter anyway. Sounds like Eris is the one you should be worried about. Or are you in love with Nola or Grilla, or whoever she is?"

"Believe me, I'm not. It was just a holiday fling, and it was six years ago. I'm sorry I didn't tell you all of this sooner. That was a mistake."

"It was."

"But I'm also telling you now because I want you to think about whether we can be a family. You, me and Eris."

She started to walk away, then came back again. "Where's that coming from? You mean, get married, house in the suburbs, a minivan. All that? I've got some friends who have that, and let me tell you, it doesn't look remotely appealing."

"We can do it differently. Try to."

"So, you kick homebody Churchill out onto the street where he'll turn into a quivering heap, and we raise a little girl whose real mother doesn't want her? You're getting way ahead of yourself, boy. You should be focusing on your tour, not on whether I'm ready to play house with you. And Eris? Bloody hell, let's cross that bridge when we come to it."

She came in front of me and grabbed my shoulders with her strong hands.

"Rowan, I could just about smack you. You're about to do what we dream of. You have no idea what I would give to be in your position. Your album is great and you're going on tour in America. This is your chance. This could end up being your only chance. This is what we imagine doing when we're writing rubbish songs in our bedrooms or playing covers at some bogan wedding, and wondering the whole time why some pathetic singer is famous and we're not. Go over there and make it happen. Everything with Eris will come after. And let me tell you, she'll find it way cooler to come to Australia with a rock-god dad than with some struggling musician who screwed up his only chance to make it and now can't afford to buy a can of baked beans."

Holly started crying. I stood up to hug her and we rocked back and forth, almost dancing.

"Whatever happens," she said, leaning back and looking up at me, "just come back. Even if every show is empty and Nola decides to keep Eris, just come back. I'll still be here, banging the drum."

"Deal. And I promise I'll keep my pants on."

Holly pulled out of the hug. "That's not what I'm worried about."

Right then, I thought the best thing for our relationship would be what Holly had just said: me failing and coming home without Eris.

Holly turned to look at the mural. "This is awful," she said, walking away. "The scribbling of one seriously deranged bitch. Probably best to get your daughter away from her."

O Christmas Tree

It's just before midnight when there's a knock on the door. A single knock, the fist resting momentarily on the door, dampening the knock's resonance.

She's ready, and has been for nearly an hour. She's dressed for the sub-zero temperatures outside, and sat since eleven in the old swivel chair, sweating under all her clothes, turning back and forth, thinking about the last few months and feeling so glad that it was almost over. Freedom, she thinks, could be just a few days away.

She stands up and opens the door a crack.

"What took you so long, Kim?" she whispers.

Kim has her balaclava on top of her head, ready to be pulled down, and is just about giddy with excitement. "Dean kept on working. And then he came to bed horny."

"What did you tell him? Headache?"

"Period. I know he doesn't like that kind of sex, and he fell for it too."

"He doesn't know your cycles?"

Kim flashed a smile that betrayed a certain bitterness. "The only schedules that exist are the ones in his phone. I'm happy to say my monthlies are not in there."

"Give me a minute."

She closes the door, wondering again what has happened to Kim, who went from wild vandal to obedient housewife in a couple of years, and is barely a shadow of the partner-in-crime she remembers.

In the bed, her daughter sleeps on. The little girl is very still, thanks to the extra dose of Phenergan administered, and she reaches down to touch that small, soft neck and confirm there's a pulse.

There is.

She shoulders the backpack that's full with cans of lighter fluid and Christmas tree candles, thinking that it feels dangerously heavy.

Kim is waiting outside in the dark hallway, fidgety and excited. When they're both standing there, Kim says, "I have really missed this," and her teeth are shiny.

She slaps Kim in the face. "Calm yourself, K. We're not spraying graffiti on some building in Wicker Park. This is real. We're about to commit several crimes in the name of art. Keep it together."

Shocked, Kim nods. "Sorry. It's been a while. I'm out of form."

"Just focus on this moment and what we're doing. Try to forget all of this and who you are, at least for the next few hours."

"I get it. But my life is not as pathetic as you think."

"Whatever. Let's go."

"You've become a little nasty, N."

She shrugs this off, not willing to argue with Kim and more interested in building a massive Christmas tree.

They head out of the house and walk down Johannes Müller Strasse. Twice, she has to tell Kim to slow down and walk at a normal pace. At the Riehl Kinderkrankenhaus station, they time it perfectly, arriving on the platform as the train pulls in. They get on backwards and stand in the doorway.

"Keep looking at the floor," she says. "We don't want to get on camera."

"I know what I'm doing."

"And no eye contact."

Kim's hands are shaking a little as she grips a pole. "Will you stop it?"

"And relax. You're making me nervous."

"I can't, N. I'm buzzing."

She smiles. "It's a nice feeling, isn't it? And we haven't even got to the good stuff yet."

"We got about five hours," Kim says, checking her watch. "Maybe four. The locals start the day early here, even in the winter darkness."

The train makes three stops, including at the end station at Sebastian Strasse.

"Walk normally," she says as they get off the train. "Maybe even pretend you're a little drunk. And keep your head down."

Kim does as she's told.

It feels colder in this part of Cologne, outside of the city centre. A chilly wind is funnelling down Sebastian Strasse from the Rhine River. But it means that the rolled up balaclavas on their heads and the black gloves on their hands don't garner attention. The few people on the streets this late at night are also rugged up against the early January cold.

The apartments still have Christmas lights and decorations on the balconies, lending the street a festive air the time of year doesn't deserve.

At the corner of Scheiben Strasse, there's a huge pile of discarded Christmas trees.

"This'll be easy," Kim says. She bends down to take a trunk of a tree in each hand.

"Leave it. We need a truck first. And we need to stay off the main roads."

It was her idea to come to this part of the city. The arcing Scheiben Strasse, at the north end of a racecourse, has a lot of trucks parked on it, because the parking is free and there are plenty of spaces. She scoped the area two days ago and was glad to find so many trucks here.

Tonight, many of the trucks are branded with company names. Kim stops at the first one and prepares to break into it.

"Wait. We need a plain truck. Something that witnesses won't remember."

"Yeah, that's probably right."

They continue along the street until they reach an old white truck that's seriously dirty.

"This one," she says. "Oh, it's so perfect."

Kim gets to work jimmying the door open, sliding a flattened shoe horn down the window and popping the lock.

"You still got it, K," she says, recalling those glorious years in her late teens when the two of them and the W-Crew raised so much hell in Chicago.

Kim gets in and leans across to unlock the passenger door. "The things you learn as a kid, you never forget."

She moves around the truck and gets in as well, putting her backpack on the floor, between her knees. From the top pocket, she takes two orange vests.

"Here, put this on," she says, handing Kim one. "In case anyone asks, you can tell them in your flawless German that we work for the city. And the balaclavas are because it's really freaking cold."

It takes about a minute for Kim to get the truck started. The engine makes the kind of struggling, clanking sound of a vehicle not terribly well looked after. The cab is messy and dirty.

"Make sure you remember where we parked," she says. "We want to bring the truck back to this exact spot."

Kim smiles. "Or we could park it further down the street. Screw with the owners."

"No, let's keep it clean and focus on what we're doing. The truck is just a brush, to help us paint the canvas. The brush goes back in the jar at the end."

265

"You know, N, you're much more intense about this than you used to be."

"Oh yeah? You should get serious about this too. You just committed grand theft auto, whatever the German word is for that."

"Kraftfahrzeugdiebstahl."

"See? Sounds very serious. Five words in one. So, get with it."

Kim pulls her balaclava down over her face. "Game face on."

They start in the quiet Weidenpesch district, working both sides of Neusser Strasse and sticking to the smaller streets. Rather than stopping each time to pick up single Christmas trees, they look out for large piles. The diligent, orderly locals have obliged, piling trees close to the street, allowing for easy pick up.

There are a few people around, walking dogs or getting home late from work, sport or something, but they don't give her and Kim a second glance. She was worried the balaclavas might attract the wrong kind of attention, but it appears the locals are far more interested in their own concerns. She assumes the orange vests are also doing the trick.

The truck fills quickly. Pine needles stick to her gloves and jacket.

They zigzag towards the city centre, collecting discarded trees in Mauenheim and Nippes and stacking them on top of the others.

She finds it fascinating that an object that people gather around and lovingly decorate one week can be cast out onto the street the next.

When they can't fit any more trees in, they drive down Merheimer Strasse, towards the centre of Cologne. Kim drums the steering wheel with her gloved hands.

"I keep thinking I should be tired, but I'm wide awake." Kim says. "I can't remember the last time I stayed up this late."

"It's the adrenaline."

"It's like doing a really small bit of ice, without all the nasty side effects."

"You should know," she says softly.

"It makes me feel like I've been sleeping for years. Don't get me wrong, I like my life here, but it could really use a bit of spice added to it."

"You were the last one I expected to become a housewife, K."

"Things change. Being poor sucks. I couldn't spend my whole life getting high and living in squalor. Remember how we pretty much

266

stank of spray paint all the time? About what about those winters in the squat on Wabansia? We had to go out and steal pallets to use as firewood."

She smiles, enjoying the memory. "It was fun at the time. We were scavengers, improvising and creating. Every single day was a work of art."

"That's not how I remember it. Every day was about basic survival and getting the next hit. But you've inspired me to shake up my life here. Get active. Stir up the city."

"You can't. You know that. Living in one place and trying to do stuff like this, you'd get caught. Don't forget that back in the day we had cops coming to the squat so often, we got to know their names and offered them coffee, when we had it."

Kim laughs. "I slept with one. You remember that? Officer Doolan. Can't remember his first name."

"Don't do anything stupid here, K. If you want to pull off something like this, you need to be gone the next day. You have to move around and go to places people wouldn't expect. And try not to leave any kind of a trail."

"Still, I need to shake things up somehow."

"You already have. Tonight."

"You mean you have. You're the tornado, blowing into town unannounced and leaving everything in disarray."

"You're welcome."

"That wasn't a compliment."

Kim turns the truck onto Innere Kanalstrasse and parks off the road, half on the bicycle path. There are no cars on the street. They both look towards the park, where the trees are shrouded in darkness.

"The old fountain's on the other side of those trees," Kim says.

"Then it's time to get to work."

"What if someone sees us? What's the back-up plan?"

She looks both ways down the road. "K, it's three in the morning on a Wednesday. It's freezing cold. There's not a car on the road. If by chance a cop car cruises by and stops, we run for it and meet back at your house. Okay?"

Kim nods, and they get out of the truck.

The octagon-shaped fountain looks like it hasn't seen water in years. It's still holding the charred remains of a few fires.

That's something she hadn't reckoned on: that there might be homeless people camping here. But there's no one, as it's too cold to be sleeping rough tonight.

They get to work, dragging the trees from the truck to the fountain and piling them up, working to shape the pile to look like a Christmas tree, which isn't easy to do without a ladder. It's not as big as she hoped, but still impressive.

It's hard work. The dried-out trees leave a trail of pine needles and short branches.

When they're just about finished, a light snow starts to fall, covering the tree-shaped pile with glittery tinsel.

"Can you believe it?" Kim asks, holding out her gloved hands to catch some flakes.

"This isn't the first time that everything has fallen perfectly into place. Looks like the chaos gods are on our side tonight."

Kim clips the candles to the tree branches.

She empties the cans of lighter fluid, circling around the pile and splashing it halfway up as well. The empty cans go into a plastic bag.

"Hey, was macht ihr da?"

Blowing steam, the runner is clad in skin-tight, reflective clothing and has a light attached to his head. He also has a phone in a special sleeve on his upper arm. He pulls up a flap and removes the phone.

She's the first to react. She spins the plastic bag a few times in her hand, getting the empty cans closer together, and swings this at the runner's head. He hits the ground, unconscious, the screen on his phone illuminated.

"Jesus, N, was that necessary?"

"He was calling the cops, so yes it was. I didn't see you trying to do anything."

Kim bends down to see if the man is still alive. As the blood slowly seeps through his yellow hat, it glistens.

"He's breathing."

"Of course he is. I hit him with a few empty cans of lighter fluid. The guy must be made of paper."

"You could've killed him."

"Who the hell goes running at four in the morning? In winter?"

Kim picks up the phone and presses the screen. "The call went through. Let's light this thing and get out of here."

"Do it. Do it. You have the lighter."

Kim drops the phone and starts darting around the pile, lighting candles.

She bends down and retrieves the phone, tapping the screen before the screensaver activates. She presses the camera icon and prepares to start filming.

With the candles lit and the snow falling, she says, "That's good."

Kim stands next to her. "Can we go now?"

"Here, take this," she says, handing Kim the phone. She realises making a video will save her from having to take a photograph, which is good because she's found the Polaroids never come out very well at night.

"Are you out of your mind?" Kim asks.

"Start recording, but keep me out of the shot."

"We don't have time for this, N."

"Do it."

She takes a card from her pocket and holds it in front of the phone. Her G-symbol is on one side. On the other is "O Christmas Tree", written in bright red pen and decorated with holly and presents. She shows both sides of the card, then flings it towards the pile.

The snow starts to get heavier, and the wind blows out a few candles. She realises the whole thing may not catch fire on its own, so takes a box of matches from her pocket.

On the ground, the runner starts to stir.

"Come on, N."

She jams six matchsticks into one end of the box and pushes the flammable tips together. She lights a match, then lights the other six, which quickly fuse together and make a bright flame. She tosses the box onto the pile. The lighter fluid ignites with a loud whoosh and encircles the pile in flames. The trees burn quickly and there's a lot of smoke.

"It's beautiful," she says. "Merry Christmas."

The runner gets slowly onto one knee and puts a hand to the back of his head.

"I'm outta here," Kim says, dropping the phone and running for the truck.

She watches the flames for a few more seconds and inhales some of the smoke. "A natural high."

Then she runs as well. When she gets in the cab, Kim is struggling to start the truck because of her shaking hands.

"You got it, K. You can do it." She looks between the trees at the bonfire and the stream of rising smoke. "This is spectacular. Imagine if we'd got more trees."

"I don't care. I just want the truck to start."

When it does, Kim bangs the steering wheel and pulls the truck onto Innere Kanalstrasse.

She pulls off her balaclava and puts her boots up on the dashboard. The outline of the fire is still there when she closes her eyes.

"Don't speed," she says.

"Stop telling me what to do."

Kim keeps her balaclava on as she takes the K4 to Parkgürtel. Both of them are silent until they reach Scheiben Strasse and the truck is parked in the same spot. Kim turns the engine and lights off.

They sit there, both staring straight ahead.

"I can't believe you knocked that guy out," Kim says, breaking the silence.

"Collateral damage. And anyway, he survived. Think of the fire. Its colour and smell."

"Yeah, it burned. Big deal."

"I once met a guy who had hair the colour of fire," she says.

"Like Eris?"

She nods.

Kim takes off her balaclava. "Is he her father? Because you never said anything about him."

"I'm going to meet him again. In Berlin."

"Is he German? Can't be. A red-headed German?"

"He's Australian."

"And he's coming all the way to Berlin to meet up with you? Does he know about Eris?"

"He's already here, touring Europe. He's a musician." She finds it interesting that she's bragging about this. "His name is Rowan Davidson."

"Never heard of him," Kim says, shaking her head.

"He's just starting out. You should give him a listen. He's alright."

"Yeah, whatever. But why Berlin?"

"I'm giving him Eris," she says, and it feels good to confess this, as telling someone makes it more than just an idea in her head.

"Are you joking?"

"I can't do it anymore. I've had enough."

270

"You can't just stop being a parent," Kim says. "You're in it for life."

"There are other ways to do it. I'm not giving up my entire life for a kid the way you have."

"That's really unfair. Freaking low, N. Don't forget how much we completely screwed up when we were teenagers. We flunked out of high school. We didn't go to college. We were pathetic and going nowhere, wasting our lives. It took me nearly two years to get clean. I was really lucky to meet Dean and to have him pull me out of the quagmire we were living in. Even better was when he got transferred over here and I could leave all that crap behind. Like, close the book for good. I mean, come on. Who the hell wants to be a middle-aged vandal?"

"Is that what you think I am?"

"I don't know what to think of you. You're frozen in time. Same as always. Completely self-involved, trying to make every single thing you do a work of art. All you care about is your next project. You nearly killed that runner and you couldn't care less about him. You don't even care about your own daughter. You're gonna palm her off to some guy you barely know."

Kim gets out of the truck and slams the door. As she walks down Scheiben Strasse, the balaclava and orange vest both get tossed against the fence.

She gets out and picks both items up, putting them in the top pocket of her backpack. It's tempting to walk in the opposite direction, away from Kim and her petty concerns, but all her stuff is still at Kim's house. So, she runs to catch up.

"I'm not frozen in time," she says. "I just need new inspiration."

"What makes you think this Ronan will even take Eris?" Kim asks.

"It's Rowan."

"You don't think he gets a say in this? Maybe he doesn't want Eris either. Then what? No one wants the poor little kid. I know you get a real kick out of telling people what to do, but you can't just order him to take her."

"He's a good guy. He'll be a far better parent than me."

"That won't be hard, because you set the bar seriously low. What about Eris? Have you even considered what she might want?"

"She wants to meet him."

"Okay, she knows. Wow. That's something," Kim says, ramping up the sarcasm.

"I had to tell her. I'd be giving her to a stranger otherwise. She likes his music too."

They reach the corner and cross the street.

"What planet are you living on, N? In case you haven't noticed, Eris just about worships you. It's almost unhealthy."

"She just wants attention."

"It's pretty clear she doesn't get enough of that."

She sighs, hating the conversation. "Well, she'll get more from Rowan."

The train is waiting at the station, already with passengers sitting inside. The display shows the train leaves in four minutes.

"Stand in the doorway," she says as they get on. "And keep you head down."

Kim ignores her and takes a seat. "It's over. I don't care about that and I'm not taking orders from you."

She sits down as well and puts the backpack on the seat opposite. "Fine. It's finished anyway. But at least stop shouting like a crazy bag lady. You're bringing attention to yourself."

"Why not? We can make this train ride a work of art as well. Screw up people's lives with chaos."

A few passengers look in their direction.

"Stop it."

Kim calms down, then gives her a hard stare. "I can't believe you are just gonna abandon Eris. What if Rowan's a paedophile or something?"

"Jesus, K. Relax. Rowan's good. And I'm not abandoning Eris. Like I keep telling you, she'll be better off."

"I hope so. What about Helen? I thought she was helping."

This makes her laugh. "Helen is so far beyond help. Eris was with her for the summer and it was a disaster. Helen forgot about Eris on a daily basis. The day-care centre had to call me, because Helen wouldn't even answer the phone. I had to leave my job early and go back to Chicago to sort things out. Then I get there and Helen tells me she's sold the house and is going on a road trip to New Mexico."

"What about the other two? The couple?"

"Warren died and Cyril met someone else. And now Helen's gone off to chase rainbows and moonbeams in the desert. There's no one left for me in Chicago, and I can't take Eris with me when I do my ranger work. Rowan is the only solution."

"Or you settle down somewhere."

She shakes her head. "I'm not doing that. I'll wither and die."

The train slowly pulls forward.

"What about boarding school?" Kim asks. "Eris is due to start this year. Send her somewhere."

This gives her reason to pause, as it's an option she never considered. "Would you do that? Would you want that?"

"I guess not. I'd want to stay with my parents."

"Rowan is Eris's father and right now, he's the best option. The only option."

Kim nods slowly. "Leaving you free to pursue your chaos art, and to search for new inspiration."

"I think the chaos thing is over. I need a new direction."

"Was Eris part of that? Was she a bedlam project? Chaos life with daughter?"

"No, of course not. It just happened. I met Rowan and then I was pregnant."

"I don't believe you," Kim says.

"Believe whatever you want."

At the first stop, a few commuters board the train, dressed for work. They shake the snow from their jackets.

"What if he says no?" Kim asks.

"He won't. He knows the importance of being a parent."

"Good. Because you clearly don't." Kim looks out the window. "What happened to you, N? We all thought you'd be the one to go on and do something amazing. Something memorable. That's why we followed you. We wanted to be part of it."

"I've done a lot of memorable stuff."

"You think so? If you want my opinion, you're wasting your talents. What you're doing isn't art. Setting trees on fire? That's just vandalism."

"You were very into it a few hours ago."

"It was a prank. You're no better than a ten year-old kid dropping rocks from a bridge onto a freeway. There's nothing artistic about playing pranks on people and hurting them, or mindlessly destroying stuff."

She's too angry to reply. She finds it frustrating that Kim has completely missed the point, and thinks it would be a waste of time to get her to understand it.

"I want you out of my house," Kim says. "This morning. You pack your stuff and go."

She nods. "Fine."

"And if Rowan doesn't take Eris, I want you to bring her to me. I'll take care of her."

"That's very generous of you, but I won't be doing that. The absolutely worst thing for Eris would be to grow up in your house. I'd be just about alright leaving her with you, but Dean's a douchebag, K. He always was and always will be. Yeah, I get it that he saved you from the street and good on him. But that doesn't mean he gets to hold that over you forever and that you have to keep your marriage going when you don't love him anymore."

Kim almost starts crying.

"I'm sorry, but you don't see it, because you're living it," she continues. "Or maybe you just don't want to see it. But it's there. You're both going through the motions, and I bet your kids know it too. Kids aren't stupid. So, don't point your finger at me and call me an irresponsible parent, because that's you. There's no love in your house. There's just frustration and compromise and loneliness. I know I'm a bad mother and I know I'm not cut out to be a parent, but at least I'm honest about it. That's why I want Rowan to take care of Eris. Because it's the best thing for her."

"You're a beast."

The train pulls into the Riehl Kinderkrankenhaus station. Kim stands up and gets off.

She follows, but walks slowly, happy to put some distance between the two of them. As she watches Kim march down Johannes Müller Strasse, she's reminded that the one thing that often causes the most chaos in life is the truth.

"There'll be fallout," she says, but hopes it will be good; that Kim will stand up and try to fix things.

She thinks of that beautiful fire they made. That mesmerising moment when the trees were orange and the fountain was full of flames. She wonders if the fire has already burned out, or been put out. Are the police there? Have they watched the video? Is the runner okay?

Not much chaos, she concludes, but a thing of beauty, and it was captured on film.

There's nothing left to do now but leave; no point trying to talk things out with Kim. Just pack and leave. She doesn't want to be there when Dean and the kids wake up. The only problem is she'll have to carry her sleeping daughter, the big backpack and the small daypack.

She decides to take a taxi to the train station. It's a relief to think that, after all the miles they've done, Cologne to Berlin will be their last journey together.

She imagines leaving Berlin on her own: at the train station, with just her backpack and no plan. This image fills her with an inexplicable amount of happiness.

Dancing Star

Leipzig was an end station. The train pulled in, then pulled back out again, meaning I was facing the wrong direction. This made me feel queasy, but I didn't move. I let the queasiness turn into sleepiness and closed my eyes, leaning my head against my guitar case. My hope was that sleep would help me stop thinking about last night's gig in Nuremberg, the final show of the tour, playing to exactly five people; two were friends of the barman, and they'd sat at the bar with their backs to me, talking loudly the whole time, while the other three were regular lone drinkers, who nursed their drinks, stared straight ahead, and didn't seem to have anywhere better to be.

I stayed in this position, head against case, eyes closed, trying not to think, trying not to hate myself and the world, and trying not to envision how things might play out in Berlin.

But my brain stayed active. I was filled with uncertainty: about my music, my career choices, my impending role as a parent, my relationship with Holly, and what the year would bring. Perhaps a more substantial crowd last night would have provided the required icing on the cake I'd been slowly baking over two months of touring, but the five people added a sprinkling of poison instead. I'd felt pathetic on stage, like a lonely drunk hogging the karaoke machine. My voice had echoed around the empty bar. No one present cared, no one listened, no one even looked in my direction. So, why on earth should I care?

I wanted to focus on the good gigs, where I'd sold CDs and been interviewed by local press. But what stood out from the tour were the empty rooms and nonplussed drinkers.

And then there was the feeling that after all of it, I was good and not great, and this meagre tour was perhaps the best I was ever going to achieve.

A forceful tap on my shoulder made me open my eyes. A middle-aged woman, with a round face and rather fluffy hair, spoke to me in German. Amongst the confusion of words I heard Berlin, pronounced "Bear-lean", and looked out the window at the grey platforms.

People milled around the doors. Those getting off had little luggage, beyond a shoulder bag, small backpack or wheelie suitcase, which struck me as odd. It was as if they were all only here for the day.

I waited with my backpack, guitar case and box of CDs, and was the last to exit the wagon.

I followed the people up the escalators to the S-Bahn platforms and got myself on the right train going to Zoo station.

It was cold and I was tired. I was also fed up with carrying the box with one arm and my guitar case with the other. I put both down on empty train seats and stood with my pack on my back.

The tour was over, I could barely talk, my ears were ringing worse than ever, I was just about broke, and all I wanted was to go home. While the tour had been just successful enough to make me think I should keep trying, I hadn't made any money and I wasn't sure if continuing was the right thing to do. To break even at a show felt good. I'd managed this by earning enough from CD sales and sometimes getting some of the bar-take to cover my travel expenses as well. Unfortunately, that hadn't happened enough.

But what I felt most uncertain about was Eris. In early November, Nola had sent a postcard from Berlin. Churchill told me it didn't have a five-fingered hand on it: just a date, January 10. There was no place or time. It was an assumption that the meeting place was Berlin. Other postcards followed, from places around Europe, but they just had the hand on them.

I was a day early. How was I supposed to find them in this foreign city, when I wasn't even sure they were here?

Through the window of the S-Bahn, the city looked interesting. The train-line followed a canal and park. Despite the cold, the sky was cloudless, the sun bright and low on the horizon. It was so bright, it filled the sky. A big, white winter sky, like what the woman had described on the way to West Yellowstone. A sky that was all sun.

Though tired, homesick and low on money, I kept telling myself to feel positive about things. I was doing it. I was a musician, even if that meant playing for five people in a Nuremberg dive. People had seen me play live and had handed me their own money in exchange for my CD. Maybe someone somewhere was listening to my CD right now, bopping their head and smiling as my music went into their ears. The police drama might yet decide to use *Chasing a Shadow* and I might get the kind of royalty cheque Charlie had talked about; one with a least four zeros on it. And maybe I'd head back to the States later in the year to play all the same venues again and record a second album with Charlie.

Would I take Eris with me? Touring like this was no life for a six year-old. I wasn't sure it was a life for me either.

I checked the map on my phone and decided to walk to the hotel. From Zoo, I carried all my stuff down Joachimsthaler Strasse, passing nothing but shops.

My lower back hurt. It was tempting to start giving all these CDs away, so I wouldn't have to carry them home.

Once off the main street and onto Schaper Strasse, the area was residential, leafy and attractive. The Metropolitan Hotel was in what looked like a converted apartment building. As I wasn't sure what would happen, I'd booked a single room here for two nights, wanting to save as much money as I could, but not willing to bunk in a hostel room with eleven others.

The receptionist was welcoming, the room close to luxurious. Everything felt new, which was a nice change, given I'd stayed in plenty of worn, over-used hotels in the last few months and slept in a handful of closets beneath or above bars. I'd learned early on during the tour that staying in hostels was a mistake, because I couldn't get a decent night's sleep in a dorm room, as I came in late, people snored, and some got up very early. I needed my own room. It was lonelier and more expensive, but definitely more comfortable.

I put all my stuff down and went into the bathroom to wash my face and hands. In the mirror, I looked old, which wasn't necessarily a bad thing. In the last year, I'd had so many experiences, enough to make me stop feeling like a teenager and more like an adult. I had a few lines on my face. I looked rumpled and worn. My hair was long. If I'd been in a more positive frame of mind, I might have ventured that I looked cool. Not quite a rock-god, but a hard-working musician, which I thought was far better than being some pen-pusher or music shop monkey.

As in all the rooms I'd stayed, I put my picture of Eris on the night stand. This picture was the screenshot taken by airport security in Salt Lake City, and I kept it inside a plastic sheath. Nola hadn't been cut out, as I wanted to be sure I'd recognise her again and cutting her out of the photo seemed too harsh, but the picture was folded so only Eris was visible.

I connected my phone to the hotel's Wi-Fi and sent a message to Churchill that I'd arrived. He called immediately.

"Guten Tag," he said.

"You know more German than me, Church."

"The benefit of a private school education. You won't believe it, but my German teacher's first name was actually Heidi."

"How's it going?"

"Same old. More important, how are you?"

"I'm in Berlin. Just got here."

"And you contact me first? What about Holly?"

"It's Tuesday. She's playing at Clancy's."

"Ah, yes, right you are. She told me about that."

"She did? When?"

"Hold your jealous horses, Rowan. She just came over for dinner on Sunday with me and Janette. Those two have become pretty close in your absence. I am fully okay with that, as some of Janette's friends need replacing. Holly's whacky, but she's one very good human."

Hearing Churchill say this reminded me how much I missed Holly.

"Rowan? You still there?"

"I'm here."

"Level with me, mate. Have you been a good boy?"

"Church, I've been so finished each night, I've fallen straight into bed. I don't know how other guys do it with groupies. I don't have the energy. And I want to be with Holly. I'm not willing to throw away what I've got with her for a night with some college girl in Wisconsin who thinks I'm sexy because I play guitar."

"When you say it like that, you take a lot of the gloss off life on the road."

"Did Holly order you to ask me about it?"

"That's from me. I like Holly."

"Any new postcards?"

"One. From Amsterdam. But it just had the hand on it again. Nothing else."

"How's the map looking?"

Churchill laughed. "It's wild. Another eight-pointed star. The last stop was Cologne. I know that because Grilla did something there. Two days ago."

"What was it?"

"A Christmas tree bonfire. There's a video of it online. You should check it out. It's pretty impressive."

"So, she's in the country. Berlin could be next."

"It is," Churchill said. "There's no doubt in my mind. That's where she started, and going back there closes the star."

"How am I supposed to find them? This city is huge."

"Maybe you should let them find you. Hit the streets and do some busking."

"I'm planning to do that anyway, to make some cash. But it's freezing."

"You need those gloves with the fingers cut off."

"Like a homeless man, Church?"

"I'm thinking more wandering minstrel. Wander that great city and play on every corner until you find them. Crap, you're in Berlin. Can you believe it?"

"Right now, it's just another hotel room. There have been so many places, they've kind of blended together."

"Well, you're done now. It's time to come back in from the cold."

"Gladly. By the way, what was on the Berlin postcard? Maybe the picture's a clue of some sort."

"Hang on."

I heard Churchill move through the house. The familiar sound of the creaking floorboards made me very homesick. I'd been on the road for too long. I missed Holly. I missed Churchill. I missed Perth. I wanted summer.

"Okay," Churchill said, "it's like a half-ruined church tower. The top's missing. It's called the Kaiser Wilhelm Memorial Church. Looks like it was bombed during the war."

"I think that's nearby. Might be a good place for me to start."

Churchill was silent for a moment, then asked, "How does it feel?"

"What? Finishing the tour?"

"Eris. You're going to meet her tomorrow. Hopefully. Your daughter."

"I'm nervous, Church. I'm also worried that it's all some kind of prank. Nola setting me up for disappointment. Maybe it's all some act of Grilla, with me as the target."

"Doubt it."

"Well, I won't believe it until Eris is standing in front of me. I really hate the way Nola has toyed with me, with these stupid postcards and making it so hard to meet up."

"Rowan, this girl went to all the trouble of collecting old Christmas trees, stacking them in a big pile, putting candles on the branches and setting the whole thing on fire. And that's just one example. She clearly does things in strange ways."

"She does."

"And you can be sure you'll find each other, if that's what she wants. In fact, the most likely outcome is that she'll find you. So, get out there and make yourself visible."

"I will. Thanks, Church. Really nice to talk."

"Take care."

He hung up, in that abrupt way that was so typically Churchill.

I changed into my warmest clothes, including the thermal underwear I'd bought in Milwaukee, and grabbed my guitar case. The front pockets of my jacket were large enough to hold five CDs each. While I didn't expect to sell any, I thought they'd give me more credence when displayed.

Downstairs, I asked the receptionist for advice about busking. She suggested the square in front of the Europa Center, and marked this on a map.

"There's a, how do you say, Brunnen," she said. "You know, with water."

"A fountain?"

"Yes, the Weltkugelbrunnen. The world ball fountain. Many people sit there. And there are some restaurants too."

"Even today, when it's so cold?"

"This is not cold. It's a beautiful day. It can get much colder than this."

"That's comforting." I picked up the map.

"Good luck."

"Thanks. I think I'll need it."

From the hotel, I got onto Ranke Strasse, heading for the fountain. There was a bargain store along the way; I bought a wool hat, fingerless gloves and a scarf. It was all in one packet, with each item in zebra stripes. I put everything on, not caring how I might look. As long as I was warm and I could play the guitar without my fingers turning blue, I was happy.

It was the middle of the afternoon and the streets were busy. There were lots of pedestrians, which was something I was really enjoying about the European cities I'd been to so far. It wasn't just people in cars. There was life on the streets, even in winter. I thought this gave the cities a vitality and sense of community that Perth lacked.

At the end of the street was the tower of a ruined church, flanked by two strange-looking buildings made of huge square tiles. I wondered if this was the church from the postcard. It had to be. How many ruined churches did Berlin have?

I could see the fountain and crossed the street. The Weltkugelbrunnen was half below ground, but there was no water trickling through or around the large, brown, ball-shaped structure, which made it look rather barren and decrepit. The dated Europa Center backdrop also wasn't helping, with this section of Berlin exhibiting an early-eighties version of cool. A building across the street was undergoing renovation and fronted with scaffolding.

Keen to redeem myself for last night's awful gig, I set myself up, with my back to the windows, concrete and brands of the Europa Center. I had a place in the sun, and the large mall acted as a wind break. I opened my guitar case, took out my guitar and scattered the CDs I had in the bottom. I blew on my fingers and started playing Beck's *Lord Only Knows*, using a pick to get more volume. The gloves made it a little difficult to play bar-chords, but also created an interesting, muffled sound. The real problem was my voice, which was haggard and rough. The cold, dry air wasn't helping. I had to choose songs that were easy to sing and didn't require me to stretch my limited range.

Coins landed in my guitar case, dropped by people walking past. I assumed this was more out of sympathy: that I was out here in the cold, having a go and perhaps needed the money. Whatever the reason, as I worked through some covers, the coins piled up and they spurred me on.

I found it interesting how the locals might be more generous to a street musician than to someone playing in a bar or club. After barely half an hour, I could see from the coins that I'd already earned more than I had in Nuremberg. This was satisfying. It was also fun to play covers again. I'd grown weary of playing my own songs over and over.

One woman, in large sunglasses and a baggy wool hat that was so low on her head to be under the frames of the glasses, came up to me and asked in English how much the CDs were.

"Ten euros."

She bought two, handing me a blue twenty-euro note which I pocketed.

"Can I make a request?" she asked, keeping her head down.

"Of course."

"Play *Two Sticks*. I really love that song."

This gave me a buzz. "You know it?"

"I heard it on the radio." She turned the CD over in her hands. "Nice cover. I like the title too."

"Thanks."

She walked to a nearby pylon and sat down, facing the church and not looking at me. I played the song and sang it as best I could in my current condition. At the end, she turned to me and clapped with her hands just under her chin, where someone might hold them in prayer.

I'd seen that clap before. And that mischievous grin.

It was Nola. It was rather stunning to see how well she had disguised herself, but then I thought of Grilla, and how Nola was probably some kind of master of getting around undetected.

I saw the recognition; she knew that I knew that it was her. I thought she might run, but she continued to sit there. She took her sunglasses and hat off, and gave her hair a shake.

This gesture come across as a summons of sorts, so I scooped up all the coins from my guitar case and filled the pockets of my jeans with them. The weight felt good. The remaining CDs went into the pockets of my jacket and the guitar into its case.

Nola made room for me at the pylon and I sat down next to her. It seemed strange to be this close to her, and I thought finding her had been a little too easy.

"That was nice," she said. "I thought about asking you to play *If You Leave Me Now*, but wanted to hear one of your songs. They're really good, Rowan. You should be proud."

"Thanks." I paused for a moment. "Chicago. That's where you're from."

"You forgot that?"

"The song reminded me. I was there a few weeks ago."

"What did you think?"

"I liked it. I only had a one night, but I thought it was a pretty cool place."

"It's a nightmare," Nola said. "A cemetery for dreams."

This was an odd thing to say, so I didn't reply. We sat there, looking at the church. There was something both sad and hopeful about the ruined tower.

"So, here we are," Nola said. "In Berlin. A bit earlier than planned."

"Yeah. Where's Eris?"

"At the hotel."

"You just left here there? You can't do that."

"She's sleeping. I locked the door. She's safe."

"You mean she's imprisoned. What if she wakes up and needs help?"

Nola smiled. "I'm happy you think like that, Rowan. That's what she needs. Someone who puts her first."

"Let's go. I want to meet her."

"Not today." Nola looked at the CD again. "How was the tour? I followed the online updates, but I want to hear it from you."

"Good and bad. I did really well at the start in Bozeman, but that was because I got a lot of help from a friend. In most of the other places, I was too much of an unknown."

"I bet that you really tried though. Really worked for it. I know you'd do that."

Nola's presumptuousness made me uneasy. "I did my best, but some nights, it just didn't happen." I sighed, breathing out a cloud of steam. "It's been a good experience, but I'm glad it's over."

"And how's the Metropolitan?"

"How do you know I'm staying there?"

She smiled, giving me an almost imperceptible shrug. "It's pretty easy to find people these days. You just need a phone tracking app. You gave me your number last year, just before you left Isle Royale. I tracked it. I followed you everywhere you went, including last night in Nuremberg, today at the Metropolitan, and here."

I felt just a little bit violated. "Well, you're not the only one who can do some tracking."

"What do you mean?"

"I know who you are. Maybe it's better to say I know who you pretend to be."

She raised her eyebrows at me.

I mouthed: "Grilla."

She laughed. "What makes you say that?"

"The postcards. We matched them to everything Grilla did in those cities. Turned out all of those pranks were around the same dates as the postcards sent from those places."

"They're not pranks," she said forcefully. "Don't you dare call them that. And who's we?"

"Me and Churchill."

"Your buddy? Ground control?"

"Yep. He's a fan. We figured out that all your postcards formed an eight-pointed star when joined together on a map, just like what you have on your symbol. And you've done it again on this trip in Europe."

"Well, aren't you clever? You better keep it a secret or I'll cut your balls off with a butter knife."

"We've known for months, me and Churchill. Like I said, he's a fan, and I didn't want to put Eris in any potential danger. So we kept it to ourselves."

"How noble. But what about you? Aren't you a fan?"

"I used to like one of your murals, the one of the shark kissing the man in Fremantle."

"That's my early work," she said, dismissing it. "I've done better since then."

"But someone made me see it differently. As for the live stuff, I really don't get the point of it. Are you protesting or something? I mean, I saw you cause a car crash in Austin. I was there, on the street when it happened. You could've killed somebody."

"It's art."

"What is?"

"The action, and the chaos that results."

"How is that art? That's like throwing a pie in someone's face and calling it art. It basically gives you license to do whatever you want, and you can get away with it by saying it's art. Don't you think there's something wrong with that?"

Nola looked straight ahead. "I'm getting really sick of hearing this. If you don't get it, I'm not explaining it to you."

"Why don't you go back to painting murals? That's art."

She stood up. "Holocaust Memorial, tomorrow morning. 10 o'clock. Don't be late."

She started walking quickly across the square, weaving between other pedestrians and even pushing a couple aside. I stood up to follow her, but figured it would be useless with my pockets full of change and CDs, and with my guitar case to carry.

As I watched her cross the street and dart between moving cars, I decided that whatever Nola had planned for tomorrow, I had to get Eris away from her.

→←

I drifted in and out of sleep. Each time I woke, I opened my eyes to check they were both there. But the last time I did this, I saw that Nola wasn't.

This didn't strike me as necessarily a bad thing.

When Eris woke up, she got dressed and went by herself to the bathroom. She left the door open while she brushed her teeth. I wondered if this was normal behaviour for her. Didn't kids her age need help with this kind of stuff?

She came back out and stared at me.

"That's impressive. You already do a lot of things by yourself."

"I'm hungry," she said.

We went downstairs for breakfast. I let Eris choose the table.

"Where's mommy?" she asked, after she'd sat down.

After waking to see Nola gone, I'd thought for a while about how to answer this question, as I knew it would come at some point. I'd decided to be honest. I didn't want to start our relationship with lies.

"She's gone. On a really long trip."

"Like Warren?"

"Who? Uh, yeah, like Warren. Your mother asked me to take care of you. It's very important for her, because she wants you to have the best care in the world. Is that okay, that I take care of you?"

It was hard to read her expression.

"She told me to take you back to Australia. To Perth. That's where I'm from. I have a house there. It's a great place. The sun always shines and there's a beautiful beach nearby. There are lots of animals too. Birds and kangaroos and emus."

"What about Helen?"

I really wished Nola had told me more.

"Well, she's, you know, she's also on a long trip. It's now my job to look after you. Eris, I promise I'll take really good care of you. Now, what would you like for breakfast?"

Eris stood up and went to the buffet. She did this with the confidence of someone familiar with hotels and buffet breakfasts. She put together a bowl of cornflakes, pouring the milk herself, and asked me to put some banana on top. I did so, using half a banana which I then sliced on top of the cornflakes I made for myself.

I smiled at her before I started. "We're eating the same thing. We're cornflake buddies."

Again, her expression was very hard to read.

We ate in silence. I sensed that Eris was a little unsure around me, which was to be expected. I felt the same way. I had no idea how to put her at ease, and I had no idea about Eris's particular preferences and habits. We needed time to get used to each other. Still, she wasn't screaming or flipping out or shouting for help, and she hadn't run away. I thought she understood that she was with me now, but that she didn't fully know what that would mean.

"Tasty?"

She nodded.

"What shall we do today?"

"I want to go home."

"You know what? So do I. It's a long way to Perth. Are you ready for that?"

"It's okay."

I wondered if Churchill would lend me the money to buy Eris a ticket. I couldn't ask Holly. I had a feeling Nana would be the best one to ask. I didn't want to stay in Berlin, and I thought we needed to get to Perth and settle into our new life together.

With her strawberry hair hanging loose and her round, pixie face, I thought she was the most beautiful thing on the planet. I couldn't believe I'd had a part in her making. The red hair and green eyes made a stunning combination.

For the rest of breakfast, she said nothing. She drank three glasses of orange juice, always lifting the glass with both hands.

When she was finished, she said, "Can I watch TV?"

"How about we go for a walk and see some of the city?"

He shoulders slumped a little. "Okay."

Upstairs, while Eris put on her jacket and hat, I sent a message to Churchill, asking for ground control's financial and organisational help to get Eris on my flight tomorrow, and saying that if he didn't have the money, he should ask Nana for it.

"I like your scarf," Eris said.

"You want to wear it?"

She nodded.

"You already have my gloves. It matches nicely, I think. And I'll wear my hat, so we match as well."

She seemed to like this, and let me loop the scarf a few times around her neck.

This time, as we walked down the stairs, we held hands. Her little hand was lost inside my large, fingerless gloves.

In the lobby, the receptionist called out to me: "Mr Davidson, there's a postcard for you."

"Uh, thanks."

On the image side was a line of bears, standing upright, with their front paws raised, and each bear decorated differently. On the other side, "Dennewitz Strasse, enclosed U-Bahn bridge" was written in blue pen. There was no stamp, but my name was written in the address box, care of the Metropolitan Hotel. Nola, and it could only have been her, must've left this when she fled this morning.

I found the street on the map. It didn't look far.

Eris was playing with a rack of business cards, moving them around, shuffling and disorganising the decks.

"Are you ready to start?"

She nodded.

"I'll carry you if you get tired."

"Okay."

Outside, it wasn't as cold as yesterday, but it was cloudy. It felt like it might snow.

I plotted a route that kept us off the main streets. Having never walked with a child before, I had to catch myself and keep an eye on her, and stop my mind from wandering off onto other distractions.

We had an ice-cream at Viktoria-Luise-Platz, sitting near a circular pool that was frozen over, then walked the length of Winterfeldt Strasse, until it ended. It felt good to see Berlin in this way, on foot, in an area where there were no tourists.

Eris asked to be carried and I put her on my shoulders, her skinny legs dangling in front of my chest. Every few steps, a heel hit my ribs, like I was horse being told to go faster. She was very light. When she said she was sleepy, I carried her piggy-back style. She wrapped her small arms around my neck and rested her head on my shoulder. I felt her breath go down the collar of my jacket and heard her snoring softly.

We went through a small park and came out onto Dennewitz Strasse. Up ahead, I saw the enclosed bridge, which led into a building. It looked like people lived there. As a train rumbled through, I couldn't imagine what it would be like to be a resident here, even in one of the buildings that flanked the bridge.

I'd thought Nola might be here, waiting for us, but there was no one.

As the snow started to fall, I took shelter under the bridge. Eris continued to snore.

I looked around, wondering why Nola had brought us to this place. The wall had some graffiti on it, names written in unintelligible squiggles. Near an exposed pipe, there was a small cartoon-style painting: two red stars, one large, one small, with arms and legs, holding hands and dancing together happily. Slightly above, there was a moon shining down on the two stars. Written in black underneath was a quote: "You must have chaos within you to give birth to a dancing star" – Nietzsche.

I touched the smaller of the two stars; the paint wasn't completely dry.

With Eris asleep on my back, I stood under the bridge, waiting for the snow to stop.

The flash of a camera made me turn around, but there was no one.

To find the soundtrack to the book, go to http://rippplemedia.com/music/rowaneris/

Travel Page (cont.)

Lightning Source UK Ltd.
Milton Keynes UK
UKOW06f0346231217
314915UK00008B/449/P